shing
ing.com

Shadow Lands

Book One

by
Simon Lister

Spire Publishing
www.spirepublishing.com

Spire Publishing, January 2008

Second edition. This edition first published in Canada 2008 by Spire Publishing.

Spire Publishing is a trademark of Adlibbed Ltd.

Note to Librarians: A cataloguing record for this book is available from the Library and Archives Canada. Visit www.collectionscanada.ca/amicus/index-e.html

Printed and bound in the US or the UK by Lightningsource Ltd.
Cover photo/design © S Lister

ISBN: 1-897312-62-8

Simon Lister was born in Twyford and raised in Berkshire. He studied and lived in London for several years before travelling and working around the world. He now lives and writes on the North shore of Loch Tay. His Arthurian saga comprises of *Shadow Lands*, *Causeway* and *Haven*.

For information on ordering the books in this series please visit:
www.simonlister.co.uk

Shadow Lands

is for

Rick

- here's to all those early stories

Acknowledgements

Thanks to Rick who co-wrote the earlier Shadow Land stories when we were kids and who helped editorially in these later versions. Thanks also to: Anna and Stan for Loch Tay. Tish and Bren for all the support and encouragement, and Mark too, who was there with the original inspiration back when I was doing a primary school essay. Paul Biggs and Jenny Grewal for the valuable feedback, and Steve Forrow for the re-reading, critical assessments and editorial input. And a final thanks to the folks at PABD for all the effort and patience in getting these books to print. Any errors that remain are, of course, solely of my own doing.

Characters

The Wessex

Arthur – Warlord of Wessex
Merdynn – Counsellor to King Maldred
Ruadan – Arthur's second-in-command and brother to Ceinwen
Trevenna (f) – Arthur's sister, married to Cei and a warrior in the Anglian war band
Ceinwen (f) – healer and ex-tracker for the Wessex war band, sister to Ruadan
Morgund – Captain in the Wessex war band
Mar'h - Captain in the Wessex war band
Balor – Wessex warrior
Morveren (f) – Wessex warrior
Ethain – Wessex warrior
Cael – Wessex warrior
Tomas – Wessex warrior, married to Elowen
Elowen (f) – Wessex warrior, married to Tomas
Tamsyn (f) – Wessex warrior, sister to Talan
Talan – Wessex warrior, brother to Tamsyn
Llud – Wessex warrior
Laethrig – the Wessex Blacksmith
Kenwyn – Wessex Chieftain

The Anglians

Cei – Anglian Warlord, childhood friend to Arthur and married to Arthur's sister, Trevenna
Hengest – Cei's second-in-command, son to Aelfhelm
Cerdic – Anglian warrior
Aelfhelm – Anglian warrior, father to Hengest
Elwyn – Anglian warrior and boat captain
Aylydd (f) – Anglian warrior and boat captain
Lissa – Anglian warrior and boat captain
Leah (f) – Anglian warrior

Saewulf – Anglian warrior
Cuthwin – Anglian warrior
Berwyn – Anglian warrior
Roswitha (f) – Anglian warrior
Herewulf – Anglian warrior
Osla – Anglian warrior
Wolfestan – Anglian warrior, brother to Elfida
Elfida (f) – Anglian warrior, sister to Wolfestan
Godhelm – Anglian warrior
Thruidred – Anglian warrior
Wayland – Anglian warrior
Ranulf – Anglian warrior
Leofrun (f) – Anglian warrior
Aelfric – Anglian youth
Henna (f) – Anglian healer
Aelle – Anglian Chieftain

The Mercians

Maldred – King of the southern tribes
Gereint – Mercian Warlord, brother to Glore
Glore – Mercian warrior, brother to Gereint
Dystran – Mercian warrior
Unna (f) – Harbour master of the Haven

The Uathach

Ablach – Uathach Chieftain of the lands to the North of Anglia, father to Gwyna
Gwyna (f) – Uathach warrior, daughter to Ablach
Ruraidh – Uathach Captain
Hund – Uathach Chieftain of the lands to the North of Mercia
Benoc – Uathach Chieftain of the lands to the far north

The Cithol

Venning – Cithol Lord and ruler of the Veiled City, father to Fin Seren
Kane – Commander of the Veiled City
Fin Seren (f) – daughter and heir to Lord Venning
Terrill – Captain of the Cithol

The Bretons

Bran – Chieftain of the Bretons
Cardell (f) – Advisor to Bran
Charljenka (f) - Breton child
Nialgrada – Breton child

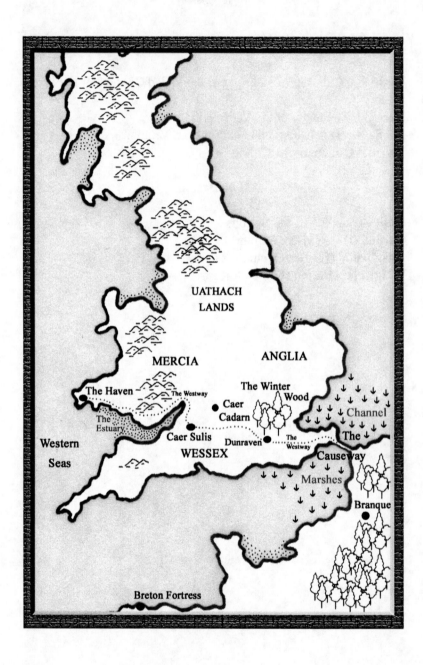

Chapter One

Winter was coming and with it the long darkness. Andala could feel it; a sharper edge to the late autumn air as he stood on the village wall scanning the hillside. His shadow stretched out across the long grass, cast by the low sun that hung above the eastern horizon. Soon the sun would set and the land would be abandoned to the darkness until it returned once more in the spring. He stared out across the western valley floor searching for any sign of the overdue Anglian war band that was to escort them over the Causeway to Britain on the first leg of their long journey to the Western Lands.

He switched his gaze back to the hillside trying to quell the foreboding sense that something was wrong. His disquiet had been gradually deepening over the last few months. There had been no single event to trigger or warrant alarm but the steady accumulation of unexplained occurrences had brought him to the point where he would be glad to leave behind his responsibilities to his village, if only for the six months of winter darkness. With nothing definite to point at he had kept his unease from everyone but his wife, Ceinwen, who had been relieved to discover she wasn't the only one feeling that something was amiss.

He tried to clear his mind and turned his gaze back to the hillside to resume his search but it was another long hour before he finally saw the lone rider approaching.

The horseman was picking his way down the steep slope towards the river that flowed lazily from the long, sinuous lake that the village was perched beside. The horse under him skittered on some loose scree and slid forward, scrabbling to find a firmer footing. The rider jumped off and looked to be cursing the horse. Andala recognised the horseman with a sudden stab of apprehension and turned around anxiously to look at the ordered chaos within the village below him.

Every year, as the sun set in the East, the villages on this side of the Causeway and those on the other side in southern Britain prepared for the journey to the Haven and the crossing of the Western Seas. This perennial migration cut the months of winter darkness down to three and allowed for a short but critical growing season in the Western Lands. Not everyone travelled on to the lands across the sea, some would remain in either Caer Sulis or the Haven, the two main towns of Britain, but no one stayed behind to endure the harsh winter in their own village.

As head of the village of Branque, the largest village south of the Belgae lands, the unenviable task of ordering the local communities fell to Andala. Had one of his sons lived to come of age then he would have gladly passed on the responsibility some years ago despite only being in middle years himself. He had always said to his wife that at the first signs of grey in his hair he would pass on the leadership of the village and spend his days out on the lake with a fishing line but his hair had turned gradually from brown to grey and then prematurely from grey to white, and his fishing line had stayed coiled up in his roundhouse by the lakeshore.

Perhaps next year, he mused, his daughter Caja would be able to shoulder at least some of the responsibility. He looked for her and spotted her easily enough, not so much because of her long red hair but because she was always at the centre of any activity. Andala raised an arm and called out to her, 'Caja! Rider across the river!'

She looked around to see where the call had come from and saw her father on the stockade wall. 'Who is it?' she called back.

'Come see for yourself!'

She quickly finished her suggestions for tying down the covers for the wain in a burst of hurried commands and rushed towards the steps at the base of the stockade wall. The wain master looked after her with teeth clenched and lips tight together. Breward, the awkward youth standing next to him, laughed and gave him a gentle push, 'Go on Jac, say it. She won't hear you and I won't tell.'

Jac relaxed and smiled, 'No. She's only trying to help.'

'Only trying, you mean,' Breward said as he finished tying off the ropes and added, 'She's nervous about the journey west.'

'My gods, who isn't?' the older man muttered.

'I hate this time of year.'

'It'll seem better tonight when we start on the harvest wine,' Jac pointed out.

'I suppose so. It doesn't seem like a year has passed does it?' Breward asked, thinking happily about how he and Caja had increasingly spent more time together over the last year.

They both moved on to the next wain and threw the cover across the top. Breward collected up the ropes then pointed towards the sun that hung low on the eastern horizon and answered his own question, 'And yet, there's the proof.'

'Do you think it's Cei coming?' Jac asked innocently, nodding his head to where Andala stood watching the approaching rider. Breward just gave him a sour look in reply. Caja was not a girl to keep her feelings hidden and the whole village knew of her youthful infatuation with the Anglian Warlord. Indeed, it was a source of no little amusement - most of which was aimed directly at her more plausible, if less heroic, suitor.

Caja remembered her composure and climbed the steps up the stockade wall more slowly, not wanting her father to see her obvious excitement. Warriors always escorted the villagers on their yearly journeys to and from the Haven and Caja had become hopelessly infatuated with Cei, the easy natured Anglian Warlord, during the last such journey. She knew it was unlikely that Cei would be among the escort this time but she could not stop herself from hoping and in any case, the prospect of meeting and riding with the proud and strutting warriors of Britain was cause enough for excitement. By the time she got to the top Andala was grinning broadly at her.

He had married Ceinwen a year after his first wife had died in childbirth; the child, a son, had died a week later – his second son to have died within weeks of being born. Ceinwen, like many others, was unable to have children but Andala had fallen in love with her and insisted that her inability to have children was no obstacle. There had been those who had frowned upon a marriage based on such incompatibility believing that it was Andala's duty to seek out a woman who could bear children with him but he had overridden their objections and most people had realised that Andala and Ceinwen needed each other, if for quite differing reasons. Fate gave them a daughter three years later when an Anglian warrior's wife died in childbirth leaving the infant motherless and the father with little inclination to raise her. Cei had taken the child to them and they had named her Caja and raised her as if she were their own. Even having one child was more than most couples were blessed with and Andala had doted on her; his love for her was only matched by his pride in her. He smiled at the irony that Caja should have become infatuated with the man who had brought her to them so many years ago.

'Wipe that knowing smirk off your face, father, and tell me who it is.'

The rider had nearly reached the bottom of the slope but he still seemed to be vilifying the horse.

'I think he's having words with his horse.'

Caja turned and tugged at his arm, 'Tell me!'

'Though the horse seems remarkably unconcerned.'

Caja cursed in frustration.

Andala casually clipped her on the back of the head, 'That's no way to talk, young girl.'

'Sorry, father,' Caja replied as she attempted to straighten out her unruly mane of hair, 'but you know I can't see that distance!'

'Well then, it looks like Arthur of the Wessex war band.' The levity had vanished from his voice and Caja's face fell.

'Oh,' she said, her buoyant mood collapsing immediately. 'Why Arthur?' she asked, puzzled.

Andala was asking himself the very same question.

'Well, I'd better warn the others,' Caja said, slightly concerned by the look on her father's face.

'And you'd better let your mother know first,' he said trying too hard to sound off-hand.

She climbed back down feeling both deflated and a little uneasy, her previous excitement firmly replaced by a nagging worry that perhaps she had overlooked some essential detail in the preparation for the journey west; a detail, she thought, that the Wessex Warlord would undoubtedly spot immediately.

Andala watched her retrace her steps back past Jac and Breward and he noticed their different glances. Jac braced as if expecting another outburst from her and relaxed once she was past, while Breward's eyes followed her until she entered the village's main hall. Caja was well aware of his gaze. Breward glanced up to where Andala was watching him and guiltily busied himself with some unnecessary re-positioning of ropes and ties. Andala made a mental note to watch Breward during the journey west – Caja's harmless fascination with Cei was one thing but the growing bond between his daughter and young Breward was another altogether. He turned his attention back to the rider who was walking his horse towards the fording point on the river. It was unmistakably Arthur.

Taking a deep breath Andala started to climb down from the wall. He surveyed the scene before him and thanked the gods that the weather had remained dry. The compound seemed to be under a permanent haze of dust but that was infinitely preferable to the mud and standing water of the previous year when the rains had made the whole process almost impossible. Order was definitely coming out of the chaos – twenty-five wains, more or less secured and all fully loaded with maize, corn, vegetables and the various fruits of the summer harvest. The cattle, sheep and goats were paddocked inside the stockade wall and ready for the journey, their noise and smell competing with those of the people crammed too tightly into the confines of the village in preparation for the migration.

Another twenty wains were heaped with feed for the animals. Ten more were packed with dried meats and smoked fish; two others had cages of hens piled high and still more were packed with the belongings from the other four villages that had gathered here. A few remained empty to be loaded at the last minute with his own village's belongings.

As in the other settlements to the North, and across the Causeway in Britain, villagers were collecting their harvests and preparing to abandon their homes as the summer sun set in the East heralding the onset of the long night of winter. They would return with the rising sun in the spring, once the snows and deep ice had thawed and melted, to start the whole cycle all over again. We do it every year and yet it never seems to get any easier, Andala thought to himself as he made his way out of the East Gate to meet Arthur.

Behind him word was spreading that the Wessex Warlord himself was across the river and was going to lead them across the Causeway and west. Andala could feel a noticeable change in the atmosphere of the busy villagers behind him. The boisterous levity of the hectic last few days seemed to be dissipating quicker than the rising smoke from the main hall. Andala forced himself to pick up his pace. Arthur was already crossing the ford. He decided to stop and wait for him. He had met Arthur twice before in person, though he had seen him twice each year for as long as he could remember, always at Caer Sulis in the West during the Gathering of the Tribes at Lughnasa, the harvest festival, and at Imbolc, the festival for the Wakening of the Sun.

Across the Channel Marshes and over the Causeway the three main tribes of Britain gathered in the West at Caer Sulis in late autumn with all their livestock and summer harvest to celebrate Lughnasa and invoke blessings for the journey across the Western Seas. The King of the Britons, Maldred, held his council at that time, where the chieftains and counsellors of each tribe gathered to settle disputes and to plan for the journey ahead. Caer Sulis was the king's seat and by far the largest settlement in Britain. Andala remembered the first time Caja was old enough to take it all in; the look of wonder on her face as she gazed at the two storey stone buildings and the wide streets between them still made him smile.

There had been serious trouble with one of their guards on a previous journey to Caer Sulis some years ago on one of the rare occasions when Arthur's war band had escorted them. Andala had worked up his courage and gone to see Arthur to remonstrate. Arthur had asked him some short questions then summoned the guard involved. Andala could not remember the man's name and he frowned, trying to recall it. Arthur had questioned the man and woman concerned in front of Andala and then without hesitation he had drawn his sword and killed the man where he stood. It did not seem right that he could not even remember the man's name. Brynstan? Berwyn? No, but something like that. It did not seem right that he should feel guilty about the man's death either, yet he did. Andala was lost in thought. That was the day he first met Arthur in person. This was to be his last.

'His name was Breagan and neither you nor yours have had any trouble since from any warrior.'

Andala started, Arthur was standing no more than five-feet away and staring into his eyes. Arthur's horse snorted and stamped the ground, shaking the water from the ford off its fetlocks. Andala stared at Arthur half in fear, half in bewilderment.

'No Arthur, no trouble since.'

'It wasn't a question.'

Andala swallowed in a suddenly dry throat. Arthur stood a head taller than he did, and Andala was not considered to be a short man. Arthur's long black hair was straggled and his beard was unkempt. An ugly white scar ran from his broken nose to below his right ear. That wasn't there the last time I saw him, Andala thought as he felt another unbidden well of unease rise inside himself. The fear wasn't prompted by the war gear that Arthur carried – the longbow strapped to his horse, or the round shield slung across his back, nor even the sheathed sword idly hanging from his belt although all these were uncommon enough sights in the villages. He feared the *man* standing before him; he feared his staring eyes, gray and empty of life. That was how he remembered Arthur's eyes during the questioning of Breagan in Caer Sulis, empty and flat, lifelessly staring as he judged guilt and punished with death.

Arthur spoke again and life returned to his eyes, 'How's your daughter, Caja?'

Andala fell into step with Arthur as he made his way toward the East Gate of the village. He was aware that Arthur was making a conscious effort to make him feel more relaxed but the casual tone just made him feel all the more nervous and he replied, 'Well, Arthur, well thank you.'

'How old is she now?'

'She's seventeen this Imbolc, seventeen times she's made the journey west,' Andala replied.

'Married yet?'

'No, Arthur, n-not yet,' Andala felt his anxiety rise another level and tried to lighten his tone saying, 'I think she was rather hoping Cei might be coming to take us west.' He regretted it as soon as he said it.

'Indeed? Cei has married my sister, Trevenna.'

Andala mentally brought his fist to his forehead and blurted out without thinking, 'Excellent news, she'll be glad to hear it.'

Arthur turned to look at him and smiled, 'I doubt it, Andala. I very much doubt it.'

They were approaching the gate now and most of the four hundred villagers had crammed themselves into the open square at the centre of the village to see Arthur enter. Andala did not want his people to see him nervous or silent with Arthur and forced himself to ask, 'Was it a good journey here, Arthur?'

Arthur looked at his horse and grinned, 'Not with this bastard it wasn't.' The horse just raised its upper lip in apparent derision.

Arthur stopped on the edge of the square and casually scanned the

17

gathered villagers. They were completely silent. He handed the reins of his horse to the nearest person and said, 'See that it's fed and watered.'

Andala gestured to the main hall and the crowd parted as Arthur strode towards it. Andala followed behind with the villagers standing and staring at Arthur as he passed through them.

When he had entered the hall and was safely out of earshot, the noise of conversation started up once more as the dispersing crowd began to recount the tales they had heard of the Wessex Warlord. They went back to their allotted tasks swapping stories of Arthur as they made ready for the journey to the West.

Breward and Jac decided to take an early break and get some food before the midday bell signalled it was time to eat. It would only be for a day or two but while the populations of five villages were confined to this one place it was all very cramped and meal times inevitably became chaotic.

It was sunny and still fairly warm so the trestle tables were set up outside to serve breads and fish for everyone and they sauntered across to the one that seemed most prepared for the midday meal. It also happened to be the one that Jac's wife Bri was preparing.

She saw them approach, 'Had a busy morning of it then, Jac?'

'Usual chaos – but as always, it's getting there,' replied Jac, helping himself to some bread and cheese.

'Luckily Anda's daughter, Caja, was there to organise us,' Breward said, keeping a straight face. Jac just grunted.

'Well, that kept you happy then,' Bri said pointedly to Breward and continued, 'though I've no idea what she sees in you.'

He poured himself a drink from a flagon of water and said ruefully, 'I don't think she sees anything in me at all sadly. Ever since that Cei took us back home from Caer Sulis after Imbolc she's had moon dreams running around in her head.'

'Well the sooner she wakes from them the better. It's never done anyone any good getting messed up with that type – though Cei seemed more civil than others,' and she glanced across at the main hall.

'Do you think there's any truth to that story about Ceinwen being with Arthur when she was with the Wessex war band, before she married Andala and moved across here?' Jac asked tucking into the food.

Bri stared at him with pursed lips.

'Probably not, just asking,' he added hurriedly, noticing the disapproval on his wife's face.

'That was all a very, very long time ago. And you should know better than to go dredging up gossip,' Bri said in a tone that clearly closed the subject.

'I don't suppose that Andala is enjoying his midday meal much. A war band leader! For us! And Arthur of Wessex at that,' Jac said round a mouthful of bread and cheese hoping to distance himself from his wife's scorn.

'Don't talk with your mouth full,' his wife replied automatically.

'Makes me nervous just knowing he's here, let alone poor Andala having to sit and talk with him,' Breward said.

Jac resumed, having swallowed his mouthful of bread, 'Why Arthur? Why here? A few from a war band to protect us against any Uathach looking to raid our supplies, fine, but a warlord? And of all the warlords to have, did it have to be Arthur of Wessex?'

'Perhaps he's come to take your little redheaded Caja away with him,' Bri suggested to Breward.

'Don't even joke about that kind of thing. I wouldn't let him,' Breward replied. The other two laughed out loud. Breward looked offended but did not reply.

'Now clear off the both of you, I've got work to do here and you'd better make sure those wains are perfect, Jac – I don't want to have to defend you from that monster in there,' and Bri nodded to the main hall.

'Listen well young Breward, if my wife doesn't want to cross our guest and protector then you'd be truly out of your depth. At least the Uathach won't try to raid us – once they see Arthur with us they'll turn around and find a softer train.'

They both ambled off to find a quiet place to finish their meal and Bri continued slicing the bread and laying out fruits. They were right about the Uathach, the lawless roamers from the northern tribes of Britain, but it was not the Uathach who were making their way towards the village.

Arthur looked around the main hall. It was large by village standards, almost seventy yards long and over thirty wide. The far end was raised and there were heavy wooden tables down each side. A small fire burned in a circular hearth in the middle of the hall with various spits and cooking implements lying around it. Most of the smoke was channelled out of the hall by a wide funnel suspended above the hearth pit. Five or six people were moving up and down the tables beginning to make the preparations for the Lughnasa festival. Arthur unslung his shield and unbuckled his sword, propping them against the lower hinges of the heavy double doors of the main entrance. He unfastened his travelling cloak and put it on a hook above his weapons. Seeing the washbasin he ducked his head under the water and shook the water free then scrubbed the dust and dirt of the road from his hands with the washing stone.

'Would you like something to eat first Arthur, or would you rather rest?' Andala asked.

'Some food first, you can tell me about your preparations,' Arthur replied and started to walk up the hall to the raised main table where three figures sat waiting for him. There were wooden slat-covered windows down each side of the hall. Although those on the West side were covered, the low sun shone through the open windows on the East side sending smoke-lit shafts across the hall. Those at the table watched Arthur approach as he alternated between the shadows and the shafts of light. They stood as he reached the table.

'Greetings, Arthur of Wessex,' Ceinwen said, managing to keep her voice strong and steady.

There was an uneasy silence around the table as Arthur studied her. Ceinwen was a strong-willed woman and she held his gaze for as long as she could but eventually her eyes flicked away and settled on the food laid out on the table before defiantly returning to meet the gray stare. They were in the shadows but even in the filtered sunlight, and the soft glow from the candles that were set at either end of the table, he noticed how much older she looked; grey streaked her shoulder-length brown hair and her thin face carried the lines of the intervening years. Her sharp features had softened little with age and Arthur was pleased to see that her eyes still held some of the fire he remembered. Twenty years had passed and in that time they had exchanged no more than the obligatory pleasantries that their infrequent meetings had necessitated.

Andala watched them both but, like the others, felt unable to intervene to break the silence; whatever the silence meant, or whatever either of them were thinking, everyone else was excluded. He had never felt so distant from his wife.

'Some food and drink?' Ceinwen finally asked, gesturing to the food laid on the table.

'Thank you, Ceinwen, blessings on your homes and families,' Arthur completed the formal greetings and they all sat and began to eat. Arthur continued, 'The years begin to tell on you, Ceinwen. Are you well?'

'As well as the years allow, Arthur. It's been many years since we last spoke and I'm not Merdynn,' her eyes held Arthur's and the others stopped eating at the mention of Merdynn. Merdynn was the King's Counsellor, every successive King's Counsellor and a great deal of suspicion and myth surrounded him. Arthur was known to be one of the few whom he counted as a friend and the two had often been seen travelling together or deep in conversation at the great feasts in Caer Sulis. The villagers told their young sons and daughters that the two of them met to decide punishments for those children that had behaved badly but in truth many of the adults wondered if they weren't the ones being judged.

The tension increased as Arthur continued to study Ceinwen. Finally, he answered her, 'Merdynn outlived your father. He'll outlive you. He'll outlive your child but don't think the years don't weigh on him heavier than on any other.' Arthur's tone lightened as he continued, 'Besides, Merdynn has always looked as old as the seas and I certainly don't remember him dancing to the Bard in the Great Hall of Caer Sulis, unlike you, Ceinwen. Many years have passed since then, for us all, eh Narlos?' Arthur said turning to the old warrior who sat to his left quaffing down a mug of beer.

'Far too many. I remember that night in Caer Sulis. Well, some of it at any rate. I was in the Anglian war band back then. Great days.'

'Were they?' Arthur asked smiling.

'No. No, they weren't. Constant fighting with Uathach bands. That's why I spent most of my time drunk whenever I got to Caer Sulis. But I do remember Ceinwen dancing there – that was where you two met wasn't it?' Narlos gestured towards Andala and Ceinwen, his aged, liver-spotted hand trembling slightly. Ceinwen wondered if the old warrior was tired of life or just too feeble-minded to realise how thin the ice under him was becoming.

Andala placed a hand over hers wishing to bridge the distance which he felt had opened between them, and said, 'Indeed it was. Amongst that great throng and you picked me out. I still don't know why to this day, Ceinwen.'

'That's why,' Ceinwen answered as she poured a beaker and handed it to Arthur.

'And what of you Bernache? Has your apprentice wain-master managed to do as good a job as you used to?' Arthur asked.

Bernache was as old as Narlos but he sat a little straighter as he replied, 'Yes, well, Jac's still learning of course.'

'Are we on time to start the journey west?' Arthur asked. He said it casually enough and looked briefly at Andala.

Andala shot a quick glance at Bernache who nodded, and then he replied, 'We are. Everything should be finished tomorrow and then we can start.'

'Good.' Arthur began slicing into a joint of meat and everyone at the table visibly relaxed. Caja came across to the table with an armful of bread. Arthur watched her and his gray eyes became lifeless once again. Andala followed Arthur's gaze. Arthur sat back in his chair and took another drink from the beaker, his eyes still on Caja. She looked directly at Arthur and then quickly retired back to the kitchen area that was behind the dais.

Andala cleared his throat and said, 'We were expecting ten or more of Cei's warriors, Arthur. Is there anything wrong?'

'Cei hadn't heard from the Belgae villages so he sent some of his warriors there to see if anything was wrong. He asked me if the Wessex could escort you instead. I came across the Causeway with twenty warriors and I was going to keep ten with me at the Eald villages to the North and send the other ten down here.'

Ceinwen leaned forward at this news and exchanged a glance with Andala before asking, 'There's been no word from the Belgae? We haven't heard anything from the kingdoms to the East either. There haven't been any traders coming through for the last few months and it's usually the busiest time of year.'

Arthur looked at them both, his food forgotten. 'No news at all?' he asked. They shook their heads.

'You brought twenty warriors with you?' Andala asked, wondering again why Arthur had come to Branque alone.

'Yes, but Eald doesn't have Bernache, his apprentice, Ceinwen, or you Andala. They weren't ready. I had to leave those that came with me at Eald to sort out the mess and get them moving. Every year the villages have to do this and every year it's the same, you're on time and they aren't.' An edge had crept into Arthur's voice as he spoke.

Ceinwen remembered the tone and what it used to presage. She hastily tried to dispel it, 'Well, they have much more to harvest of course.'

'And many more to do it,' Arthur replied. 'Next year their chieftain's son will stay with you for the Gathering. What he learns he can take back and teach. If they don't learn quickly then they can wait behind for the darkness and be damned. There's worse things in the Shadow Lands than the Uathach.'

Narlos shuddered and added, 'Indeed there are. Thankfully I'm too old to ever have to travel in the darkness again.'

'Or perhaps your daughter Caja can travel to Eald and show them how the village of Branque prepares. She's learnt from you how to organise this business. Then we wouldn't have to wait until the year after next to see an improvement,' Arthur directed his comment to Andala but it was Ceinwen who answered.

'She's only seventeen, Arthur, she's too young for that responsibility.' There was a slight quaver to her voice and she didn't look Arthur in the face, speaking with her gaze on the table.

'Daughters are always too young in their Mother's eyes,' Arthur replied.

'Indeed, but seventeen...?' Ceinwen's voice trailed away.

'At seventeen you were dancing barefoot in the Great Hall and captivating everyone including the king. Did your Mother think you too young?'

'She did. Perhaps she was right. And I was nineteen, not seventeen, as you well remember,' Ceinwen said putting down her food. She put her hands in her lap and stared at Arthur but the challenge failed to mask the worry in her eyes.

There was a brief silence as Arthur went back to his food, 'Well. Think on it. I wouldn't suggest it if she wasn't capable enough but it's a mother's choice. For now.'

'We will Arthur, we will,' Andala said, not wishing a confrontation.

Outside the hall they could hear the hour bell being rung. Most villages had a bell of one kind or another with which to ring out the hours. There was usually a rota among the villagers to keep the hourglass, or read the sundial, and the responsibility often fell to those who spun the wool or to those whose turn it was to nurse the young. Twenty-four turns constituted a day and the passage of the days could be followed during the summer by the sundial that each village usually placed outside their main hall. They normally only slept between four and six hours a day during the long summer months but any length of time spent in the darkness of winter was characterised by idleness and long hours of sleep.

Arthur drained his drink and stood up saying, 'Perhaps you could show me to a place where I can rest?'

They all stood and Andala said, 'Of course, you've journeyed far. You'll join us for the Lughnasa festivities later?'

'Yes. Until then,' and Arthur took his leave of those at the table and followed Andala down the hall. Ceinwen watched him walk away, once again alternating between the shadows and shafts of sunlight.

Once Arthur had left the hall, Narlos put a hand on Ceinwen's shoulder and said, 'Don't fret yourself yet, a year is a long time and much may change before the next Gathering. Besides, he left it up to you to decide.'

'Did he?' responded Ceinwen, clearly not believing so. Bernache mumbled something about checking on Jac and his work on the wains and hobbled from the hall. Narlos sat back down and within minutes his chin was resting on his chest as he nodded off. Ceinwen sat staring sightlessly down the hall her hands twisting together where they lay in her lap. Caja quietly moved out of the shadows and left the hall by a small back door.

Andala led Arthur along a path that bisected an enclosed crop field towards his roundhouse, which was built over the lake. Serried ranks of carrots, onions and potatoes had already been harvested from either side of the path. There was a pasture field to one side of the crops with the bright yellow of buttercups strewn through the long grass.

'You can rest in my house. It's away from the noise of the village so you won't be disturbed,' Andala said.

Dust rose from the path about their feet as they neared the bridge to the roundhouse. Both the bridge and the house were supported by cut tree trunks sunk into the lakebed. Logs were laid out laterally along most of the bridge's short span but in the middle was a section of ten-foot logs set end by end. Unlike the others, they were not lashed in place and could be easily removed and on this section the intertwined hazel-latched sidewalls of the bridge could be pulled back too. Several dugout canoes lay on the stony lakeshore, beached for the winter and secured by thick ropes to the supports of the bridge. Inside the canoes were the village's fishing nets, freshly mended and folded away. Everything about the village spoke of departure.

Arthur studied the roundhouse. Around the walls of the stilted house ran a wooden platform about three-feet wide, which served as a walkway encircling the roundhouse with a low wall of hazel-latched fencing to the lakeside. The conical, reed-thatched roof spread down almost to the platform surface, overhanging the circular walls that were constructed of double layered tight bound trellising, daubed on the outside and filled with fern insulation between the layers. He recognised the many similarities to the homes in Britain, particularly Wessex, although he had rarely seen one built over water like this.

Andala held the door open for him and he entered. It took a while for his eyes to become accustomed to the dim light. As Andala cleared some belongings from one of the partitioned rooms Arthur gazed around the house. The floor was carpeted with dry fir needles and green fern bracken making it soft underneath his boots. In the middle of the roundhouse was a raised clay square centred by a large hearthstone. Three stout branches, tied at the top, formed a tripod above the fireplace and an iron cauldron hung above the embers suspended by strips of blackened leather. On the stones surrounding the fire oatcakes and unleavened wheat bread slowly cooked, filling the large room with the familiar smell of baking. By the hearth was a wide flat stone to grind the wheat on and a fireboard of pinewood together with the strung bow and oak spindle used to fire embers. There was no hole in the thatching above the fire but as the roof was so high above the hearth the smoke rose and dissipated through the reeds without filling the room.

25

Four small rooms faced the central hearth like open-ended boxes also made with, and separated from each other by walls of interlaced hazel branches. Andala gestured to the room he had been clearing where a low bed laid with soft fern and sheepskin could be seen through the goatskin hangings that draped across its open front. The roofs of these small inner rooms afforded extra storage space and bundled reeds and various farming tools, many old and needing repair, were stacked high enough to reach the thatching of the roof. From oak crossbeams hung leather gourds, pots, tied bundles of juniper to scent the room, and the various clutter accumulated by a family.

'Rest well. I'll send Caja to wake you when the feast starts,' Andala said.

Arthur settled down on one of the low beds. The roundhouse was still and he could hear the gentle lapping of the water fifteen-feet below as he drifted into sleep.

Caja was looking for Breward. She searched through the crowds that had gathered to take their midday meal in the main square before the hall but to no avail. She wandered off to the crafts buildings on the far side of the village, once again without success. Finally she asked the stores master and someone who overheard the question said Breward and Jac had gone out the East Gate before the midday bell had been rang. She went to the gate and saw them sitting on the grass with their backs against a cartwheel, watching the late autumn sun as it hung suspended over the flat, harvested crop fields of the narrow valley to the East. She strode across to them. They both turned to see who approached. She smiled inwardly at their contrasting faces, 'Don't worry Jac, I haven't come to nag.'

'Good. Want to sit down with us and steal some food then?' Jac stretched across Breward and offered her his plate. She took it gratefully and quietly.

'Gods, she's gone quiet. Doom is at hand if the wind's gone from her sails,' Jac said.

'Jac! Gods man, you can't say things like that with the journey across the Western Seas at hand,' Breward said sounding genuinely appalled then turned to Caja, still frowning, 'What's wrong Caj?'

'That bastard in there wants to send me to Eald for next year's Gathering,' she replied.

'Language girl,' Jac admonished idly and picked an apple off Breward's plate.

'Father told me off earlier for saying that, cuffed me actually – I'm a bit too old to be cuffed aren't I?'

'And you're old enough to know not to use that kind of language in front of your father,' Jac said then added, 'He's a braver man than me mind.'

Breward was still staring at her, 'What do you mean 'go to Eald'?' he asked.

'I'm not entirely sure. He's angry that Eald messed up their timings again. They weren't ready so he wants me to go and help them.'

'Organise them more like,' Jac said.

'He can't just decide that. You're too young. He doesn't even know you – he's only been here an hour!' Breward did not sound any less appalled but to his surprise Caja jumped up and with a muttered 'thanks very much' she strode off back to the village gate.

'What did I say?' Breward asked in exasperation.

'Well, first you said she was too young to do it and secondly that if Arthur knew her better he'd realise she couldn't do it,' Jac answered.

'No I didn't, I just said... but Eald, that's miles away – she can't want to go that far?'

'I wouldn't have thought she did but she's probably feeling quite proud that a warlord could just walk in here, take one look at her and then suggest it to her parents.'

'Oh.'

'You stick to ropes and wains my lad, you know where you are with them.'

'I'd better go and explain,' Breward said half-heartedly.

'Explain it later at Lughnasa, wine always makes things clearer. Less painful anyway,' Jac said then they lapsed into silence. The sun disappeared behind a bank of growing clouds coming towards them from the North East and a breeze whispered around them. They both noticed the drop in temperature immediately.

'Looks like Lughnasa will be held inside. It'll be raining and colder in a few hours,' Breward said.

Jac stood up and brushed the crumbs from his front before saying, 'Typical isn't it? Two fine weeks then the day before we head off a storm blows in. We'd better make doubly sure the wains are all secured and watertight. Come on.'

They walked back to the gate, the long grass around them swaying in waves before the stiffening breeze.

The wind softly nudged at an unfastened wooden shutter in the roundhouse where Arthur slept. The door opened slowly and Caja entered. Ceinwen had sent her to close and fasten the shutters in the roundhouse. Everyone knew what a wind from the East brought at this time of year. She crossed to the shutter and latched it firmly closed. She glanced across to the small room where Arthur slept and walked softly across to it, annoyed that her father had shown Arthur to her room. She turned back the goatskin curtain and crept in to collect her dress for the festival. She looked at Arthur and saw he was sleeping soundly. With her back to Arthur she quickly stepped out of her trousers, unbuttoned her top and shrugged it off. Reaching for her dress she pulled it on over her head and moving her long hair to one side, fastened it at the back of her neck. She glanced at the sleeping figure and started with surprise when she saw Arthur staring back at her. She took a step backward, her heart racing and she nearly clattered into a chair against the wall. Arthur's stare did not follow her. For a brief moment she thought he was dead but the covers across his chest were rising and falling with each breath. She realised he must be sleeping with his eyes open. She shuddered and quickly and quietly left the room. She wiped her suddenly sweaty palms on her hips and tried to control her breathing before crossing to the entrance and hurrying back across the bridge.

Arthur woke about an hour later. It took him a second to remember he was in a soft bed in Andala's roundhouse and that it was Lughnasa. He automatically scanned the room to find his weapons and then noticed the wind had picked up outside and was buffeting the wall of the house. The eastern wall. The roundhouse was filled with the roar from the wind-driven waves of the long lake. He cursed and swung his legs off the bed. He sat on the edge of the bed and rubbed both hands up his face and through his hair. Then he remembered the dream. He wished he had not. It was about Caja, but not the redheaded, untroubled, laughing girl who was no doubt already celebrating the festival. No, the Caja in his dream was in wretched misery, tormented beyond sanity. He crossed to a basin of water and splashed cold water on his face but the image remained and he sighed looking down into the water as his reflection reformed. He cursed and picking up his weapons he put out the oil lamp and left the house to find Andala.

As he stepped outside the wind whipped around him, snowflakes were already being blown horizontally out across the lake and through the air around him. It was snowing heavily further to the East and the water below the house was being driven against the stilts. Arthur strode across the bridge and back into the village, head down and leaning into the wind. He looked around the main square as he strapped his sword to his side noting how dark and gloomy it was even for this time of year. People were scurrying between the wooden buildings, all dressed in their best clothes and heading towards the main hall. Various foods and ewers of wine were being brought into the hall and everyone seemed carefree enough despite the sudden turn to cold. Arthur decided to check on his horse and caught sight of the new wain master, Jac, making his way to the hall. He called out to him but the wind snatched his words away.

Arthur ran across to him, nearly crashing into a small group of scampering children. They saw who it was and fled into the hall. He caught up with Jac by the doorway and put a hand on his shoulder. Jac turned and his already cold face froze further.

'My horse!' Arthur shouted above the wind, 'Where is it stabled!'

Jac pointed to a hut near the East Gate, 'The stables are by the gate, Lord!'

Arthur nodded his head and made his way to the gate, the wind wrapping his cloak around him. He reached the stables and slammed the door behind him. He looked around the stalls, it had become gloomy outside but inside it was almost dark. His horse was at the back. He untethered it and walked it up to the entrance and put the reins around a hook close to the door. He searched around in the dark and found his saddle and a spare saddlebag. He filled the bag with feed and saddled his horse. He checked the longbow was fitted correctly and that the quiver was full of arrows. He checked the horse's shoes then stood beside her, his hand absently rubbing his forehead. Uncharacteristically he patted the horse's neck. As he left the stable the horse gave him a look of deep suspicion.

He made his way to the main hall battling against the wind. Fewer people were now making their way in. Arthur assumed most were already inside. As he reached the doorway a small figure bumped into him. It was Caja. He opened the door and she dashed in, throwing back her hood and dusting the snow from her cloak. Arthur followed and stood his shield and sheathed sword against the wall.

'Mother had just sent me to the roundhouse to wake you! Gods it's getting bleak out there! But you must have already woken because you weren't there and I couldn't find you...' she spoke too quickly and fumbled with the clasp of her cloak. Arthur reached out and unfastened it for her. She was wearing a simple flowing white dress under the cloak. Caja felt even more nervous under his gaze and gestured awkwardly for Arthur to join the gathering at the top of the hall.

The hall was packed with the people from the five villages and Arthur did not notice that Breward had watched the interchange by the door. Nor did he notice how people made way before him as he walked to the tables at the top of the hall. People were already eating and swilling down the harvest wine and he realised he must have missed the formal part of the ceremony and the blessings for the Harvest Gathering.

Caja joined Breward who was sitting with Jac and Bri. She imitated wiping sweat from her brow, 'Gods, I feel uneasy near him!' she said to them, 'He even sleeps with his eyes open!'

Jac handed her some wine as Breward spluttered his out over his food.

'What?' he managed to say before Caja continued,

'I had to close the shutters in the roundhouse and collect my dress and when I turned he was just staring at me with those dead eyes! My heart nearly stopped!'

'But did your mouth?' Jac asked, already having finished several cups of wine. He got a clout from Bri for his trouble and consoled himself by taunting a hopeless cat juggler from a nearby village.

Bri scolded him for that too and pointed out, 'He may be hopeless but it's damned difficult and at least he's trying. He's quite sweet actually.'

'Gods woman! He's at least twenty years younger than you!' Jac stood up unsteadily and went in search of more affable drinking company, muttering something inaudible about kitchen girls.

Breward had recovered from his misapprehension and attempted to explain what he had and had not meant earlier when they spoke by the wain. He made heavy going of it. Caja elected not to tell him about undressing in front of the sleeping Arthur.

Arthur joined those at the top tables. He greeted the heads of the other villages and sat down next to Andala with his back to the wall and facing the thronging hall. As before, Ceinwen, Narlos and Bernache were seated at the table. The table was piled with foods and more was being brought from the central hearth, now in full blaze. The hall was warm, hot even, and lit by burning brands lined along each wall. The wooden shutters were all down but not latched so occasionally they would lift slightly as the wind buffeted the hall. The snow was becoming thicker in the air outside.

Arthur turned to Andala and asked, 'Do you have any guards for this village or any warriors?'

Andala shook his head vaguely, 'Barely – we set watchers if there's news of trouble nearby but any ex-war band are old like Narlos here or maimed. Ceinwen's trained a few of the younger men in hunting and tracking but they aren't really guards.'

Arthur leant back and surveyed the carefree scene before him. These people had worked hard all summer to raise their crops and then harvest them and now they had an arduous journey to Caer Sulis before them, or even further on to the Haven and across the sea. This was their local celebration of Lughnasa and they feasted, as they should, in their own homes among their own people. The festivities at Caer Sulis would be far grander but they would not enjoy it as much, they would be among strangers there and they would feel unimportant. Yet, despite the casual celebrations of the villagers, he felt uneasy, uneasy enough to have saddled his horse and packed extra feed.

Andala was watching him and growing more concerned as his own pleasant wine-induced shroud drifted away from him. 'Surely you don't expect an Uathach attack? In this storm? At Lughnasa?' Andala asked softly but urgently amidst the din of the hall.

'It would be an excellent time to do so. A drunk, defenceless village piled high with supplies...' Arthur took a drink from his beaker of wine, 'but no, we've spent the last two months in the North Country making sure that wouldn't happen. Still... something concerns me here.'

Ceinwen had noticed their quiet conversation and the look of worry on Andala's face. She asked Andala what the matter was but to her annoyance he held up a hand to stop her questions.

Arthur spoke again, 'Get seven of your watchers or hunters, make sure they're still sober, and put three on the eastern wall, one each on the other walls. Give them sheltered brands to keep near them but not so close so that they'll be lit-up by them. Place one watcher in a central point and have them signal him regularly. Have another seven stay sober to replace them in four hours time. Do it quietly and do it now.'

Andala got up ashen faced and went down into the throng of feasting villagers. Ceinwen took his vacated seat and leaned towards Arthur, 'Is there something wrong, Arthur?'

'No, I merely had a dream, just taking some caution.'

'What was the dream?' Ceinwen asked anxiously.

Arthur looked at her but did not answer. Ceinwen suppressed a shudder and resisted the urge to make the habitual sign to ward off evil spirits. Below them someone had struck up a lively tune on a lyre and the more drunken began to caper and dance in a small space before the raised part of the hall. Ceinwen recognised Jac dancing with one the kitchen girls and smiled despite her concern. She was a good-looking girl and holding Jac's hands they had began to spin in a tight circle. Others gathered around them and started to clap in rhythm to the lyre. It ended inevitably with them both crashing to the straw covered floor and, much to Jac's obvious delight, with the girl sprawled on top of him. The others helped them up and the space was cleared for some more accomplished dancers to pick up where they had left off.

Andala returned and took the empty seat next to Ceinwen and nodded across to Arthur to indicate it was done. Arthur forced himself to appear relaxed and started to eat from the piled foods on the table but he drank sparingly. Ceinwen heard from Andala what Arthur had ordered and her concern returned. Andala drained his beaker and refilled it then suitably emboldened, leant across Ceinwen to make himself heard above the music and spoke to Arthur, 'Can I ask you a question that's troubled me for years, Arthur?'

Arthur turned his attention to him and after a moment said, 'He was guilty, why think more on it?'

'That's just it! How did you even know what I was going to ask? How did you know he was guilty when it was just my word against his?'

Ceinwen watched them puzzled, and then it dawned on her that Andala was talking about the incident with the warrior and the girl on the journey west years ago.

She wanted to stop her husband asking any further questions but Arthur was already replying, 'And the girl's word.'

'Even so, she could have had an axe to grind.'

'And did she? Did you?' Arthur half-smiled at Andala as he asked.

'No. Every word we said was true but you weren't to know that.'

'I did know that.'

Andala ran out of courage to carry on and drank deeply from his beaker of wine. Ceinwen tried to indicate to her husband to drop the subject but in a rare misunderstanding Andala thought she was encouraging him and he continued, 'Some say that Merdynn gave you the Gift of Sight at your birth.'

'Do they? It's what I can't see that concerns me and the only gift Merdynn ever gave me was a cursed horse.'

'That you can see into people's hearts...' Andala persevered before his courage ran out completely.

Arthur turned to face him, 'Merdynn gave me no such gift.'

Andala tried one last time, 'Then how could you know, how could you be so certain so quickly?'

'Enough. Breagan was guilty. There's been no such incident again from any of my warriors. Nor will there be.' The subject was closed though not Andala's curiosity. Ceinwen rested a hand on Andala's arm to make sure he understood not to ask anymore.

Arthur stood up and said directly to Ceinwen, 'Heat some broth for those on the walls and get someone to take it to them, and bring them extra winter cloaks.' With that he made his way off the raised area and strode through the increasingly inebriated villagers to the main door. As he left the hall a dense swirl of snowflakes circled inside the doorway. Ceinwen issued the necessary instructions.

Arthur could barely see fifty yards ahead of him in the gloom and swirling snow. Eventually he saw a man huddled in the shelter of a doorway. He crossed over to him. There was some heat coming from the blacksmith's forge behind him and he had a timer glass on the floor beside him.

'What's your name?' Arthur asked once he was in the lee of the wind.

'Colban, my Lord.'

'Well Colban, is everyone signalling on time?' Arthur asked.

'Yes Lord, they're due to signal again now,' Colban motioned to the timer on the floor, its sands having run through the glass. He picked up a brand, which had a tubular, holed metal extension to protect the flames from the wind, and they both walked out into the exposed square. One by one the watchers signalled and he returned the signal. They retired to the lee of the blacksmith's and Colban turned the timer.

'Stay alert Colban. I'll make sure that you and your family get good quarters in Caer Sulis to make up for missing your festival. If any signal fails to be returned don't go to see if he's fallen asleep but come to me straight away. It's very important you understand that. Do you?'

'Yes, Lord.'

'And call me Arthur, I'm not your Lord.'

'Yes, Lord,' he replied automatically then realised what he had just said. They smiled and Arthur fought his way to the East wall. Behind him the first of the broths and cloaks arrived.

Breward was not delighted about being asked by Ceinwen to have to ferry supplies out to the watchers – he had been making good progress with Caja he thought. He had finally managed to convince her that he did not think she was either too young or incapable of helping to organise the Eald villages. He did have to agree he was just probably jealous of not being asked himself even though the thought hadn't crossed his mind but if it repaired some of the damage then he did not mind too much. He saw Arthur talking to one of the watchers as he carried around the supplies and was soon back inside the warmth of the hall. He felt the contrast sharply. Outside was gloomy, bleak and cold – a far cry from the merry making inside. He looked round for Caja and to his relief saw she was with her parents at the top table and not chatting to any of the lads from the other villages gathered here. He made his way with difficulty back up the hall and sat down heavily at the table.

'Done?' Ceinwen asked.

'Yes, and it's wretched out there. Only the gods know why he's decided to put watchers out in this weather, he must be mad,' Breward said and helped himself to a spare cup of wine from the table.

'Did you see him out there?' Andala asked.

'Yes, he was on the eastern wall.'

'And did you ask him why he set the watchers?' Andala queried.

'No – it was windy, couldn't hear a thing,' Breward explained.

Narlos tapped Breward on the arm, 'That's his wine your drinking lad.'

Breward nearly dropped it in his haste to put it back down and Caja laughed. He looked shamefaced at his haste but smiled broadly when Caja came across the table and sat in his lap offering him her wine.

'Are you going to dance, Caja?' Ceinwen asked.

'Shall I?' Caja asked Breward who groaned and said,

'You will anyway – best get it done.'

Caja jumped up and skipped back to the kitchen area where she had put her daisy-chain circlet ready for the dance. Arthur was making his way back up the hall having completed his circuit of the walls. Breward quickly refilled Arthur's wine cup and then theatrically examined his fingernails. Narlos laughed and clapped him on the shoulder.

Arthur took his seat and Ceinwen said, 'You're just in time to see our daughter dance, Arthur.'

'And does she dance as well as her mother used to?' he asked.

'You may judge that.'

The bard plucked a sequence of notes on the lyre and a tambourine rattled as Caja made her way barefoot to the small area before the top tables. She wore the daisy chain circlet around her long red hair that hung down the back of her simple white dress. She smiled up at Breward as the first chords of the song started on the lyre and, as the tambourine set the rhythm, she began to dance. The music grew louder, slowly developing with soft minor chords. The dance told of the sun's slow passage to the eastern horizon, the onset of autumn and the coming of the darkness.

Arthur sat back and leaning towards Ceinwen said, 'Just like her mother, twenty years ago.'

Ceinwen stared at him unsure whether he was cruelly taunting her or complimenting them both; she was not the girl's real mother, she could never have children – a fact that Arthur was all too aware of. Arthur watched the dance.

Gradually the noise of shouting and laughing died down as more began to watch the dance. People craned for a better view as word spread that Caja was dancing. Everyone knew her mother had silenced the Great Hall at Caer Sulis many years ago with a dance that had woven a tale into the music. They wanted to be the first to see if her daughter would do the same here. As drunk as they undoubtedly were, the onlookers became spellbound. People were standing on benches and tables to get a better view.

The funnel for the circular hearth in the centre of the hall obscured Arthur's view of the main doorway. He did not see it open. He did not see Colban stand there panting or see him sprawl forward to the floor, arms outstretched as if someone had pushed him violently from behind. Those nearest the main doors turned in irritation to see which drunken fool had left the doors open and let the cold air sweep in. They looked at Colban sprawled face down on the floor. They saw the crow-feathered arrow protruding from between his shoulders. They stared blankly at the prone form and just could not register that he had been killed by an arrow. Fully ten seconds passed and the dance continued. Then four black armoured, squat figures thrust the double doors open and stood in the doorway, curved swords held before them. Bri, standing near the door stared at the new horror then let out a terrified scream that tore through the hall and silenced the music. Arthur jumped to his feet, sending his chair flying behind him just as the nearest attacker to Bri leapt at her with his sword already swinging through the air. The sword cut her scream dead and she fell backward, blood showering from her neck. The wooden shutters along the eastern wall were flung open and black-clad, squat figures scrambled through like locusts spilling into the hall. A dozen more appeared at the main door and the mayhem started. People were screaming and trying to get away from the doorway and from the eastern wall where still more attackers scrabbled in.

Arthur shouted to Andala and Ceinwen, 'Get out! Make west!' and he leapt for the tables running down the West side of the hall, he landed and slid straight off the greasy surface into the villagers cramming themselves against the wall. He jumped back onto the tables and ran towards the main door where his sword stood against the wall.

Breward came out of his shock and tried to make his way toward Caja. Andala took Ceinwen's hand and pulled her toward the kitchen area where there was a small side door. There were screams coming from the kitchen and as they approached three assailants burst through, their curved swords already bloody. Andala turned and pushed Ceinwen back the way they had come as a sword took his legs from under him. Ceinwen turned in horror to see the swords hack down on her husband. She turned and fled back into the bloody chaos of the hall.

Breward had battled his way to Caja who still did not seem to understand what was happening around her. She grabbed his hands but before either could say anything a curved sword swung down over her shoulder and cut deeply into Breward's face. He slumped to his knees then fell forward, his bloody face smearing down Caja's white dress. She screamed as hands snatched and held her arms and legs, dragging her back toward the eastern windows.

Arthur reached the last table and slid to a stop. Before him the attackers were wading into the villagers, cutting a bloody swathe before them. Still more were pouring in through the doorway. He shot a look across to the other side of the hall to see even more scrambling through the windows and into the hall. There were already a hundred of them inside and a good thirty between Arthur and his sword.

'Out! Out the windows and run!' he shouted to those around him and hurled himself at the nearest wooden shutter. He flung it open and as he dived out he grabbed the wooden stake used to prop it wide. Others followed him as the slaughter continued behind them. He sprinted around the corner of the hall and joined the throng of attackers running towards the entrance. They were not looking for someone running with them and he made it to the doorway before cries went up all around him. He swung the wooden stake into the face of an attacker just behind him and sent him sprawling into those following. Lashing out with his foot he cleared the assailant just inside the doorway. He dived for his weapons and slipped his hand through the shield hold and brought it around just in time to catch the downward slash from a sword. Rolling across the earthen floor he swung his sword and the scabbard flew free and toward his attacker's face who ducked but could not avoid the sweeping sword that followed cutting his left leg off below the knee.

The attackers that were trying to stop the flight through the western windows began to turn to see the commotion behind them. Arthur did not hesitate, roaring he rushed at them and cut down two in as many seconds. They faltered and he lunged at another who tried to turn Arthur's blade but was not quick enough. Arthur dragged the sword back out of the falling body.

In front of him a single line of the attackers turned to face him, they had been pressing their slaughter on the villagers along the western side of the hall who were still desperately trying to get through the windows. Behind him a band of twenty to thirty attackers were closing on him from the doorway. The eastern side of the hall was a chaotic bloody mess with bodies everywhere and the attackers moving on to those crammed up against the West side. In the moment it took to take this in Arthur saw Ceinwen among those at the top end of the hall trying to escape the massacre through the western windows.

He leapt at the single line ahead of him in a howling rage. The attackers were unprepared for his fury and he cut his way through. Once again he ran the length of the tables, standing on friend and foe alike as he tried to reach Ceinwen. He saw Jac as he drunkenly laid about him with a wooden stool but was already beyond him and did not see the arrow fired at close range that tore into Jac's throat.

As he neared Ceinwen he lost his footing on a blood soaked table and flew off crashing into a group of attackers. Before he could recover, a curved sword slashed down into his shoulder and blood flew into his face. He lashed out blindly and rolled beneath the table as more swords thumped down into the earth where he had been. Once on the other side of the table he leapt up and turned the table over as the attackers began to clamber over it. He looked to see where Ceinwen was. She was only fifteen-feet away but as he watched an attacker ran at her with a spear. At the last second she twisted away from the thrusting spear and it just missed her stomach and embedded itself in the wall. She kicked out at her attacker who staggered backwards. Arthur hurled himself at the spearman and took his head clean off with one full-blooded sweep of his sword.

He looked at the wreckage of the hall. Where a few minutes earlier there had been feasting and dancing now there was carnage. It seemed that the only ones standing were the black armoured attackers. He turned quickly and hoisted Ceinwen through a window that already had its shutter torn off and dived after her. The freezing wind chilled him immediately and shouting for Ceinwen to follow he started for the stable by the East Gate.

'Wait! My daughter, Caja!' Ceinwen shouted and turned back to the window. Even from where she stood she could see that the panic and bloody slaughter continued unabated inside. She screamed her daughter's name again and again.

Arthur ran back to her and, circling her waist with one arm, half-carried and half-dragged her away from the hall. She struggled to free herself from his grip, her legs kicking in the air and still screaming for her daughter. Arthur set her down and held her at arms length.

'Where was she?' he shouted above the wind. She stared at him blankly and he had to repeat the question. She pointed back to the hall and Arthur had to reign in his impatience. 'Whereabouts in the hall? Near the West windows?'

Ceinwen shook her head.

'Where was she when you last saw her?'

'Nearer the East side,' Ceinwen said regaining control of herself and understanding what her answer meant.

'Everyone still in that hall is now dead,' Arthur said still holding her shoulders.

She looked towards the hall and, as if to prove Arthur's words, she saw someone being dragged back from the window as he tried to escape through it.

'I can't leave her, Arthur,' she said desperately.

An arrow flicked between their faces and they instinctively broke apart and turned to see four Adren charging towards them. Arthur met them and killed two almost instantly. He pressed forward and Ceinwen followed, stooping down to claim a sword from one of the dead. They dispatched one each but more were coming from the hall's entrance.

Arthur grabbed her by the arm and ran for the stables. As he neared the entrance an arrow thudded into the back of his right thigh and he crashed to the snow-covered ground. He crawled to the entrance and Ceinwen pulled him through. He looked at the arrow with blurred vision and decided he could not push it all the way through. Ceinwen came to the same conclusion and swiftly snapped off half the protruding shaft. She leapt up onto the horse and leaning down helped Arthur as he hauled himself up in the saddle behind her. He nearly passed out leaning forward to untether the reins as the remaining part of the arrow shaft caught on the saddle. He clung onto Ceinwen as she spurred the horse out of the stables. There were black-clad figures running everywhere, looting whatever they could find and setting fire to the insides of wooden buildings. There were screams and shouts still coming from inside the hall and Arthur could hear the desperate screams of a woman from one of the wooden houses across the square. Ceinwen half-turned the horse towards the screams but two arrows sped past to either side of her and she urged the horse forward again. Arthur spat on the ground and they rode out through the East Gate leaving the slaughter behind them.

Chapter Two

It had stopped snowing. The low, dark clouds still barrelled in from the East but the gale had subsided. They were near the top of the hill across the river from the village. Arthur clung to his horse's neck as it stood and pawed at the snow; Ceinwen was standing some distance away, staring down at Branque.

Arthur tried to clear his eyes and focus on the ground where his steadily dripping blood was already staining the snow. With an effort he slid off the horse and immediately crumpled to the ground as his leg gave away beneath him.

Ceinwen turned at the sound of Arthur's curses. She instinctively checked to make sure that the horse was not silhouetted against the sky and then returned to scanning the hillside for any sign of pursuit. She absently brushed at the tears stinging her eyes and noticed her hands were trembling. She knew she was in shock; that her mind was lagging a long way behind the events of the last hour.

Only a few hours ago she was the healer in a peaceful village, the wife of the village tain and mother to a vivacious daughter whom she loved more than life itself. She gazed down at the village and told herself once again that her husband, daughter and village were all dead. The last twenty years of her life had been wiped away in the horror of the last hour but she was not yet able to accept it or to understand where that left her now.

She had seen others experience what she was now feeling, or not feeling, but that had been over twenty years ago when she was with the Wessex war band. It wasn't difficult to remember the scenes from the villages that had been attacked by the Uathach but even the brutal raids of that time didn't compare to what she had just witnessed.

She had been a teenager back then, fearless because she had nothing to fear losing, courageous because life stretched before her with endless possibilities, but she had left that life behind a long time ago and was now a very different person. She turned and looked at the man sitting in the snow: the man she hadn't talked to in twenty years and the reason why she had left the Wessex war band.

Arthur looked across to her, 'Are they following yet?'

She shook her head.

'Then give me a hand here.'

She stayed where she was.

Arthur turned his attention back to his leg and using both hands he gingerly examined the arrow still embedded in the back of his thigh. He could not remember if any of the spent arrows he had seen had barbed arrowheads and cursed himself for not noting it. Without looking over to Ceinwen he asked, 'Did you see if any of the arrows were barbed?'

'No, they were just two-sided,' she replied without thinking.

Kneeling up he took a small vial and a water bottle from one of his saddlebags then drew his knife and cut a slit along his ox-hide trousers where the arrow had penetrated. He poured water around the arrow shaft that protruded from his leg to clear away some of the blood then tore several strips off his cloak using the knife.

Ceinwen looked back down the hill to see if there were any signs of pursuit but it seemed the attackers were still busy in the village below. She crossed over to Arthur and stood beside him. He ignored her and putting the torn strips in his mouth and clamping his teeth on them, he eased the knife into the arrow wound until he could feel its tip. Opening the wound with his knife he gently pulled the arrow free, grunting in pain as he did so. Blood pulsed out but did not spurt and Arthur breathed a sigh of relief through the strips clamped firmly in his mouth.

Ceinwen knelt beside him and folding some of the strips into a solid pad she pressed it against the gash in his thigh and soaked the area with the liquid from the vial that he passed to her. The muscles in his thigh spasmed and he grunted again as the liquid burned in the deep cut. Ceinwen tightly wound the other strips around his leg to hold the pad pressed against the wound.

Next he examined his shoulder where he had taken a blow from one of the curved swords. It was bruised and ugly but the cut was not deep, his heavy leather jerkin having taken most of the force from the blow. He repeated his actions with the water and the vial but did not try to bandage it. Using a stirrup as a handhold, and with Ceinwen's help, he hauled himself upright. With the horse on one side and Ceinwen on the other, he hopped on one leg to where Ceinwen had been studying the village below.

As he studied the hillside for any sign of movement he absently felt for his sword. Neither it nor the scabbard hung from his belt. He remembered losing the scabbard in the hall when he had to free his sword quickly but did not remember leaving his sword at any point. He looked around the blood-covered snow but did not see it there either. He thought it must have flown from his grasp when the arrow had sent him sprawling. He saw no movement on the hillside. He had hoped that perhaps some of the villagers had made it across the river but without horses... he left the thought unfinished and tried to make out what was happening in the village below.

'Can you see what's happening down there?' he asked her.

It was not easy to see much in the gloom but the whole village was crawling with the assailants. Some of the buildings were already on fire and she could see flames springing from the thatch of her roundhouse down by the lakeshore.

'They've found the loaded supplies, I can see them being dragged out of the barns and oxen being yoked to them. Some of the houses are being fired,' she answered, surprised at how emotionless her voice sounded.

'The main hall?'

'No, that's still intact. There seems to be one figure on a horse directing the others.'

'But no mounted warriors?' Arthur asked.

'No,' she answered, unable to take her eyes away from the desecration of her village. As she watched, the full horror of what had happened began to sink in; her family, her friends, her home – all dead and destroyed.

Arthur took her by the shoulders and turned her away from the scenes below, 'I swear to you we'll hunt down every last one of those bastards, even if we have to hunt them through the winter and through the Shadow Lands, we'll hunt them down and we'll kill every last one of them. We'll track them to their homes and we'll slaughter their women and children and then we'll burn their homes to the ground in payment for what they've done here.'

Ceinwen looked at him and, for the first time since he had arrived at her village, she saw him for the man he now was and not as the man she once used to know. She saw the hatred burning in his eyes and knew he meant to do exactly as he said. She had seen him fighting in the hall and, staring into his gray eyes now, she felt sure that the man standing before her could and would kill the families of his enemies for what they had done to her village. She realised she wasn't the only one to have changed over the last twenty years; for all the emotions she had once felt for or about Arthur, fear had not been one of them but as he stared down at her she suddenly realised she was afraid of him.

She stepped away from him, leaving him clinging to the saddle for support, and said quietly, 'We need to get away from here.'

Arthur motioned for her to mount the horse first, 'We'll make for Eald and warn Ruadan and the others about this Shadow Land army.'

Ceinwen stared at him in surprise, 'My brother's at Eald?'

'He rode with me across the Causeway. He and the others are getting Eald ready for the journey – I told you this back in the hall.'

'You didn't say Ruadan was leading them!'

Arthur shrugged and impatiently gestured for her to mount the horse. She did so and Arthur painfully pulled himself into the saddle behind her and they made their way across the hillside on one last sweep before leaving the scene behind them. They found no fleeing survivors on the hillside. Neither had expected to but both had wanted to make sure.

Arthur told her to take the main way that ran through the forests from the now dead village of Branque to Eald. It was more open but it would be much quicker and he wanted to get the warning to his warriors as quickly as possible. They rode for several hours without speaking; Ceinwen weeping silently for the dead and Arthur fighting the pain from his leg. In an effort to take his mind from the flaring agony of each jolt he pondered the attack on Branque. It had been years since anything similar had happened. He remembered when he was no more than a young teenager the Uathach had raided a North Anglian village. It was the first time he had seen such a slaughter since his own childhood. Even then they had not slain so indiscriminately. He had only seen the aftermath and while many had died more had been taken as slaves, particularly the women with children. Most of the dead had been killed trying to defend their young. Less than half the marriages produced any children and every birth was regarded as a precious blessing just as every child taken represented the stealing of an already tenuous future.

What he had just witnessed did not make sense. Through the waves of pain he tried to think it through: they must have been after the harvest supplies – that made sense with the sun setting and the long winter ahead, but why the senseless slaughter in the hall? There must have been close to five hundred armed attackers – that was nearly as many as the combined warriors of Britain. Where did such an army come from and why? All for one undefended village? The questions repeated themselves and Arthur realised he was close to delirium. He struggled to remember where the next way-station was on this road. It would be abandoned for the winter but it would offer them shelter and a place to re-examine his wounds.

They rode on for several hours, down the rough, wide path between endless rows of tall pine trees, the sun low in the sky and hidden by the forests to their right that stretched further than either of them knew. He fought the delirium but the questions kept returning. No such Uathach army had existed since he was a child. They raided in clans, no more than twenty or thirty and never across the seas to this part of Middangeard.

The assailants were not Uathach, he was sure of that. They had all worn similar armour, black and uniform – no Uathach raiding band had ever worn uniform armour. The black shields he had seen all had the same device on them, a white vertical stripe with three prongs radiating from the top, possibly a star he thought. The attackers had displayed a feral, ferocious quality that had reminded him of the way he had once seen rats, maddened by winter hunger, attack a lamb. He tried to remember the ones he had seen without their helmets on and was fairly certain that they had all had black hair, so black it was almost blue, and their facial features set them apart from any peoples he had seen before. He shook his head fearing that his delirium was clouding his memory and turning them into something they weren't.

He was relieved to see the way-station ahead in a wide clearing to the side of the road. He pointed it out to Ceinwen and she directed the tired horse towards it. Arthur gently lowered himself down to the ground while Ceinwen opened the stable doors and walked into the darkness. The horse followed her and Arthur, with one arm crooked around the pommel of the saddle, let it half-carry him into the stable. Ceinwen automatically emptied some feed into a trough and taking the saddle off the horse began to wipe the sweat off its flanks.

Arthur watched her for a moment then taking two buckets hanging from the wall he limped out to find the well. He came back seconds later and collected the longbow and quiver from his saddle then resumed his search for the well, using the stout longbow to take the weight from his right side. When he had collected the water and put one bucket before his horse, Ceinwen set about building a small fire on the floor and started boiling some water.

Arthur cleaned the wounds on his shoulder and leg and re-dressed them with fresh strips. He re-applied the liquid from the vial while Ceinwen made a light broth from his rations and the water. When the meal was ready they ate in silence. They had both been preoccupied with their own pain and had barely spoken to each other since leaving the hill above Branque but now that they were sitting opposite one another and sharing a meal the silence seemed to weigh heavier and both were aware of it. The two decades since their parting had taken them each down very different roads and, for all that they might have shared in the past, it seemed they had little common ground now – except for Branque, and neither wanted to talk of that yet.

Eventually it was Ceinwen who broke the silence, 'How's your leg?'

'Better now I'm off that horse.'

She nodded in reply and Arthur saw how pale and drawn her face was. Her eyes were red and puffy and her voice sounded flat and lifeless.

'Can I look at what herbs and ointments you have?' she asked.

Arthur pointed to one of the saddlebags and she got heavily to her feet and inspected his supplies.

'There's not much here,' she said picking through the meagre supply.

'You've kept up your practice as healer?' Arthur asked.

'Yes, for all the good it can do anyone now,' she replied bitterly.

Arthur was thinking quite the contrary but he kept his thoughts to himself. 'You should try to get some sleep. I'll keep watch for a while then we'll ride on to Eald.'

Ceinwen felt too exhausted to disagree; all she wanted to do was curl up and go to sleep hoping never to wake again. She watched as Arthur forced himself to stand and collect a blanket before limping out of the stable with the aid of his longbow. She knew it was unfair to blame him for what had happened at Branque, it had just been coincidence that they had been attacked while he was there, but neither was she able to thank him yet for saving her life during the attack: she wished that he hadn't.

Arthur felt overwhelmingly drowsy but forced himself to cross into the forest on the far side of the roadway. He found a sheltered place some way back in the trees and slumped down awkwardly with his back against a trunk and watched the road leading back to Branque.

He awoke with a start. Through the trees he could see horses and figures moving about the stables. The dark grey clouds still scudded in from the East and the light was poor. He quietly got to his feet and quickly leant against a tree for support as the pain hammered through his body from his wounded leg. Wiping the sudden sweat from his brow he strung his longbow and drew an arrow from his quiver. Moving silently and slowly he worked his way closer to the roadway. There were five horsemen, two had dismounted and he presumed that they were around the back of the stables. The horses had been ridden far and were blowing hard.

Arthur crept closer, half-drawing the longbow. The two figures emerged from the side of the stables and briefly conferred with the others then one approached the stable door and readied to open it. Arthur recognised the tall, thickset figure with his wild thatch of brown hair that had increasingly grown to resemble a crow's nest as the years went by.

It was Ruadan, his second-in-command and Ceinwen's brother. The two of them had joined the Wessex war band as young teenagers, over twenty-five years ago now, and they had immediately fallen in with Arthur and Trevenna, and the young Anglian, Cei. The five of them had been inseparable for several years but other duties had gradually taken them apart; Cei had growing responsibilities in Anglia, Merdynn would take Arthur away for months at a time, and then the chain of events had started that ended with Ceinwen leaving the war band and living across the Causeway in Branque. Arthur and Ruadan had since been through many battles and many raids together but their friendship was never on the same footing after Ceinwen had left.

Arthur watched the group by the stables. They were all from the band he had left at Eald and he wondered where the others were and why these five were here. Ruadan was talking to Mar'h and Balor and, as he watched, Morgund sauntered across to join them. In many ways the four of them constituted the heart of the Wessex war band and Arthur was about to call out to them but he rarely got the chance to observe his second-in-command and two of his captains without them knowing he was nearby, and he was curious enough to wait and watch for a while.

Mar'h was the elder of the two captains, a few years younger than both Arthur and Ruadan. He was a tall man with a dark complexion and a slight stoop to his wiry frame which, together with his long, straight black hair and hooked nose, gave him something of the appearance of a vulture or a raven. It was a resemblance he vehemently denied whenever Morgund cheerfully pointed it out to him.

Arthur had taken a risk when he made Morgund a captain in his war band. It had been a few months since his selection and he hadn't yet stopped strutting – much to Mar'h's and Balor's amusement. He was slightly shorter than Mar'h but of a much heavier build and his black-skinned, shaven-headed, muscular appearance was nothing if not imposing but the warrior's most striking feature was his pale blue eyes. People seeing him for the first time couldn't help but stare at the unexpected contrast between the blue eyes and dark skin, and, depending on whether it was a man or woman, it often gave him the opportunity to find either offence, where none had been intended, or encouragement, where none was actually being offered. At twenty-eight he was relatively young to have a captain's responsibility but Arthur had gambled that the only way to curb the young man's natural recklessness and explosive aggression was to force upon him the sense of responsibility he so patently lacked. Largely it had paid off; the only aspect it hadn't changed was Morgund's complete lack of conscience or restraint when it came to women, indeed, if anything his new position had encouraged those particular and relentless pursuits.

The fourth member of the cadre was Balor but where the other three had been warriors from an early age he had only been with the war band for the last ten years. He had joined about the same time that Morgund became a fully-fledged member of the war band. Only Arthur knew the whole story behind Balor leaving his life as a woodcutter in the Wessex forests at the age of thirty-five and requesting to join Arthur's warriors. Mar'h and Morgund had spent many drunken hours in the long winter months speculating about Balor's story and the more favoured theories revolved, of course, around a hypothetical woman. Typically enough, Morgund's more colourful speculation involved two women and a young girl but even he had to concede his theory was flawed when Mar'h simply pointed to Balor and asked if he really, honestly thought so. Balor was not cut from the usual warrior mould. He was a broad, bald, angry five foot four with a grey beard and blue eyes, and he only had two moods; either he was in a sullen, brooding sulk or incredibly good humoured and barking out his infectious laugh. He wasn't known for his subtlety and his loud, argumentative and generally combative social skills rarely left anyone in any doubt where they stood with him.

He had immediately formed a friendship with Mar'h, seeing in him a kindred spirit when it came to pessimism and recognising in him an enviable capacity to brood. They spent many happy hours trying to outdo each other on the expected and worst possible outcomes of any given event. Balor was the kind of man to gloomily keep checking exactly when it would be mid-summer and as soon as the sundial suggested that mid-summer had passed then he would cheer up immeasurably and take great delight in telling everyone that the dark winter months were already drawing in.

It was an attitude that Mar'h admired despite Morgund's mocking scorn who maintained, with good reason, that the two of them would only truly be happy and content once the worst had happened and they were dead. For their part, they thought Morgund lived with his head in the clouds and his feet in clover and absolutely no good would come of it. All of which left Morgund at a loss to understand why Mar'h was just so disappointed with the world, and why Balor was so angry at it. With Ruadan usually siding with the more optimistic Morgund and despite their apparent differences, or perhaps because of them, the four of them got on like a summer barn on fire with the hay feeding the wood and the wood feeding the hay until the whole thing was blazing away merrily and producing an endless supply of hot air.

But as Arthur watched them from the cover of the trees there was no sign of their usual levity. Each of them were grim-faced and their usual banter silenced. He turned his attention to the last of the riders and saw why: the youth was splattered in blood. Clearly it wasn't his own and equally clearly they had been in battle. Arthur cursed quietly at the implication and called out to them.

They all turned to the trees at the sound of his voice. Using his bow as a staff he picked his way towards them and those still on their horses quickly dismounted. They stopped short when they saw Arthur step up onto the roadway; his leg was heavily bandaged and his clothes were still covered with the blood from the fighting back at Branque.

Ruadan cursed and crossed the path to Arthur, 'It's what I feared when I saw your horse's tracks on the roadway. Were you ambushed on your way to Branque?'

'Are the Eald villages on the way west yet?' Arthur asked, ignoring Ruadan's question for the time being.

Ruadan's look of relief at seeing Arthur alive changed to anguish. Mar'h stepped up next to Ruadan and replied for him, 'They're gone Arthur. The Eald villages are gone. Some army from the Shadow Lands attacked us. We sped here to warn you...' his voice trailed off.

Arthur's heart grew colder at the news and he leaned heavily on the longbow, 'Gods,' he muttered then addressed Ruadan's earlier question, 'I'm not on my way to Branque. I made it there in time for their Lughnasa festival. So did an army from the Shadow Lands. The Branque villages have been butchered too. I was on my way to warn you.'

They stared at him as they took this news in, realising what it meant. Arthur looked at each one in turn. Ruadan was swearing vengeance and gripping the hilt of his sheathed sword tightly. Suddenly he looked at Arthur, 'Ceinwen? Her family?' he asked, fearing the worst.

'Ceinwen's in the stable. Asleep.' Arthur said, nodding to the closed doors behind Ruadan.

He exhaled heavily in relief and then asked softly, 'Anda? Caja?'

'Dead. They're all dead.'

Ruadan swore, caught between feeling relief for his sister's safety and despair at the fate of her family. The others had clustered around the two of them. Balor and Morgund were offering what sympathy they could to Ruadan while pointing out that at least Ceinwen was safe. Mar'h and Arthur were looking at each other both thinking of the wider implications behind the synchronised attacks on the villages.

The last of the group and by far the youngest, Ethain, was still standing by his horse, some way apart from the others, alternately looking north up the road toward Eald then south toward Branque.

'Are you the only survivors? Did any of the villagers escape from Eald?' Arthur asked Ruadan.

'We got about twenty-five of the villagers away. Elowen and Tomas are taking them to the Causeway. Once we put a safe distance between ourselves and the Shadow Land army we rode south to warn you,' Ruadan answered.

'As I rode north to warn you,' Arthur grimaced as his balance swayed and he inadvertently put weight on his injured leg. 'So then, the others are dead and we stand on a roadway between two Shadow Land armies.'

'Not the best place to be really,' Mar'h said casually.

They all turned as the stable doors opened and Ceinwen emerged from the darkness shading her eyes against the late summer light. She had a brief look at the gathered warriors before Ruadan engulfed her in an embrace. They may have been brother and sister but their physical appearance couldn't have been much more different; where Ceinwen was small and slight, Ruadan was tall and thick limbed. Their only common feature was their dark eyes, usually so full of life and amusement but Ceinwen's eyes were still red and puffy while her brother's were full of sadness for her.

Arthur turned away from them and spoke to Morgund, 'Get my horse saddled and bring it out.'

Balor, in a rare show of sensitivity, moved away from the siblings too and stood by Arthur and Mar'h who were watching the road back to Branque.

'Did he fight well?' Arthur asked them, nodding at the lone figure of Ethain.

'Well enough for a youngster. I had to dig him out of a hole – that blood soaking him should've been his,' Balor replied.

'He'll learn,' Mar'h added.

'He'll have to learn faster,' Balor said, thinking about the sudden onslaught at Eald. 'What's our next move, Arthur?'

'We'll ride west through the forests then north to the Causeway and meet up with Tomas and Elowen,' Arthur said as Morgund brought his horse out to him.

Ceinwen and Ruadan joined them, both looking equally miserable.

'How's your injuries?' Ceinwen asked in a hollow voice, gesturing to Arthur's bandaged leg and bloodied shoulder.

'The shoulder will be fine but the leg could be a problem. Small price to pay for getting out of that massacre. Ruadan you take the lead,' Arthur said and repeated the plan that he had already outlined to Balor and Mar'h.

'I'll ride with Ruadan,' Ceinwen said over her shoulder. Arthur thought it would make more sense for her to travel on Ethain's horse as he was a good deal lighter than Ruadan but he said nothing and hauled himself painfully back onto his horse.

The others mounted their horses and one by one they slipped into the gloom of the forests on the West side of the roadway. Arthur held back to ride with Ethain, 'Tell me what happened at Eald and how it ended for the others.'

The woodlands were fairly open at first and Ethain recounted the attack on Eald in his soft voice as he rode by Arthur's side. He occasionally brushed at his clothes and watched in fascinated distaste as dried crusts of blood fell away. His black hair, which usually stuck out at every angle, was matted down with sweat and he seemed nervous as he talked to Arthur. Every now and again he would falter in his story and cast a glance back over his shoulder, and whenever he did so Arthur would ask him another question concerning the assailants and how they had attacked. Gradually Ethain stopped looking back but something about his manner worried Arthur and he would have looked more closely at the young warrior if he hadn't been constantly distracted by the pain that was flaring up from his leg again.

After several hours they descended a slope and stopped by a stream running north. The woodland on the far bank looked to be much more dense. Arthur decided to rest where they were for an hour or two. The raw throbbing from his wound was worsening and each jolt sent searing pain up his leg and spine. Ruadan went across the stream to see how far the thicker patch of forest extended while Mar'h built a small fire from dry, dead wood. Arthur examined his injured leg and redressed the wound.

'Lucky it wasn't poisoned,' Mar'h said without looking up.

'And fortunate the arrowhead wasn't barbed,' Balor chipped in.

Morgund shook his head as he sat down next to Arthur, 'I'd swear that between them they could find the dark side of the sun.'

Arthur looked up at him and was struck once again by the pale blue eyes that contrasted so sharply with his dark skin.

Ceinwen fetched a small satchel from Ruadan's saddlebags and picked out a packet of powder which she handed to Arthur saying, 'This will stop any fever and dull the pain for the next few hours.'

Arthur emptied the powder onto his tongue and took a swig of water. Grimacing he wiped the back of his hand across his bearded face then said, 'We'll take two hours to rest here,' he stopped as Ruadan came back across the stream.

'It's dense, probably too dense to walk our horses through,' he said and ran his hands through his thick hair, dislodging snapped twigs as if to prove the point.

'Then we'll follow this side of the stream north,' Arthur continued, 'Ethain – take the first hour on watch.'

'And I'll take the second,' Morgund offered and with that they unrolled their bedding and slept as best they could.

Ethain busied himself with doing a wide circuit of their makeshift camp then giving the horses some feed from the supplies they carried. The wind from the East had either died down altogether or the forests protected them from it. The clouds had cleared but the sun was too low on the eastern horizon to send any shafts of sunlight through the trees or to provide them with any warmth. He collected all the water bottles and filled them from the stream and as he did so he noticed that while most of them slept soundly enough, Ruadan and Ceinwen were talking quietly to each other. He replaced each water bottle on the respective saddles then added some more wood onto the fire. He watched it for a few minutes to make sure it didn't give off any smoke then sat down near the group. He found himself staring at the dried blood on his clothes and reliving the events at Eald in vivid and repetitive detail.

Ceinwen wrapped the blankets more tightly about herself and Ruadan watched her with concern. She had a distant look in her eyes that suggested to him that she was looking anywhere but at the recent events.

Finally she stirred and looked at him, 'You should be getting some rest – I slept back at the way-station but gods know when you last got some sleep.'

Ruadan shrugged to indicate it was completely unimportant and Ceinwen smiled sadly.

'I thought I'd left all the killing and dying behind me,' she said, staring at her brother as if imploring him to somehow undo all that happened. His heart went out to her but he could think of nothing to say that would alleviate her pain. She looked away clearly distraught and muttered, 'They're dead. What am I going to do now? My family gone, my village gone... I've nothing left.'

'You've still got your big brother,' Ruadan pointed out with a clumsy attempt at humour. A ghost of a smile crossed her face and she laid a hand on his leg.

'Come back to the war band, you'll always have a home with us – you know you'd be welcomed with open arms,' he added quietly.

'I wouldn't know any of them now. Twenty years. How many are still alive from the old days?'

Ruadan was about to say there were many from the old days but he brought himself up short. He hadn't really thought about it before but now that he tried to name the survivors who would remember her he found that there weren't many at all. Not all of the old names had died or been killed in battle but the war band had changed completely since Arthur became the Warlord sixteen years ago.

'I probably know more of the Anglian warriors these days – more than the Wessex ones anyway,' Ceinwen said.

Ruadan thought she was probably right especially as it had almost always been the Anglians who escorted the villagers from across the Causeway but he didn't want her thinking she would be better off joining the Anglians.

'I don't know any of these for a start,' she said indicating those around them. Both of them were conscious she had included Arthur in that statement.

'Well, you won't know Balor or Morgund. Balor joined us about ten years ago and Morgund would have been too young then for you to remember him,' Ruadan said.

'And the young one...'

'Ethain?'

'Yes, I doubt he was even born when I left the Wessex.'

'But you must remember Mar'h, surely.'

'I don't think so.'

'He was that teenager who spent his whole time chasing after Della – the blacksmith's daughter. You must remember the antics he got up to. One time he nearly burned their home to the ground...'

'That Mar'h?' Ceinwen asked looking over to the sleeping figure. Ruadan was relieved to see her taking some interest and even more relieved to hear a touch of life in her voice again.

'What happened to Della?' Ceinwen asked, curious now that the old memories had been stirred.

'She married Mar'h! They've got three children now.'

Ceinwen smiled, 'So he got her then, good for him. She had a witch of a mother if I remember right.'

'You do. She's living with them now; she left old Laethrig.'

'Lucky Laethrig,' Ceinwen replied with a laugh. It was a soft laugh and didn't last long but Ruadan would have been happy to barter everything he owned just to have heard it. He had been afraid that the mention of Mar'h's children would have sent her plummeting back into her darkness.

'So what about Balor and Morgund?'

'There's not much to say about them really; they're warriors. Morgund's outlook on life is very simple – as long as there's pretty girls in the world and someone to fight, then he's happy. Balor's is even simpler – as long as there's a world then there's something to complain about. Good men both of them, you'll get to know them soon enough.'

Ceinwen smiled but the emptiness had returned to her eyes and silent tears were soon coursing down her cheeks once again. Ruadan held her, mercifully unaware it had been his comment about 'pretty girls' that had brought a picture of Caja right to the front of Ceinwen's mind.

Ethain had been staring at his bloodied sleeves and too absorbed in reliving the brief battle and flight from Eald to hear or notice Morgund sit up and stretch.

He stood up, crossed to Ethain and asked, 'Got the hour glass?'

Ethain looked up in surprise and then handed him the small time-keeper.

'Get some sleep, Ethain – and 'keeping watch' doesn't mean what you seem to think it does, eh?'

Ethain retreated to his bedroll in guilty silence and watched Morgund take his longbow and quiver and move away from the sleeping group. He sat with his back to a tree trunk and wrapped his cloak around himself. Within seconds his dark skin and worn clothes had faded into the gloom to become part of the forest. Ethain had excellent eyesight but if had not been watching Morgund leave the camp, he would have been hard pressed to point out the warrior who had so effectively blended in with his surroundings.

Morgund woke them sometime later with a hot drink then they packed up the makeshift camp in silence, each occupied by their own thoughts.

They followed the stream north for several hours before stopping for a hurried cold meal and then riding on, always staying close to the stream as it gradually turned to the West.

The forests were quiet and they neither saw nor heard anything of the wildlife that inhabited the woodland. Even the birds that made their summer home there had already started their own long journey to the West. It was as if the forest was anticipating the setting of the sun and the long, cold winter to come. The few animals that stayed in these woodlands were either already prepared for hibernation or keeping their distance from the passing horsemen. Even the ground over which they passed seemed to be bracing itself for the deep frosts and heavy snows now only a month away. Soon the land would be locked fast by cold.

The stream they followed tumbled over itself and swirled in agitation around the smooth, glistening rocks that stood in the way of its last desperate surge to the sea as it vainly tried to escape the moment it would become stilled. The deep forest waited in a crouched foreboding of the coming winter that was creeping closer with each passing hour.

At length the broadening stream led them to the edge of the forest. Before them lay the Channel Marshes and beyond that, the cliffs of Britain. The marshes stretched for a hundred miles both to the North and to the South West before they succumbed to the sea. Over the years a broad causeway had been built, raised above the surrounding impenetrable and treacherous marshes, connecting the outermost settlements of Middangeard to Britain. This was the Channel crossing over which the villagers of Eald and Branque took their journey to the West in autumn to Caer Sulis and on to the Haven then back home again in the spring when the sun rose once more from the West.

Arthur and his band were still some way from the crossing and they rode north along the ragged edge of the forest for several hours until they eventually came to the roadway that led down to the Causeway. Ceinwen dismounted and circled the area studying the ground while Mar'h rode some way down the path towards the East and back into the edges of the forest. Ethain stood in his stirrups and studied the Causeway looking for signs of movement. He saw none and turning back to Arthur shook his head.

'Ceinwen?' Arthur asked.

'Fresh wain and horses' tracks. All heading west. It's the right number too, as far as can be told, and they passed here, perhaps within the day.'

'Perhaps you could be vaguer?' Balor grunted. Ceinwen studied him for a moment then just gestured to the surrounding ground, inviting him to be more accurate. Balor declined the offer by clumsily turning his horse away and joining Ethain who still stared out along the Causeway.

Mar'h returned down the roadway and joined the group, 'No sign of anyone coming, only gone.'

'Then they're either already across or they're not coming at all,' Arthur said and turned his horse and began to head down to the Causeway.

The others followed him with Ruadan and Ceinwen lingering briefly behind and facing the roadway east, back to the forests and the now dead villages. Eventually Ruadan turned their horse around and they rode past the others until he had caught up with Arthur. They rode in silence and studied the marshes that spread to either side. The whole valley was in shadow, untouched by the sun suspended above the horizon behind them. The first slither of the new moon was rising in the West to begin its slow fourteen-day journey across the skies. Over the next five days it would wax to its fullest, when it would shine down brightly on the land for a further four days before gradually waning once more as it sank to the eastern horizon.

The marshes stretched out on either side as far as they could see with myriad small channels of salt water snaking between tall rushes and into stagnant, scum-lidded pools. The rushes grew up from waterlogged sand that looked solid enough to bear a horse and rider but which would suck both under within a minute. Wider channels of water looked navigable but they led nowhere except back on themselves or dissipated onto reaches of sand that would only bear the webbed footing of the birds that dwelt there in summer. High tides would swell the streams and create new waterways but they followed interminable courses and led only astray.

They all turned at a growing sound behind them and watched as a flight of noisy geese approached them from the East in a straggling V formation. As they flew low overhead one broke away and circled them once before hurrying off to catch up with its departing family. Ethain looked around at the others to see if they thought it was as strange as he thought it was. 'Perhaps it's a blessing?' he suggested.

'It was just a goose, Ethain,' Morgund said patiently.

'Curious goose,' Mar'h added as he passed Arthur and Ruadan.

As Ethain rode ahead they heard him say to Balor, 'Did he mean 'inquisitive goose' or 'strange goose'? Some people would say it was bad sign it circled us like that.'

Morgund turned and rolled his eyes to Ruadan and Arthur who were now bringing up the rear. Ruadan made a slapping motion to him and he duly slapped Ethain round the back of the head. Mar'h and Balor laughed as Ethain reeled in the saddle and they all began to talk again.

'That's the first time I've seen them laugh and talk lightly since Eald,' Ruadan said.

'It's because they're nearing home, or at least nearing Britain. Familiar and safe. But I don't think we will be safe there for much longer,' Arthur replied.

'Perhaps we should have taken the whole war band to the villages,' Ruadan ventured, at last saying what had been on his mind since the attack on Branque.

'Had we known that for the first time in hundreds of years a thousand strong army was going to unleash a timed attack on the villages then we should have undoubtedly taken all the war bands. And even then we would have been outnumbered. Did you know this was going to happen?'

'Of course not, Arthur...'

'Nor did I, not until it was too late.'

'Where did they come from?' Ceinwen asked.

'And why slaughter every man, woman and child? We'll talk to Cei – he may be at the Causeway Gates, he sent some of his warriors across the sea in their longboats to bring in the Belgae villages. He may know more.'

'What if...' Ruadan left the question unfinished and it hung in the ensuing silence as they thought about the fate of the Belgae.

The laughter up ahead seemed ill-timed and they slowed their pace to distance themselves from it. Ahead now they could see the Causeway Gates and behind them the chalk cliffs lit golden by the setting sun.

Ethain turned and shouted to them, 'We'll go ahead and see if Tomas and Elowen are there yet!'

Arthur raised a hand in acknowledgement and the others galloped off down the Causeway to the Gates.

'Do you think they made it?' Ruadan asked.

'There only seemed to be their tracks back on the roadway,' Arthur said and glanced at Ceinwen.

'I think so. I haven't had to look closely at those kind of tracks for some time,' she replied.

'Well, whether they made it not, we'll bear grim tidings for the council at Caer Sulis,' Ruadan added.

'King Maldred will have more to ponder than the usual disputes and arguments,' Arthur replied.

Ceinwen heard the underlying scorn in Arthur's tone and wondered just how badly the Wessex Warlord's relationship with the king had deteriorated over the years. She hadn't spent as much time with Ruadan as she would have wished but he had always made a point of seeing her at least once each summer and she had always looked forward to his visits, almost as much for hearing the news from Britain as the pleasure of her brother's company.

During the early years of her life in Branque, Ruadan had made a point of not mentioning Arthur at all to her but when he became the Wessex Warlord it had become impossible to talk of Britain without talking about Arthur. Besides, as the years passed and Ceinwen settled more and more into her new life, her past with Arthur became less painful and less relevant and Ruadan felt freer to talk about what Arthur was changing and how the king viewed the young warlord.

The king had been a good friend of the previous Wessex Warlord and he had been outraged by the way that his tenure had ended when Arthur took control. Those events had sown the seeds of their enmity and when King Maldred had invited the raiders from the Green Isle to Britain, to aid him in his ongoing war with the Uathach of the North, Arthur had stood violently opposed to his decision and any remaining pretence at cordiality had been stripped away. It hadn't comforted the king when Arthur had been proved entirely correct in his assessment of the raiders' motives.

Ceinwen decided she ought to find out more of what had happened directly from Arthur, when she could summon the energy to face anything other than her grief. Judging by Arthur's tone he at least still viewed the king with distrust and antipathy and she had no doubt it would be mutual.

Up ahead the others were nearing the Gates when they swung open and a horseman came out to meet them. They spoke briefly and the horseman rode on towards Arthur. It was Cei, Warlord of the Anglian spear riders. Like most of the Anglians, he wore his straw-coloured hair long and crowned with a bronze band that ran across the forehead to keep the flowing hair from his face. He was a tall man and his face was deeply and permanently etched by the alternating sun of summer and the cold of winter. His weather-tanned arms seemed as if they were carved from hard wood and his dark blue eyes rarely shifted from the person he was talking to.

He cantered towards them at an easy pace and Arthur recalled the time when as children Cei had taught both himself and his sister, Trevenna, to ride ponies. Arthur never had been a good pupil and though he could ride well enough he had not been able to emulate Cei's natural ease on horseback. Arthur had always maintained that it was because Cei's parents were warriors and he had been born into the war band where he was carried on horseback before he could even walk. It had been the same with the sea; Cei had been too young to even remember the first time he had sailed the seas in the Anglian longboats. He was equally at home whether on horseback, galloping across the fens or fields of his home, or on the sea, with his longboat heeled-over close to the waves and running before the wind. Arthur was neither and suffered both only as a means of necessary transport, an attitude that Cei took great delight in mocking. They picked up their pace to meet him. As they got closer

Arthur could see Cei was grim-faced, his usual cheerfulness replaced by a seriousness that spoke of bad news. Arthur leaned out of his saddle and clasped Cei's hand.

'Thank the gods you're alive, Arthur.'

'Thank this truculent bastard more like,' Arthur replied slapping his horse's neck. Cei grinned and the seriousness left his face momentarily. Arthur continued, 'And thank Ceinwen for dragging me to the truculent bastard.'

Cei looked at Ceinwen and then back to Arthur; he seemed uncertain which of his many questions to ask first. Arthur saved Ceinwen from having to retell the ordeal by asking him about Tomas and Elowen and the villagers from Eald.

'Yes, they came across the Causeway several hours ago. I was going to send people out to try to meet you but half of my spear riders are up the coast awaiting the longboats and I didn't know if you'd take the road or go through the forests,' Cei said.

'We left the roadway and came through the forests,' Arthur said.

'So no one else made it out of Branque?' Cei asked softly, addressing his question directly to Ceinwen.

Ceinwen shook her head, unable to meet Cei's eyes. Cei looked just as pained and he turned a worried look to the North, fearing for his men who had left in the longboats. Turning back he said, 'It's good to see you, Arthur.'

'Likewise, Cei, likewise.'

'And you Ceinwen. I'm sorry about your family, and the others...'

Ceinwen nodded miserably, wondering how many times she would have to hear those words and wondering if she would ever hear them without wishing to abandon life herself.

Cei had noticed Arthur's injured leg and seen how fresh blood was staining the bandaging. He had also seen that Arthur carried no sword and wondered how desperate the fight at Branque must have been for Arthur to have left his sword behind.

'Come. We'll get that leg looked at, get some food in you all and then you can tell me why the gods have turned their backs on us,' and with that Cei tugged on his reins and led the way back to the Causeway Gates.

The gates were set into a wooden wall that was twenty-feet high and stretched across the breadth of the Causeway and then down the slopes on either side. The sidewalls were set into the marshes and paralleled the Causeway for two hundred yards before climbing back up the slopes to form a rectangular fortification with the Causeway running down its centre. A parapet eight-foot wide ran around the inside of the walls where defenders could stand with the top of the wall at shoulder height. Inside the Causeway Gates were two wooden buildings set either side of the Causeway, which provided shelter and living quarters for those stationed there.

This was the Anglian tribe's territory and as Cei was their warlord it was his men who garrisoned the Gates. The Anglians were a separate people from the other two southern tribes. Their tales and legends spoke of a homeland across the northern seas. A land bound in ice and snow where the sunlit summer was short and cold. A land where the gods of the earth fought to repel the onslaught of the ice giants from the furthest North. Their myths told of a time when the earth gods lost their battle against the giants and how their ancestors had been forced to take to their longboats in search of land still free from the grip of winter. Some had gone far into the West, others into the southern oceans, and no one had ever returned from either journey.

Some of their people had settled in the lawless lands to the North but most had accepted the offer of the southern tribes to live in the East of Britain and they had become known as the Anglians.

While they spoke the same language as the Britons their customs, accents and beliefs had all been distinctively different. As one generation followed another many of their old ways were diluted and eventually forgotten. Despite trading with the other tribes and living alongside them, there had been few inter-tribal marriages and the characteristic tallness, fair hair, fair skin and blue eyes of the original settlers remained to this day. So too did the accents and some of the traditions of their forebears. It was usually easy to see that someone was from Anglia and always obvious when they spoke.

During the Gathering time and for the beginning of the journey west it was common for most of Cei's spear riders to be collecting the various villages from further north in Eastern Britain and from the Belgae tribes across the sea. Half of Arthur's warriors would be in Wessex gathering the villages there and taking them to Caer Sulis. This year the other half were divided between helping the Anglians further north, where the risk of an Uathach raid was always greater, and the Gathering of the villages of Eald and Branque from across the Channel Marshes. Arthur had taken twenty of his warriors across the Causeway and sent thirty further north to help protect the Gatherings from Uathach raids. Twelve had died at Eald under the Shadow Land army.

There weren't many villages near the marshes and the few that were relatively close were already empty, their peoples either already at Caer Sulis or on their way there, and those stationed at the Causeway Gates had been casually preparing for the onset of winter, the majority of their work already done. That had changed with Tomas's arrival and his news of the attack on Eald and now the camp was busy with renewed activity. Weapons were being seen to and the superficial damage of neglect was being hastily repaired.

There were about twenty-five of Cei's warriors in the compound and on the walls. They had just heard from Mar'h and the others the news from Eald and of Arthur's escape from Branque, and they all stopped to watch Arthur ride in. Ruadan had lost thirteen of twenty warriors in the flight from Eald whereas Arthur had been alone at Branque; still he had fought his way out.

While much of the separate war bands' campaigns against the Uathach were co-ordinated they rarely actually fought or worked side by side and for many of the younger Anglian warriors this was their first close look at the Wessex Warlord and they watched him in silence. Arthur ignored their scrutiny as he climbed painfully off his horse.

Balor took the reins of his and Ruadan's horses and Arthur asked him if the villagers from Eald were already on the Westway. The Westway was the main track-way that crossed the width of the country. It ran from the Causeway in the East, looped south of the great Winter Wood, followed the Isis Valley to the foot of the Downs then cut west to Caer Sulis and the head of the Estuary before finally running along the North side of the Estuary until it reached the Haven in the West.

'Yes,' Balor answered, 'Tomas decided to take them on to the Westway and make for the Haven.'

'Won't see them for years then,' Cei said, and Balor laughed in agreement; Tomas had got lost on more than one previous journey.

'Elowen too?' Arthur asked.

'She's inside with the others,' Balor hitched his thumb over his shoulder pointing towards one of the huts, 'stuffing down all of Cei's supplies and running her eye over his men.' Balor led their horses away chuckling to himself, partly at the thought of Tomas losing himself on the Westway, partly at the chaos that Elowen could cause among the Anglians but mostly in relief; he had feared the Anglians would blame them for the deaths at Eald.

The fact that Arthur too had fled from the attackers had assuaged the sense of shame Balor felt in front of these Anglians. His pride and sense of honour had been punctured by their hasty retreat from Eald and their inability to protect most of the villagers, and it only made matters worse that it was usually the Anglians who escorted the Eald villages. He felt, to some extent, that the Wessex warriors had failed and had thought that the Anglians might well have felt the same way but having seen the way they had looked at Arthur, and the way he had nonchalantly ignored the stares, he knew that no one would be accusing anyone of having failed in their duty.

He need not have worried as none of the Anglians thought him anything less than courageous and even if they had, few would have dared tell him so. To the Anglians he looked like a man who was equally short on both height and temper and few would be prepared to risk enraging him or goading him into using the heavy, single-bladed axe that he still carried from his days as a woodsman.

Balor was not known to shy away from casual trouble, although most of the fights he got involved in were usually instigated by Morgund, and he was more often than not in the forefront of any battle. Some put his eagerness in battle down to his wanting to justify Arthur's faith in accepting him, others felt it was just because he was short and that he wanted to prove to the taller warriors around him that he was every bit as good as they were. Both opinions held some truth but it was Morgund who got closer to the real reason when he pointed out that Balor just had a vicious temper.

Cei led them to the central building where there were about fifteen people gathered around a table piled with food. The lively conversation between Arthur and Cei's warriors stopped as Arthur entered. Twelve years previously, before Cei became the Anglian Warlord, there had been a fierce argument between Arthur and the Anglian Warlord over some captured Uathach. That same night two of the Anglian warriors had ambushed the weaponless Arthur on his way to the sleeping quarters. He had killed them both bare handed and then, taking one of the swords, killed the eight Uathach prisoners.

Some of Cei's current spear riders had witnessed what followed: Arthur had walked back into the feasting hall and emptied the ten decapitated heads from a sack at the feet of the Anglian Warlord and said, 'If you have a message for me, bring it yourself. I've settled the dispute over the Uathach.' Then he turned to the Anglians, who had all jumped to their feet and drawn weapons, and stared them down saying, 'Choose a leader more fitting for you.' He had gestured to Ruadan and those of his own war band there to leave the hall. Ruadan had hesitated but with one look from Arthur he had hurriedly joined the others filing from the hall. Laying the sword on the table in front of the Anglian Warlord and turning to the stunned warriors he had added, 'And do it tonight,' before walking out of the silent hall.

None had dared to challenge Arthur, least of all the Anglian Warlord, and so they had thrown him out and chosen Cei as their new warlord. Over the years any ill-feeling between the war bands had been put to rest but many of the Anglians still remembered that night and they had no love for Arthur.

Hengest stood and poured a mug of beer and offered it to Arthur. Hengest, the son of Aelfhelm, was Cei's second-in-command and although he was many years younger than Cei and Arthur, he too had been in the hall twelve years ago. He had been seventeen then and if it had not been for his father's steadying hand he would have rushed at the Wessex Warlord and then Arthur would have killed him. Arthur recognised the narrow face and thought how much he looked like his father. Like Hengest he was remembering the night twelve years ago and he stepped forward and accepted the brimming mug.

'It's been a long journey,' Arthur said and raised the cup to Hengest before draining the beer. As Cei gathered some food from the table the talking struck up again. Elowen was telling the Anglians about the attack on Eald and though they listened avidly about this new enemy and continually interrupted her with questions, it was clear that the atmosphere in the room had changed. Few of the Anglians had been so close to Arthur and Morgund smiled as he watched them sneak glances and try to match the various stories they had heard with the man standing before them talking casually to their warlord.

Ruadan had started telling his version of events to Hengest, which left Ceinwen standing alone amongst the warriors. She felt entirely out of place and quietly joined Cei and Arthur. Cei made room for her and introduced her to some of the warriors nearby most of whom barely nodded to her. Cei shrugged in an offhand apology and Ceinwen grimaced, 'I'm never going to remember all these names.'

Cei laughed, 'Just do what Balor does – don't acknowledge anyone by name for at least a year.'

She looked at him enquiringly.

'He reckons it isn't worth getting to know a new warrior until they've been around for a while.'

She nodded in understanding but didn't look any the happier.

'Besides,' Cei continued, realising his lack of tact, 'you'll soon know them all well enough to be thoroughly sick of them.'

Cei's attention was diverted away by Arthur and Ceinwen gazed around at the gathered warriors feeling, if anything, less encouraged than she previously was. Her eyes settled on Balor who was berating the young Elowen for exaggerating her tale of Eald and he took over from her, reasoning that if anyone was going to tell the bad news it should be him. The noise level grew as curses and questions rallied back and forth but one question remained unasked despite it being at the forefront of most their minds; how did Arthur escape from Branque and a five hundred strong Shadow Land army. But not one of them, Anglian or Wessex, had even entertained the idea of directly asking him.

Arthur and Cei moved closer to the doorway to get away from the babble around the long table and Ceinwen automatically followed them. Cei noticed how miserable and alone she looked. He put a hand on her shoulder in a gesture of understanding and the three of them left the overcrowded room. Arthur was still using his longbow as a crutch and the pain from the wound was evident on his face. Ceinwen noticed fresh blood was seeping into the bandaging around his thigh.

'Arthur, your leg will need looking at again – if you can't rest it then it ought to be stitched.'

'Your powder has taken away any fever.'

'Still...' Ceinwen replied.

'Very well, but first I need to talk to Hengest and Ruadan. Ask them to join us on the East wall.'

She nodded but it was Cei who went back into the building to get the other two. The five of them walked to the eastern wall and climbed the steps up to the parapet. Arthur struggled to get up the steps and arrived last.

'How's Trevenna?' he asked Cei once he had joined them.

'She's fine, Arthur, fine. But I'm worried, she's further up the coast waiting on the longboats.'

'We should have heard by now,' Hengest added.

'Then you've had no news,' Arthur said, leaning against the wall for support.

'None,' Cei replied.

'I don't think the longboats will be coming back, Cei,' Arthur said, looking back down the Causeway towards the East.

'You think they were attacked too?' Hengest asked.

'Two Shadow Land armies attacked Eald and Branque at the same time and when all their harvest and supplies were ready for the journey. It wasn't chance. If you could co-ordinate that, wouldn't you hit the Belgae at the same time and take their supplies too?'

Cei and Hengest exchanged looks.

'But we sent thirty men – all experienced and good warriors,' Hengest said.

Arthur lowered his head and rubbed his hand across his eyes. 'Thirty against five-hundred with the sea to their backs and nowhere to go,' Arthur said and turned to them, 'Perhaps some will make it back but I believe we've lost the Belgae villages too.'

'You can't know that, Arthur,' Cei said, more in appeal than with any real conviction.

'Keep your hope Cei but whether the Belgae have fallen or not we have greater concerns now. We'll be next. And they'll come this way,' Arthur said, pointing to the Causeway leading from the East.

'So many dead. Where did these Shadow Land armies come from? Are they Uathach?' Cei asked.

'They aren't Uathach,' Arthur said.

'They couldn't raise an army that size,' Ruadan joined the conversation, 'how can you support such an army? How would you feed that many warriors? They weren't even like us...' Ruadan trailed off, unable to explain further what he meant.

'Questions for the King's Council at Caer Sulis,' Arthur said, but privately he hoped Merdynn might have the answers.

'I just can't believe all at Eald and Branque are dead. Andala? Old Narlos too? Everyone?' Cei asked turning to Ceinwen.

'I saw Andala die. Narlos too. I saw dozens die. We looked for people who might have fled the slaughter but...' Ceinwen shrugged and turned her eyes away from them.

'Caja?' asked Cei softly.

'She was dancing when they came through the windows and main door,' Arthur replied for her.

'Dead too?' Hengest remembered the happy redheaded girl from last year's journey and could not keep the disbelief from his voice.

Ceinwen nodded, trying desperately not to break down crying in front of them.

Cei looked sick, he remembered the girl chatting to him and asking him endless questions as they covered the miles back to her village, and he remembered taking the same girl to Branque back when she was just an infant.

'We've heard what happened at Eald but tell us what happened at Branque, Arthur,' Cei asked.

Arthur rubbed his eyes once more and told them the details of the sudden attack. Again Cei and Hengest were appalled, Ruadan had seen similar at Eald. Arthur finished by saying, 'Understand this and make sure all your warriors understand this. This is not some Uathach border raid. Whatever this Shadow Land army is and wherever it's come from, it will bring unremitting war to us, our families and all our peoples. They have shown no mercy and we can be certain they will not treaty. We already know that all the warriors we have, even combined with the king's war band, are still outnumbered by at least two to one. And this is the way they will come first,' Arthur pointed once again down the Causeway to the East. 'Send word for all the gathered villages that haven't already left to move immediately to the Westway and journey to Caer Sulis. The thirty of the Wessex war band with your men in the North shall remain with you here at the Gates. Ruadan, you stay here too and help Hengest plan and construct how to defend this Causeway against an army. Cei, we need to journey to Caer Sulis and inform the King's Council of what's happened.'

Ruadan and Hengest stayed on the parapet and started to plan the defences that would best hold against a concerted attack while Arthur and Cei climbed back down the steps. Ceinwen waited at the top reluctant to leave Ruadan but he and Hengest were already deep in conversation debating the pros and cons of various defences and eventually she too climbed back down. Cei had gone to organise his warriors and was nowhere in sight but Ceinwen saw Arthur resting by a water trough and, taking a deep breath, she made her way towards him.

Arthur looked up as she approached. She sat down beside him without saying anything and he began unravelling the bandage from his thigh.

'I'm sorry for what happened at Branque – sorry you lost Andala and Caja.'

Ceinwen nodded, 'You did what you could. We weren't prepared.'

'And thank you for dragging me into that stable.'

Ceinwen looked up at him surprised by his tone. She shrugged but was unable to return the gratitude; she felt that she too had died at Branque.

'The Anglian's healer is called Henna – I saw her over by that building,' Arthur said and indicated which one he meant.

Ceinwen realised he was telling her to go and fetch whatever she needed to see to his wound and she was almost relieved that his previous gentleness had vanished. She got to her feet and went to find Henna wondering if perhaps she had mistaken Arthur's earlier tone.

She found the healer and got all she needed. She strolled back to where Arthur was still sitting reminding herself that no matter what memories or feelings their unexpected meeting had re-woken she hardly knew this man at all; and she was fairly certain she didn't want to get to know him any better.

She told him to lie on his front so that she could work on the wound to the back of his thigh. She laid a clean cloth under the leg and washed the deep cut with alcohol before closing the gash with eight stitches. When she had finished she smeared an ointment around the wound and rubbed it thoroughly into the flesh. Taking a fresh length of cloth she firmly wound a bandage around his thigh and told him he could sit back up again. She handed him the pot of ointment, 'You'll need to change the bandage every day and rub this around the stitches. And don't stop the powders yet either – they'll help prevent any fever.'

Arthur smiled, but it wasn't a smile of amusement, 'You should join the war band again.'

Ceinwen looked at him, suddenly seeing him as he was twenty years ago. Even then he had the knack of saying something that wasn't quite an ultimatum, or a command or even a suggestion but it came across somehow as an inevitable conclusion to an already thoroughly debated argument and it only made it more exasperating that he was invariably right.

Before she had the chance to contradict him he continued, 'You're a natural warrior: in the hall at Branque you fought back; you knew to check my horse was not silhouetted against the skyline on the hill above the village; you'd seen that the arrowheads weren't barbed even though you weren't looking for it; you can still read tracks in the ground as well, or better, than anyone in the war band; your healing skills are better than ever. And you're younger, fitter and more capable than our current healer. We need you, now more than ever. Britain stands on the brink of war and I want you with us,' Arthur got awkwardly to his feet and looked down at her, 'but you'll need to get used to our short bows and you'll need to start practising your sword work again if you want to survive and be of any use to us.'

Ceinwen watched him as he limped away, 'What a bastard,' she muttered softly. He had praised, complimented, insulted and challenged her but more than any of these he, of all people, had given her a purpose, a cause, a reason to live and that was something she desperately needed; and he had known it.

After they had rested for several hours Arthur and Cei left the Causeway Gates and took the paths up the cliffs. Ceinwen had decided, at least for now, to travel with them. Riding with them were Mar'h, Balor, Ethain, Morgund and Elowen from the Wessex war band and Aelfhelm, Cerdic and Leah from the Anglian warriors. Word had been sent north and west to move all the remaining gathered villagers onto the Westway and make for Caer Sulis. Ruadan remained at the Gates where he would be joined by the other thirty from the Wessex war band from North Anglia once their villagers were on the Westway. Together with the Anglians there would be about a hundred warriors to help prepare the defences on the Causeway under the joint command of Hengest and Ruadan.

When they reached the top of the cliffs they were bathed once more in sunshine. They all turned their horses to look back at the shadowed marshes that stretched back to the East. The Gates below them looked more like a child's toy, tiny in the expanse that lay before it. The Causeway leading from the Gates cut a straight line through the marshland and pointed back to the forests that were beyond their sight.

The sun hung suspended just above the eastern horizon and in the clear late autumn sky they could already pick out one or two of the brighter stars of winter. Leah pointed one of them out to Ethain and Elowen who were next to her and she began to softly sing one of her people's songs telling how the star had lost her way in the heavens and was doomed to sail the cold winter skies forever. Reluctantly they turned their backs on the setting sun and with Leah still singing softly, made their way northwest toward the Westway.

Much to Balor's disappointment Tomas hadn't gotten lost and they caught up with him and the surviving villagers from Eald at the end of their first day's ride and Arthur decided they should make camp together. The country was open grassland and they rode some miles out of their way to camp on a hilltop that was crowned with a small grove of beech and oak trees. As they rode into the sheltered copse hundreds of crows and ravens took to the air in outraged alarm and Mar'h immediately named the copse 'Dunraven' and the name stuck. Some of the villagers stretched canvas between the trees to create a more sheltered place to sleep while others set about cooking the last meal of the day. Arthur and Cei were feeding their horses and watching the villagers.

71

'It's as if they're just sleep-walking,' Cei said quietly.

'They've seen their neighbours and families slaughtered. They're wondering how and why they got out alive,' Arthur said.

'Because Ruadan and your lads were there. That's why.'

'Have you seen Tomas since we made camp?' Arthur asked, suddenly remembering he had not talked to him since the attack on Eald.

'I think he went off with Elowen to find a quieter place,' Cei replied smiling.

Elowen and Tomas were both young, neither had reached twenty yet but to the disapproval of their two families they had fallen in love. Elowen's family had not wanted her to marry a warrior while Tomas's had insisted that her family were too poor for a son of theirs. The pair of them had decided the only fair solution was to insult both families equally. Tomas had married Elowen and she had joined the Wessex war band. Together they made a handsome couple and held the promise of becoming good warriors.

Arthur had not noticed Cei's smile and his thoughts had already reverted back to the attacks across the Causeway, 'There must have been six-hundred villagers gathered at Eald. This is all that's left. None from Branque, other than Ceinwen, and none from the Belgae,' he said.

'They had no warriors, Arthur. Living on the borders of Middangeard they should have had their own war bands.'

'And how long do you think their warriors would have held out against those Shadow Land armies? How long will we hold out against them?'

They moved away from the camp and walked in silence to the North edge of the copse. On the lip of the hill they saw Ceinwen and Leah. Ceinwen had appropriated some old weapons from the Anglians and was sitting cross-legged on her upturned shield. Leah was lying on her cloak, one arm propping her head up and she twisted around to see who approached. She flicked her long, fair hair from her round face to reveal sky blue eyes set wide of a long nose above her full, pale lips. Even lying down it was obvious she was a tall woman, strong limbed with long, well-muscled legs. She looked to be quite the opposite of the slightly built Ceinwen beside her.

The two of them had formed a friendship some years back during one of the long journeys from Branque to the Haven and having talked through the recent events they now sat in companionable silence. Leah made to get up when she recognised them but Cei motioned for her to remain where she was.

'They've got some food by the fire back there,' Cei said.

'Thanks Cei, we've already brought some food here – help yourself,' Leah answered. She replaced the circlet round her head that kept her long, straw-coloured hair off her face and made room for him to sit down on her spread cloak. He sat next to her and accepted the offered cup of wine.

'How's your leg, Arthur?' Ceinwen asked.

Arthur was staring down on the shadowed woodland that stretched below them. He still leant heavily on his unstrung longbow. Leah loosened the silver-embedded leather band that encircled her throat and looked across to Arthur waiting for him to reply to Ceinwen and when it became clear no answer was forthcoming she turned to Cei, 'We were just talking of the legends about that place.'

Cei reached across her and selected an apple from their unfinished meal.

'The Veiled City. The Cithol. Star Walkers of the Ghost Woods. I've heard the tales and myths since I was a child,' Ceinwen said.

'Ever been tempted to travel through those woods when you were younger?' Leah asked her.

'Gods no! They may just be tales but I'll take the longer roads thank you,' she replied.

'They aren't just tales,' Arthur said, still standing with his back to them. Both Leah and Ceinwen looked at him to see if he jested.

'The Star Walkers are very much there, and always have been,' Arthur continued.

Cei stood up and said, 'Let's not talk of them here, eh? The shadows are long enough and there's a fire to warm ourselves by.'

Leah shuddered involuntarily as she and Ceinwen stood up. Cei led them back toward the camp. Arthur stayed behind lost in thought and gazing down on the expanse of shadowed woodland.

Chapter Three

After several hours rest the camp stirred into life and the first meal of the day was made ready. Ceinwen collected a bowl of food from one of the villagers who looked like he had spent the last few hours weeping. The villagers reminded her of the refugees she had seen from Uathach raids all those years ago when she was with the war band, and she wondered if she could really face that life again.

She looked around to find someone to sit with hoping to see a familiar face and feeling a little lost without Ruadan nearby. Arthur was not among the scattered gathering; Mar'h and Balor were eating in silence and neither seemed particularly approachable; Leah was nowhere to be seen; Ethain was chatting to Elowen and Tomas and Morgund was missing too. She remembered what Ruadan had said about Morgund and somewhere at the back of her mind she connected his absence with Leah's.

She ate her breakfast miserably, thinking of her dead husband and daughter. Those around her were just as quiet. When she had finished she returned the bowl, nodding to Mar'h and Balor as she passed them, and wandered out of the camp. She walked through the trees with her arms folded and her head lowered feeling drained and empty; almost everything that had constituted her life had been taken away from her and it left a hollowness, a deep well that echoed with sadness and despair every time she thought about her family.

She realised she hadn't felt anything like this low for the last twenty years, not since leaving the war band, not since Arthur had left her. The comparison made her recoil in self-admonishment, horrified that she could compare her current loss to the one of twenty years ago. Yet, at the time, it had affected her in just such a manner – so much so that she had left Britain and married Andala, a gentle, caring man who couldn't have been more different from the man Arthur was; and now she faced the choice of returning to Britain and Arthur's war band.

She eventually found him where she had last seen him, standing beyond the trees and overlooking the dark expanse of woodland below. She stood on the edge of the copse, uncertain whether or not to approach him. He turned to look at her and she walked to his side.

A light wind was gently blowing from the West and the chill made her eyes water as she left the shelter of the trees. The skies were overcast, heavy and grey, and there was already rain in the air. The breeze ruffled her hair as she shot a quick glance at Arthur's face, trying to determine his mood. He seemed distant, either lost in memories or weighing the options ahead. Ceinwen was unsure how to start, if she was going to re-join the war band then she needed some questions answered first; she needed to put the past firmly in the past.

'Have you been standing here long, Arthur?' she asked.

He nodded, 'I've been thinking about how many times Merdynn and I travelled through the Ghost Woods and into the Veiled City. He was known and accepted among the Cithol but on the last visit they asked that I never return, either alone or with any other. Until now I have kept their wish and not even spoken about them but the time is coming when these woods will no longer provide a haven for them.'

Arthur continued staring out over the shadowed woodland below them. It spread east and west as far as they could see and stretched north to the rim of hills in the distance. They could catch glimpses of the wide river that ran through the woods and on down to the marshes beyond. It swelled each spring with the melting of the snows and flooded much of the woodland valley. Even in the twilight of the setting sun they could see the stained colours of the unshed autumn leaves.

Ceinwen stared down into the woodlands thinking the city was well named for she could see no sign of it from where they stood. She remembered childhood tales of condemned spirits wandering lost, cursed to walk the shadowed woods and unable to ever cross into the afterlife. They were told as children that to trespass into the Veiled City was to be damned to walk with the ghosts there. She did not believe it now of course, nonetheless she felt uneasy just being this close and she knew of no one who had travelled through them, until now. She felt the first drops of rain on her face as she looked up at Arthur again and he seemed to come out of his reverie.

'Will you join us?' he asked.

Ceinwen folded her arms and stared out over the woods trying to find the courage to ask him what she had asked herself countless times: why did he leave her all those years ago? They had been together for about two years but she had borne no children. She had heard that a woman from a Wessex fishing village had borne him a child less than a year later but she didn't know if that was true or not.

'Did you leave me because I couldn't have children?' Ceinwen finally asked. She was surprised how steady her voice sounded; there was no hint of accusation or reproach.

'It was all a long time ago. We were little more than children ourselves at the time.'

'Nonetheless, I deserve an answer.'

'Then your answer is yes,' Arthur replied, turning to look directly at her. It was far from the whole truth but it was the answer that Ceinwen was expecting and she seemed satisfied by it.

Arthur shifted his weight and leaning heavily on his longbow he turned away from the woods below, 'We'll make for Caer Cadarn, perhaps Merdynn will be there. Morgund can follow behind us with Ethain, Tomas and Elowen and take the villagers onto the Westway. We'll meet up with them at Caer Sulis for the festival and the council.'

Ceinwen nodded, relieved to have asked the question and equally relieved that Arthur had turned the subject back to matters at hand.

'Do you want to go back and join Ruadan on the Causeway?' he asked her.

That was exactly what she had intended to do but now that Arthur asked her it seemed somehow cowardly. She was miserably aware that her old life was truly over and even though the thought of starting a new life filled her with fear she realised she needed a purpose, and where better to start than where she had began so many years ago.

The fear left her eyes and she relaxed, 'I'll go to Caer Cadarn with you and the others – and join the war band if you think I'll be of use.'

Arthur watched her walk lightly back to the trees and as he laboriously followed her he noticed for the first time the smattering of rain on the cold breeze blowing in from the West.

Within thirty minutes the band making for Caer Cadarn had left the villagers behind and were skirting around the southern fringes of the woodland. The trees here were well spaced apart and the ground between them was covered in short grass. The light breeze caused the leafed boughs to nod back and forth, whispering softly in the light rain as the riders passed below them. The first frosts of winter would follow soon after the sun slid below the eastern horizon and the gold and burnished leaves would be gone within a week or two as the trees readied themselves for the long, cold darkness. The frozen ground would be covered in snow disturbed only occasionally by the few woodland animals not passing the winter in hibernation.

The riders kept clear of the denser woodland to their right and all but Arthur were uneasy being this close to the source of such dark myths. As they passed through the edge of the Ghost Woods they formed into two distinct groups: Mar'h, Balor and Aelfhelm were riding ahead with Arthur and Cei discussing the attacks on Eald and Branque by the Shadow Land army while Ceinwen rode with Leah. Their friendship had developed during the perennial journeys to the Haven and they had developed a mutual respect for each other's skills. Ceinwen's ability as a tracker and her knowledge of curative herbs and plants had impressed the younger woman just as the latter's skilfulness with both sword and spear had impressed Ceinwen. Cerdic, who had been scouting behind, rode up at a canter and joined them.

'I still can't believe Eald and Branque have gone,' Leah said sadly.

'We never stood a chance. We had no warning of the attack at all, and even if we had it would still have been a bloody disaster. They just swept in and started slaughtering everyone in sight. They were everywhere at once. I lost everything there.'

Cerdic brought his horse alongside them. 'At least Ruadan got some of the villagers to safety. More than Arthur managed,' Cerdic kept his eyes on the woods to their right as he spoke and didn't see the flash of anger in Ceinwen's eyes. She looked across at him and studied the young man before replying. Although he was only a young warrior he was highly regarded among the Anglians. Like most of his people his straw-coloured hair was encircled at his forehead by a bronze band and he held his head high as he scanned the woods. He had the pride-fed swagger of confidence about him, a certain assuredness in the set of his beardless but strong jaw and she took an instant and strong dislike to him.

'Arthur was one, there were at least five-hundred of the attackers,' she finally replied.

'Yet he spirited himself away,' Cerdic said still not looking at her.

Ceinwen took a deeper breath to calm herself before replying, 'Well, the next time a five-hundred strong army arrives at my door I'll be sure to petition the king to send for you to defeat them.'

Cerdic finally turned to look at her, 'I meant no offence, just that I wouldn't have left the villagers defenceless.'

'Then you'd have died with them,' she replied through clenched teeth.

'Such is a warrior's duty.'

Ceinwen was furious, 'It has never been a warrior's duty to die needlessly, and it certainly isn't a warlord's. Clearly a distinction you don't appreciate. Perhaps you'd better think on that and take a care with your words, others would have killed you for what you've just said. Your vaunted bravery may stretch to accuse me of cowardice but if you think for even a moment that Arthur is a coward then please, ride ahead and tell him so, he's not far ahead – just out of earshot.'

Aware of the insults and seeing hands were on sword hilts, Leah rode between them saying, 'Enough enemies behind us without making more for the road ahead.'

It was a common saying among the Anglians and it served to calm the two protagonists but it did not make the peace. Without another word Cerdic spurred his horse and rode ahead.

'Don't take offence Ceinwen, he's young, proud and hot-headed but he's a good man.'

'And that's the way he'll die if any of the Wessex hear him say that again.'

Leah was by no means a natural peacemaker but she regarded them both as friends and did not wish to see them set against each other. She reached out and put her hand over Ceinwen's saying, 'He meant nothing. Arthur's a strange man to us. He's not like the other Wessex warriors, we understand them. But Arthur's different.'

'That's why he's our warlord and why we'll need him in the months before us,' Ceinwen said, rolling her shoulders and letting the anger drain from her.

'Truth of it is that he makes us nervous, there's so many stories about him – he faced down one of our previous warlords and more or less the whole war band.'

'I know, Leah. My brother was there that night and neither he nor any other from the Wessex would have dared thought about crossing him. No one would, not when the killing mood's on him.

'Our last warlord, Saltran, was a right bastard – he lorded it over Wessex like a king, and not a good king either. After one particularly bloody incident in a Wessex village Arthur decided it had to stop and he challenged him for the leadership. Arthur wasn't a great deal older then than Cerdic is now, and it all happened a few years after I'd left the war band, but Ruadan told me what happened.

'Saltran laughed at the challenge. He was a bear of a man, vicious and cruel, and next to him Arthur didn't seem to be much more than a boy. The combat was held outside the hall on Whitehorse Hill under a late autumn moon. Saltran chose an axe as his weapon but Arthur chose no weapon, he just faced him in the circle empty-handed. No one gave anything for his chances and no one could understand why he chose to stand with no weapon. Ruadan implored him to at least take his sword but he would not do so. The challenge lasted fifteen minutes, every move that Saltran made, every swing or feint, Arthur anticipated it. Saltran cursed and goaded Arthur at every turn but it was the silent Arthur who was doing the taunting. Finally Arthur ended it and though Saltran begged for his life, Arthur killed him slowly, using Saltran's own axe to hack him to pieces. And he took his time too, hacking him limb from limb.

'Ruadan told me this and swears every word is true, he says he's never seen anything so truly frightening or such cold, deliberate cruelty in all his life. They had all seen worse, of course, but that was in the fury and rage of battle and not like this. Ruadan called it a dispassionate hatred, the coldest killing he ever witnessed.

'I remember Ruadan trying to explain why Arthur had acted so coldly, he said that when the challenge had started the gathered warriors had bayed for blood, but as each minute passed one by one they fell silent. By the end the bloodlust of the whole war band had drained away to appalled silence. When Arthur had finally finished his butchering he looked around at the silent warriors and what truly frightened Ruadan was that it seemed to him that Arthur wanted to continue, that he was only just getting started. Fearless warriors stepped backwards and stared at the ground when Arthur looked at them. Then he quietly asked if there were any other challenges. There weren't. And there never will be. Saltran had led a bloody and violent life and he died as he had lived.'

Leah was quiet for a moment before replying, 'I've heard different versions of the same story at feasts in our hall – one claimed it lasted four hours and there were ten challenges, that Merdynn had given him a magic sword and he had killed all ten challengers - yet the truth is a better tale. Strange that he and Cei should be such friends when they seem so different. Cei's anything but cold, he's well liked by everyone, anyone can just talk to him – we'd follow him into hell if he asked.'

'They are different. Arthur wouldn't ask us to follow, he'd just expect it of us – and we would follow but we'd believe we'd be coming back too. But in other ways they are strangely similar. The only people I've ever seen truly comfortable with Arthur are Cei and Merdynn, and his sister, Trevenna, of course. I've known Cei since childhood and love him like a brother, and don't misunderstand me here – he's a great warrior – but if there was one person I'd want to be near me in a hall that's being attacked by hundreds, well, it'd be Arthur.'

Leah frowned.

'What?' Ceinwen asked.

'Nothing. Just a bit a surprised to hear you defending Arthur – and speaking so highly of him.'

Ceinwen sighed before replying, 'Whatever happened between us happened a long time ago and it doesn't seem very important now, does it?'

Leah held her hands up at Ceinwen's tone.

'Anyway,' Ceinwen continued, 'the same holds true about who I'd want to be leading us against this new enemy. From what Ruadan has told me over the years, I gather that Arthur's become an even more ruthless bastard and I think we're going to need someone like that. Arthur and Merdynn - we'll need them both.'

'Gods, Arthur and Merdynn, now there's a pair to give anyone nightmares,' Leah smiled and shuddered over-dramatically, but she wasn't entirely jesting.

'If they belong in nightmares then their time is coming. I think he believes the Shadow Land armies want the whole of Middangeard destroyed and if he's right then you'd do better to put your faith in Arthur and Merdynn than the king and all the chieftains.'

'That and these,' Leah replied, patting the sword at her side and the long spear cradled in her saddle. Ceinwen nodded her agreement.

After a few minutes Leah asked, 'Everyone's curious how Arthur got out alive. He fought his way out, didn't he? How many did he kill?'

Ceinwen didn't answer immediately. She was depressed by having to acknowledge that Leah, whom she liked, was just the same as the other warriors – more concerned with how many of the enemy had been killed rather than what had happened to her village and family. She realised this judgement was unfair but couldn't help wondering if she had made a mistake in thinking she could re-join the war band after so many years. Leah was still looking at her, expecting an answer.

'I don't know – I wasn't counting,' she finally replied. Leah looked disappointed and Ceinwen felt a little guilty at her harsh words so added, 'Perhaps fifteen, maybe twenty. Maybe more, I don't know really. He certainly saved me, another few seconds and I'd have been speared.' *And I would be at peace now with my family*, she thought. They rode on in silence.

It took them three days to reach Caer Cadarn, their stronghold on Whitehorse Hill. They had followed the edge of the Ghost Woods until they struck the River Isis that wound its way on through the shadowed woodlands. They followed the Isis some miles west upstream and away from the woodlands before fording it and joining the Westway. The Westway was busy with various villages on the move, their stores and belongings all piled onto wains and being carted west to Caer Sulis where they would be re-organised before heading on to the Haven. They continually met groups who they knew from previous Gatherings. The news of the attacks on Eald and Branque had spread all along the Westway. Speculation about the Belgae villages was rife and villagers constantly stopped them asking for information on what had happened beyond the Causeway. The general rumour was that the Uathach had raised an army and, knowing that the Anglian and Wessex villages were too well protected, had gone across the sea in boats to raid there. Some took it as confirmation of the ill tidings that the Wessex and Anglian Warlords rode together to Caer Sulis. Others were reassured by seeing their warlords riding to the West, seeing it as a sign dispelling the rumours that the Uathach army had already crossed the Causeway. All the warriors noticed that none of the villagers on the Westway were tarrying and the customary festive air was replaced with a palpable anxiety. Everyone was hurrying to get to the safety of Caer Sulis.

They followed the increasingly busy Westway for about sixty miles then turned north along the Ridgeway up onto the Downs and towards the Whitehorse where the Wessex warriors had their main base. It was situated in the north of their territory as the major threat to their lands came from the Uathach of the North, although in recent years the Uathach had only raided the northwest Mercian territory and the northern Anglian lands. There were other, smaller camps deeper into Wessex near the main settlements and strung along the coast but these were only garrisoned in the summer months. Caer Cadarn was populated all year round by those not on duties elsewhere, and by their families and the various craftsmen necessary to support a war band.

Their camp was placed at the top of a hill which had a chalk engraved white horse on its northeast side that could be seen for many miles. A roughly circular wooden wall standing on a ring of raised earth encompassed the top of the hill. It was twenty-feet high and had two gateways, west and east, wide enough for two wains to pass through side by side. Two towers stood by the gateways. Within the compound were cattle sheds for the winter stabling of stock, various buildings for blacksmiths, metal and wood workers, lodgings and roundhouses and in the centre, the main hall.

The Ridgeway ran by the camp and as Arthur's band approached they could tell by the subdued activity that the camp was half-empty. Most of the war band were gathering villagers in the West and in Anglia, a few would be at Caer Sulis already, some would be at the Causeway Gates now, others would never come back from Eald. A crowd of families had gathered outside the gate when word was passed that Arthur was coming up the Ridgeway, many hoping the scant news they had heard regarding Eald was inaccurate and all hoping that it was not their own who had died across the sea. They waited silently as the band drew nearer. Overhead the gathering clouds dropped scattered showers across the landscape but the sun still clung to the eastern horizon and cast their shadows long across the stubbled cornfields.

Arthur and the others reached the gates and dismounted. The assembled crowd waited silently for the news, only Della rushed forward with her children to embrace Mar'h her husband. Arthur told them all to gather in the main hall and Cei led his Anglians to one side and they busied themselves with stabling the horses as Arthur and Ceinwen made their way to the hall.

It was about the same size as the one at Branque but the woodwork around the entrance and within the hall was far more ornately carved with intricately looping and spiralling designs interlocking with each other as they ran up pillars or around the frames of windows. There were raised steps up to the wide entrance and on either side of the doorway there were two flagpoles, the king's red dragon flew from one and the other flag bore the white horse emblem of the Wessex war band. The warriors carried the same device on their shields, a stylised white horse in mid-leap on a green background.

Arthur sat on one of the trestle tables that ran the length of the hall and the group collected around him. He listed those from Ruadan's band who had died at Eald and as he named each one he spoke directly to their respective families and told them how they had died. Most accepted it with stoicism. It was a rare year when they lost no one from the war band but they had not lost twelve in one battle since the last full Uathach border raid and that had been several years ago. The young wife of one of the dead warriors broke down and Ceinwen led her from the hall and offered what comfort she could.

Arthur then told the group the whole story from when he had left Ruadan and the others at Eald. They listened with growing anxiety as the full implications of the timed attacks and the silence from the Belgae villages began to dawn on them. Arthur made it clear this was no border raid but a new enemy. He finished by making it equally clear that he expected Britain to soon be at war with this new foe. The group left the hall and dispersed back to their homes talking amongst themselves with a mixture of grief, anxiety and excitement, speculating on what King Maldred would do about this new threat and what part they would have to play in it.

Mar'h entered the hall with Cei and Balor and they approached Arthur who was still sitting on the long table, his head bowed.

'How did they take it?' Cei asked.

'Well enough. They'll take some time to truly realise what it will mean,' Arthur replied.

'It'll mean many more dead if they come across the Causeway,' Mar'h said.

'And the Anglians won't be able to stop them,' Balor added dismissively. Cei looked at him sharply and Balor hastily qualified his statement by saying that there were just too many of the enemy for the Anglians to hold the Causeway against them.

'Then I won't wait for them to do so,' Arthur said, lifting his head to look at them.

'But winter's almost on us,' Balor replied, aghast at Arthur's implied intent.

'You want to cross the Causeway in the darkness of winter?' Cei asked.

'The king won't agree to that,' Mar'h said shaking his head.

'No one's taken a war band across the Causeway in winter since, well, ever,' Cei said. Someone sitting behind them cleared their throat unnoticed.

'At least they won't be expecting it,' Mar'h replied considering the prospect.

'And it would be better than waiting for a time of their choosing,' Cei conceded.

'Excellent! Carefully laid and thought-out plans. Splendid. Nothing hasty here I see. Needn't have bothered journeying here really, I might as well be on my way then.'

Cei and Mar'h spun round and Arthur jumped off the table. Balor nearly fell off his chair at the unexpected voice.

'Merdynn!' they exclaimed more or less in unison and with a variety of oaths.

'Always nice to be recognised. I got word you were crossing the Causeway and heading here. But it seems I'm not required for counsel,' he nodded to them as he passed between them and made for the door. 'Good luck in your meticulously considered venture,' he said over his shoulder as he reached the door.

Arthur smiled at the others and took a step after the departing Merdynn,

'But you'll share a flagon of beer with us before we leave for the Shadow Lands?'

Merdynn turned at the doorway, 'You'll be needing all the beer for yourselves to help refine this masterpiece. The fumes might cover some of the gaping holes in your inspired strategy.'

'Some beer and Wessex cheese then?' Mar'h upped the offer.

'Well,' Merdynn hesitated, scratching his head in mock contemplation and hesitation.

'Right. Ale, cheese and Cornish bacon,' Cei made the final offer.

'You have Cornish bacon here?' Merdynn asked tilting his head back and raising both eyebrows.

'I've no idea, Merdynn - do you think I live here?' Cei replied laughing.

Merdynn laughed softly, 'No Cei, no one could mistake you for one of these barbarians. Mar'h, grab some suitable victuals and we'll eat like kings in Arthur's hall as you three tell me your news. And close your mouth Balor – at least until the food arrives.'

Balor and Mar'h went in search of food and Cei collected some ale then joined the others who had sat at the top table in the raised end of the hall. Merdynn noticed a shadow cross Arthur's face and looked intently at him.

'Arthur?' he asked, still staring into Arthur's grim expression.

'The last time I sat at the head table in a hall was in Branque. Just before the slaughter,' Arthur replied holding Merdynn's eyes.

'And what are you contemplating?' Merdynn asked leaning forward, 'Revenge?'

'I will not let it happen again,' Arthur replied, deliberately not answering the question.

'Good,' Merdynn said and sat back in his chair, straightening the folds in his worn and ancient brown cloak. Cei looked from one to the other discerning that something had passed between them but not knowing what.

'How's your leg – I saw you limping,' Merdynn asked.

'It'll be fine. Ceinwen's seen to it but even so, I'll be limping for the winter.'

'Ceinwen, eh?' Merdynn asked with interest.

Mar'h struggled up to the table laden with various breads, cheeses and meats. Merdynn clapped his hands and stood up to pick out a slab of cheese from the armful Mar'h was precariously holding.

'Thanks, that's a help,' he said to Merdynn.

'Don't mention it my boy,' Merdynn replied cutting a large corner off the slab and popping it into his mouth. Cei laughed and helped Mar'h unload the foods onto the table.

'Where's your partner in pessimism gone?' Merdynn asked Mar'h.

'Balor?'

'The one and only.'

'He's gone.'

'Gone? Why?'

'I think you make him nervous,' Mar'h replied smiling.

'Good. Serves him right for chopping down so many trees. Never trust a man who lives in the woods and talks to trees, and then cuts them down.'

The others laughed and Merdynn's ancient face creased into a broad smile. They fell into the carefree talk of local news and gossip as they ate and drank.

It was some time before Merdynn finally broached the subject that had never fully left their minds, 'So, Arthur, Ceinwen the only survivor from Branque?' he asked around a mouthful of cheese.

'Yes. Ruadan got twenty or thirty out of Eald.'

'Who were they – who attacked you?'

'Not Uathach.'

'No?'

'No. They were different from us, different from anyone I've seen or encountered in Britain or across the Causeway,' Arthur said, unsure of how to describe the attackers.

'I've not seen their like in Middangeard before,' Mar'h added.

'Were they generally short, with straight black hair, round-ish flat faces, black armoured, curved swords, merciless and careless for their own lives? And, more significantly, did they carry the three-pronged device on their shields?' Merdynn asked leaning forward.

Arthur and Mar'h nodded, 'You've seen them?' Arthur asked.

The levity had dropped from Merdynn's face and he looked at Arthur as he spoke, 'Yes. Many times.'

'What do they want?'

'Everything.'

'Where have they come from?' Arthur asked.

'The past.'

'Merdynn...'

'They call themselves the Adren and they come from the East, the Shadow Lands. Many years ago I saw them when I journeyed far into the East, into the Khan's lands, where the plains stretch on for ever and the sky never ends. They have mounted captains who command them. The captains are from the Shadow Land City but the Adren are from further east and their like hasn't been seen here for such a time that none but a few remember the stories of them now. I had not guessed they had come so far west and so quickly. I didn't believe he could organise them in so short a time, just a few hundred years and yet they're already within our lands.' Merdynn had become distant, lost in past memories and the silence was only broken by the soft rapping of his fingers on the tabletop.

They realised it had begun to rain heavily outside too, and the driving rain drummed down on the hall's roof as Merdynn continued to tap the table seemingly unaware of those around him. Mar'h carried on eating unperturbed by the silence. Cei always assumed these lapses of silence by Merdynn were due to his old age. No one knew how old he was but the eldest amongst the tribes remembered him as an old man when they were but children. Arthur knew him better than anyone else did and knew him to be lost in his memories – searching through the Ages for the information he needed. He signalled the other two away from the table and told them to get everyone together in the hall later on for the evening meal and that they would head west to Caer Sulis tomorrow. When they had left he sat back down and drifted into sleep while waiting for Merdynn to return.

Merdynn had indeed been lost in his memories. He had been trying to recall all he once knew concerning the kings of old. His memory spanned millennia and one image from the past triggered another until he became lost in reliving the events and ancient histories that only he in the whole of Middangeard could remember. Over recent years he had pondered and fretted over the possibility that two others may still be in the world, two others who would remember all that he himself did. They had passed from his knowledge long ago but he felt with a certainty that could not be defined or explained that one or perhaps both were somehow linked to the reappearance of the Adren, the soldier slaves of a distant master. With an effort he brought his wandering mind back to the question that had haunted him for centuries. Who was the heir to the ancient realm? Had the bloodline continued through the dark and sudden chaos of the ending of the last Age? Who was the one person who could unite the disparate peoples of Middangeard, unite them long enough to face the darkness that had come from the Shadow Lands?

He had cursed the fate and treachery that had seen him imprisoned during the glorious rise and devastating fall of the last Age for it meant he had lost all trace of that which he was charged to protect. Only the unimaginable scale of the carnage of that fall had set him free from his imprisonment. He had wandered through the debris of a people in utter ruins, collecting the scant few who had survived those dark years and setting them on a course to recreate their world in the image of the one he had last known.

He searched for centuries vainly trying to find the thread that linked the Ages together. He had the patience of oceans and hope unfathomable but the countless years had whittled both to a brittle splinter. Then on a soft summer's day he had strode into the burning wreckage of an Uathach raid. The marauders had departed leaving only smoking ruins and death. He had sat on the edge of the village well, wrapped in despair and weighed down by hopelessness when he heard the echo of a baby crying. It had taken him four hours to coax the young boy from the bottom of the well where he had hid from the raiders with his infant sister huddled close to his chest. The only things the raiders prized above harvested crops were children and childbearing women.

When the four-year old boy had finally climbed out and stood defiantly before him Merdynn had felt a surge of joy. He had recognised something in the gray eyes of the boy that brought the faces of ancient kings flashing back into his mind. He had knelt before the boy and asked him his name. When the boy replied, Merdynn had turned his face to the skies in the West and relief was etched into every line of his worn face.

That boy now sat sleeping in the chair opposite him, the Warlord of Wessex. The time had come to put his beliefs and hope to the test, to discover if all he felt to be true was indeed true. He had to take the boy who had climbed from the well to the Halls of the Kings.

Arthur stirred back to wakefulness when Merdynn waved a mug of beer under his nose.

'Thought that might do it. Now grab your cloak, there's a gift waiting for you outside,' Merdynn said as he stood and clasped his own threadbare cloak around himself. Arthur got up and followed him to the doorway at the far end of the hall with images flashing through his mind of the slaughter at Branque.

Merdynn strode straight out of the hall, his staff in one hand and the rain bouncing off his bare head. Arthur stopped at the doorway, cast a glance back inside the dry hall then pulled the hood of his cloak over his head and followed Merdynn who was already half-way to the gate.

Leah, standing outside Della's home with Ceinwen, watched them leave and shuddered. Arthur, still limping and using his bow for support, caught up with Merdynn as he joined the Ridgeway track and turned towards Delbaeth Gofannon. The clouds had come in from the West and the rain fell in straight lines obscuring the views down into the vale of the white horse. The setting sun was hidden by the black-bruised clouds that now stretched from horizon to horizon. Puddles and pools of water were already collecting along the chalk-clay track reflecting darkly the skies above. The stunted trees and straggling bushes along the track-way were twisted and bent by the force of the prevailing winds that normally swept across the Downs. Now they were still, collecting the hard rain and spilling it onto the heavy clay path making each step more arduous than the last.

'Is this gift better tempered than the last?' Arthur asked.

Merdynn turned to look at him, 'Has the horse not served you well then?'

'I don't believe that horse would serve anyone, but it took me out of Branque alive and I'm grateful for that.'

'Quite right. Well, this gift is tempered perfectly.'

The rain hardened, throwing mud up from the track-way as it hammered down on the gathered pools.

'How far are we going?' Arthur raised his voice to make himself heard.

Merdynn pointed up ahead to the ring of tall trees that circled Delbaeth Gofannon. Arthur nodded and bent his head against the rain. As they approached the grove the pathway, sunken between the sodden fields on either side, grew more flooded and Arthur found himself wading and having to drag his damaged leg through thick, muddy water as he followed on behind Merdynn.

They turned off the Ridgeway and followed a short path to the circle of trees. In the centre of the ringed grove stood an oval burial mound, edged by standing stones with three rough-cut blocks at one end as an entrance. Merdynn stopped by the low doorway into the burial mound and absently ran his hand over the wet stone. He stood there lost in his own thoughts as the rain swept around them.

'Now is not the time to examine your memories old man.'

Merdynn took his hand from the worn stone and turned impatiently to Arthur, 'I was trying to remember how to get in, so now is exactly the right time to examine my memories.'

'More of your runes and chants perhaps?'

Merdynn looked at him sharply before replying, 'Actually, I'm fairly sure we just walk through the entrance. Follow me.'

He ducked down and disappeared into the darkness inside. Throwing back his hood Arthur followed. After crouching along behind Merdynn for two or three yards he found the passageway widening to either side. He reached above his head expecting to feel the damp earth of the ceiling but his hand touched nothing and he straightened up. He looked back the way they had come but despite having taken no turns he could no longer see the twilight outside.

He could hear Merdynn ahead of him stumbling in the darkness and cursing to himself. Gradually a light grew in the darkness and Arthur found himself in a chamber with what appeared to be smaller and darker rooms branching off to either side. Merdynn was slowly pacing along the walls and peering at them as if looking for something. Every now and again he would stop and touch his staff against the wall and a dim light would start emanating from the spot he had touched.

Arthur watched him and when he had finally completed his circuit the chamber was lit by a flickering light from all four walls. Merdynn placed his staff on the earth floor and stood by Arthur with his arms crossed and his head bowed. Arthur thought he sensed movement around him and the silent burial tomb seemed to hold the distant echo of voices balanced just on the edge of his hearing.

'What is this place, Merdynn?'

'You know it as Delbaeth Gofannon. The Blacksmiths. It is an ancient burial mound. Kings, queens and masters from the ancient world lie at rest here. Every land has its heart. Here lies Britain's for this is the heart of the whole of Middangeard.'

Arthur looked around at the damp earth walls and the puddled floor, 'Why bring me to this place of the dead?'

'Because it's not just the bones of the dead that lie here.'

Merdynn crossed to the far end of the chamber and beckoned Arthur to follow. Arthur felt a slight breeze to his right and he turned expecting to see a ghost from the past but there was no one else with them, just the distant sound of voices. He joined Merdynn at the far end where one of the smaller rooms led into blackness. Merdynn went inside and came out carrying a long bundle of oiled cloths, which he laid carefully on the floor.

'What is it?' Arthur asked, wondering if Merdynn was desecrating the bones of the dead.

'It's a sword. One that was carried into battle by the ancient kings. It's yours now.'

'I'm not a king.'

'Nevertheless it is yours.'

'No sword that's lain here for any time would be of any use now.'

'Nevertheless it is yours.'

Arthur stared at the bundle then at Merdynn but made no move to pick up what Merdynn claimed was his. Merdynn knelt down and unwrapped the cloths to reveal a sheathed sword with a magnificently crafted hilt and intricately worked scabbard with inlaid silver wreathed along its length.

Arthur leant forward and picked it up. He drew the sword from the scabbard and he saw it was masterfully forged. Faint tracings ran down the entire length of the blade. He held it closer to his face as he tried to see the etching more clearly in the dim light. The distant voices fell silent and he felt the faces of those whom time had silenced staring at him from across the centuries.

Standing, he sheathed the sword and faced Merdynn, 'This is the gift. And it's mine.'

'Yes. If I wasn't sure before, I am now. It is an ancient sword. It was forged long ago and in every Age it has been wielded by one from your lineage. Now it comes to our turn. I have waited a long time for what I hoped would never come and watched as others took up the burden. Yet now the moment has come I feel the need for their counsel.'

'Can you not go to them and take counsel?'

'No, not now. Two from my order left this world long Ages past. Two went into the East and I fear for them both now.'

'What do you know of the Eastern Lands, Merdynn? What do you know of those who guide them?'

'Everything and nothing. This Land has lain suspended for centuries, adjusting and recovering slowly after the ruinous end of the last Age. We now stand at the true beginning of our Age, Arthur. Should we fail then it will be an age of darkness. We stand between the shadows and the light, and it may be that in defeat is our only chance of victory.'

'If our fate hinges on riddles then the gods mock us.'

Merdynn's sharp eyes watched Arthur keenly as he buckled the sword to his waist, 'It wouldn't be the first time that fate has hinged on a riddle, Arthur.'

'Then may it be for the last.'

'It may well be so. Now, we must leave, it doesn't do to tarry in these places.'

Merdynn picked up his staff and as he did so the flickering light from the walls dimmed and died. Suddenly they were back in the narrow corridor with the entrance to the mound before them. They stepped back outside and with the rain hammering down on them Arthur cast a glance back at the entrance. It seemed no more than a sodden burial mound. He looked down at the sword buckled to his side as if to confirm what had happened only moments before. It still hung there, rain running down the magnificent scabbard. He pulled his cloak around it and glanced about the familiar grove with its tall trees standing silently sentinel. He looked at Merdynn who was watching him.

'I've been here countless times. I've even hid inside there when I was child but it's never been more than what it seems to be now,' Arthur said as he gestured towards the burial mound.

'But it's the first time that you and I have been inside.' Merdynn smiled, 'Did you know that it was once said that if your horse lost its shoe you could leave the horse here and it would be re-shod by the gods?'

'And would it?'

'Of course not, it'd be stolen. But in myths lie many ancient truths. The sword you carry has been broken before, yet you'll find no trace of it now.'

As Merdynn finished speaking, an image flashed across Arthur's mind – he saw himself standing on a rain-lashed beach with the wind howling about him. Blood and sweat streaked his smoke-blackened face. He was surrounded by the dead and he was holding the bloodied sword aloft in desperation. Merdynn watched him as the life returned to his eyes.

'Is that the place where it will all end?' Arthur asked.

'No fate is set in stone,' Merdynn replied quietly.

They left the grove and Merdynn turned to Arthur, 'I must leave you now. The King's Council is set for the day after tomorrow and much needs to be considered. I am bringing the Cithol Lord to Caer Sulis. None of their kind have left the Veiled City for longer than anyone can remember, but we need their knowledge. King Maldred has much to ponder on and many decisions to make.'

'Caer Sulis then,' Arthur said and Merdynn turned off the path and strode eastward across the soaked, pooled fields.

Chapter Four

A rthur rode into Caer Sulis with Cei and Ceinwen. The others had already gone ahead. The Westway was thronged with the wains from the last of the villages gathered from further east. Like most of the towns and villages in the West and South of Britain, Caer Sulis was not fortified. The Uathach had never raided this deep into the southern lands so there had been no need for walls or gates around the largest settlement in Britain.

The town was nestled in a valley ringed by rolling hills and the Westway ran straight through its heart and onto the Haven further to the West. To the North of the town and along the hillsides stretched the long barns and paddocks for the winter stabling of the cattle, goats, sheep and pigs from the combined villages of the southern tribes. The wind rarely came from the North but when it did the townsfolk claimed the stench from the penned animals was enough to melt the winter snow.

Most of the town's farms and crop fields were across the river that ran along the southern edge of town. A light mist rose from the river course and its drifting tendrils felt their way across the stubble fields and paddocks. The hills obscured the setting sun but the sky was clear after the recent rains although the cold wind from the West promised further rain to come. Smoke rose above the town from every building and every dwelling, most of which were set along the town's broad, earthen roadways.

The settlement was several miles long and was spread along either side of the Westway. Without encompassing walls the town had spilled year by year into the adjacent fields and now encroached upon the slopes of the surrounding hills. It was loosely divided into various quarters with most of the blacksmiths, wainwrights, craftsmen and butcheries to the North and the living quarters strung along the main thoroughfare and stretching down towards the river. The King's Hall stood imposingly in the centre of the town.

Where the broad roadway entered the town, members from the king's war band noted all the wains and their contents that were coming into Caer Sulis and took charge of them. The livestock were registered and led either through the town or to the northern paddocks while the harvest crops were divided between the local store houses, for those staying behind for the winter, and that which was to be taken through Caer Sulis and onto the Haven to be loaded there aboard the ships that were being readied to sail across the Western Seas.

As they rode by the lines of wains waiting to be recorded and allocated Arthur and Cei called greetings to various harried members of the king's warriors. The king's men were the only war band to wear anything resembling a uniform, a red tunic under their leather jerkins that matched the red dragon device on their shields and flags.

They stopped briefly to talk to Gereint, the chief captain of the Mercian warriors. It was his duty to organise the westward journey and this was a trying time for him. His short, iron-grey hair was ruffled from where he continually ran his hand through it and his brow was deeply furrowed as he stamped back and forth cursing, shouting and generally bullying everyone into some kind of working order. He only turned his full attention to them when they answered his questions about the attacks across the Causeway. He promised to talk to them at more length during the festival after the council and returned to the perennially impossible task before him. He was not a happy man.

Almost all the villages of Britain had now been gathered and about twenty thousand people were crammed into Caer Sulis, sharing the houses and preparing themselves for the last leg of the yearly journey to the Haven from where they embarked on the month long crossing of the Western Seas. Neither Arthur nor Cei were concerned with these preparations for it was now the responsibility of the king's men to organise the rest of the journey for the villagers and their supplies.

Arthur and the others slowly made their way on horseback along the main way into Caer Sulis. The ground had been churned to clinging mud with the recent rains and the continual passing of ox-drawn carts, horses and people. The two storey buildings rose above them on either side as they rode further into the heart of the town. The stone buildings stood out imposingly from their wooden counterparts which had been covered in wattle and daub and painted in pale blues and yellows with diluted pigments. Even though Ceinwen had been there hundreds of times before she still looked with wonder at the buildings, much as Caja had done when she was a child.

They gradually made their way through the crowded roadways to the area where the Wessex villages had been quartered. Arthur wanted to give his account of Eald and Branque to the Wessex chieftain, Kenwyn, and then get some rest before being summoned to the King's Council. As they approached the main building in the quarter, crowds of the Wessex villagers gathered around Arthur, relieved that the news of their warlord's survival was true and eager for more information on what they still believed to be the Uathach attacks across the Causeway. Arthur told them the news in brief and word quickly spread that the villages across the sea had indeed been massacred and only a handful of survivors would be arriving in Caer Sulis.

Cei suddenly let out a cry and hurriedly dismounted. Trevenna was standing on the steps to the main building and smiling at them. She was tall and slim, with paler skin than her brother but with the same dark hair. She would have been a striking woman in any case but her eyes caught and held people's attention. They were a clear, turquoise blue and seemed to be always carefree and smiling. Cei swept her up in his arms, grinning broadly as Arthur and Ceinwen joined them. She flashed a smile at the other two and embraced them both.

Trevenna took Arthur's hands in hers and said, 'Thank the gods you got out safe Arthur, and you Ceinwen. When I heard the news of the attacks, well I needed to see you to believe you were safe.'

'Have the boats returned yet from the Belgae shores?' Cei asked.

A shadow crossed Trevenna's face and she slowly shook her head, 'There'd been no news when I left with the last of the coastal villagers but many things could have delayed their departure. Perhaps they're making their way down the coast to the northern edge of the Channel Marshes – maybe they had a problem with some of the boats or the seas were too heavy.'

Hope returned to Cei as she spoke but Arthur just bowed his head.

'I'm so sorry about your family, your village,' Trevenna said turning to Ceinwen.

Ceinwen grimaced and then set her expression to the now familiar portrayal of gratitude, sorrow, acknowledgement and stoicism. She would rather that people just stopped voicing their sympathy to her but at least with Trevenna, a friend since childhood, she knew it was wholly sincere.

Trevenna guessed some of what she felt and smiled sadly at her before turning to touch Arthur's arm and say, 'You should go inside and talk to the counsellors.'

Arthur nodded, 'We'll catch up with you at the festival, in the King's Hall. You can go with them, Ceinwen, if you want.'

Ceinwen shook her head and the other two walked away. She turned to Arthur and looking up at him she said, 'There may yet be hope for the longboats, Trevenna might be right.'

'Trevenna would find the light in the darkness or warmth in the cold winter and I love her for that. But without the moon there is no light in the darkness, and without a fire there is no warmth in the winter; her hope is not founded on anything other than hope. Everything across the Causeway belongs now to the Shadow Land armies. We need to stop the same happening in our own land.'

'Can you stop that happening here?'

'Yes, I will. We will,' Arthur replied and guided Ceinwen through the doorway and into the building. They were greeted warmly by those in the main entrance room and directed to the back of the building where the Wessex counsellors were already talking to their chieftain.

It was the custom in Wessex for the people to choose a chieftain and four counsellors. The counsellors each had their own area of responsibility; Fianna was the head counsellor and she was in charge of all matters that related to farming, crop stores and provisions throughout Wessex. TiGwyna was the second and she was learned in healing and medicine; it was her duty to pass on that knowledge to the villages and it was she who had taught Ceinwen as a child about the curative properties of various wild plants and forest moulds. The third counsellor dealt with crafts and building work while the fourth was the official bard whose duty it was to keep the tribe's history and create new sagas as events merited.

Together they advised and answered to the chieftain who in turn answered to the king. Most disputes and decisions were settled within the tribe either by the counsellor responsible for that area or by the chieftain. Occasionally there arose a dispute between tribes or a decision had to be made that affected more than one tribe and these matters were brought to the King's Council by the chieftains.

The warlord was considered to be the fifth counsellor and it was his duty to keep the peace within the tribe and with the other tribes, to train and maintain a war band and to protect his people. The warlord was chosen by the warriors according to their own customs.

The whole Wessex Council had held their positions for many years and were highly respected by all the people of Wessex. The system had served them well. Each village was self-sufficient to a greater or lesser extent but it was common for villages to pursue local activities such as fishing, mining or tending livestock while others would specialise in one craft or another and this led to a healthy bartering trade. The council would set the relative value of goods but more often than not trades were exchanged to local satisfaction irrespective of official values. Even though the war band had their own farms they were on a much smaller scale than those of the villages and the council collected tithes to supplement their produce.

The Wessex Council rose and greeted Arthur when he entered, they had all known each other for many years and each relied on the other's knowledge and wisdom. Kenwyn sat at the head of the table. He was a short, rotund man approaching sixty but he was still quick-witted, persuasive and never anything less than honest. He had known King Maldred since childhood, both having been under the tutelage of the Royal Bard, Ossian, and the king trusted his judgement. Once greetings had been exchanged, Arthur began relating the story of Eald and Branque and of the silence from the Belgae villages. Ceinwen poured him a goblet of wine as he spoke and stepped back to lean against the wall and watch Arthur as he told the news to the Wessex Council.

Arthur told them about the attacks on the villages and other recent events but refrained from telling them that Merdynn had gone to the Ghost Woods to bring the Cithol Lord to the King's Council. He concluded by saying that he had left Ruadan and Balor with Hengest to organise a defence of the Causeway. At the mention of Ruadan, Ceinwen quietly slipped out of the room noticed only by Fianna who watched the departing figure with interest before looking back to Arthur.

'So you believe that the Belgae and Cei's men are lost?' Kenwyn asked.

'Yes. The attacks were too co-ordinated. I see no reason why they would not have attacked the Belgae at the same time and they must have soldiers to spare or they wouldn't have committed so many to the attacks on Eald and Branque.'

'And you fear they will come across the Causeway next?'

'Why would they not? Perhaps they want our land. Perhaps they have other reasons. Merdynn may have the answers at the King's Council. After the ships have sailed for the West I'll take the war band across the Causeway and see what can be learnt of this enemy and what the fate of the Belgae was.'

'You'll do this in winter?' Fianna asked, clearly surprised. Arthur turned his eyes to her and nodded. She was white haired and becoming more frail as the years passed but her voice was clear and firm and her wisdom was valued as much by the Wessex villagers as it was by the council.

Kenwyn cleared his throat, 'King Maldred won't agree to that, Arthur.'

'I hadn't thought to ask his permission.'

'He won't like the idea of taking the Wessex warriors across the Causeway when his lands are threatened. A treating party, perhaps, but not a war band and not in the winter darkness.'

'He can take his counsellors and lead a treating party if he'll forego the sunlit lands in the West. I'll lead the war band. You can choose the next king as he'll not be returning from the parley.'

'Arthur! You must not speak of the king like that!' TiGywna said.

'Be careful at the council Arthur, he has had no love for you ever since you challenged Saltran for the leadership of the war band and if you speak to him that way at the council-'

'Saltran was a cur and died like one.'

'Nonetheless, he was friend to the king.'

'Then the king should choose his friends more carefully,' Arthur replied.

'It seems to me that we need peace amongst ourselves more than ever. Both you and the king will need to put your hostilities aside, Arthur,' Fianna said.

The conflict between the king and Arthur had started long before he had become the Wessex Warlord and killed Saltran. It had begun almost forty years ago when Maldred had been crowned king about the same time as Merdynn had found Arthur as a young boy. As Merdynn was the King's Counsellor, Maldred believed that he had exclusive access to the old man's advice and he had expected his continual presence. He had grown to resent the time Merdynn spent with the boy from Wessex.

He had been a young king, only twenty years old, and he had felt uncertain and insecure when Merdynn was away for long periods and he had turned more and more to ambitious, cruel men like Saltran for guidance. Maldred had thrown his support behind Saltran when he had positioned himself to become the Wessex Warlord and had been delighted by his success.

Maldred's line was from Mercia and so it followed that the Mercian war band acted as his own guard and warriors, and when his ally, Saltran, became Warlord of Wessex Maldred effectively controlled two thirds of the warriors from the southern tribes. With that kind of military strength he no longer felt the need for the counsel of the absent Merdynn and he happily turned a blind eye to the havoc the ill-led warriors wrought throughout the country.

Arthur couldn't do likewise and as the atrocities continued Arthur realised something had to be done. Maldred had been delighted to hear that Arthur had challenged Saltran for the leadership of the Wessex war band. While Arthur had gained renown as a young warrior, Maldred was confident he would be no threat to the seasoned and murderous Saltran. The king's resentment had curdled to hatred when the news had reached him that the youth had slain Saltran.

Merdynn had continued to spend more time with Arthur than he did with the king and Maldred's hatred of Arthur hardened over the years and he grew to fear the power of the warlord and his growing reputation. Arthur had reformed the Wessex war band and forced the Mercians and Anglians to do likewise and he led them in battle as the king never could. Maldred feared the warriors owed more allegiance to Arthur than they did to him and in an effort to regain some of the authority he had lost, Maldred had brought the warriors from the Green Isle across the sea to help fight the Uathach - with nearly disastrous consequences. If anything, his ill-judged strategy had only strengthened Arthur's position in the land.

Maldred had considered throwing his Mercians against Arthur's war band in what would effectively be a civil war but he couldn't be sure that Gereint would lead his warriors against Arthur and he realised that even if he did then Arthur would more than likely win and he would have then lost everything so he contented himself with more petulant acts; he slighted Arthur at every opportunity hoping to goad him into a rash attack where he could be justifiably killed and sought to disrupt whatever plans he attempted to implement, no matter how innocuous or beneficial they might have been, in an effort to undermine his increasing authority.

Every one of the Wessex counsellors knew the turbulent history between the king and Arthur and none of them wanted to exacerbate the situation any further.

Arthur put both hands on the table preparing to stand, 'So be it then, I'll keep my peace with Maldred but the time is coming when the king will need to prove his judgement.'

'The council is set for tomorrow before the feast,' Kenwyn said.

'Then I'll see you there,' Arthur replied.

'Come. I'll show you where we are quartered,' Fianna said and led the way from the room. Behind them the others looked at each other worried by both the news Arthur brought and his words about the king.

Fianna led Arthur across the busy courtyard to a long row of low buildings. These were the living quarters, built especially for the Gathering times when the town's population increased tenfold. They had small windows, widely spaced apart to keep the rooms dark and cool in summer and to lessen the harsh elements of the long, cold winter.

Fianna stopped at the doorway to the first building and turned to Arthur, 'You can rest here - I'll send someone to tell you when the council is ready to start.'

Arthur opened the door but Fianna stopped him, saying, 'Arthur, what's wrong? I've never heard you talk openly like that about the king before. For all your differences do you actually doubt the king has the land's best interests at heart?'

'No, but no king in living memory has had to face what we are about to face.'

'He may well rise to that, you can't judge him, not yet – he is the king after all.'

Arthur looked away then back again directly into Fianna's eyes, 'And if he cannot face it, if he fails, are all my people to be butchered too?'

Fianna tried to read Arthur's face but he turned and stooping down, entered the building. Fianna stood uncertainly by the doorway before making her way back to the other counsellors. Ceinwen watched her from across the courtyard until she was out of sight then she too made her way to the living quarters and ducked inside. She hesitated by Arthur's door, her hand raised to knock softly then she turned and walked quickly on down the corridor.

Arthur awoke some hours later as the door to his small room clicked closed. By his bed was a tray of food and a hot drink. He ate as he dressed then headed out into the courtyard.

Mar'h was leaning against a wall watching the busy activity in general and a group of chatting girls in particular. One of the young women kept casting glances across at him. In her estimation any warrior was worth looking at and this one with his dusky skin, long black hair and pale brown eyes was certainly no exception. It was not the large, hooked nose or his lean, wiry frame that made her quickly lose interest but, on closer inspection, he was not as young as she had at first hoped. She guessed, quite accurately, that he must be in his mid-thirties and probably married. She had made that mistake before and was not about to repeat it again. Not yet anyway. Had she known that he had already fathered children then she would have quickly put her reservations to one side in the hope that they too might produce children. A warrior and a potential father would have been a fine catch but she didn't know about his children, so she looked away from Mar'h and re-joined the conversation with her friends. Mar'h sighed and rubbed the hard stubble on his chin, knowing that Morgund wouldn't have accepted the dismissal so easily – he'd have strolled right across to them and no doubt he would have invited them to join him at the festival in the Great Hall; it galled him that they would have accepted Morgund's invitation too – they always did.

Arthur had seen the brief exchange of looks between Mar'h and the girls before his attention was averted by a swirl of swifts as they darted overhead, changed direction with a flick and then wheeled away in the late autumn skies like a pall of smoke snatched by conflicting winds. Arthur watched them for a while, surprised they had not yet left for the West. He followed their twisting, unpredictable flight until they were lost to his sight over the stream to the South where they swooped for food in the drifting mists that rose from the river like gentle steam.

He walked across to Mar'h, 'How are Della and the children?'

Mar'h straightened up and turned around looking surprised and guilty, 'They're fine Arthur, bit worried like. We thought it'd be best if they took the journey west this year.'

Normally the families of the warriors stayed at Whitehorse Hill or in Caer Sulis. Arthur just nodded, understanding.

'Fine look out I make, I was supposed to watch for you and take you to the council.'

'There's less distractions on most watches,' Arthur replied and Mar'h laughed and looked across at the small group of girls still chatting in the corner of the courtyard.

'If I were ten years younger.'

'Ten?'

'Twenty then.'

'And not with Della.'

'And not with Della.'

'Or have any children.'

'All right, Arthur, all right. I was just imagining I was a young man again.'

'Nothing wrong with your imagination then.'

Mar'h laughed, 'You don't have to take it out on me just because you can't stand to speak to the king.'

'Lead on then. Is Merdynn there yet?'

'Not yet.'

Mar'h led the way to the council. It was not being held in the Great Hall as Arthur had thought but in one of the king's houses down by the river. The royal houses were set off by themselves, away from the other dwellings that stretched along the riverbank. The cluster of two-storey buildings and low stables had all been painted some years ago but the red dyes and pigments had washed out to leave no more than a thin wash of pink over the daubed walls. They backed onto the river and the mist edged its way between the houses, hugging the ground as it crept its way over the fields towards the town. On the far bank Arthur could hear the murderous clamour of squabbling crows, their coarse screeches piercing the autumn mists as they fought over the last of the easy pickings before winter set in.

Ceinwen was waiting for Arthur outside the main house with Leah. Normally the war band's second-in-command would attend the council with the warlord but as both Ruadan and Hengest were at the Causeway, Ceinwen and Leah would attend in their place.

'If the king steps out of line, just set Leah on him,' Mar'h said under his voice and turned to go.

Arthur stopped him and said quietly, 'I've told Ceinwen to stand-in for Ruadan because I want you to get the warriors together Mar'h, we may be heading for the Causeway a few days earlier than we planned.'

Mar'h nodded and strode off. As Arthur approached the king's house the twenty guards from the king's war band stood straighter and faced him.

Arthur greeted Ceinwen and Leah, 'Everyone inside already?'

'Everyone but Merdynn,' Ceinwen answered.

'He'll come.'

They walked up the steps and one of the guards spoke, 'Only the king's warriors can bear weapons in the king's house.'

'That's a new law isn't it?' Leah asked.

Arthur stopped and stared at the man who quickly lowered his eyes.

'Is he not my king then?' Arthur asked.

The guards stirred uneasily. 'He is king to us all,' one of them ventured warily.

'And am I not a warrior?'

The guards became more uncomfortable and remained silent.

'Then I too must be a king's warrior.'

The guards looked at each other for support and Arthur walked into the king's house unopposed. As Leah went through the doorway she puckered her lips at the guard as if blowing him a kiss and patted the sword at her hip. Ceinwen hurried her through. They were led to a large, high-ceilinged room dominated by a heavy wooden table ringed by chairs with a carved throne at one end. Two large fires burned brightly in grates against opposite walls, throwing their heat across the room. Most of the smoke was drawn up iron flues built into the walls but enough of it escaped to rise up to the high ceiling where it clouded the soot-stained rafters. The strong scent of wood smoke filled the room overpowering the smell of the roasted meat that was laid out on the table for all the chieftains and counsellors of the three tribes to feast on. The room was full with people standing in small groups and talking. The king and two of his counsellors stood apart. He wore a narrow gold crown set with jewels and a long, blood red cloak. He had been king for decades but neither his age nor his responsibilities had bowed him. He stood straight and though he was not tall he had the habit of tilting his head back as if looking down on whomever he was talking to. His neatly cropped beard was silver as was his long, well-groomed full head of hair.

He saw Arthur enter with the two women and he strode to his throne with a sour expression on his face. The room went quiet and the counsellors and chieftains from the three tribes went to their places around the table, many of them greeting Arthur as they did so. Arthur looked around the gathering and nodded to Gereint who looked no less harassed than when he had seen him organising the influx of villagers. Cei caught Arthur's eye and gestured towards the king, grimacing. Clearly the king had been waiting for Arthur to arrive and he hadn't been waiting patiently. He had tried to start the council without him but too many had pointed out that Arthur's news was more important than the usual fare they dealt with and that it would probably be best to wait for Arthur's arrival before they began. Maldred's mood had only gotten worse and many around the table cursed Arthur for putting them in this position.

King Maldred looked across at Arthur, 'Unavoidably detained were you, Arthur of Wessex?' he asked, looking pointedly to either side of Arthur at Ceinwen and Leah with an unconcealed sneer. Those near the king laughed softly, others looked at the table.

'I meant no delay, but are we not waiting for Merdynn?' Arthur replied, ignoring the insinuating leer.

Maldred cast a glance at the empty chair beside his own. 'Do you suggest we await his pleasure as we have yours, Arthur of Wessex? Kings have grown old waiting for Merdynn to appear.'

105

Ceinwen turned her head to Arthur and muttered so only he could hear, 'Older but rarely wiser.'

Arthur didn't bother to suppress his smile and replied, 'As you wish, but he does have news that concerns us here.'

'I don't wait on anyone,' Maldred said in an effort to dispel the impression that he had indeed already waited for Arthur. A servant immediately filled his goblet with wine while the counsellors unhooked their cloaks and took their seats. As Arthur laid his cloak on the back of his chair the king shot to his feet, sending his wine spilling across the grained oak as he planted both fists on the table.

'And were you not instructed to leave your weapons outside the Royal House?'

Once again the room fell silent. Ceinwen noticed none of the others bore their swords. Even Cei across the table had left his outside not seeing it as important one way or the other. He shrugged as Ceinwen glared at him. All eyes turned to the sword hanging at Arthur's side and gasps and exclamations rippled around the table. None had seen it before and all marvelled at the workmanship that could be seen on the hilt and scabbard.

'It was said that the king's warriors could bear their arms.'

'And it's such a fine sword too, Arthur of Wessex, fit, indeed, for a king. Do you bear it as a gift?'

'It is a gift - it was given to me. But I can't offer it on – the receiver would be insulting the giver if a gift were to be passed on.'

Maldred's face reddened and a vein stood out on his neck as he said, 'You would rather insult me than whoever gave you this gift? Do you seek to belittle me, Warlord of Wessex?'

'Not I, Lord.' Arthur replied with a smile that implied Maldred was doing that himself without any need of Arthur's help. Half the room stood, some to pacify the situation, others taking offence from one side or the other.

One strident voice cut through the room, 'Silence! Is this any way to act before an honoured guest from the Veiled City?'

Merdynn stood just inside the doorway to the room glaring at the silenced counsellors. Cei marvelled at how Merdynn could give the impression of being a jovial old man one day and then the next be the commandingly powerful figure who now stood staring at them with fury in his eyes. By his side stood a tall, slender figure robed and cowled in a winter cloak. Those in the room not already standing got to their feet and stared at the tall figure. None in the room save Arthur had ever seen anyone from the Veiled City; many had thought the city only existed in fables. The Cithol Lord slowly reached up and lifted back the cowl covering his head. The skin on his hands and face was a translucent, pale white that contrasted sharply with his black robe.

The gathered counsellors, the wisest of the southern tribes and representatives of their peoples all started in horror and alarm. Gasps of shock and oaths to ward off evil sounded louder in the suddenly small room than had their previous shouting and arguing. The initial shock of seeing a child's tale manifest itself before their very eyes quickly gave way to a deep unease brought on by something unknown and beyond their experience. Many of those around the table were paralysed with uncertainty believing they were faced by a long dismissed childhood ghost.

Arthur studied the Cithol Lord in the complete silence that followed. His hair was very fine and completely white and the pale skin seemed stretched over his high cheek-boned face. His eyes were entirely black with no visible iris or pupil. The Cithol Lord took a step forward and those around the table backed away feeling for weapons that were not there. He gradually looked around the room, studying each face in turn before finally settling on the one person who had not recoiled from him.

'You I know,' his voice was surprisingly deep and sonorous coming from such a slender frame.

Arthur stepped forward and inclined his head, 'Welcome to Caer Sulis, Lord Venning. Welcome to the King's Council.' Arthur gestured towards the king, 'King Maldred of Britain.'

The king, desperate not to lose face or to appear less composed than Arthur gathered his wits and stepped forward and looked from Merdynn to the Cithol Lord, 'Greetings from the peoples of Britain, Lord Venning,' he managed to say in a normal voice. In his mind he was shouting to himself that he was the king, that all the civilised land of Britain obeyed his rules, that this was just some conjuring trick of that old fool Merdynn. He continued aloud in a stronger voice, 'We had not expected your arrival,' and he looked poisonously at Merdynn. 'What brings the Cithol

Lord to the King's Council?'

'An army has arisen from the East, it threatens all who live in Middangeard,' replied Merdynn.

The council erupted in renewed uproar at this declaration but the demands for an explanation were soon muted, as if they feared the Cithol Lord were directly responsible for this army and had the power to summon them forth even here.

'If either of you can tell us more about this new army then take a seat at the council,' Arthur indicated the vacant chair next to the king. The Cithol Lord made his way to the head of the table and those he passed turned to face him but they leant back to put as much space as possible between themselves and the apparition.

Cei glanced across to Arthur with a bewildered look as the Cithol Lord took his seat. Arthur held up the palm of his hand to calm him. Leah had to force herself to stop making the sign to ward off evil while Ceinwen stood rooted to the spot, staring wide-eyed at the spectre among them. Merdynn drew up a chair and sat down next to Lord Venning.

'You know more about the attacks on my villages across the Causeway?' the king asked Merdynn, already suspicious of the link between the Cithol Lord, Merdynn and the army across the Causeway.

'We know something of those behind the attacks but we should start with an account from one who was there,' Merdynn said and gestured toward Arthur.

Arthur was looking intently at the Cithol Lord and Ceinwen noticed how Arthur's gray eyes had become glazed and seemingly sightless. As the silence lengthened the Cithol Lord slowly raised his bowed head and looked directly back at Arthur who jolted back as if stung. Arthur blinked and the life came back to his eyes. It had only been a few seconds but everyone in the room was watching the two of them. Lord Venning bowed his head again and as Arthur looked away from him Cei thought he saw surprise in Arthur's eyes. Arthur clasped his hands in front of himself on the table and related the story of the attacks on Eald and Branque as he had done earlier to Kenwyn and the Wessex counsellors. All in the room listened as he spoke, nodding at various points as parts of the tale tallied with what they had already heard second or third hand.

When Arthur finished speaking Maldred leaned forward and said, 'You left them to their fate then?'

'I could not change their fate,' Arthur replied.

Ceinwen stared at the king incredulously, fearing a repeat of the accusation she had heard from Cerdic when they rode through the edges of the Ghost Woods.

'Could you not? Not even you? Are we to understand that the Warlord of Wessex turned and fled?' the king asked.

Ceinwen felt her anger rise again that Arthur should be accused of abandoning her family and friends, and by inference that she too had abandoned them. She turned to the king to speak her mind but her attention was drawn to the Cithol Lord sitting by King Maldred's side who looked calmly at her with his black eyes. She felt the anger drain away to be replaced by fear and she kept silent.

'I could not change their fate,' Arthur repeated, not rising to the insult.

'You left that you might yet change others' fates.'

All eyes turned to Lord Venning as he spoke. A pervasive dread of the Cithol Lord had settled on those around the table and they were unsure if he had spoken in Arthur's defence or accused him of something.

'Yes, Lord Venning,' Arthur replied.

'It would only have served the enemy to stand and die there. Had they known who you were you would not have left alive,' Merdynn added.

'A mistake they will have cause to regret,' Arthur said.

King Maldred leant back in his throne and took a drink from his replenished goblet of wine, trying to regroup after the shock of seeing someone walk out of the songs of myth. He had hoped to use this council to undermine Arthur's authority after the disasters across the Causeway but he had lost control of proceedings even before the council had begun and he had no clear idea how to wrest it back.

He turned to the Wessex Chieftain, 'Kenwyn, are you and the Wessex counsellors content with this account?'

Cei was about to stand and remonstrate against the suggestion that anyone here doubted Arthur but Kenwyn raised a hand to stop him and said, 'We are, King Maldred. In these matters we place ourselves entirely at Arthur's judgement. Perhaps it would benefit us all to learn more of these attackers?' His eyes flickered between Merdynn and the Cithol Lord as he spoke.

'Indeed it would, sensible Chieftain of the Wessex.' Merdynn stood up, 'Contrary to popular misconception, they were not Uathach. No, would that they were. I can tell you a little about them but Lord Venning will explain more in due course.

'The armies that attacked Eald and Branque and possibly the Belgae villages were Adren. They come out of the East and are of a different race to those in Middangeard. I have reason to believe they are the Khan's army. They are a new race of people to you and yet they are an ancient race. Their like has been seen before in these lands but no living person remembers that time except for myself - and possibly those who lead them. They are commanded by captains who probably number in the hundreds but the Adren are likely to be many thousand strong. Many years ago I travelled far in the East looking for others of my Order and the Adren were growing in number even then, ever stretching further west, ever seeking more land to support their burgeoning numbers. Perhaps I am at fault for not realising they could trouble us here so soon. There were signs but like so many signs before I hoped they were false. But false they weren't.'

The Anglian Chieftain, Aelle, spoke up, 'Is it just land they want? Surely there's enough and more to spare?'

Merdynn looked across at Aelle and shook his head slowly before saying, 'No, Aelle. No to both questions. A thousand years ago your own people came to this Island from shores to the North of the Belgae looking for good land to farm in peace. You were granted the lands you now live in. But the Adren come with a different purpose. Lord Venning?' Merdynn sat as if weighed down.

Everyone's attention was fixed upon the Cithol Lord as he slowly stood. Their dread of the stranger among them was becoming mixed with wonder that they should be the ones to see the legends come to life.

He was by the king's side but he spoke directly to Arthur, 'Our two peoples have had little to do with each other for many thousands of years. Yet it was not always so. Deep in the past we have a shared history, when the world was younger, when day followed night and night followed day, before the sun and moon slowed to their unhurried cycle. Those who lived in the world at that time were our common ancestors. The world was not always as it is now, yet our paths diverged when the world changed to as we now know it. We left these lands just before the last

Age crashed in ruins.

'Merdynn awoke to this world of darkness and toiled without cease to reform some order. It was he who brought you together in councils and tribes for you were but scattered and desperate remnants before. It was he who dragged your ancestors from their underground hovels and caves. It was he who brought you once more into the light and re-taught you all you had forgotten. It was the work of centuries and although it was only his appointed task yet it remains a tale unmatched in the history of the Ages.

'Yet there were wondrous things in the world before the terrible times that plunged it all back into the darkness. We returned to find all the wonder gone from the world. Almost all gone. We could not remake the world as it had been before we left and what little knowledge we had withered away until it was no more than a sad memory of what had been. But there remained two places that we knew of that still held something from the past. One here, one in the East. We chose to remain here, in the Veiled City in what you call the Ghost Woods though we name it the Winter Wood and here we kept alive something of the old wonder.

'You have had many names for us. 'Ghost Walkers' or 'Star Walkers', those that remain behind in the dark and walk like ghosts under the stars in the Winter Wood. Some have tried to find and enter the Veiled City. Few have succeeded for our halls are under the earth, lit and heated by a legacy that existed before the long darkness descended, and that we brought back into the world. We have no fear of the winter darkness for it is never winter and never dark in the Veiled City. With the lore we hold we have no need of fields for our crops, nor do we need the sun and rain to make them grow.

'Many hundreds of years ago your peoples used to journey east in the search for the sun but you were careless of your histories and much of what you knew has been lost. We preserve some of it, tales and maps from lands you once travelled, for in those days there was some contact between our peoples and long ago the city in the East was open to you too. We believe the Khan sent his lieutenant to command the Shadow Land City and he closed it to you forever and their borders grew and passage was denied to you. No longer able to take the eastern road you turned to building the tall ships that would take you across the Western

Seas and, in time, forgot the eastern lands or Shadow Lands as you came to call them. And you forgot the City in the East. And you forgot the Lord of that City and you forgot how his people closed the road east and put up gates to bar the way. But he learned of the Veiled City from your tales and myths and guessed that it too held a power from the past like his own City. He did not forget. He sent word to his Master and bided his time and his army grew and his control spread westward. His time has come and only our peoples are left to stop him taking the Veiled City and controlling all the land from Middangeard to the far eastern sea.

'I would not be here amongst you but for this matter for it concerns both my people and yours. It may well be that we have been idle for too long. Had we seen the danger earlier perhaps we could have forged alliances with the kingdoms that have already fallen to the East. If Merdynn is to blame then I too am guilty for we have long closed our City to you, choosing instead to be among only ourselves. Our only hope is that we have not left this too late.'

Lord Venning concluded and sat back down in the silence that engulfed the room. Some were still trying to grasp the strange, unfamiliar history laid before them. Others had become spellbound by the cadence in the resonant tones of the Cithol Lord's voice.

'Couldn't this army just be raiders from the Shadow Lands? We've faced such before,' Kenwyn had a dogged, persistent mind that allowed for little imagination. Sentiments and higher purposes that he did not understand he simply ignored and until now his uncomplicated approach had served him well.

'Haven't you been listening? Do you think Arthur and Lord Venning dreamt up the account of the attacks on the villages and the history behind them?' Merdynn shouted at him in exasperation.

The king stood to speak, 'This history is unknown to us. How could we have travelled east chasing the sun and yet now have no knowledge of it? How can your history go back before time to an Age where day followed night? The sun crosses the sky in these lands during the summer months between Imbolc and Lughnasa, the winter is ruled only by the cold moon. Has it not always been so? How could it be otherwise? How can Merdynn be the founder of all we know? Even with his deep enchantments, how could he live the lifespan of centuries? Taliesen, Cwenfled, is any of this possible?' Maldred asked, addressing his last question to the bards of

Wessex and Anglia.

They glanced at each other and Taliesen said, 'Lord, we know nothing of this. None of our tales speak of such times, yet these events happened many hundreds or thousands of lifetimes ago. Who is to say what tales have been passed down and which have been lost?'

'Lord Venning apparently,' Cei said from across the table.

Arthur leant forward in his chair and said, 'Lord Venning either tells the truth or not. Who here thought the Veiled City truly existed? Who here thought the Star Walkers merely lived in children's stories? If the Cithol Lord claims his city is beneath the earth and untouched by winter by some sorcery from the past who are we tell him that it is not so? If they've kept themselves in secret for so long, why break it now if the need weren't great and the threat not true? Some of what Lord Venning speaks of I have seen and know it's true, for the rest I believe it to be the truth. I've seen these Adren and their attacks speak of a design.'

'You've been to the Veiled City?' King Maldred asked incredulously. Others around the table were looking at Arthur with astonishment too.

'I have and what Lord Venning says of it is the truth,' Arthur replied. The king glanced at Lord Venning then back to Arthur and though his suspicions grew he did not voice them.

'Merdynn, can you speak of these times?' Aelle asked.

'Well, yes and no really,' Merdynn looked uncomfortable.

'Yes and no? Did you see or do you know of these things?' King Maldred asked.

'I, ah, missed quite a bit of it actually. Indisposed.'

'Indisposed?' the king shouted. It was his turn to become exasperated.

Arthur's voice rose above the growing confusion, 'Merdynn! Now is not the time for your riddles. Now is the time to share your knowledge.'

Merdynn's indignation suddenly subsided and he sighed heavily, 'Very well, I shall tell you what I know to be true though only a few of you will believe even a part of it. Where to begin?' he genuinely looked lost.

'Tell us your tale from the beginning, Merdynn,' Arthur said.

All around the table the counsellors, chieftains and warriors leant forward eager to hear at last the mysteries of Merdynn explained. Even the Cithol Lord turned with curiosity towards him.

'Indeed? My tale? Your lifetimes are too short, far too short. This much will have to suffice:

'I, like others, was sent into this world for a purpose, to see through a task until its end. Some of those who walked the Ages with me have passed from this world having either fulfilled their part or fallen from the path. I witnessed the histories of the Ages unfolding and I took my path through those times and stayed true to my course. Of those times there are no longer any records nor are there any alive who remember the tales that shaped the Ages. None except for I and perhaps two others. They may be behind this new threat but I don't know for certain or even, indeed, if they still walk this world. The tale of those Ages is not for here.

'Before the last Age ended in ruins I walked amongst men, guarding the line of kings that traced all the way back to the beginnings of your time here. I shaped events as best I could but one came who was as powerful as I. One of my kind who had strayed from the path but who came in a cloak of kinship that veiled the treachery beneath. His name then was Lazure Ulan and I hope he passed from this world when the last Age fell in ruins. Working through others he imprisoned me in a timeless place not wholly of this world and yet not wholly removed from it either. For the first few centuries of my imprisonment I could still discern something of what was happening in the world that I could no longer touch, but gradually my sight dimmed and the events of the world faded from my eyes. There I languished for years beyond counting and would still be languishing but for the events that caused the last Age to crash so utterly. So cataclysmic was that ending that it broke the spell that had entrapped me.

'And so I walked the world once more at the beginning of this Age and it was a terrible time of ruination. How long I had been under the enchantment I do not know but I saw the wreckage of a time that must indeed have been wondrous for the world had changed beyond my recognition. I must have lain under the spell for thousands of years for such wonders don't come into the world under a short span of time. But the fall was even greater than the rise and all that was left were a handful of people scattered and lost.

'When I had last walked these lands, day did indeed follow night. The sun traversed the sky in the time it takes for one of your hourglasses to be turned twelve times and night reigned for the same duration before the sun returned once more. But no more. For long years the sun was hidden and at first terrible floods washed over the land. These were followed by the years of ice and snow. Those that remained were desperate survivors who were on the brink of being snuffed out altogether. I worked without cease to keep that flame alive. Year by year and decade by decade the heavens cleared and the long summer day and the long winter night held sway. I helped where I could and taught what I knew. I could not recreate the wonders that the fading ruins spoke of so I recreated the world as I had last known it. The world I knew before I succumbed to the treacherous act of one I had counted as a friend.

'The few who had lived through those nightmare times adapted to the new world, and the people, the animals, the plants and the forests either died or grew into their new surroundings, finding ways to survive the long winter and make the most of the long summer. I re-named the hills and valleys and rivers, some with the names of old when I last walked the land and some with the newer names that came as I watched from my prison. I learned the language of this land for it was new to me and I named the few children born to those survivors, but the children were so few. The woods and fields used to ring to their laughter and the new world seemed so bleak and silent without it. I taught the survivors the old crafts, the old ways for they were the only ways I knew. The flame flickered in the vast darkness stubbornly refusing to go out and, as time crawled on, the flame grew stronger.

'The Cithol returned at this time but they too were unable to rebuild what had been so utterly cast down and gradually they withdrew into the home they had built for themselves and had less and less to do with those dwelling above ground. I, for my part, continued to guide you as best I could until you were able to once again determine your own paths and I began my long search to find the descendant of the ancient kings.

'All that Lord Venning has told you about the city in the East and how your people once travelled that way to stay in the sunlight is true. When that city was closed to you and the way barred, that was the start of the long road that takes us from then to now. I do not know who counselled the city's ruler to close the East Road. I fear that the Khan's lieutenant, Lazure, was the power behind the city's ruler and I fear that as the years passed it was he who assumed complete control of the Shadow Land

City. I only hope my fears are baseless. It is clear to me now that the one who closed the East to you is the one who has brought the Adren to your shores. How you face that is now the decision before you.'

Merdynn finished and after a moment's pause everyone started talking to each other across the table, debating all they had heard. How could such an unlikely tale be true? Surely some tale or myth would remain if what Merdynn and the Cithol Lord had asserted were true? Why had the Adren army come to their shores? The questions fired back and forth, few of them entirely believed all Merdynn had said and they used different parts of the tale to support whichever argument they were putting forward.

Lord Venning sat with head bowed as small groups debated noisily around him. Merdynn looked oblivious to his surroundings, lost once again in the tales he had not told. Arthur looked across at Cei and shook his head then got up and poured himself a cup of wine, his back turned to the room.

The debating continued for hours and more food and wine were brought in. The gathered counsellors put question after question to Merdynn and Lord Venning but their answers only seemed to deepen the divided opinions. Arthur left the council for an hour or so and walked down to the river looking for peace and quiet in which to ponder the best course ahead.

Once he had decided he returned to the council room and made his way to Ceinwen. He leant down and whispered to her, 'Find Mar'h and get the war band saddled and on the Westway. Do it quickly, there's no time for them to tarry or to say their farewells.'

Ceinwen nodded and left the room unnoticed. Arthur raised his voice and the debating died down, 'We must decide what is to be done.'

'And what would you suggest Warlord of Wessex?' the king replied.

'Cei and I will take our warriors to the Causeway, some we'll leave there to help build and defend the Gates while the rest of us will ride across the Causeway to discover what happened to the Belgae and to find out the strength of these Adren armies and what their designs are.'

'And leave Britain unprotected?' Maldred replied.

'No, I suggest that half your war band go across the Western Seas with the people who take the journey west and the rest stay at Caer Sulis to protect the winter stores and those that remain.'

'Do you indeed? Surely a plan the Uathach will much admire.'

'The greater danger now lies to the East. We need to know if the Belgae were attacked and if any survived. We need to know how many Adren we face, and we need to know when we will have to face them. We have no other choices but to cross the Causeway or wait like animals selected for slaughter. Half your warriors will have to suffice against any Uathach raiders.'

Much to the surprise of the gathered counsellors and to Merdynn's suspicion, the king agreed.

'Then so be it, Arthur of Wessex. I'll take the peoples west with half of my warriors after the Lughnasa festival. If you're to travel the Shadow Lands in winter then you best leave now while the roads are still free of snow.' The king waved a hand as if to dismiss both Arthur and all that had been said at the council. His mind was turning over the strategy he had long pondered and he marvelled at how such ill tidings could prove to be so well timed.

Cei, Leah and Ceinwen stood to leave but Arthur stared sightlessly at the king. Lord Venning watched Arthur intently as the king said, 'We hope to see you at Imbolc when we light the flame of sunrise.'

Arthur stared at Maldred for a second longer, understanding now why he had agreed to his plan, then turned his back on the king and left the council.

Chapter Five

Mar'h was outside the king's house waiting for them. He had brought Arthur's horse with him. Arthur strode up to him while Cei collected his weapons from the king's men.

'Are they gathering?' Something in Arthur's voice or appearance made Mar'h take a step backward.

'Yes, Arthur, Ceinwen's leading them onto the Westway.'

Arthur turned to Cei and Leah, 'We'll head for the Causeway straight away. Get your spear riders together and catch up with us on the Westway.'

Cei nodded and left with Leah to gather his war band together.

Arthur turned back to Mar'h, 'We're going into the Shadow Lands. We'll collect our winter provisions from Caer Cadarn on the way but I want you to speak to the blacksmith, Laethrig. He cannot make the journey west. I want him and his people to start making ready for war. We'll need swords, shields, spears, and arrows – he'll know what to prepare and we'll need as many as he can possibly make over the winter. Get him to try to convince the Anglian smith to do the same as well. And we'll need battle jerkins – the kind with strips of hardened iron woven into them.

'The king doesn't need to know about any of this. When you've done this, requisition any extra supplies you can and take them to the Causeway. We may still be there and if not, we'll be back at some stage to replenish our stores.' As he finished saying this he jumped up onto his horse and taking the reins brought it around, 'I'll see you at the Gates.'

Mar'h started to reply but Arthur was already riding for the Westway. As Arthur departed, Merdynn and the Cithol Lord came out of the king's house.

'Well, that all went fairly smoothly I think,' Merdynn said, brushing imagined dirt from the front of his cloak. Lord Venning turned his cowled face to Merdynn but Mar'h couldn't see his expression.

'So, Mar'h, where's the best, darkest and quietest place to get some food in Caer Sulis these days?'

'I can show you if you'll wait for Laethrig to join us, I have a message

118

for him.'
'From Arthur?'
'Yes.'
'Thought there might be.'
'What happened in there? Arthur came out looking like he wanted to murder.'
'Did he indeed? Murder whom?'
'It didn't look like he was overly concerned who he murdered. And I wasn't going to enquire of him either.'
'Yes, well, it appears there's a conflict of interest within the council. Ah, here's the smithy. Laethrig! Join us for a meal.'
Laethrig looked over and strode across to join them. He was the war band's blacksmith and armourer and as befitted his trade he was a big man, broad across the chest with thick muscled arms that were invariably bare to the elbow and covered in a dense growth of black hair that was frequently singed by the searing blasts from the furnaces as he tamed and moulded the unwilling metals to his designs. His luxuriant black beard fared little better.
The four of them walked off into the gathering gloom of Caer Sulis. The presence of Merdynn kept inquisitive villagers away and Lord Venning walked through the town with no one the wiser that the Cithol Lord walked amongst them.

Arthur's war band had gathered on the Westway just outside of the town. With some of their number at the Causeway and others fallen at Eald there were less than sixty waiting for Arthur. They were standing in small groups by their horses and speculating on why they had been brought together only hours before the Lughnasa festivities began. Any farewells they had managed were rushed and their families had been unhappy at the sudden and unexplained departure. Some had asked Morgund what the rush was all about but, knowing as little as they did, he had just shrugged and told them to wait for Arthur. They did not have to wait long.
The small crowd that had formed, curious to see why the Wessex warriors had gathered, suddenly divided as Arthur's horse thundered through them. Arthur brought his horse up sharply in front of Morgund

who had been talking to Ethain and Tomas.

'We're riding east,' Arthur said to them.

Morgund, seeing the look on Arthur's face just nodded.

'East?' Ethain asked, clearly surprised and taken aback. Morgund closed his eyes.

Arthur stared at Ethain then said loud enough for those around to hear, 'Whitehorse Hill then on across the Causeway into the Shadow Lands.'

As the warriors mounted their horses and Arthur rode to the front to join Ceinwen, word spread that they were going east. Morgund looked across at the hundred or so who witnessed their departure. He thought that this many mounted warriors must look impressive to them but privately he thought that sixty warriors riding east was a pitiful number. He had seen the strength of the enemy at Eald and the war band simply was not strong enough to be going east to meet them but he kept his thoughts to himself and caught up with Elowen who was riding with Tomas and Ethain.

As they rode up the gentle slope away from Caer Sulis and into the surrounding hills he cast a glance backward. He could hear the clear bell of the Great Hall calling out across the valley summoning the peoples to the feast. In the descending gloom he saw the fires and torches congregating around the King's Hall as the peoples of Britain made ready for the celebration of Lughnasa. He wondered idly what next Lughnasa would bring. Would they be celebrating still or would the Shadow Land army have carved their way to Caer Sulis? He took a deep breath and scratched at his growing beard. Either way, he thought, he would make damned sure he would be around to see in next Lughnasa.

'You don't look too happy about crossing the Causeway, Morgund,' Tomas said smiling at him. Morgund just snorted.

'He's old, he's worried about the cold. Looking forward to a comfortable winter fire weren't you?' Elowen chided.

'You children haven't been east to the Shadow Lands in winter have you?' Morgund replied.

'No, but it's about time we did – there's nothing to do here in the winter months but listen to you ancients recount unlikely tales from your travels. It's time we made our own unlikely tales,' Tomas said.

'Gods! Weren't you three at Eald? Have you forgotten already?' Morgund was normally quite happy to exchange banter with the younger warriors but none of them had travelled east in the darkness before and he harboured serious doubts about the wisdom of going across the Causeway to fight an uneven battle and his concern showed in his voice.

Ethain remained quiet but took a long look at Morgund. Morgund glanced at him and noted how scared he seemed. He looked away cursing to himself; two youths too stupid to realise the danger and one who will be paralysed by fear. He had a sudden urge for the company of Balor or Mar'h. Elowen was trying to work up some enthusiasm from Ethain and Morgund decided to drop his pace and slip back to the group behind them.

They breasted the low hill and the strengthening wind from the West blew his cloak around him with the promise of the cold to come. He shivered and fastened his light cloak around himself. Before them the sun had finally met the distant horizon, weakly lighting the eastern clouds in pale yellows and washed reds. Morgund had been east before in winter and had no wish to do so again. The wind pushed at his back as if urging him towards the East and the journey across the Causeway.

Ethain too was questioning the merits of heading east and he could feel the beginnings of panic welling up inside him. He nodded and grunted at appropriate points as Elowen spoke excitedly to him but his mind was elsewhere. He was comparing his own feelings to those of the rest of the war band. The riders near him, all seasoned veterans apart from his two friends, seemed genuinely in high spirits. Their talk was confident and loud, punctuated with laughter and derisory remarks to each other.

Ethain was puzzled and worried by this. He could not dispel the memory of the nightmare attack on Eald or the unexpected suddenness of it. The memory of the vicious and unmerciful slaughter made him feel sick again and he consciously swallowed back the rising bile. He had seen people he had known all his life hacked down in the initial onslaught. He had seen villagers just stand stationary in shock as the Adren swords cut them down. He could not match his own feelings with the good-humoured nonchalance surrounding him. Only Morgund struck him as not being excited about the prospect of going east. He cast a glance back at the big warrior now riding behind them. He certainly did not seem scared, brooding perhaps, but not afraid. Ethain realised he was scared, scared sick at the thought of it and finally came to the same concluding thought as Morgund: was it wise to confront an enemy that outnumbered them, in winter and far from home. And did he have to go? He spent the rest of the journey to Whitehorse Hill pondering on ways to avoid the expedition into the Shadow Lands and trying to hide those same thoughts from Elowen and Tomas.

Ceinwen was riding up front with Arthur and Llud. They were talking about the supplies they would need for travelling in the Shadow Lands. Ceinwen knew Llud from years ago - he had been with the war band all his life and Ceinwen was glad to find someone she knew from the old days. His father and grandfather had been with the Wessex warriors before him and no doubt his young sons would follow too. He was older than both Arthur and Ceinwen with short strands of gray hair above his ears and around the back of his head. He had not questioned Arthur why they were heading east or what the aim of their mission was. It was enough for him to know they were going and he only wanted to make sure they had everything they might need for winter travelling. Together with Arthur he listed all they should take and made a mental note of the various items to ready once they reached Caer Cadarn.

Ceinwen observed them quietly, watching as the outward signs of Arthur's unspoken anger slowly ebbed as he dealt with the practicalities before them. She herself still felt angry with the king. From the first he had taunted Arthur, seeking retaliation from him and she didn't really understand why. Nor had she been at the council at the end and wondered what had been said to so anger Arthur. She no longer knew Arthur as well as Trevenna and Cei did, but she knew what his anger was like. She knew that his rage either broke upon people like a sudden, violent storm or burned with the slow, hidden flames that would not be quelled until the source was consumed. It was the source that concerned her for she feared it was the king himself and that's what she failed to understand: why would the king court such anger?

She wondered if perhaps Maldred wished to have Arthur removed as the Wessex Warlord. It was true that he had never forgiven Arthur for challenging and killing Saltran but the king only had the right to depose the Wessex Warlord if Arthur directly crossed the throne. Ceinwen shuddered involuntarily; if Maldred was the source of Arthur's anger, if the king had finally goaded Arthur into opposing him, then it could only go ill for the king, and Britain would be plunged into chaos. She felt she needed to talk to Arthur away from the others to try to determine how much of what she feared was true. She knew this would be difficult. Unless Arthur had changed dramatically over the years she knew he rarely talked openly of what he thought, felt or planned and while he listened to other's opinions he invariably kept to his own counsel on most matters. Ceinwen felt it was a curious contradiction that it seemed he could see into other people's hearts and thoughts almost with ease yet few or none could claim the reverse.

She looked across at Arthur as he talked to Llud and allowed herself to recall the time when as a young woman she had fallen in love with him. He too had been young and yet, in spite of Saltran's obvious disfavour, he had already been a captain in the Wessex war band for over three years. She had admired the way he held the older warriors' respect yet felt drawn by his vulnerability as a young man leading those much older than himself. They were together for some time but, in retrospect, she realised he had always seemed distracted and never truly open to her. It felt to her as if he were waiting for something or someone else but she had convinced herself otherwise and came to believe that Arthur returned what she felt for him.

They had had no children and after one winter apart, when she had gone across the Western Seas and he had stayed in Britain, she had returned to find that he had left her for some woman from a Wessex fishing village who was in her mid-thirties with three grown sons of her own.

It had broken her heart and it gave her little comfort that Arthur didn't stay long with the Wessex woman, although it was rumoured he stayed long enough for her to become pregnant. Years later when time had finally convinced her that, like so many others, she was unable to have children she had begun to wonder if that was the reason why Arthur had left her.

By then she was married to Andala. They had met in Caer Sulis and he had fallen in love with her immediately. She had settled for his love and she had no regrets even though she never felt for him as she once had for Arthur. Andala loved her and she had needed that. He had never stopped loving her and she had been happy enough in her home across the Causeway raising her adopted daughter, Caja, and helping to run the village. Every day she had told herself that she didn't miss the war band or her old life. Occasionally she would cautiously admit to herself that if she did miss the excitement and unpredictability of her former life she certainly didn't miss the violence and death that so often accompanied it. But even in the quiet life across the Causeway she had ultimately been unable to avoid the violence and death; the irony sickened her.

'Gathering wool, little Ceinwen?'

Ceinwen started, both Llud and Arthur were looking at her. Llud, who had spoken to her, was smiling, Arthur just watched her. She felt unnecessarily panicked, clearly a question had been asked and she had no idea what it was. She couldn't shake the feeling that they both knew what she had previously been thinking about and she could feel her cheeks flushing with guilt and turned defensively on Llud, 'I'm not so little that I couldn't run rings around you old man.'

'True, you could run rings around me. If dancing in rings were the contest, little Ceinwen!' Llud said still smiling at her. They continued their banter and Arthur stared ahead at the sun on the horizon, setting over the Shadow Lands in the East. It would sink below the horizon within a few days, the ships would leave the Haven for the West and darkness would steal, day by day, over Britain. Arthur scratched at his beard and looked behind him at the sound of thundering hooves. Elowen and Tomas went galloping by. They were not that far from Whitehorse Hill and clearly a challenge had been issued. Cries of encouragement or derision followed them. Arthur was surprised that Ethain was not also in the race but paid it little attention.

Morveren rode up beside Ceinwen. She was a dark haired, pretty girl from the far West of Wessex and she regularly won any horse race among the warriors just as she more often than not won any foot race or swimming contest. She was only nineteen and had come to the war band two years ago to be closely followed by the persistent rumours that she was a bastard child of Arthur's. Her mother had died giving birth a year after Morveren was born and her father had died at sea some years prior to that, his small fishing boat caught in a storm off the coast of Wessex. Her older brothers had insisted that she forsake the fishing boats of her family and marry a local farmer but she could not face a life devoid of excitement so she had traded the unpredictable nature of the sea for the danger and exhilaration of a warrior's life. Some of the others had been surprised that Arthur accepted her so quickly and took it as confirmation of the rumours, but with both her parents now dead and no one willing to enquire of Arthur, they resigned themselves to never knowing the truth of the matter.

'I hear you used to be fast on horseback, reckon we can still beat them both?' Morveren said and slapped Ceinwen's horse on the rump. Ceinwen reacted automatically and dug her heels into her horse's flanks and they both sped off after Elowen and Tomas while wagers started amongst the other warriors. Ceinwen knew there would be many such challenges before the war band accepted her as one of them. She had already noted how Arthur's captains had watched her closely when she had been discerning the tracks on the far side of the Causeway and when she had been tending to Arthur's wounded leg. She didn't resent it either, she knew it was the natural way of things and she concentrated on closing the gap to Elowen and Tomas. Morveren had already caught up with them.

'She's a fine lass that one,' Llud said watching the riders galloping away and doing a bit of fishing himself.

'She is indeed,' Arthur replied but they were not talking about the same woman.

Those that had backed the long odds on Elowen, Tomas or the largely unknown Ceinwen all lost although Ceinwen ran Morveren a reasonably close second. There was much good-natured cursing as wagers were settled. Arthur watched them bicker amongst each other and smiled briefly. He noticed Ethain leading his horse off to the stables and wondered again why he had not raced his young friends. He talked again with Llud who turned and picked out Talan and his sister, Tamsyn, to help him start preparing the various winter supplies. Each of the warriors would be expected to gather their own winter gear but some provisions were more general and Llud would make sure everything needed was taken and that each warrior knew what they were expected to take.

Most of the war band's families were at Caer Sulis, having expected to celebrate Lughnasa together there, so the camp at Whitehorse Hill was as deserted as it ever got. Arthur crossed to the main hall. The ground was already hardening in the colder air and the tracks of the pigs and goats that freely wandered the camp were already beginning to set into rigid casts. One of the camp's dogs trotted alongside sniffing around the group heading for the hall and Elowen, still smarting from coming last in the race, kicked out at it.

The company gathered in the main hall and Arthur told them they had eight hours to ready their gear, eat, drink and sleep. There were groans that they were missing Lughnasa and they would need more than eight hours for drinking let alone for anything else. Arthur pointed out that how they divided the time was their choice, which was greeted with cheers, then added that anyone leaving behind vital winter provisions would be sent back to spend the dark months with the king's men at Caer Sulis and the theatrical groans returned. He hoisted a tall urn of beer onto a nearby table and poured himself a jar full.

He raised it to the gathered warriors and cried out, 'We go across the Causeway to the Shadow Lands in winter to face the Adren armies. If those in Caer Sulis knew of this they would have lined the Westway and saluted you. But they know nothing of this, so I salute you! The Wessex!' and he drained his drink.

Cheers and speeches erupted from the company as each sought to find and fill their own mugs. Arthur strode through them towards the top of the hall where he had his quarters. Various cries of 'Arthur!' 'Warlord!' 'The Wessex!' and one of 'Miserable bastard!' rang out around him.

He grinned at them and stopped by Morgund and Ceinwen, 'Talk to Ethain, something's not right – probably nothing but have a talk to him and see what's bothering him. And find the bastard who called me 'miserable' and hang him from the gate.'

They grinned and Arthur strode on up the hall. Ceinwen watched him leave while Morgund sought out Ethain.

Arthur opened the door to his room off the hall and stooped slightly to enter. It smelt dank and unlived in. He lit the two oil lamps hanging from the wall, unhooked his cloak and threw it on the low bed to one side. He opened the shutters on his window and started a large fire in the hearth before sinking into a chair as the room warmed up and wood smoke permeated the dankness. He picked up his sword and unsheathed it. He sat there staring at it lost in thought as the fire flickered and occasionally cracked, spitting out an ember unnoticed. The muffled sounds of the war band celebrating Lughnasa and making the most of being at home for the last time before going east suddenly became louder as the door to his room opened. He looked up and Ceinwen was standing there. She put a plate of food and two goblets of wine down on the floor by the fire.

'Thought you might want some food, I presume you're not joining the others in the hall?' she said, not looking at him and kneeling by the fire.

'No. Better they celebrate tonight without me being there,' Arthur replied and Ceinwen turned to stare into the fire as he continued, 'Let them let lose their cares for tonight.'

'You're not concerned things will get out of hand?' Ceinwen asked still gazing at the flickering flames.

'No. If they did you or Llud would calm things down.'

'They're talking about the rumour of the stranger with Merdynn.' News of the appearance of the Cithol Lord at the council had spread quicker than fire throughout Caer Sulis to be met equally with disbelief, anxiety and curiosity.

'And did you tell them it was the Cithol Lord from the Veiled City?'

'No, but someone has. Others were guessing that he or Merdynn gave that sword to you.'

'I don't think Merdynn gave me the sword, he only led me to it. Others judged if I should take it,' Arthur replied, thinking once more of the indistinct voices in the Halls of the Dead.

Ceinwen looked to Arthur for an explanation but when none was forthcoming she resumed watching the fire. Arthur watched her face in the firelight. Her almost delicate features had not changed much over the years. There were streaks of grey in her shoulder-length, wavy brown hair and deepening lines radiating from the corners of her small, dark, lively eyes, but she somehow seemed younger, more alive, than when Arthur first saw her in the hall in Branque. She was by no means a striking woman but her eyes still held the merriment and mischief of her youth. Despite her recent bereavement she had a natural energy and love for life that defied both her sorrow and her years, and those qualities leant a strength to her character that made her undeniably attractive. It suddenly struck Arthur that the young Morveren shared the same kind of love for life and he wondered why he hadn't seen the similarity before.

She looked up at Arthur and held his eyes. Her thin lips parted to speak but Arthur spoke first, 'Did Morgund speak to Ethain?'

She drew a breath, clasped her hands in her lap and returned her gaze to the fire putting aside what she had been about to speak of.

'Yes, we talked about it briefly, before I collected this together,' Ceinwen said, gesturing to the food on the table before lapsing into silence, unsure how to continue.

'And?'

'He's young, Arthur.'

'He is. So too are Elowen and Tomas to name but two.'

'And he was at Eald - and Morgund said it was as bad there as anything he's seen. It wasn't good.'

'Battle never is - and Elowen and Tomas were there too. What is it, Ceinwen?'

'Well, he didn't say as much but I got the impression he thought Ethain was scared, scared to go East.'

'Any sensible person would be, especially if they'd already met a Shadow Land army.'

'I think he was more than scared, Arthur, he was almost panicked.'

'I saw that in him when we met on the road between Eald and Branque. I'd hoped it would pass. He'll need to steel himself. That or he'll die in the Shadow Lands.'

'Arthur! He's only a boy!'

'He's a member of the Wessex war band. That makes him a warrior. He can't suddenly choose to be a farmer once battle comes. Before we're finished I'll be asking farmers and craftsmen to be warriors. This is not the time for warriors to decide to be farmers. He goes east.'

'Well, will you at least talk to him?'

'Of course.'

Ceinwen reached for a goblet of wine and Arthur did the same. They drank in a silence punctuated only by the crackling fire.

At length Ceinwen said, 'But you're not worried about going east are you, you're not afraid?'

Arthur looked at her directly, 'No, I'm not. Nor are you. We've seen what the Adren can do and I won't wait to see it happen here too. Nor would you.'

'But it's more than that isn't it? You want to go east, you want to face them don't you?'

'I'd rather they weren't there, Ceinwen. I'd rather they had never come west. I'd rather your village still lived in peace and I'd rather it wasn't necessary to defend this Isle against them.'

'Yet they are there, and they are coming and you want to face them don't you?'

Arthur once again looked directly at her and his face changed and his voice quietened, becoming harder and edged with hatred. Ceinwen felt her flesh crawl as she sensed the danger.

'Yes. I want every one of them dead. I want to burn their lands and homes. I want to kill their families and young. I want to slaughter their very race and leave no trace of them. They have no place in this world and I'll do what I can to rid them from it. I'll do whatever I have to, to protect my people and my land.'

Despite his quiet tone, or perhaps because of it, the force behind what he said stunned Ceinwen and she suddenly felt unsafe sitting in front of him.

She summoned her courage and replied quietly and without looking at Arthur, 'Your people. Your land.'

Arthur sat back in his chair, the moment passed and he said, 'They're your people and land too. Isn't that why you've joined us again? Isn't that why you'll go east?'

Ceinwen's gaze remained fixed on the fire as she replied, 'No Arthur. My people are dead and what had become my home, my land, is now gone. I go east because that's what the Wessex Warlord decides is the best course to take.'

'And would you disagree?'

'No, perhaps not,' Ceinwen paused, wondering what made Arthur's implacable stance different from that of the Adren.

'Andala didn't form an army. He didn't march it into the Shadow Lands. He didn't slay everything in his path. That's the difference.'

Ceinwen sat back, stung by Arthur's words and cursing herself for not being more guarded. She hurriedly sought to placate and divert his obvious anger, 'I don't disagree with you, Arthur, or think you're wrong but why did the king agree to it? What happened at the council after I left?'

Arthur took a drink of his wine, 'The king wants me dead and he counts all the Wessex and Anglian warriors as expendable to have it so.'

Ceinwen looked aghast, 'What? Dead? All of us? Why?'

'No, he just wants me dead, perhaps the warriors too but I don't know that yet.'

'But why? He needs us now more than ever.'

'I'm not sure why yet, I haven't seen his design, only his intent.'

'But how can you know this?'

Arthur held her gaze for a few seconds and Ceinwen looked away.

'I'll know the rest the next time we meet.'

'And what then?' Ceinwen asked, dreading the answer.

'Then I'll judge him. But it's a long road from now to then and who knows when or if we'll see King Maldred again?'

Ceinwen finished her wine and stood up, 'You already know, Arthur, and you've already passed judgement.' Ceinwen looked at him a moment longer and then left.

Llud was the first to raise himself from the ale-induced slumber in the hall. He was the oldest active warrior in the Wessex war band, those of his companions who had survived to his fifty-plus years had retired to help run the camp and arm the younger warriors. Some had even sought out a more sedate life in the villages of their choice along the coast or deep in the Wessex countryside. He had been fifteen when Merdynn had walked into the camp on Whitehorse Hill with the boy who called himself Arthur and who carried his baby sister in his young arms. He remembered the day well, the day that two orphans had joined the community on Whitehorse Hill. Even then he, and others, had suspected there was something different about the boy. At first they had put it down to the trauma of the raid on his home village but when they heard how he had lowered his sister in a bucket down the well and then shinned down the rope himself just as the Uathach had struck they realised that perhaps this was not a four-year old child like others of his age. He had watched the child grow and was proud that he now held a position of responsibility under the boy that he had regarded as his younger brother and who had become his warlord.

Llud roused the company an hour later and they set about collecting and stowing their winter gear. Thick undergarments where donned under hide and leather trousers and sheepskin jerkins. Fur-lined boots were pulled on and heavy fur cloaks were bundled onto their horses together with sheepskin caps and gloves. Snowshoes, designed to both spread weight and to enable the wearer to slide across hard snow or ice were strapped to their burdened horses. Each rider carried several weeks' worth of dried foods, feed for their horse and a leather water bottle. An oiled cape was tied over these bundles to keep rain and snow off them.

This was the first time in six years that the entire war band would stay for the winter. Normally lots would be drawn and half would take the journey west, though much swapping of lots and deals were struck so that various groups could stay together or indeed be apart. Only a few had gone across the Causeway before in winter. Some were wary of leaving their lands in the hands of the king's men, others were anxious about the journey ahead but all were keen to learn more of why they were going east.

They eventually set off, filing out through the gate of their camp and onto the Ridgeway to head south for the Westway. Llud brought up the rear leading several cartloads of their winter supplies. They left in a more serious and quieter mood than when they had arrived and each was conscious of it. The breeze had stiffened from the West and clouds covered the setting sun. Only a handful watched the war band depart into the twilight. The only sound left behind them was the barking of dogs and the slapping of the ropes on the flagpoles where the two flags of the white horse and the red dragon snapped in the wind. It was the last winter that both flags would fly side by side.

When they reached the Westway they found it deserted. All the villagers had already passed on to Caer Sulis and all that remained to tell of their passing were the ruts of the wain wheels, rain-filled parallel lines stretching both west and east. They followed the wheel tracks heading east and Arthur dropped back to Llud and those leading the wains. He explained to him that he would be going on ahead to the Gates to talk to Ruadan and Hengest about the defences they had prepared. The rest of the company would travel with the provisions and he expected they would have to stop twice before reaching the Causeway. He hoped to only stop the once, at Dunraven on the hill above the Winter Wood. Arthur reminded him that Mar'h should be following close behind and left it to his discretion whether or not to send back a party to help escort any extra supplies he may have acquired. He unnecessarily told him to post flanking riders in case any Uathach had ventured this far south hoping to raid any late trains heading for Caer Sulis. Llud bore it patiently knowing Arthur was only thinking aloud to make sure everything was covered. It was usually a sign that he had other things on his mind.

Arthur then moved slowly up the line explaining to various groups of riders what had transpired at the council and why they were going east, how long he expected to be across the Causeway and what he planned to achieve. As he moved up the line the change in those he had already spoken to was immediately noticeable. The seriousness was still there but now they had substance rather than speculation to debate and talk through. They were warriors and they were going to war. It was what they lived for and they could not have been in better spirits. The news that there was a Cithol Lord present at the council, that he had arrived with Merdynn and that Arthur himself had once been to the Veiled City amazed them greatly and was a completely new source for debate.

Llud watched the transformation from his position at the back of the line and he snorted and smiled. He had seen three warlords lead the Wessex war band and he was glad it was Arthur who was now leading them into the Shadow Lands. If that was where they had to go, then there was no one better to go with, he thought to himself. The usual pre-campaign apprehension evaporated and his natural confidence reasserted itself. By the time Arthur rode ahead of the column with Ceinwen, Morgund and Ethain the previous journey's banter was back again. Llud started chatting and laughing with Talan and Tamsyn on one of the other wains and forgot to post the flanking riders.

Arthur and the others made good time once free of the slow pace of the column and its supply carts. He decided they could make the Causeway with the one stop for rest so they pushed on for the hill overlooking the Winter Wood. They travelled east under a heavy, grey sky that sagged above them and threatened more rain. He had ridden with Ethain for a few hours and they had talked about how the other warriors were feeling about the journey ahead.

Arthur had gradually turned the conversation around to the attack on Eald and how Ethain felt about it now that it was in the past. Ethain had guardedly admitted that he had had trouble sleeping since the Adren attack and Arthur had reassured him that many warriors felt the same way after their first battle. He had told him that every warrior, at one time or another, needed to draw strength from their companions and that it was important to know when to lend that strength and when to draw upon it; that no one in the war band had to face anything alone. If he felt out of his depth then he only had to look for help – someone would be standing on firm ground and next time the positions would be reversed, but if no one reached out then each would drown individually. He told him that a war band was bound together and that each needed and relied upon the other's strength. That it was all right to be scared but it must be controlled, to put his faith in the people who stood by him and to remember that they had put their faith in him.

Arthur told him he was proud that he and the others had managed to bring out some of the Eald villagers safe against those odds and that other, older warriors in the war band envied him his feats. He told him that all he needed to do was believe in himself, trust his companions, use his training and draw on his newly acquired experience.

By the time Arthur rode ahead to catch up with Ceinwen, Ethain did believe in himself and was prepared to face the journey east with more confidence. It would not be until they were crossing the Causeway a few days later that the doubts would steal back, working on him with the inevitability of rust, flaking away the brittle layers of his newfound confidence.

They eventually approached the temporary camp at Dunraven where they planned to rest. Their horses were tired and fractious from the long ride so they decided to walk them up the hill rather than give them the final burden of carrying them up the steep slope. Ceinwen jumped down lightly and chided the others as they dismounted stiffly.

The cold wind had been strengthening all day and they had seen squalls and showers tracking across the country throughout their journey. It gusted from the northwest, whipping their cloaks out behind them as they stood by their horses.

They struggled up the hill, tugging at the reins of their reluctant beasts as dead leaves, scythed from the trees above them, were snatched from the long grasses and sent flying through the gloom. Low, dark clouds scudded overhead and the first spattering of rain, borne on by the wind, began to sting their faces. Halfway up the hill Arthur's horse refused to go any further. Arthur cursed it and hauled with all his might but not even his strength could budge it as the horse straightened and dug in its front legs. Morgund handed his reins to Ceinwen and went back to help. He stumbled forward onto his knees as the wind forced his tired legs to move too quickly down the steep slope. The rain fell harder as Morgund picked himself up and joined Arthur. Together they tried to force the stubborn horse forward. Lightning tore through the clouds and down into the Winter Wood to their north. Seconds later the thunder shook the ground beneath them as Arthur roared at his horse, the veins standing out on his neck and his long hair plastered across his face. The horse's resistance broke with the thunder and they laboured up the hill after the other two who had already reached the darkness under the trees.

They tied their horses' reins around a fallen tree trunk and began unloading their gear in the crashing rain with the wind now splintering through the trees around them. Without trying to talk they doggedly fixed the oiled capes around their unloaded supplies in an effort to keep them dry, keeping two free to try to fashion a makeshift shelter from the storm. Lightning seared through the muggy twilight on three sides of the hill, momentarily lighting their rain-swept faces. All four of them involuntarily flinched as the following thunder whiplashed around them. Arthur secured one cape and stepped back just as Morgund fixed the other in place. The other two dived into the relative cover. Arthur grinned at them and raised both arms outstretched to the turbulent skies. The rain swept in opaque curtains through the copse and ran down his upturned face and beard as he shouted out his defiance to the elements. Fractured lightning screamed down and shattered into the trees only a hundred yards away as thunder detonated all around them. Ethain cowered further back in to the shelter and Morgund covered his ears with his hands. Ceinwen dashed from the shelter towards Arthur, who had both fists raised to the heavens, and tried to drag him back towards the cover of the shelter.

'Why do you defy the gods?' she screamed at him.

Over her shoulder Arthur suddenly saw Ethain pointing and Morgund half-draw his sword. He quickly spun round, freeing himself from Ceinwen's hands and putting her behind him. As the lightning rent the gloom once more he saw dozens of cloaked and hooded figures standing amongst the trees.

The same storm hit the war band two hours later. Llud was trying to make up for their slow pace and had not yet made camp. As the slow journey had worn on, the mounted warriors had inevitably drawn away from the trundling carts and they had become strung-out in a line along the Westway covering almost a mile from the riders at the front to the loaded wains at the rear. Llud had sent ten warriors back down the Westway to find Mar'h soon after Arthur had left them. They found him several miles behind the column leading another four wains of supplies that Merdynn had promptly requisitioned at Caer Sulis. Mar'h had left the ten warriors with the wain drivers and ridden ahead to the war band with a message for Arthur only to find him already gone ahead.

He joined Llud and the dark skinned Talan and his sister Tamsyn at the rear of the column with Morveren cantering around them. She was teasing Talan about being stuck on a wain while his horse plodded behind on a long rein. Her long, dark hair was blowing about in the wind as the heavy grey clouds stretched over the sky from the northwest. As the rain began to spot the canvas tied across the wain in front, Mar'h suggested to Llud that they close up the company. It had become gloomy between the trees that ran along either side of this stretch of the roadway and as the rain came down harder, the visibility dropped further.

The Uathach raiding party had chosen its time and place well. They had been hoping to find the odd straggler making their way to Caer Sulis, laden with their summer harvest. Although well armed there were only twenty-eight of them and when they saw the war band they had thought to turn away and leave them well alone but the temptation of the supplies loaded on the wains persuaded them to follow the column from the cover of the trees on the North side of the broad track. They bided their time as the column stretched out. They waited as the visibility diminished under the greying skies. When the rain started to fall in sheets they rode ahead to set their ambush at a point where the roadway dipped and began a broad swerve to go around a small lake. Their plan was simply to take as many of the wains as they could and ride back down the Westway to the wide path that ran north through the forest. If the war band was in close pursuit and they became quickly outnumbered then they would abandon the wains but if they could get a good head start then perhaps they could get away. They hoped to attack the isolated wains and get away with the supplies without the main body of the war band realising until it was too late to stop them. It was more opportunistic than planned but with winter about to fall on the land they felt it was worth the risk.

Mar'h was riding alongside Llud's wain cursing the weather when the Uathach arrows flew from the trees edging the roadway to their left. The last two wain drivers were killed outright as the arrows found their marks. Llud was sent flying into Mar'h's horse, lifted clear off the wain by the force of the two arrows that slammed into his upper arm and the side of his head. An arrow flashed inches past Mar'h's face as another smashed through his left forearm, splintering the bone. He screamed in pain as he dug his heels into the horse's flanks to spur it forward. As he did so a second hail of arrows sped from the trees. His horse collapsed under him and he leapt for the shelter behind the wain. Llud lay dead before him, the rain washing the blood from the side of his face as his horse thrashed nearby in the churned mud, three arrows buried deep its flank. He looked behind him and saw Talan and Tamsyn already sheltering behind their cart, shields held out and their swords drawn. Someone was screaming nearby but he could not see who it was. Morveren was galloping madly down the Westway, slung low in her saddle as arrows flashed past her.

Riders were coming from the trees in two groups, one heading for the rearmost wains and one speeding after Morveren, trying to overhaul her before she could get word to the warriors up ahead. Mar'h reached for the iron pin on the crossbar that released the harnessed ponies from the cart.

He pulled it free and flung it away into the mud so that the raiders could not draw the cart away. Tamsyn saw what he had done and did likewise. Two of the wains already being hauled away by the raiders. Those chasing Morveren gave up and raced back to the driverless wains. Mar'h and Talan sprinted towards the nearest carts, slipping and sliding in the mud. Mar'h held his injured arm close to his body to protect it as he ran. At some level he knew that the shock was still blocking most of the pain and he worked frantically to pull another pin free. The ponies shied away taking the crossbar with them and he tugged his sword free as the returning horsemen swept through the wains. One of the Uathach raiders swung his sword down on him. He ducked and the sword struck the wooden side of the wain. Mar'h pivoted on one foot, hooking his sword round in an arc that sliced through the raider's sword hand and he was gone, leaving the sword still stuck in the wain with his detached hand still gripping it. Mar'h regained his balance and looked round wildly but it was over. The raiders were gone just as suddenly as they had attacked. Five of the wain drivers from Caer Sulis lay dead. Four of the wains were gone. Llud, who for so long had seemed beyond mortal injury, lay dead in the mud. Mar'h turned to Talan and Tamsyn and groaned in despair. Tamsyn knelt in the rain silently rocking back and forth over the body of her dead brother.

Mar'h sheathed his sword and slowly walked towards her, cursing as he held his dangling left arm, the arrow still embedded through his forearm. Great pulsing waves of pain washed over him and threatened his consciousness. Behind him he could hear Morveren and the rest of the warriors fast approaching. Mar'h had seen death and slaughter before but he watched with a heavy heart as Tamsyn stroked the rain from her brother's face.

Arthur gazed round at the ring of figures surrounding them. One of the intruders crossed to the horses and gathered the reins. Morgund stood to intervene but Arthur stilled him with a hand gesture. Another approached Arthur and he stepped forward to meet him. A double flash of lightning jagged above the grove and the hooded figures all turned away as one from the brilliant light. The cloaked figure stopped in front of Arthur.

'You are Arthur of Wessex?'

Arthur tried to see the man's face but it was shadowed by the hood he wore.

'I am,' Arthur replied.

'Lord Venning offers you shelter below,' he said, gesturing towards the Winter Wood.

Arthur looked around at his companions. Ceinwen was faintly shaking her head as the rain lashed down, pooling the ground around her. Morgund was nervously watching the figure by their horses. Ethain stared at the proceedings wide-eyed and open-mouthed.

'We would be glad to accept Lord Venning's offer,' Arthur replied at last.

The figure before him nodded and led the way from the copse. Others picked up their bundled gear and dismantled their brief and ineffective shelter. As the four of them moved off the others fell in to either side and behind them. Ceinwen had told the other two about Lord Venning's appearance at the council but the recent revelations of living legends did nothing to calm the fear they felt in their company.

'I don't like this, Arthur,' Morgund said.

'Nor I,' Ceinwen added.

'They're the Cithol aren't they?' Morgund asked.

Arthur looked around at the cloaked figures surrounding them and nodded his reply.

Overhead the thunder rumbled back and forth in echoes as they left the trees and started the steep walk down into the Winter Wood. By the time they entered the wood the storm had started to move away to the West leaving in its wake a persistent rain and the distant rolling of thunder.

The wood was thick with undergrowth, ferns and briars tangled between the mix of close-packed firs that ringed this edge of the expansive woodland. As they continued on the firs gave way to wider spaced oak, birch and elm trees. Each branch, stem and twig was jewelled with droplets of water. The wooded canopy collected the rain and, with every gust of wind, spilled it down upon them in heavy, sudden showers. The shadows of the woodland seemed alive with the splashing water that bounced and glistened off every surface as the rain sought the deep roots of the forest.

The Cithol had split into two groups, one leading Arthur and his companions, the other bracketing them and bringing up the rear. They followed a narrow track that wound a circuitous route deeper into the dark woodland. The path was veined by the wet, moss-wrapped roots of the trees that overhung them, making the passage difficult in the half-light under the dull, storm-bruised skies. Their Cithol guides walked surefooted and swiftly along the path in contrast to their guests, who frequently slipped and stumbled on the dimly seen, wet path. Arthur's efforts to move the stubborn horse had aggravated his injured thigh and he was limping once again.

Ethain tugged at Morgund's cloak and said quietly, 'Do you see them?'

Ceinwen heard him and turned around quickly, 'See who?'

'Not who but what. There are ruins all around us, large cut stones and walls, all in ruins.' Ethain gestured to their left and the others could make out a tall stone façade wreathed in vines and split by the roots and trunks of towering trees. Spilling around its base lay the tumbled wreckage of cut blocks of granite, their cut edges and flat sides almost indistinguishable under the deep, velvet covering of emerald moss and verdant lichen. Saplings had tentatively edged their way through the narrow gaps in the debris and, as the years had passed and their strength had grown, they had gradually heaved the fashioned boulders to one side. As the centuries had passed, the soaring giants of the Winter Wood had returned once more to the forest floor for the cycle to start over anew and the remains of the ancient city had been patiently crushed, broken and buried by time. Over the next hour of their journey they glimpsed more and more of these vine-wrapped ruins edging the pathway.

Suddenly there was a high stone archway in front of them. Arthur and the others stopped, staring at the stonework of the arch and the high granite walls that stretched to either side of it. The wild and tangled woodland butted straight up to the walls and branches over-reached the top in several places. The Cithol leader indicated that they should come through. As she walked through, Ceinwen ran her hand over the side of the arch as if to make sure it was real.

Once through the archway they were struck by the open space. The high walls encompassed the first open ground they had seen since entering the Winter Wood. Arthur could see that the walls, each several hundred yards long, formed a square. It was difficult to tell in the half-light but it seemed that the archway behind them was the only entrance. Three magnificent, tall cedars grew in the square but there were no other trees. It was as if the high walls around them were designed to keep the woodland out. The ground was laid to lawn and three small streams, admitted through low grilled gaps at the base of the walls, fed ornate, cascading stone fountains. Late autumn flowers lined the banks of the rills and their scent in the rain seemed to refresh them after the closeness of the woods beyond the walls. They breathed the sweet air deeply. Paths of stone trailed across the lawns and all seemed to emanate from the centre where a domed half-sphere rose twenty-feet from the ground.

Their Cithol guide approached Arthur, 'I am Terrill, Captain of the Cithol.' He cast back his hood. Although his skin was black it had the same translucent quality as Lord Venning's and he had the same entirely black eyes. Morgund took an involuntary step backward. He had not expected any of the Cithol to have the same skin tone as his own and Ceinwen's description of their eyes had not prepared him for the reality.

'You and your companions may rest here, Arthur of Wessex. Lord Venning and the Traveller will meet you here after you have rested.'

Arthur nodded in reply.

'Is this the Veiled City?' Ethain asked forgetting himself as he looked around with wonder.

Terrill turned his eyes to him slowly and spoke patiently, 'This is the Winter Garden. Some of us come here when the darkness is complete and gaze upon the stars as they slowly wheel before us. The Veiled City lies below. I shall send some food to the bower for you.'

Terrill indicated the nearest corner of the square where a marble pavilion stood, carved in the shape of interlocking tree boughs.

'You may tether your horses to the side,' Terrill said with a wary glance at the horses they led. The other Cithol had made their way to the central dome and were going inside. Terrill inclined his head and left them to make their own way to the bower.

They found that feed for their horses was already provided. Soft mattresses were laid out under the shelter and cushions were arranged around a low trestle. A shallow dip in the floor served as a hearth and dry wood was stacked to one side. Two vents opened at either end of the bower and warm air gently rose from them.

Once out of the rain they took their cloaks off and shook the water from them. They looked at each other in silence. Ethain ran his hand over the carved marble boughs in wonder and stared in puzzlement as he felt the warmer air from the vents.

'Have you seen this place before, Arthur?' Ceinwen asked.

'No. Merdynn led me by a different way. This is the first time I've seen this.'

'It's wonderful, just wonderful. How do they build in stone like this? How do they carve it?'

Arthur had no answer for her.

'Perhaps you can ask,' Morgund said and nodded towards a small group who were walking across the wet grass carrying platters of fruit and bread.

Arthur stared at the young woman leading the group. She was beautiful. She wore a flowing black dress drawn in at the waist by a simple cord. Over her shoulders was a cape of dark green, clasped around her throat by a light silver chain. The blackness of her dress contrasted starkly with her flawless ivory skin. A thin leather cord circled her throat and a clear-cut jewel glittered from the centre. Her eyes were green, a shade darker than her cape, and they smiled at Arthur as she stopped before him.

'Welcome back to the Winter Wood, Arthur of the Britons. And welcome to your companions too.'

Arthur stared at her, lost for any reply. A smile played on her lips and her eyes danced in amusement.

'Do you not remember me, Lord?'

'Seren? Fin Seren? But...' he said as it dawned on him who she must be.

She turned to her attendants and said playfully, 'It seems the years have clouded Lord Arthur's memory, or perhaps he's aghast at how Lord Venning's young daughter, who last brought him food in the Veiled City, has grown so ill.'

'It's just that you've...'

'Changed?'

'Indeed.'

'It would be a sad world where children remained children, would it not?'

'It would indeed have been a sadder world were you to have stayed a child.'

Seren smiled and keeping her eyes on Arthur half turned to her attendants once more saying, 'Lord Arthur has regained his gallantry, do you think he will soon introduce us to his companions?'

Arthur tore his eyes away from her and indicated the others as he introduced them. She smiled at them as she greeted them and laid the platter she was carrying on the trestle. Her attendants followed, setting down flagons of wine and clear, cool water then they lit a small fire in a hearth on the floor. She dismissed those that had come with her and she helped herself to a cup of wine as the others started on the food arrayed before them. She engaged Ceinwen, Morgund and Ethain in conversation about their homes and the outside world, occasionally turning her smiling green eyes to Arthur who gazed at her, still trying to equate the young child he had met on his previous visits with the woman before him now. Gradually she put the others at ease and when they had eaten all that they wished too, Seren turned to Arthur and said, 'Would you care to see the rest of our poor Winter Garden before you rest?'

'The garden is an amazement, certainly not poor,' Arthur replied standing up and offering his hand to Seren. She took it and she linked her arm through his as they walked out of the bower. As they left Ceinwen heard her say, 'Then Arthur you should see it in mid-winter when the trees hold the snow and ice holds the fountains. When the marble is lit by only the deep winter stars or when the cold full moon shines on the frosted grass and is reflected in the frozen streams...'

Their voices dwindled in the rain as they moved out of earshot.

'I never thought such a place could exist!' Ethain said, still wide-eyed and staring around himself.

'Yet we aren't invited into the City itself,' Morgund remarked as he lay back on the soft mattress.

Ceinwen sat there silently while Ethain and Morgund discussed the strange Cithol, Ethain's wonder and enthusiasm the perfect foil for Morgund's uncharacteristic wariness. Ceinwen hugged her knees to her chest, watching Arthur and Seren as they disappeared in the twilight and rain.

Silent lightning still flashed across the low clouds casting the surrounding forest in brilliant light for the briefest of moments. The rain had eased to the point where it was almost no more than a mist seemingly suspended in the still air of the forest and the only noise was the water settling through the trees to join the rivulets now coursing throughout the woodland.

Arthur could feel Seren's warmth next to him as they walked arm in arm. She drew her cape around her to keep the rain off but left the hood back. She tilted her head back and laughed as the rain ran down her face and through her long, purely white hair.

'I so rarely feel the rain, I forget the simple pleasure it affords.'

Arthur, who was soaked through, just smiled down at her as he watched the rain trace lines across her face. His concerns for the world beyond the Winter Garden seemed to slip away unnoticed in that moment. The image of her face turned to the sky with the rain gently spilling down her neck and throat burned itself on his memory.

'You don't agree, do you Lord?'

'It loses its appeal quickly, but I've never seen it so beautiful as now. And I am no Lord, for you're the one of noble blood not I.'

'Is that so?' Seren asked and smiled. They began walking again and Arthur yearned for the moment past. Seren started to point out and name the variety of flowers and plants along the path, some of which Arthur had never seen before. In a quiet moment Arthur asked, 'Why would the High Lord Venning's daughter carry food out to wayfarers when the same wayfarers are not permitted entry to the Veiled City?'

Seren stopped and looked down at the path abashed. Arthur felt an overwhelming impulse to hold her in his arms.

'It's Lord Venning's decree that none but our own should ever enter the City,' she replied still looking down, then lifting her eyes she added, 'I'm sure he will admit you all once he arrives with Brunroth the Traveller and if the guests cannot come to us then I shall go to them.'

They looked briefly into each other's eyes then Arthur began walking again.

'Is the 'Traveller' Merdynn?' he asked.

Seren stepped after him and linked arms once more.

'Yes, Merdynn as your people call him for he has many names, most of them lost to time. He has visited us many times over the years – always bearing news of the outside, and patiently answering my questions and telling me tales of the man who sometimes accompanied him – the wild Warlord of the barbaric Britons.' Seren laughed as Arthur raised an eyebrow at the description of himself.

They passed one of the fountains carved to resemble horses galloping across a stream, the water cascading up from their splashing hooves. Seren trailed a hand across the smooth stone and resumed in a quieter, more self-conscious tone, 'At first my questions were those of a child, but they changed as the years passed. Now I know all you have done, as you know it yourself. And the years passed, one after another and each time the Traveller came to us I looked for you. Yet your visits became less frequent and then stopped altogether.'

'Lord Venning banned me from ever entering the Winter Wood again. It is his realm and it was his wish.'

'Had he?' Seren asked in surprise and looked long at Arthur as if studying his answer. 'It's true what Merdynn told me, your heart cannot be read. I can sense the others but not you. Strange that the only wayfarer to visit the Veiled City is the one whose heart I cannot read. Strange that it should be you, Arthur.'

'And your peoples' hearts are all closed to my sight,' Arthur replied glancing at the girl by his side whom he had felt an unreasoned and irresistible attraction towards the moment he had seen her approaching the stone bower.

Seren stopped once more and faced Arthur, 'Unread perhaps, but not necessarily closed to you.'

Arthur stared into her dark green eyes, which looked uncertain for the first time. He drew her closer and she put both hands on his chest. Arthur lightly brushed his fingertips across the raindrops on her forehead and cupped the back of her neck. She raised herself onto her toes and, after a moment's hesitation, they slowly kissed in the twilight and rain of the Winter Garden.

Merdynn found Arthur several hours later, asleep in a covered bower under one of the cedar trees. He coughed loudly and said, 'I see you've decided to sleep away from your companions. I've been sent to bring you and the others into the City. They're still sleeping. I'll, ah, wait for you over there,' he pointed off with his staff, hesitated and then decided to walk off in that direction.

Arthur could still feel Seren's warmth in the bed next to him and her fresh scent was still on the pillow by his head. Sitting up he looked across at the dome in the centre of the square and thought he caught a glimpse of a green cape as someone disappeared inside. Smiling he got up, dressed and joined Merdynn as he made his way to the others.

'Ceinwen snoring again was she?' Merdynn asked, looking straight ahead and carefully avoiding any insinuation in his voice.

Arthur couldn't think of an appropriate reply so made none.

'Thought so. Terrible thing that,' Merdynn added.

The rain had stopped and the sky above the square was a clear, pale blue, still lit by the sun that had finally sunk below the eastern horizon surrendering Middangeard to the dark winter.

The others were already stirring when they got there. None of them were surprised to see that Arthur had already packed his bedroll and that he had been off talking with Merdynn.

As they made their way to the dome Ceinwen gave him an inquisitive sidelong look, 'You were talking with Seren for some time,' she said casually.

'We had much to say to one another,' Arthur replied.

They entered the dome in silence and Merdynn led them down a wide, spiralling set of stone steps.

As they descended the light grew dimmer but it was not until the domed entrance was high above them that they realised that light was emanating from crystals set at regular intervals along the walls. Morgund stopped by one, his face softly lit as he studied it.

'One of the many marvels and mysteries of the Veiled City. Come, the Cithol Lord and his Commander await us,' Merdynn said and led on down the stairs. Ethain made a sign to ward off evil and followed the others.

'We are safe here, Merdynn, aren't we?' Ceinwen asked, the memory of childhood fables coming back to her.

'You're safe if you've come this far, for only the invited see what you have seen.'

The steps finally ended and opened up onto a low ceilinged hall, lit by the same large crystals they had seen along the stairway. The floor was carpeted with dry pine needles and the sides and ceiling of the hall looked to be made from the same smooth stone that they had seen outside but the dim light made it hard to tell for certain. Narrow corridors radiated out from the hall like spokes from a wheel.

Merdynn led on confidently down one of the corridors. Some of the Cithol who passed them greeted Merdynn but all stopped and stared at the strangers with him. Most had never seen people from outside and they looked warily at the intruders, studying their strange apparel and fascinated by their rough, sun-creased faces and dark hair.

The Cithol, like the people of Middangeard, ranged in skin tone from pale white to dark black yet they all had the same smooth, translucent skin quality, pool-like eyes and pure white hair that they had seen in Lord Venning and in those who had brought the food to them earlier.

At length the corridor widened and opened up onto a large hall. Broad, carved pillars rose in ranks to an unseen ceiling. It was a great feasting hall and low tables were set in lines running the length of the hall. The hall was so long and so dimly lit they could barely see the far end. The hall was busy with Cithol who stopped and stared as the strangers made their way to the far end.

'It's all a bit dark isn't it?' Morgund asked.

'Not to the Cithol,' Merdynn replied.

After a while they could make out the far end. Wide stone steps arced out in a semi circle and led up to a raised area.

'Gods,' Ceinwen whispered in awe. Ethain stopped in his tracks and Morgund drew in breath sharply. Before them, although still a good hundred yards away, they could see that the raised area was carved out of solid rock to resemble a forest. Trees towered from their carved roots on the floor straight up to the ceiling where they were lost from sight. Their branches seemed to meld into one another and looked as if they were growing into and out from the smooth rock that faced the three sides of the raised area. The scale was overpowering for them and they stopped and stared. Arthur remembered how daunting he had found it on his previous visit and even Merdynn looked at it anew through the eyes of his companions.

Morgund swore under his breath and Ethain nodded his head in agreement.

'How could... how long did...?' Ceinwen could not even decide which question to ask first.

Merdynn led on and they advanced towards the stone forest, staring ahead as the detail became more distinct. As they neared the end of the hall they heard strains of music from instruments that were entirely unfamiliar to them. Ceinwen was slowly shaking her head in disbelief. Morgund believed the whole affect was designed to rob them of their senses and to make them feel insignificant in the presence of those who could create such a stage but he was wrong. The Cithol admitted very few to this hall and they had carved out the stone forest purely for their own delight.

Ceinwen looked around her for the source of the music that seemed to surround them. She saw a small group of Cithol to one side of the broad hall, sitting in a circle and facing each other. She paused, trying to see what instruments they were playing but the gloom of the hall made it difficult. It seemed to her to be a blend of soft breathing pipes, stringed instruments whose notes soared beyond the range of her hearing and voices chanting a cadence in a language that seemed both alien and perfectly suited to the variants in the repetitious refrains. She felt uplifted and drawn towards the living force of the circular rhythms and found herself taking a step to one side away from her companions. She felt her heart rate slow to match the music's gentle tempo and she closed her eyes as the serene harmonies enveloped her. Merdynn gently took her arm and guided her back. She followed but could not turn her gaze away from the musicians.

They walked up the wide steps that led to the raised dais where a large stone table was set. There was a single throne fashioned from marble, high-backed and inlaid with precious stones where Lord Venning sat watching them with one long fingered hand covering his lips. Next to him and on his left sat Fin Seren and Captain Terrill. To the right of Lord Venning sat the Commander who Captain Terrill reported to and who was ultimately responsible for both the city's security and for guarding the borders of the Winter Wood. His pale white skin seemed even more anaemic than the other Cithol, almost albino and his eyes were a pinkish red but he was broad across the shoulders and although shorter than most of the Cithol they had seen so far he looked more powerful. He may have lacked the elegance and poise of those he sat with but there was no denying the presence or authority of Commander Kane.

Lord Venning's wife, Inis, was next to the Commander and she stood as they reached the table, 'Welcome to the Veiled City. Our visitors are too few. Brunroth we know of old, the warlord Arthur we have met before yet there are three more come from the outside.'

Arthur introduced them and Inis greeted each in turn and then addressed them, 'Lord Venning you have perhaps already seen since he has just returned from your land. Terrill, Captain of the Cithol and guardian of the Winter Wood, you have already met. The Commander here is responsible for the City's security. And this is our daughter, Fin Seren – perhaps you remember her, Arthur?'

Arthur finally allowed himself to look directly at Seren and returned her smile, 'I remember her well my Lady, though she has grown even more beautiful than when I last saw her.'

Ceinwen glanced at Morgund who continued to look straight ahead, mesmerised by actually being in the Veiled City and before the High Cithol. Inis smiled at Arthur's reply. The Cithol who had been simply introduced to them as the Commander sat perfectly still and stared into Arthur's gray eyes with a steady concentration. The visitors felt their attention inescapably drawn to him and only Merdynn was able to look away. Power seemed to radiate from the Commander's intensity and the others felt themselves inching back in their chairs feeling that somehow their thoughts and hearts were being searched.

Arthur returned his look unperturbed and with a slight smile playing on the corners of his lips. A flash of irritation crossed Kane's face and a deep frown momentarily creased his forehead before being quickly replaced by a look of mild curiosity. The sudden tension and alarm that Arthur's companions felt vanished.

'Please, sit and break your fast,' Inis said and swept her hand over the table that was laid with various foods. Merdynn had watched the exchange between Commander Kane and Arthur and he ate his breakfast in thoughtful silence. Inis once again turned her attention to Arthur as

Terrill engaged the others in conversation.

'Our captain informs me you took exception to our storm.'

'My Lady?'

'Please, simply call me Inis. He claims he came across you as you railed against the storm.'

'Ah, yes, that's true,' Arthur could feel Seren smiling at him and he was finding it difficult not to look towards her.

'Do you take issue with all storms, or just ours perhaps?'

'It was more a feeling inside rather than the storm outside, Lady.'

'And did the storm obey you, Arthur?' Commander Kane asked, still studying him.

'So it seems. It passed.'

Seren laughed softly giving Arthur the excuse he wanted to turn his eyes towards her.

'As all storms tend to,' Inis added dryly.

When they had finished the breakfast Inis suggested that Seren show their guests the Summer Lake and she agreed eagerly before realising Arthur was to stay at the table.

Merdynn came back to the present when the others left the table, led away by Terrill and the reluctant Seren. Arthur watched her go.

'What happened between you?' Merdynn asked. Arthur turned to look at Merdynn and he hurriedly continued, 'Between you and the king at the council?'

Lord Venning leant forward, waiting for the reply. Kane watched Arthur as he pushed his chair back and absently rubbed the back of his thigh where the arrow had penetrated.

'He wants me dead. That's why he agreed to the war bands going east in winter. He doesn't think we'll be coming back.'

'But why? What purpose would that serve? Despite his obvious animosity towards you, to lose you and Cei and your warriors would be a disaster for Britain at this time,' Merdynn said, clearly puzzled.

'I don't know his purpose yet, only that this much is true. For some reason he wants the Wessex and Anglian warriors far from home,' Arthur replied.

'I don't believe he intends to take the journey west,' Lord Venning suggested.

'That would surprise me, he usually takes a care with his own safety,'

Arthur replied.

'He believes we have formed an alliance, one designed to overthrow him.'

Arthur and Merdynn stared at Lord Venning.

'Good God, the man's finally gone mad,' Merdynn muttered.

'He's my king, how can he think I'd betray that?' Arthur said.

'He's not mad but he could be a danger to the land if you are abroad Arthur. I don't know what he plots, his heart is secretive and his will is strong but his designs have been prepared over the years and he feels now is the time to bring them into the open,' Lord Venning said staring at the table. He brought his black eyes up to Arthur's and added, 'Is going east wise?'

'I see no choice. Do we wait for the Adren attack, not knowing where it will fall, or how many will be coming at us or even when? Do we abandon the Belgae as lost? I see no choice. We will have to face King Maldred and his designs when we return.'

'And? There's something else, what is it?' Merdynn said, sensing that Arthur had held something back.

'We need to know if the Adren are intent on invading Britain – and why. Is it just the land they want? Do they intend to enslave the peoples of Britain? Or is their true design to take the Veiled City and what it hides?'

Merdynn looked uncomfortable and shot a glance towards the two Cithol.

'What?' Arthur asked.

'You remember what we were saying in the council?'

'Yes,' Arthur replied impatiently.

'Well, I believe Lazure was sent to the Shadow Land City many, many years ago. It seems likely that the Khan in the East sent him. At that time his Adren armies probably would not have been strong enough to take that city by force so Lazure took it by guile. He positioned himself to council the Shadow Land City's rulers and over the centuries gradually took control himself. Once he had control over the ancient power of the city he was able to use it to effectively feed the Adren armies of the East. And their number grew until Lazure felt confident enough that nothing in the West could withstand them,' Merdynn paused and looked again to

Lord Venning.

Arthur stared at him impatiently, 'This is more or less what was said at the council.'

'Yes, yes it is. But we felt that the next bit perhaps ought not to have been mentioned at that stage. The Shadow Land City is very much like this city. The source of its power, while different, is still a legacy from the same past. And, well, that's not the only similarity – it's a Cithol City too,' Merdynn concluded, nodding to himself.

'Lazure runs a Cithol City? The city that supplies his Adren armies?'

'Hmmm, yes, it would seem so,' Merdynn replied.

Arthur stared at the two Cithol.

'We don't know anything for certain yet. It may be that once he took control of the city the Cithol there were either killed or sent east to the Khan. We just don't know,' Lord Venning said, adding his shrug to Merdynn's.

'It may be that the Adren captains are Cithol,' Merdynn said brightly.

'That's just speculation – there's nothing to support that,' Venning added angrily.

Commander Kane spoke for the first time since the others had left, 'This city must not fall. To the best of our extensive knowledge there are only two cities that still have the ancient knowledge, the legacy power. Whoever controls the two cities controls everything from the far east to the western oceans – and no one would ever be able to challenge their control.'

Arthur held his eyes and said, 'I would rather this land from the Causeway to the Haven and everything in-between be burnt to ash and utterly destroyed than to see it in the hands of the Adren and their Master.'

His words chilled both Merdynn and the Cithol.

Chapter Six

Arthur took his leave of Fin Seren in the Winter Garden. He had gone ahead of Merdynn and the others to prepare the horses for the next stage of their journey to the Causeway. Seren had left her guests to say their farewells to the Lord of the Cithol and hurried to the Winter Garden hoping to meet Arthur there.

Arthur had saddled the horses and was just saddling Merdynn's pony when he heard Seren behind him.

'Going so soon, Arthur?'

Arthur turned to look at her. She was smiling in the same playful way as when they first met but her eyes betrayed an uncertainty. Again he felt an overwhelming urge to embrace her but turned back to secure the last strap on the horse's saddle.

'I must go east, Seren.'

'To the Shadow Lands?'

'Yes.'

He had heard the fear in her voice and was loathe to turn around and see it in her face.

'They say it is dangerous to go east in winter.'

'There's danger at every turn now. Both here and there.'

Seren stepped closer to Arthur and rested a hand on his shoulder. He turned to face her.

'Then we will both have to be careful.'

Her voice was stronger again and they embraced, holding each other tightly. She stepped back and bowing her head, lifted off the clear stone that hung on a leather cord around her neck.

'Take this.' She offered him the jewel.

Arthur took it and looked at her enquiringly.

'We call it Elk Stone, it brings the wearer good fortune, or so they say,' Seren said. 'And be sure not to leave it another ten years before you deign to visit us once more,' she added, lightly mocking him. He laughed and holding her face in both hands, kissed her.

'I'll be back before Imbolc.'

'And when, pray, is that particular strange festival of yours?'

'Before the sun rises.'

They heard the others leaving the dome and making their way across to them. Their short time alone was slipping quickly away. Seren moved as if to embrace Arthur one more time but she stopped herself. Arthur smiled at her and her dark green eyes said everything they no longer had the time to voice.

As the others neared she said, 'You'll miss the Gardens in the starlight.'

'It's not the Gardens that I will miss, Seren.'

'Look for the winter moon Arthur and when you see its cold face remember I too will be looking on it, remembering this moment.'

The atmosphere changed as the others arrived talking excitedly as they started to untether their horses. Arthur shrugged almost indiscernibly to Seren and then led his horse out of the shelter. Terrill suggested they walk their horses out of the woods and the group moved to the archway, Terrill and Merdynn leading, the others next and Arthur and Seren last.

They filed through the gateway with Seren bidding them farewell and when the others were through Seren leaned up and kissed Arthur saying, 'I'll look for you when the snows melt and the streams run once more.'

She turned and was gone. Arthur was through the archway and following the others. He fought the desire to turn back. All he wanted in that moment was to stay in the Veiled City with Fin Seren, to be at peace, a peace he had not known all his life. As the distance increased between them he feared with a cold certainty that it would never happen. If they were fortunate they might yet steal moments together but they would be desperate moments in a time of despair.

Minute by minute he became more aware of his surroundings. Ahead, Ceinwen had just asked Terrill about the ruins they could see to either side in the woods.

'Our tales say that a great city once stood here. Thousands upon thousands lived here in gleaming towers amid treasured gardens with walls higher than the eye can see.'

'What happened to them?' Ceinwen asked trying to imagine the scene and the downfall that Merdynn had talked of at the council.

'All I know is that they are long gone. The city died in ages past, I don't know how and I don't know why. The lore keepers know more of these things. If you come back this way perhaps you can ask Lord Venning if you can talk to them.'

Ceinwen was unsatisfied with the answer but realised that Terrill would say no more and she lapsed into silence. Arthur's thoughts returned to the Veiled City. He remembered seeing the Summer Lake on his previous visit. The lake was situated in a cavern the size of a valley with houses strewn around its shore. The cavern roof was hundreds of feet high and lined with crystals that lit the whole valley like miniature bright stars. The lake itself was black, unfathomable and utterly still except where the occasional long canoe cut rippling arrows across its inky surface. Fresh, chilled air blew gently from regularly spaced large fissures in the walls. It was a setting that could not possibly exist in the imagination of someone from outside and even seeing it did not seem to make it any more possible or real.

Equally amazing to Arthur were the caverns where the crops were grown. Endless lines of earthed-plants were suspended above equally endless troughs of water for their roots to trail in. This had been the brightest place in the whole of the Veiled City; strings of lights lit the cavern as if it were high summer. Ethain had attributed it to dark magic when he had seen it and the other two had been inclined to agree with him. Arthur felt the City now held a different type of treasure and once again he felt drawn to turn and go back but he continued on down the winding path.

The trees were becoming more spaced out and the path became wide enough for them not to have to keep to single file.

Terrill turned to them, 'The path goes on and will take you to the hill where we met. If you return this way, find this path and we will meet you along it.'

He raised an arm in farewell as they mounted their horses, 'Journey well in the Shadow Lands, may your way be lit by the stars.' He turned and headed back down the path. The others looked at Arthur who was watching Terrill take the path he so keenly wanted to take himself. He brought his horse round, turning his back on the Veiled City and the peace it offered. He looked at the others and said, 'We tarried here too long.'

They reached the Causeway only a few hours before Mar'h and Cei arrived leading the Wessex and Anglian warriors. Arthur was on the eastern wall looking out to the Causeway with Ruadan and Hengest when Cael ran up the ladder behind them with the news.

Cael had been with the Wessex war band in North Anglia helping to gather the villages there. He and his detachment had come straight to the Gates to help with the defences once they had safely seen their villages onto the Westway as Arthur had requested. Cael was too stout to be running up ladders and he had to pause to catch his breath before he could tell them the news. Arthur and the others watched him, shaking their heads sadly at his condition. Their levity vanished when he finally got out the news that the Wessex war band had been raided.

They went to meet the warriors that were still milling around the gate on the far side of the fort. Cei was still marshalling the wains down the steep cliff path. Trevenna was off to one side with Mar'h.

'Hengest, sort this rabble out,' Arthur said abruptly and strode towards Mar'h who was sitting at a table with Ceinwen bent over his arm.

'What happened?'

Mar'h flinched inwardly at Arthur's tone.

'Please, Arthur, his arm needs setting,' Ceinwen said attempting to mollify his anger.

Arthur brought his fist crashing down on the table, 'How in the name of all the gods did my war band get raided?' Those around the table instinctively took a step backward.

All except Trevenna, his sister. She stood slowly and walked around the table towards Arthur, hands held up before her and said, 'He's in enough pain Arthur. We joined up on the Westway an hour after the raid. I know all that happened. The column had become strung out. Llud did not set any flanking riders. A rain storm blew in, visibility dropped and they were ambushed by probably thirty Uathach.'

'Where's Llud?' Arthur asked, keeping his voice level.

'He's dead Arthur. They buried him at the edge of the Westway with Talan and five wain drivers.'

Arthur closed his eyes briefly.

'Mar'h, Talan and Tamsyn disabled most of the wains during the attack, that's when Talan died, but the Uathach took four wains. Llud and the drivers were killed in the initial hail of arrows. That's when Mar'h's arm got smashed and his horse was killed under him. Morveren managed to outpace the Uathach riders and she brought back the rest of the company. We arrived a short while later and together we went after the Uathach raiding party. We slew ten of them before they abandoned the wains.'

'You recovered the wains?'

'Yes.'

'And pursued the Uathach?'

'No. We had the wains. Any more would have cost us further. In the light of recent events across the Causeway Cei decided we could not afford to lose more warriors hunting down a raiding party that can do no more damage now the villagers are at Caer Sulis.'

Arthur nodded.

'It was the right choice Arthur. The Wessex and Anglians have fought side by side now. They fought well.'

Arthur replied quietly, 'They'll need to, Trevenna. We have the Adren to the East, the Uathach to the North and the king's men to the West.'

'Any chance of heading south for the winter?' Mar'h asked grimacing as Ceinwen manipulated his forearm.

Arthur sat down opposite Mar'h, refilled his mug of beer and passed it across to his good hand.

'How's his arm?' he asked Ceinwen.

'It's not good at all. The bone is smashed – the arrow must have been fired from close range.'

Mar'h winced and nodded, 'Twenty, thirty-feet.'

'I can clean it and splint it. There won't be any infection but...'

'But what?' Arthur asked.

Ceinwen looked at Mar'h, 'You may lose the movement in your left hand.'

'As long as I can strap on my shield with my right hand,' Mar'h said and screwed his face up as Ceinwen poured liquid from a vial over his forearm.

Arthur rubbed a hand over his eyes and let out a deep breath and said, 'Llud was a good man. We'll miss him. Why didn't he set the flankers? It's been too long since we've been at war – everyone's too casual. We'll have to change that.'

Mar'h nodded, his long, straight black hair hanging around his face and hiding his pained expression.

'You did well, Mar'h. I should have left Morgund with the column or I should have stayed with them myself - or made them wait for you. It was a mistake, knowing the enemy was in the East, I felt too safe in our own land. No longer can anywhere be seen as a haven. And there will be no more mistakes.'

Hengest, Cei's second in command, had sorted out the new influx and their horses were being stabled as Cei rode in ahead of the wains. He jumped down and Arthur went to meet him.

'You heard?' Cei asked.

'Yes and thanks for getting our supplies back, we'll need it all before summer comes.'

'That's what I thought. I was tempted to go after the rest of the bastards.'

'No, you did the right thing – they're the king's problem now. Come, see what you make of the defences,' Arthur said and as they made their way to the East wall he called out for Ruadan and Hengest to join them.

As Ruadan strode towards them Arthur asked, 'Is there a watch posted at the far end of the Causeway?'

'Yes, Arthur, any sight of the enemy and we'll see the beacon warning.' He pointed to a guard on the wall watching through the twilight to the East.

'Good,' Arthur replied and started to climb the ladder up to the wall. His leg was still too stiff to bend comfortably and he hauled himself up using his arms and hopping with one leg from one rung to the next.

'The only way up to the wall are these ladders now – if the walls get breached we bring them down stranding the attackers on the wall,' Ruadan said, half-apologising for Arthur's discomfort and half-explaining why it was necessary.

Arthur looked back at the twenty-foot drop, 'They could jump that.'

'We are going to stake the ground,' Hengest replied, 'and we've added a second inner wall as you can see.'

The second wall was five-feet high and paralleled the three outer walls before funnelling back towards the West Gate. There was at least thirty yards between it and the outer walls.

'You plan to stake all the ground between the walls?' Cei asked.

'Yes. If it gets to that stage then clearly we'll have to abandon the Gates and we'll have to buy as much time as possible to get out – anything to slow them down and allow us to pour arrows into them,' Hengest answered.

Arthur turned his attention forward again. The East wall ran across the Causeway and down either side into the marshes before joining with the two lower walls running west. He could clearly see that the East Gate had been heavily reinforced. Five-feet from the East wall the Causeway had been removed, leaving a gap of over fifty-feet, which the marsh water had quickly reclaimed. Across the gap stretched a log bridge laid out on bushels and floating on the water and mud.

'It can be hauled back inside the gate,' Ruadan said, pointing to the two large, spoked wheels on drums inside gate.

'Two hundred yards further on is a smaller gap in the Causeway. It's cut much steeper than this one and a simple bridge covers the span, it too can be hauled back once crossed which should give us time to cross this one in good order if we're being pursued.

'Excellent,' Cei said, 'is there any way we can get covered platforms out to either side of this gap below us for bowmen to stop any attempts to bridge it?'

Ruadan turned to Hengest for his opinion and the younger warrior studied the terrain, 'Perhaps, I'll have to look closer. If we could run walkways out from the two corners of the East Wall to platforms supported by bushels. Roof them with fire-hardened wood. Perhaps. I'll look at it straight away.'

'Good,' Arthur said, 'unless they come by sea, which isn't likely, they'll have to attack along here. Anything that any of you can think of to help defend this Causeway then suggest it. They'll certainly outnumber us so the Causeway is our best defence, if they get past here then they'll be in Britain and gods help us then.'

Arthur turned to look at the cliffs behind them, 'What about defences on the cliff path and at the top?'

They discussed various options. Hengest went to talk to his carpenters. Warriors were sent out to bring in more wood for the construction of defences. Arthur and the others retired from the wall and went to one of

158

the longhouses that stood within the compound for a meal.

On his way across, Balor who had stayed at the Crossing with Ruadan, shouted out to Arthur, 'When are we going to get to cut down some of these Adren instead of trees?'

'Soon enough and more than enough,' Arthur called back to him. Balor rubbed his hands together and beamed at Elowen and Tomas who had been listening to Ethain talk excitedly about the Veiled City. Balor had not believed much of what Ethain had said, despite Morgund's previous corroboration, and what little he had believed had only further darkened his suspicions of the Cithol. He pointed out that living underground just wasn't natural and when Ethain had enthused about the strange lighting in the city Balor had just muttered oaths to ward off evil. Elowen was mortified to have missed seeing the Veiled City and she feigned disinterest. Ethain felt robbed that only Tomas seemed to find his journey as impressive as he himself thought it was.

Arthur entered the longhouse with the others and sat next to Ceinwen who was eating with Morgund and Leah.

'Mar'h?' Arthur enquired of her.

'I've given him something to help him sleep, his arm's not good.'

'Perhaps you should give something to Tamsyn too,' Arthur suggested.

'Merdynn's with her now. She's distraught – losing her brother...' her voice trailed off and she turned her attention back to her food. She had tried to keep as much company as she could in an effort to distract herself from her own grief and to some extent it had worked but she only ended up feeling guilty whenever her thoughts came back to her loss. She felt she ought to be grieving more openly but she only seemed to be able to weep for her dead when she was alone. She wondered if part of the reason for that was her desire to fit in with the war band and not have them think of her as another victim unable to cope with death and therefore of little use to them. It depressed her to realise that there was more than a grain of truth in that thought; she had thought she was strong enough not to have to rely upon other peoples' opinion but it appeared that that too was only a vain deceit.

Arthur was imagining how he would have felt if Trevenna had been killed. He put it to one side, there would be more death to come and it was better to concentrate on how to minimise that.

Ruadan sat the other side of Ceinwen and in an effort to take her thoughts from her family she began to tell him about the Veiled City. Around them the others were weighing the arguments for various alterations and additions to the defences of the Causeway.

Arthur was concerned about being outflanked. Merdynn had assured him that the Adren were unlikely to undertake a sea crossing. Their homeland was landlocked and he did not think they had anything like the craft or knowledge to build ships to transport a large army across the sea. If Merdynn was right then the only way into Britain was across the Causeway. Everything depended upon holding the Adren here but he wanted to be sure of a retreat route should it prove necessary. Being trapped would be the worst disaster of all. He asked Cei about the conditions in the marshes in mid-winter. Would it all freeze over? Could the Adren by-pass or surround them? Apparently it depended on the local weather. The water level dropped in the winter and less of the waterways were in constant flow so during a cold blizzard with the wind from the East the marshes often froze over despite it being mainly seawater in the channels. Even then they were considered too treacherous to cross. The more Arthur heard about the conditions in winter the more he wanted to delay the Adren until spring when the only sure way would be across the Causeway.

Cei had moved his base to the Gates and the additional families were already helping to make arrows and sharpen weapons. The compound had never been so busy. Between the Wessex and Anglian war bands there were over one hundred and fifty warriors all readying their winter gear, honing weapons and preparing for the journey to the East. Hide tents had been set up against the West wall and there was a constant hum of activity as people sought food or a place to rest. Hengest was working hard to get matters organised but he was beginning to lose patience. Cei left the table to help him and together they finally put some order into proceedings around the camp.

Arthur turned to Ruadan and interrupted Ceinwen's tales of the Winter Wood, 'We'll need another gap in the Causeway between here and the cliff path, with a retractable bridge too. If we retreat we'll need time again.'

'Very well, I'll set about doing that next. Ceinwen was telling me about the marvels of the Veiled City.'

'Including Lord Venning's daughter, Fin Seren. She's very beautiful isn't she?' Ceinwen looked to Arthur for confirmation.

Arthur had been trying to put her from his thoughts but this sudden reference immediately brought the image of her face, upturned to the rain, forcibly back into his mind; his heart jolted at the memory.

'Her name means 'Fair Star', the bright Winter Star to the North. Merdynn was present at her birth and Lord Venning asked him to name his daughter. He named her well,' Arthur replied.

'Oh yes, I'd forgot – she wears this clear cut crystal jewel in a silver band around her throat. I've never seen anything like it, the way it reflects the light!' Ceinwen had to raise her voice almost to a shout to be heard over the arguments of the warriors surrounding them.

Arthur's hand went to his chest where his tunic concealed the Elk Stone that hung from around his neck. He forced Seren's image from his mind and stood up, 'Come you two, let's talk somewhere quieter.'

Outside they met Merdynn on his way in.

'How's Tamsyn?' Ceinwen asked.

'The trouble with the young is that they think they'll live for ever. Disappointing for them to find they're wrong. Bit of a shock too,' he replied.

'Probably better to give her something to do rather than let her dwell on it,' Ruadan suggested, thinking of his sister by his side.

'Put her in charge of making the stakes for inside the walls. And tell her they're to welcome any Uathach raiders and not the Adren,' Arthur said.

'That should guarantee they'll be nice and sharp,' Merdynn said and ambled off to the longhouse.

'Ceinwen, could you go and check on her and if she's up to it then get her started. She'll need others to help her,' Arthur said.

Ceinwen nodded and left to find Tamsyn. Arthur walked on out of the West Gate with Ruadan walking beside him.

'The only initiative defenders have in a place like this is how they prepare their defences. Once that's complete then the initiative passes to the attackers. It's not a situation I like,' Arthur said as they sat on the bank of the Causeway.

'True, but the defences are good. I can't see how an army of five hundred or even a thousand could overcome it. Only so many can attack along the Causeway at any one time and we can deal with those,' Ruadan replied.

Arthur rubbed a hand across his bearded chin and looked at Ruadan, gauging how much of his fears to tell him. Ruadan's pale face looked tired and strained. He and Hengest had been working on the defences with very little rest.

'I fear it may be more than a thousand and I'm not sure we can trust the marshes to protect us in winter. That's two reasons why we're going east. I need to know how many we face. If chance allows then I'll whittle those odds down a bit and in any case I'll look to delay them until spring when we can trust that the marshes won't betray us.'

'So, who's going east and when do they leave?' Ruadan asked.

'We must leave enough here to build the defences and man them if necessary. How many do you think?'

'How many will be attacking?' Ruadan replied, shrugging.

'Say a thousand try to storm the Gates, how many to repel them indefinitely?'

'I don't know. We're a bit limited on numbers aren't we? It's not as if we've had a battle like this for some time. Raids? Battles on open fields? Fine, but hundreds attacking us like this? I don't know.'

'We've got about one-hundred and fifty between the two war bands, it's a question of how to split them best.'

'I suppose you've considered that if they do come across in winter then anyone on the other side of the Causeway will have an Adren army between them and home?' Ruadan said.

'Yes. It's a risk, but the reasons for going outweigh those for staying.'

'If we had the time and people I'd have liked to tear down the whole Causeway and let the marshes reclaim it. That would be the best defence.'

'And we could have trained every man, woman and child in Middangeard to wield a spear or shoot an arrow - if we'd had the time. Perhaps we can yet buy enough time.'

They sat in silence for a while, each contemplating what the future might hold. The marshes below them were still, unstirred by any breeze.

The dusk air was cold and Ruadan pulled his light cloak around him. He had not had the chance yet to collect his winter garments. Arthur gazed at the brighter stars that were already emerging in the pale blue sky to the West. His eyes were drawn to the North Star hanging low over the stunted trees and the long reeds of the marshes. He drew a hand over his tired eyes and with an effort brought his thoughts back to the Causeway.

'We'll need to leave soon. I want to set up a camp in the forests across the Causeway before the winter night and snows set in. We can store our supplies there as we scout further afield.'

'You'll take the horses with you then?' Ruadan asked.

'Yes, we'll need them at first certainly. As the winter deepens and the snows build I'll probably send them back here.'

'We could suggest that Cei's spear riders stay here whilst we go across – it is their camp after all.'

'That makes sense but I want it to be a joint venture. A mix here and a mix across the Causeway. We need to act together now. We need to strengthen the ties that have been formed between the two groups. Strangely the raid on the Westway has helped that.'

'High price to pay, especially losing Llud. I thought the old bastard was immortal.'

'None of us are. Especially if we make mistakes,' Arthur said and then turned to face Ruadan,

'Cei and I will each take forty of our warriors and cross the Causeway. I want you and Hengest to stay here with the rest of the warriors. It's not enough to go east with and it's not enough to guard here but then if we all went, or stayed, it would not be enough either. It should be enough to complete the defences. You've worked well with Hengest, and Cei and I can trust you both to deal with anything as well as we could.

'It's possible that we may not return and there are a few things you need to know. Tell this to Hengest too and whomever you place as your second-in-command. The king is not to be trusted. He wants me dead and possibly the two war bands as well.'

Ruadan stared at Arthur incredulously but Arthur stilled his questions and carried on, 'I don't know why yet or what his plans are but he thinks I'm in league with the Cithol and that I plot against him. The Cithol do have a part to play in this but there's no plot against the king. The Adren possibly want to take the Veiled City for it holds a power they need. This must not happen. If it goes ill here then head for the Winter Wood.'

Arthur drew a map in the dust of the Causeway explaining to Ruadan where the path was that led into the Cithol woodland.

'The Adren almost certainly want all our land and to destroy all our peoples. If there is no hope left and all is lost then take what people you can and sail for the West.'

Ruadan still stared at him, daunted by the prospects outlined by Arthur.

'Do you think it will come to this?' he asked softly.

Arthur stared out over the marshes once more and his eyes settled on the North Star.

'Not whilst I'm alive to stop them,' Arthur answered and smiled at Ruadan. 'If Cei and I can take their numbers down and delay them until spring then perhaps we can hold them from our shores while we train an army to lead across the Causeway and then we'll send their heads back east.'

'I like that plan better.'

'That's the plan we'll follow then. But you know what to do if all else fails. Make sure everyone under your and Hengest's joint command knows what to do – but don't tell them about the king, they'll be concerned about their lands and there's nothing we can do about that until we send the Shadow Land army to their funeral pyres.'

Arthur stood up and Ruadan, with his hands on his knees, levered himself to his feet. They faced each other and Arthur stuck out his hand.

'May the gods bless your hunting,' Ruadan said as he shook Arthur's hand.

'And keep my land safe, Ruadan,' Arthur replied, 'until I return.'

Arthur and Cei led their warriors across the Causeway in two single file lines with several wains bringing up the rear, laden with supplies for the winter. The two standards of the Wessex and the Anglians, the white horse and the black longboat, were unfurled and carried behind the two warlords. Merdynn rode between them on his pony, wrapped in his brown cloak and lost in his own thoughts.

Those who were staying at the Gates watched from the East wall with a mixture of envy and relief as the lines dwindled into the twilight. They watched from the wall long after the figures had been enveloped by the dusk. They watched as behind the war bands a spreading mist rose from the marshes and crept up and over the banks of the Causeway.

They passed the Watchtower at the far end of the Causeway and Arthur exchanged some words with the guards there then they rode up onto the roadway that led into the forests that spread between Eald and Branque. Arthur sent flanking riders into the forests and posted three riders in front of and behind the column. Ceinwen rode in the vanguard with Morgund who was sporting a cut lip from a brawl back at the Gates while the young Cerdic commanded the rearguard. One from each position dropped back to the column every five or ten minutes and another took their place. In that way, even if the entire guard were attacked and unable to send warning the war band would still know something was wrong within a few minutes.

Ten miles further on the roadway split north and south, heading to Eald and Branque respectively. Following Ceinwen's lead, Arthur took the column straight ahead and into the darkening forest until they caught up with her in a clearer area in a deep hollow about two miles in from the crossroads. Behind them the rearguard erased all evidence of their passing into the forest.

They set up their first camp here while others scouted the area for miles around. Hide tents were erected in a circle around the base of the hollow. Their main marquee would not be unpacked until the snows arrived. A large fire was lit at the base of the hollow with a wide canvas supported above it on poles. This stopped the firelight reaching the top of the trees and had the welcome advantage of sending some of the fire's heat back down on those gathered around it. None of the scouts reported that they could detect any evidence of the fire from any more than five hundred yards away. One of the now empty wains was despatched to fill two water barrels from a stream a mile away and food was prepared.

The warriors were used to this kind of expedition from their previous incursions into the Uathach lands and the whole process had a routine feel to it. Mar'h and Aelfhelm, acting as respective second-in-commands for Ruadan and Hengest who had stayed at the Gates, issued most of the orders and everyone quickly knew what was expected of them. Arthur sat with Cei and Merdynn discussing the first stage of what they were going to do while the activity around them saw a secure, working camp develop within the circumference of the hollow.

'We've probably got another seven days worth of this half-light before the darkness sets in properly, and then it'll be another few days before the moon is strong enough to offer us any light,' Cei said, looking to Merdynn for confirmation.

'But how long do we have before the snows set in?' Arthur asked rhetorically.

Merdynn stared up at the sky wondering if he was expected to answer or not. 'How do you plan to use the last of this light?' he eventually asked.

'We'll start with our last contact with the Shadow Land army, Branque. Then Eald. Then arc northward up to where Cei's men were and find out what happened to the Belgae,' Arthur answered.

'We should be able to get a good idea of their strength that way and how prepared they are,' Cei said.

'I shouldn't get too comfortable here then?' Merdynn asked.

'No, we'll make a more permanent camp for the winter North of Eald. By then we probably won't be able to use our horses so we'll have to sledge any supplies we'll need for our sweep up to the Belgae lands,' Arthur replied.

Around them people were starting to eat the food that had been prepared on the fires.

'"Eat first", every warrior's creed,' Merdynn snorted and leant back on the bank of the hollow with his hands resting on his empty stomach before adding, 'and very sensible too. Talk of the devil...'

'Talking about me, eh?' Morgund said as he and Cael joined them.

'It may surprise you to learn that the world does not turn about you. I was referring more to Cael actually,' Merdynn said, watching Cael settle his considerable bulk down beside them.

'Oh?' Cael said, belching loudly.

'Have you eaten already?' Cei asked.

'No point in hanging around – always best to get in first,' Cael replied with an amused glance to Morgund.

Cei looked from one to the other, 'A private joke?'

'I should imagine it has something to do with Morgund's cut lip, a certain woman from your war band Cei and an unhappy warrior at the Gates,' Merdynn said with a sigh.

'Well, he's an unhappier warrior now,' Morgund said, inspecting his bruised knuckles.

'Was Leah involved?' Cei asked.

Morgund nodded trying not to grin.

'That woman's nothing but trouble,' Merdynn said.

'Ha! You mean *he's* nothing but trouble,' Cael laughed as he hiked a thumb at Morgund beside him.

Arthur got to his feet and left them without saying a word. Morgund cringed and swore at Cael under his breath.

'Hey, don't blame me – you're the one who gets himself in too deep.'

'From what I hear you're both as bad as each other – with any luck you and Leah will get married and that'll solve a lot of problems,' Cei said, enjoying the situation despite Arthur's obvious displeasure at Morgund's behaviour. Morgund just shuddered at the suggestion. Cei turned to Merdynn, 'And talking about the world turning around Morgund, were you serious back at the council about summer and winter alternating back and forth so quickly?'

Merdynn looked at him inquisitively, 'What made you bring that up now?"

Cei shrugged, 'I was thinking about what I said – how it'll be a bright enough moon in a few days and it reminded me that I meant to ask you about that and see if you were talking seriously back in Caer Sulis.'

Merdynn drew a deep breath before replying. 'Yes, I was serious. But it wasn't winter and summer alternating quickly, it was night and day. The twenty-four hours we have to our day is based upon the time it used to take the sun to rise, travel across the sky, sink below the horizon and then rise again. Half the day was light, half was dark,' Merdynn paused, wondering just how simple or complicated to make his explanation.

'How could the sun move so quickly then?' Cael asked.

Merdynn decided to make it as simple as possible. He took an apple from one of his pockets and began a lengthy but simple description of how the world rotated around the sun and how it used to spin on its own axis. When he finished he looked at the three of them expectantly, 'Understand?' he asked hopefully.

They all looked blankly at the circles Merdynn had made in the dirt. None of them met his eye. The silence lengthened.

'Mind if I have that apple?' Cael asked and took the apple from the ground where it had been representing the world. He brushed the dirt from it and took a huge bite from it.

Merdynn stared at him.

'So, if I understand it properly,' Morgund said, 'then Cael just ate the world.'

Merdynn stared at him too.

'Now that I *can* believe,' Cei added.

Merdynn closed his eyes and started to count to five thousand.

Rather than face Merdynn Cei looked about the camp. There was a group led by Balor picking the last of the autumn berries from some bushes, an activity that would have met with some derision back at their home camps but not so now. Food in winter was scarce at best and any attempts to supplement supplies were only regarded with approval. Cei noticed that they kept their voices low as a matter of habit even though they knew that the outer ring of guards was beyond even the sound of their horses' neighing. It was a good habit and Cei was glad to see that they had all slipped quickly into their campaign ways. He was also glad to see that groups of Wessex mingled with his Anglians and while the voices were softened, the talk was animated with excitement at the news that they were heading for Branque first. Most of the war band thought Arthur wanted to settle that score first and Merdynn quietly worried that might be the case too.

Merdynn pondered on that and the wisdom of this campaign in the Shadow Lands as the others slept. Despite the dangers and risks he concluded once again that it was necessary, then he fell to worrying about what the king might be devising whilst the Wessex and Anglian warriors were far from home. He could see no imaginable way that the king would benefit from losing the two war bands, unless he planned to throw himself and the kingdom at the mercy of the Adren and as the Adren had no mercy he could not expect to be shown any. No, it did not make sense, no sense at all. Clearly he was missing something and it worried him greatly.

After they had rested, Arthur led them south toward Branque leaving twenty to guard the camp and their supplies. Ethain had volunteered to be one of the guards but Cei had chosen others. As Ethain picked his way through the gloomy forest he felt his stomach turning over and he held his reins tightly in case his hands shook. Elowen and Tomas rode with him but any nerves they felt were only in anticipation of what they might find at the village where Arthur had nearly been killed. The raven-haired Morveren followed behind, subdued since her friend, Talan, had died on the Westway.

While every one in each company knew each other well, it was still usual to find groups of four or five riding, eating, patrolling and camping together. When it came to battle the same tight-knit groups would be standing side by side, trusting their lives to each other. Ceinwen watched the various groups remembering a time when she, her brother and Arthur had been one such group.

'Remember when we were that young?' Ceinwen asked, momentarily thinking Ruadan was near her. Morgund looked at her inquisitively and she nodded towards the younger group ahead of them.

'I was never that young – and if I wasn't then you definitely weren't,' Morgund answered, smiling at her.

'We certainly weren't that stupid,' Balor added.

'We were both – we were young and stupid. And you all know it, perhaps we were even younger,' Mar'h joined in.

'But surely not more stupid,' Balor said defensively.

'I wouldn't be so certain of that,' Ceinwen pointed to Mar'h who held his reins in his right hand only as his left was in a sling, 'I remember him as a kid spending half his time chasing Della and the other half trying to avoid her scary mother.'

'Trouble is that you catch one and get landed with the other,' Mar'h replied glumly.

'Of course Mar'h is more stupid, we've known that for years, but not us three,' Balor said cheerfully.

'It's exactly because you three are so lamentably dim that I had to come with you to make sure you don't go astray,' Mar'h replied with the air of one rlising above insults. Ceinwen was feeling quietly relieved that they seemed prepared to include her in what was a fairly obviously a tight group.

'Why did you insist on coming, Mar'h? You'd be hopeless in a fight with that arm wrapped up,' Morgund asked.

'He's hopeless anyway,' Balor said turning in his saddle before Mar'h could answer. He turned back just in time to avoid a low hanging branch.

'Someone needs to tell you when to duck and when to swing Balor,' Mar'h answered him and Balor chuckled.

The ground before them began to rise and word came back down the line for quiet. They dismounted with their heart-rates increasing and led their horses up the steepening hill, winding between the trees that grew further apart the higher they climbed.

Herewulf and Osla, both from the Anglian spear riders, took their horses' reins from them and they were told to go on up and over the ridge ahead. The dry, soft bed of fallen pine needles layered between the trees gave way to a short tussock grass, with rocks and boulders strewn across the last stretch to the ridge above them.

Keeping low they crested the ridge and fanned out ten or twenty yards down the other side, resting up behind whatever cover offered itself. Ceinwen collected Ethain and ran crouched to where Arthur, Cei and Aelfhelm were looking down into the valley. Below them lay Branque.

Campfires burned in the compound within the walls and they could see figures moving around.

'Ethain, how many can you see down there?' Arthur asked.

Ethain peered down into the gloom of the village several hundred-feet below them. His right hand was trembling and he pressed it firmly into the tough grass to still the shaking. Ceinwen noticed it and put her hand on top of his to reassure him. He flinched but only Ceinwen noticed it.

'Ethain?' Arthur asked looking at him.

'Probably about thirty around the fires outside. None on the walls – I can't see any watchers.'

'Good. Say double that inside the hall and buildings,' Arthur said.

'And they aren't expecting company,' Aelfhelm added as he shifted his tall, lean frame to ease the aching knee that was injured long ago in some youthful folly. He was over fifty years old, too old to be lying on cold hillsides he thought to himself. Only Herewulf, with his flamboyant but grey ponytail, was older amongst the Anglians and he noted sourly that

Herewulf had more sense than to be lying out in the cold but he could not and did not complain, he had been a warrior for over thirty-five years and counted himself lucky to have no worse than an aching knee. The years had however furrowed his brow into a deep, perpetual frown above his thin, bearded face, which, together with his close-set eyes, lent his face a pinched and continually pained expression.

Arthur surveyed the scene below. The steep slope they were on was matched on the other side of the narrow, tilled valley floor. The river from the lake cut along the valley and Arthur remembered the fording point where he had met Andala. He could see where the charred stakes from the remains of his roundhouse pointed skyward from the edge of the lake that stretched out in a pale silver mirror behind the village.

He waited and watched. The others, strung-out below the ridgeline, waited patiently for his orders. Even the younger members of the war band had learnt it was better to wait and be sure than to rush in blindly.

Arthur eventually turned to Cei, Aelfhelm and Mar'h and outlined his plan. He wanted five bowmen spaced a hundred yards apart on the hills on each side of the village and five more along the valley floor two hundred yards from the walls. None of the Adren were to get past them. If any horsemen tried to ride through then they were to be captured if possible or killed if they could not be taken.

There would be nothing subtle about the attack on the village itself. They would approach along the riverbank to remain concealed for as long as they could. Cei would lead his warriors through the West Gate and Arthur would take his through the East, both on foot. If possible they were to kill those outside the main hall with their longbows.

Cei suggested that they leave two horsemen further down the slope they were on in case any riders from the village made it past the bowmen. They agreed and Mar'h and Aelfhelm passed among their war bands repeating the plan and allocating positions.

They crossed back over the ridge and followed it for a mile away from the village before starting their descent into the valley. The chosen bowmen split into three groups and left the main body to take their positions. The warriors waited once more, strung along the riverbank kneeling or lying flat, allowing time for the others to reach their places. Eventually Arthur signalled for them to follow as he led the forty warriors towards the village. It took them thirty minutes to reach the point nearest the village walls. Cei took his company along another two hundred yards and as they passed the Wessex warriors the two groups grinned and exchanged good-natured insults, telling each other not to muck things up.

Even in the twilight Arthur could see that there were still no watchers on the walls. He signalled Cei and then crept over the bank's edge and ran crouched over to the village wall where he knelt down. Behind him scrambled his warriors and the Anglians did likewise. They headed for the two opposite gates. Those inside the compound were raucous enough to cover any sounds of their approach and Arthur hoped that they were drunk on the village's stored wine and ale.

Arthur looked at those around him. Mar'h was strapping his shield tightly onto his left arm. Balor was hefting his heavy war axe and itching to get through the gate. Morgund was restraining him with one outstretched hand while in the other was his longbow. Ceinwen already had an arrow strung to her bow and her eyes were flicking between Arthur's face and the gate only feet away.

Her mind had been in turmoil from the moment they had seen the village, her home. At first she had felt sick at the memories that came flooding back. Somehow she had managed to suppress many of the images from that desperate slaughter but seeing the village had brought them all back with a vengeance and she kept seeing Andala being cut down as he reached out shouting for her to go back the way they had come. But the revulsion and fear had slowly given way to blinding anger and now, as she knelt by the gateway, all she wanted was revenge for the blood of her family.

Arthur fitted an arrow to his bow and his hands were completely steady. He looked at Ceinwen and the others, smiled calmly and nodded. He stood up and walked through the gate. The others leapt up and followed, fanning out in a semi-circle as they ran through the entrance.

There were two main groups of Adren, loosely gathered around two fires burning to either side of the main hall. Some of those nearest the East Gate looked across to see who had arrived just as the first flight of arrows tore through them. As those hit went crashing into their companions, the second flight of arrows scythed into them.

Arthur drew the sword given to him at Delbaeth Gofannon for the first time in battle and charged those left standing. Five bowmen remained at the gate, searching for and finding targets to their left and right. The others followed Arthur, sprinting towards the chaos outside the hall. Arthur's sword was sweeping and hacking at the Adren in a blur, flashing red in the firelight. Balor diverted his charge to avoid Arthur's blade and made straight for the hall. He crashed full tilt through the door and sprawled full length exactly where Colban had fallen trying to warn Arthur. Ceinwen and Morgund leapt over him and charged straight into the confused Adren who had been feasting and carousing only moments before. Behind them the others poured into the hall.

As Mar'h passed Balor he leant down and said, 'Don't duck until I tell you to.'

Balor bounced to his feet cursing. Leah was foremost among the Anglians and she ran her spear through the nearest Adren, abandoned it and drew her sword as Cerdic and Aelfhelm overtook her hacking left and right with their swords.

Arthur met Cei by the entrance to the hall, both their swords bloodied, and Arthur grinned at him before walking in. The Adren furthest from the door had recovered and stood before the raised platform of the hall with their curved swords drawn. The slaughter near the door was over and the two sides faced each other. The numbers were about even now. Arthur turned and closed the hall doors slowly. Taking the long plank of wood by the doorway he then slotted it into place, barring the doors shut. The Adren, seeing this, shifted uneasily and snarled at their attackers in a language unknown in Middangeard. Arthur walked through his war band, his sword in his hand and faced the Adren.

'Who is your leader?' he asked.

They threw curses at him and inched forward. An arrow sped from the raised dais straight at Arthur. With almost impossible speed his sword flicked out and swatted it aside. Later the warriors would argue amongst themselves about whether the arrow had shot past Arthur or whether it had been misfired but few would openly admit to what they had witnessed.

Arthur advanced on the Adren and the war band advanced behind him. 'This is not your land. There is nothing for you here in the West,' Arthur said.

Balor could restrain himself no longer and leapt at the Adren, swinging his axe in a wide arc and cutting down two of them as the rest of the warriors crashed into the Adren ranks.

It was over in a minute. The dead and dying lay about the raised dais. 'Ceinwen, see to our wounded. Balor, Morgund – kill theirs,' Arthur said, wiping the blood from his sword.

Cei led the others to search the village for any Adren who had not been in the hall when they attacked. Balor went about his business dispassionately but Arthur saw Morgund hesitating over an Adren who was trying to crawl away from him, trailing blood on the earth of the hall.

Arthur strode across to him. 'Do you think they'd tend your wounds and send you back to us hale and healthy?' Arthur said to him. 'Well? Do you?'

'No, Arthur,' Morgund answered quickly.

Arthur stepped over the crawling Adren and kicked him over onto his back, 'You can kill them slowly,' and Arthur half-thrust his sword into the guts of the mewling soldier and twisted it. 'Or you can kill them quickly,' and he forced the sword through the now screaming Adren's chest, splintering the ribs and slicing into the heart. 'But kill them. It's simple. There's no mercy and no quarter here.' All the while he had been looking at Morgund. 'Now get on with it,' Arthur said and strode from the hall leaving Morgund wiping the back of his hand across his suddenly dry mouth.

Cei had rounded up twelve Adren who had been scattered among the outbuildings when the attack had taken place. Arthur went to inspect the prisoners but there was no captain amongst them.

'Kill them,' he said and turned to go and find Ceinwen. He found her bent over one of their injured who was squirming on the ground, his heels digging grooves in the dirt as he tried with all his strength not to scream. Ceinwen gingerly examined the deep bloody tear across his stomach. She felt oddly removed from the present. Somehow this was no longer her village, it certainly wasn't her home and now that her sudden thirst for revenge had been slaked she felt sickened once again.

Cael gripped the man's arms tightly, urging him to be still for Ceinwen. Arthur put a hand on Ceinwen's shoulder and motioned her to one side.

'How many died?' he asked.

'Four, Arthur.'

'And Sawan?'

Ceinwen looked puzzled until Arthur indicated the man she had been treating. She shook her head, 'He probably won't live. I'll get him some powder to dull his pain.' She made to go but Arthur reached out and held her arm.

'No. We'll need all we have this winter for those who won't die from their wounds,' he said.

Ceinwen searched his eyes and dropped her voice, 'Arthur, you can't let him die gradually in this pain.'

'I won't.'

Ceinwen stared at him in dawning realisation.

'You can't mean... hasn't there been enough death in this village?'

Arthur turned from her and knelt by Sawan. He supported his head and raised him slightly.

'Bid Cael farewell, Sawan, and leave with him any messages you have for your family. You've fought as a warrior in the Wessex war band, we'll not forget that and we won't forget your family. You need have no fear crossing over to the afterlife for you lived and died with honour. Make your peace, I shall return in a minute.'

Arthur left him in Cael's care and went to organise a funeral pyre for their dead. He returned a short while later and gestured for Cael and Ceinwen to leave them. He said a few words to Sawan and stilled his pain-wracked body with a knife to his heart. Wiping his blade on the dead man's sleeve he lifted him up and carried him to the funeral pyre. Ceinwen watched him pass with a stricken look of disbelief.

Arthur ordered the funeral fire to be lit. They stood around the blaze in a circle, watching sparks spiral with the smoke towards the early winter stars.

Cei stepped across to Arthur, 'I haven't seen any remains of the villagers that died here,' he said quietly, making sure Ceinwen was out of earshot.

Arthur nodded and called Mar'h across, 'Take some men and scout around the village – try and find where they burned or buried the villagers. And where's Morveren?'

175

Mar'h pointed to one side of the funeral pyre. Leah had started singing a song for the dead and the other Anglians joined in. Arthur strode across to Morveren. In the flickering light of the flames Arthur could see tears running down her face. He thought they were probably for Talan rather than those who had died here.

'Morveren, go fetch a horse from those guarding the valley and check on the bowmen, see if they've captured anyone. If so, bring them under guard here,' Arthur said.

She wiped the tears away with the back of her hand and left the funeral circle. The death song finished and Arthur raised his voice above the sound of the burning pyre, 'Collect the Adren dead and throw them into the hall. We'll burn it. First cut off each head and stake them in the ground near the gates.'

Some of the warriors looked at each other uncertainly. Cerdic who was standing near Arthur said, 'Is this necessary, Arthur?'

Complete silence fell on the gathered warriors and the pyre seemed to burn more loudly. Arthur stared at the young Cerdic without any emotion on his face at all. Cerdic lowered his eyes to the ground.

Arthur slowly walked up to him and put his face close to Cerdic's, 'Whatever I deem necessary *is* necessary,' he said it quietly so that only Cerdic could hear then added in the same flat tone, 'Do you understand this?'

Cerdic nodded once, still keeping his eyes lowered.

'Good. Then never question my orders again,' Arthur said and turned towards the hall. He swiftly decapitated two Adren corpses, tossed their heads to one side and threw the bodies one after another into the hall. He moved on to the next two and the others joined in. Morgund and Balor went into the hall to carry out the task in there.

'Doesn't like them much does he?' Balor said very quietly once they were inside.

'You have to respect that kind of attitude,' Morgund agreed just as quietly as they went about their work.

'Thought he was going to kill that young idiot just then,' Balor said looking around to make sure they could not be overheard.

'I just hope he hasn't,' Morgund replied.

Balor grunted in agreement and added, 'He'll live but I reckon he's learnt not to question a warlord in a battle mood.'

Mar'h walked past them, ashen faced, towards the doorway looking for Arthur. Balor and Morgund looked at each other puzzled.

Mar'h found Arthur talking to Cei, 'Arthur?' he interrupted them, 'I don't think they burnt or buried the dead, at least not all of them.'

Arthur and Cei looked at him not understanding.

'Come, you'd better see.' Mar'h led them back into the hall and over to the central hearth. He pointed at the embers still glowing brightly. Lying in the ashes and embers were bones. They could clearly see half a hand and the bones of a forearm still attached by burnt muscle and tendons. As they stared at the fire pit it became obvious more of the bones were human. Others started to gather, wondering why their warlords were staring into the remains of the fire.

'What is it, Arthur?' Trevenna said at his elbow. Then she too looked down into the ashes. She stirred them with the point of her sword, uncovering the tiny bones of a child's foot. Her hand shot to her mouth as she realised what she was looking at. They had feasted on the children too.

Mar'h spat to clear his mouth and then pointed to a nearby table and then into the corner of the hall. All around them were the remains of the villagers. The human bones that seemed to lie everywhere were what remained of several days worth of feasting.

Mar'h went outside to get some fresh air and he told the others the appalling fate of the village's children. They stepped inside, disbelieving, to witness for themselves.

Cei held Trevenna as she silently cried for the dead children. Hers were not the only tears. Balor, unwilling to weep openly, began hacking at the Adren corpses in an uncontrolled fury. As his fury spent itself, he sank to his knees, his axe clasped limply on the floor and he stared blankly at the dry earth. The more experienced warriors stared grim-faced at the remains of the villagers; even they hadn't seen anything like this before.

Arthur turned to the nearest corpse, lifted it by its hair and swept its head off. He hurled it at the doorway and it crashed with such force into the doorpost that its skull split half-open. He had already picked up the next and did the same, once more hurling the head with all his might at the doorway. The others watched his cold fury as he methodically hacked the head off each remaining corpse in the hall. He turned to them and only his gray eyes showed the hatred and fury he held inside.

'Get these scum out of the hall. We'll burn it as a pyre for the dead of Branque and leave the filth along the lakeshore for the wolves and ravens.'

He left the hall and the warriors threw the Adren bodies onto carts and hauled them down to the lake edge. Then they set about staking the heads within the gates as Arthur had said. Finally they threw dry bushels inside the hall and set it ablaze. The fire gradually took hold and eventually the flames engulfed the building. Arthur imagined he saw the red haired Caja dancing in the flames and turned away at the memory of her. He looked around for Ceinwen but couldn't see her anywhere nearby. She was sitting down by the lake next to the burnt remains of her family's home. She stared out over the cold, grey lake with unseeing eyes.

Chapter Seven

A rthur left five of the war band to watch the village and slay any messengers or small bands that came into the valley. Meanwhile, the rest of the warriors would watch the roadway from Eald. Eventually the Adren at Eald would send or expect messages from Branque. If any small bands came down the forest road making for Branque then they would be ambushed. They expected a captain would be among them and they hoped to be able capture one. There had been one at Branque but he was shot down as he tried to escape on horseback and had not lived long enough to be interrogated.

As their messengers continually failed to return Arthur hoped the Adren at Eald would send a larger force to investigate. If it were only a hundred strong then they would ambush that too. If it was larger then they would let it pass to Branque and ride to Eald to see if it had been left depleted enough to attack. With any luck such an investigating force would find staked heads at Eald as well as Branque when they returned. It had been obvious from the onslaught at Branque, and the subsequent events there, that the Adren felt no mercy or compassion to those they attacked but Arthur hoped that perhaps they could learn to fear those who attacked them. They would certainly be confused by the attacks and uncertain about the size of the force that was assailing their new outposts. At least they would know that an enemy force was loose amongst them, and perhaps more than one; and that someone was prepared to fight back. Arthur wanted to convince the Adren that they had to find and face him before they could consider crossing the Causeway.

Cei had suggested they take what supplies they would need and could carry from Branque and poison the rest. Merdynn was now working on a tasteless poison for lacing the enemy's stored food supplies.

Arthur posted scouts along the roadway and the rest of the warriors returned to their camp in the forests and waited. At first, those who had remained at the camp were surprised by the subdued atmosphere of the returning warriors. They understood better when they heard about the fate of the Branque villagers and their children.

Merdynn finished his poisons and they were taken to Branque. No one felt any remorse as they poured the liquid over the supplies they had decided not to take themselves. With the Adren feast still on their minds they had wavered over taking the smoked fish and cured meats but practicality overcame their understandable reluctance and they loaded the food onto a cart and took it back with them. Cei sensed they needed a release and assented to four ewers of wine being taken as well. The rest was poisoned and the remainder of Merdynn's liquid was packed away with the recovered supplies.

The wine was greeted with enthusiasm when they returned to the camp. Arthur had wanted to pour it away but Cei persuaded him to put half the company out on scouting duties while the other half celebrated their victory at Branque and then to switch groups at the following main meal. They drew lots, as they did for almost everything, and then fell into the usual haggling and bartering to keep certain groups together. Arthur had wanted to let the Anglians celebrate first, then the Wessex, but once again Cei suggested it would better to treat them all as one war band from now on. He realised that this would more formally make Arthur the warlord of the Anglians but he did not begrudge Arthur that. They were old friends and Arthur was known throughout Britain as Middangeard's foremost warlord so there was little point in pretending otherwise.

As the first round of celebrations got under way, Ceinwen watched Arthur as he moved from group to group, talking and laughing freely. She found it hard to accept it was the same man whom only a short while ago was killing his own wounded, staking the heads of his enemies and who witnessed the horrifying detritus of the Adren feast. She had broached the subject with his sister Trevenna but all she would say on the subject was that Arthur had always done whatever he felt was necessary, without looking for support from those around him and doing so with a certain ruthlessness. She had added unnecessarily that it was extremely unwise to cross him when he was in such a mood.

Ceinwen found herself increasingly alone again. She knew that part of the reason was simply that the warriors all had their own duties to carry out and that every single one of them took those responsibilities extremely seriously whether it was patrolling, preparing food or just collecting water but she suspected she knew the real reason – she had known those at Branque, they had been her friends, her neighbours and even her family, and no one knew quite what to say to her or how to approach her. They brought her food and spoke briefly to her but for the most part they kept their distance and Ceinwen was left to her own sickening thoughts.

She realised she wasn't the only one to have been so affected by the recent events; the warriors around had changed, or at least their attitudes had, since their attack on Branque. The war band had, without realising it, accepted in their minds that they were now at war. They were not dealing with Green Isle or Uathach raiding parties or even Uathach villages who were, after all, of the same people as those in Wessex, Anglia or Mercia. The Uathach might not have had the same order of counsellors, chieftains or a king, and they certainly lived without laws, but they had never perpetrated what the Adren had done.

The Uathach would raid, kill and enslave where they could and do so brutally but they had never senselessly slaughtered or resorted to cannibalism as the Adren had done. Until now, the worst crime had been the Uathach's capturing of children but they had never murdered them. Children were simply too precious. No, the war band was realising this was a war against another race. A war unlike any they had ever waged, where there was no right or wrong, just victory or absolute defeat. There was no place for mercy or compassion, just a ruthless determination to win no matter what the cost and Ceinwen had to admit to herself that Arthur had seen this even as early as when he dragged her from the hall at Branque. Ceinwen realised that if the Adren were prepared to kill their enemy's young then the cost of victory, no matter how high, was still cheaper than defeat because defeat meant losing absolutely everything. She became aware of the gloomy dark of the forest around her and suddenly she felt the need for the closeness of companions and she joined the group by the fire.

Mar'h smiled at her as she sat down with them. They had been laughing while Balor, red faced, was still blustering into his wine. She looked enquiringly at their faces to be let in on the joke.

'Balor...' Morgund tried to explain and doubled up with renewed laughter.

'When Balor hit the doors... of the hall...' Cael's attempt failed too as he subsided into a silent, wheezing laughing fit.

Ceinwen sat back on her heels and poured herself a beaker full of wine and drained it in one go. She realised she had some catching up to do.

'Flat on his face!' Morgund got out between gulps of breath and Mar'h and Cael fell into another fit of laughing taking Morgund with them. Ceinwen put the dark thoughts from her mind and forced herself to join in. She reached across and patted Balor on the shoulder, 'The doors were asking for it, Balor.' She comforted him and Morgund literally held his sides as he tried to stop laughing and start breathing.

'Don't you bloody start girl, bad enough with these idiots,' Balor said but he could not restrain himself from grinning sheepishly and moments later his bellowing, infectious laugh filled the hollow.

' 'Don't duck yet'...!' It was no good. Mar'h just could not get a whole sentence out without relapsing into helpless laughter. Balor threw his head back and roared with him.

'You really told him not to duck yet?' Ceinwen asked incredulously. Judging by the renewed seizure of laughter she guessed that Mar'h had. She refilled her beaker of wine and grinning at them, poured more into their beakers.

'What's the joke over there?' Tomas called from a group across the hollow.

'Balor's brave attack on the hall and how the doors sneakily tripped him at the crucial moment!' Morgund managed to reply before being drowned out again by Balor's resurfaced laughter.

Morveren, who was sitting with Tomas and Elowen, smiled for the first time since Talan had died on the attack on the Westway. With Balor's laughter filling the hollow it was impossible not to.

Elowen jumped at the chance to keep her distracted from her grief and said, 'Did you see him? It must have given the Adren a nasty shock, Balor smashing through the doors and crashing flat on his face cursing to the heavens.'

'Surprised he didn't get up, apologise and then sidle out through sheer embarrassment,' Tomas said chuckling to himself.

'He's taking it well – for Balor,' Morveren said.

'Yes, he either walks off in a huff or brings the place down with his laugh,' Elowen said, trying to keep Morveren talking.

'It's a great laugh though.' Tomas smiled as another round of laughter burst out from across the hollow.

'Shall we join them?' Elowen said, selfishly hoping they could leave the dispirited Morveren with them allowing Tomas and her to go and find a quieter place together. She justified it to herself that Morveren needed laughter at the moment. They crossed the hollow and sat with the others.

'Sane company, thank the gods,' Ceinwen said.

'We thought we might give you old ones a hand with the wine,' Tomas said, his handsome face and blue eyes smiling at them and much to Elowen's annoyance he poured himself a full mug of wine.

Balor wrapped an arm around Morveren's shoulders and started to extol his other exploits of the battle.

Ceinwen leant closer to Elowen and said quietly, 'Where's Ethain? He's not out scouting is he?'

Elowen shrugged, angry and frustrated that her own plans had not worked out.

'Elowen?' Ceinwen asked again.

'Oh, I think I saw him over there a while back,' she gestured vaguely with her hand.

'Thanks,' Ceinwen said, meaning the opposite and letting her know it by the tone of her voice. She got up and wandered towards Arthur's tent just as he climbed out.

'I suppose you haven't seen Ethain have you?' she asked him without catching his eyes.

'No, I've been resting. Have you seen Merdynn?'

'No, he's not by the fire.'

'Not much help to each other are we?' Arthur said and smiled at her as she finally looked at him. She could not bring herself to smile back and stood there awkwardly.

'If you see Merdynn?'

'And tell Ethain if you see him,' she answered and they parted.

Arthur went to the fire and picked up some roasted meat. Balor was sitting with his back to him and Arthur heard his name being spoken. He listened to Balor speaking.

'I had to charge them, thought he was going to talk them to death.' Balor had drunk a lot of wine and did not notice the others trying to attract his attention. He continued his explanation, 'I'd only used my axe on the door up 'til then so I had to...' he realised the others were looking behind him rather than at him. He turned and jumped when he saw Arthur standing a few yards behind him. He quickly took his arm from Morveren as some deeply ingrained sense of self-preservation sent an urgent reminder of the rumour concerning Morveren's parentage to his befuddled brain.

'Arthur! I was...' he faltered, flustered, then in his drunken haze thought he saw a way out, 'I never doubted you could talk them to death, like...' It dawned on him that he was not making things better and stopped.

'I'd just assumed you'd let loose another of your noisome fumes and were just leaping to get away from it,' Arthur replied straight-faced.

Morgund and Mar'h burst out laughing again.

'We should have used you to poison the food Balor, who needs Merdynn's potions when we have your arse?' Tomas added to more laughter.

Arthur tossed the leg of meat he was holding to Balor, who caught it chuckling, and walked off to find Merdynn. He found him feeding his pony.

'Why is it you ride a pony Merdynn when you could have the best horse in the land?' Arthur asked.

'Troubling you is it?' Merdynn replied without turning, 'We're in the midst of Adren armies, alone in the Shadow Lands with half your war band drunk and winter knocking on the door and your real concern is why I should choose to ride a pony?'

'Yes.'

Merdynn laughed and turned to face Arthur, 'Very well. I always have. Always. Others may choose fine beasts but a pony's always done for me. Now, what are you really concerned about?'

'What if the Adren don't send messages back and forth. Perhaps they have no contact with each other for weeks?'

'Then we're in for a very dull winter.'

Arthur rubbed the back of his neck, 'I should send a raiding party to Eald to stir them into life. Then they'll wish to contact Branque.'

'That should do the trick.'

'Yes, probably.'

'Good. Glad that's decided then,' Merdynn returned to feeding his pony with the carrot he held in his hand.

'But then they'll be aware of us when they come down the roadway. It'll make an ambush harder,' Arthur continued.

'True. Difficult one.'

'For someone fabled for their wisdom you aren't giving much advice Merdynn.'

'And that would be wise would it? Giving Advice?'

'What good is wisdom if not shared?'

'Very well, you want some sound advice? Stop your men drinking. Where do you think you are? Deep in Wessex?'

Arthur was surprised by Merdynn's obvious and sudden anger.

'They're just celebrating a victory.'

'Against a handful of surprised Adren drunk on wine and flesh. Such a great victory, surely we can all go home now?'

'They know it for what it is, Merdynn, and they're just trying to forget what they saw.'

'They shouldn't forget it. Ever.'

'Of course they won't but Cei's right, they need to dull the pain of it until they can accept what happened.'

Merdynn sighed and his anger left him. 'For what it's worth I'd wait a few days longer before you consider raiding Eald. You're right. Surprise is your only advantage out here. But you can't wait longer in case an attack is being planned on the Causeway elsewhere. It's a question of balance, of knowing the moment. You'll know when it is time.'

So Arthur waited and gradually the sunlight left the East. The skies above the forest canopy turned from pale turquoise to dark blue and the winter stars grew brighter and more numerous, strung through the branches and boughs above them. When they awoke after the first round of celebrations the heavy-headed and red-eyed warriors sat outside their tents with their breath pluming in clouds before them as they struggled into their thick winter gear. Many of them were already binding long strips of cloth around their feet and lower legs in preparation for the coming cold before pulling on their leather and deerskin boots. The ground was lightly frosted, and even the roots that spread out from the trees, like arteries jutting from the forest floor, were rimed white. The frost would be much deeper away from the protective cover of the forest and even here the leaves from the oak or birch trees, interspersed among the pines, already lay brittle and crisp underfoot.

The second round of celebrations got underway and still nothing travelled on the roadway between Eald and Branque. Arthur rode from group to group and then back again, silently wondering if his plan was flawed. A low blanket of clouds spread from the West and it started to snow lightly, sending flakes swirling around those gathered close about the fire recounting their tales from Branque. The snow settled briefly on cloaks and tents but it was not heavy enough to cover the forest floor. It seemed to stay suspended in the air between the trees, first drifting one way then blown another, getting into eyes and finding its way into unsecured tents. It made it difficult for the scouts and those on watch and they inched closer to the paths and roads they were guarding, afraid to miss those they sought in the gloom and swirling snow. The first tentative fingers of winter had begun to feel their way eastward, laying claim to the land that the sun had abandoned.

Arthur watched from the edge of the hollow as the second celebrations ended and the drunken warriors stumbled into their tents. Although he had wanted to pour the wine away rather than have the two halves of his company drunk consecutively, he did not begrudge them their release. They had done well at Branque. He knew that the Adren were surprised and drunk themselves at the time yet they had still outnumbered his warriors two to one. They had lost five people in the attack. His war band considered that a good exchange given the odds. He thought differently. Their numbers were few and if they lost five people in each engagement then it would not be long before no one was left. They just could not afford to be involved in pitched battles if they were to last the winter and get back across the Causeway.

It had not stopped snowing but neither had it become any heavier. Snow still swirled in slow eddies around the hollow, threatening to settle before being lifted off the frosted ground once again by the light wind that found its way through the forest.

Arthur absently rubbed his hands together, his fingers numbing in the cold air. The skin on his face felt tight, drawn by the early winter temperatures. He felt rather than heard the beat of hooves on the frozen earth and a horse tethered beyond the hollow neighed a loud greeting to its approaching companion. Arthur stood up quickly and realised his legs had stiffened in the cold too. Massaging his injured leg, he limped towards the rider who was speeding between the trees towards the hollow. It was Morveren. She jumped down from her horse that slid to a stop on the frozen ground, tossing its head and sending clouds of breath streaming from its nostrils. She looked around for Arthur and saw him limping towards her.

'Arthur! Five riders have just passed heading to Branque.'

'Who's following them?'

'Mar'h and Morgund are shadowing them.'

'Ride to the lookouts above Branque, tell them I'm going straight to the village and to meet me in the valley after the riders have passed.'

Morveren leapt effortlessly back onto her horse and brought it sharply around before charging off again. Arthur mounted his far less gracefully and made for the roadway at half of Morveren's pace, carefully picking his way between the trees in the half-darkness. Once he reached the broad forest trail to Branque he picked up his speed and galloped after the riders who were already some way ahead of him. He felt elated that the waiting was over, the stiffness in his leg was forgotten and he no longer felt the cold wind as it whipped around his face.

When he reached the valley floor where the road left the forest and turned to Branque he drew his horse up. The contrasting figures of Mar'h and Morgund appeared out of the darkness to his right.

'They're just approaching the village ahead,' Mar'h said.

'Good. I want to catch them off their horses,' Arthur replied and spurred his horse on to the village. Morgund pointed to the slope to their right, three riders were approaching fast. He recognised Balor's form bouncing in one saddle and the more elegant riding of Ceinwen and Morveren beside him. They met at the ford and went crashing straight across it, sending ice-cold water fountaining from under their horses' hooves.

The five riders ahead had already dismounted and were standing at the gateway staring at the staked heads before them when they heard the horses approaching.

Arthur and the others flung themselves from their horses and drew their weapons. There were four Adren and one of their captains at the gateway.

They recovered from the double shock quickly. One of the Adren reached quickly for the bow slung on the horse beside him, Balor rushed forward and threw his axe at him. It spun end over end and the head of the blade thudded into the Adren's face as he strung an arrow. He went sprawling and Balor stopped in his tracks, realising he had thrown his only weapon as Arthur and the others stepped beyond him. The other three Adren had formed a protective ring around their captain and the two groups faced each other only twenty-feet apart.

'Leave their captain to me,' Arthur said and they advanced on the enemy.

What happened next surprised them. Despite being outnumbered the three remaining Adren charged at them, shields raised and curved swords poised to slash down, while the captain sprinted for his horse. Arthur dashed to intercept him while the others met the charge. The captain reached his horse and bounded onto its back, digging his heels in to send it clear of the melee. Arthur dived full length, swinging his sword round in a wide arc and catching one of the horse's hind legs. The horse buckled under the captain and he leapt off, bringing his sword down on Arthur who was still on the ground. Arthur rolled beyond its reach and scrambled to his feet, his sword held before him. The Adren Captain cursed at Arthur and lunged forward aiming at his stomach. Arthur turned the blade and back swept at the captain's helmeted head. He ducked just in time. The captain feigned a thrust at Arthur's face then changed it to a low sweep, trying to cut Arthur's legs from under him. Arthur stepped back from the sweep and then leapt forward bringing his own sword down on the captain's outstretched arm, severing it at the elbow. He stared at his dismembered arm as Arthur brought the flat of his sword clattering back into the side of the captain's head.

Arthur looked around for the others. The Adren were dead but Mar'h was down on one knee cursing, holding his shield arm. Ceinwen was running towards her saddlebags. The other three were breathing hard but seemed unhurt.

'Morgund! Give me a hand here!' Arthur called out. Kneeling, he cut the reins from the struggling horse then killed it. He tied the leather strips as tight as possible round the captain's upper arm.

'Get his legs,' he said to Morgund and together they carried him inside the compound and into the nearest building.

'Bring me some water,' Arthur said.

Arthur propped the captain sitting up in a corner, his head hanging lifelessly, unconscious. Morgund returned with a skin of water and moved to take the silver helmet of the captain's head.

'Leave us,' Arthur said and Morgund closed the door behind him and returned to find out how Mar'h was.

Mar'h was still cursing through gritted teeth as Ceinwen wrapped his arm tightly in bandages. Morveren was looking on concerned, wanting to help but at the same time not wanting to get in Ceinwen's way. Balor had retrieved his axe and was adding to the staked array inside the compound.

'How is it, Mar'h?' Morgund asked.

Mar'h swore in reply.

'Cut deeply but it should heal,' Ceinwen answered for him.

'Same arm,' Morgund said rather obviously.

'Bloody shield slipped and the bastard's sword slid up it into my bloody arm,' Mar'h spat out as Ceinwen strapped his arm to his chest.

Screams tore through the cold air, coming from the compound. Balor, striding out of the gates with his axe hoisted over his shoulder, turned at the sound of them and shaking his head walked back to his companions.

'What's the point of torturing one of them for information when they don't speak in the same tongue?' Morgund asked the others. They shrugged as the screams came again.

'Bastards deserve it,' Mar'h said, his face still screwed up in pain.

'True enough,' Balor said.

The screams suddenly stopped and moments later Arthur came striding out of the gates towards them.

'Can you ride, Mar'h?' Arthur asked. Ceinwen noted how drawn his face was.

'Yes. Don't know how fast though,' he answered.

'You want that captain's head staked too?' Balor said indicating back towards the village.

'Yes. Put it at the front and keep the helmet on. It will be more easily recognised,' Arthur replied and Balor sauntered back into the compound.

Arthur and Morgund helped Mar'h into his saddle. Morveren led Balor's horse back to the gate for him. They rode slowly back up the slope with Arthur some way ahead.

Balor was unusually quiet as he rode beside Ceinwen.

'Still sure that captain deserved torturing?' Ceinwen said, misreading his silence.

Balor looked at her, 'Not a mark on him – except his arm of course. He wasn't even dead. I could see his eyes through the slits in his helmet and I've seen nothing like it before. Just staring in terror and twitching uncontrollably. Like he'd lost his mind,' Balor said and made the sign to ward off evil.

Ceinwen frowned at him. Balor was not known to be superstitious.

'You didn't bloody see him,' he said and pulled his horse away from her.

When they arrived back at the camp Arthur sent fresh scouts and guards out even though he knew it would be some time before the Adren Captain was missed. The snow was falling more heavily from the dark sky and beginning to settle on the outspread pine branches.

Arthur walked away from the hollow where most of the war band had retired to their tents after hearing the news of the brief skirmish and the capture of the Adren Captain. The forest became quiet as Arthur left the camp behind. He could almost hear the snow settling on the unseen branches above him. The darkness would be complete before long and travelling through the forests would become painstakingly slow. His head shot up as an owl hooted off to his right somewhere. An answering call sounded nearer to him and they traded calls for a minute before falling silent.

'We're not the only ones hunting in the forests of the Shadow Lands.'

Arthur turned to find Merdynn emerging from the shadows between the trees. He was wrapped in his brown cloak and the hood kept the snow from his eyes. 'You captured some Adren?'

'Yes, one of their captains.'

'Ah, an Adren Captain. And what did you learn from him?' Merdynn asked.

Arthur leant against a tree and ran a hand through his bedraggled hair, dislodging the snow that had already began to settle there.

'He was Cithol – as we suspected. I had to force read him and even then I only got scattered information. Nevertheless I saw enough, thousands upon thousands of Adren. Armies camped all along the coastline, waiting. And yet more coming west. I saw a broad, straight road that stretched mile after mile running deep into the East and endless trains of carts and wains bringing foods and supplies from the East to feed these armies,' Arthur stopped and hung his head.

'Did you see anything of the Veiled City?' Merdynn asked stepping closer to Arthur.

'Yes. I had to break his mind to do it but I did see. They want the Veiled City intact and they want to destroy everything else in Middangeard. They want all the peoples of the West dead. And I don't see how they can be stopped.'

Merdynn leaned heavily on his staff, 'Much as we feared then.'

'Can any of this be untrue?' Arthur asked.

'I can't help you there, Arthur, you were the one who saw. Can it be untrue?'

'No. No, it can't,' Arthur answered and stared at Merdynn.

'Don't despair, Arthur. We can yet hope.'

'What for? We have one hundred and fifty warriors. Three hundred with the king's men. Even if I had the time to train those who have gone west I would only have at the most two or three thousand. I had no idea of the size of their armies. Tens of thousands of soldiers...'

'You would abandon Wessex, Britain, its peoples, the land? You would abandon Fin Seren and the Veiled City?'

Arthur looked up at Merdynn when he mentioned Seren.

'You know?' he asked with resignation.

'There's little that passes under sun or moon in Middangeard that I do not know.'

'I will not abandon any of them. But I see no way to defend them either.'

'The hour is dark indeed.'

'Could it get any darker?'

'Oh yes. It can always get darker,' Merdynn replied brightly.

'Gods,' muttered Arthur and started pacing across the thin layer of snow covering the ground. He looked again at Merdynn who watched

191

him, 'If they come across the Causeway in those numbers we'll never hold them.'

Arthur strode back and forth with growing despair, as he desperately tried to think of any way to stop what he felt was going to be inevitable. 'If we can hold them long enough to arm the peoples of Britain. Until mid-summer. Delay them.'

Merdynn watched Arthur as he cast about hoping to find a plan or stratagem that might save his land. He sighed deeply, feeling the years weighing heavily upon him. Since talking to Lord Venning he had thought long on the possibility of what both he and Arthur now knew to be true. He could only think of one road that held any hope but he could not yet speak of it to Arthur. It was a road he had to choose for himself. And even that path held little or no hope. He faded back into the darkness of the forest leaving Arthur to pace the shadows alone in the falling snow.

The days passed and darkness settled on the land. Merdynn had left the group without speaking to anyone but Arthur was unconcerned by his absence. Merdynn came and went at his own bidding but Arthur knew he would be where he was needed. He divided the war band into three sections, alternating between watching the roadway, scouting the forests and resting back at the camp. Those watching the road were posted further up towards Eald in order to give the greatest possible warning of an approaching force sent to investigate the silence from Branque. They watched and waited with the snow persistently falling from the unseen clouds in the blackness above them. The company waited in a state of nervous boredom with nothing to do other than anticipate either the coming ambush or the race to Eald through the dark forest depending on how large the Adren force was. Scouts were sent out as pathfinders to discover the best route north and they were glad for something to occupy themselves with.

Mar'h and Aelfhelm discussed the best site for an ambush and how best to execute it. They honed the plan as they sat around the fire and dreamt about it as they slept until they could make it no more effective and no simpler. Few spoke to Arthur during this time. He had become preoccupied and inaccessible, walking the dark forests and rarely seeming to sleep. Gradually Ceinwen and the others gave up trying to engage him in conversation, he would answer their questions tersely and seemed to resent the intrusion upon whatever thoughts occupied him. He would only spend any length of time with Cei and even then it seemed to be mostly spent in silence. They thought it was the idle waiting that irritated him as it irritated most of the warriors.

A scouting party was dispatched to get as close to Eald as possible to try to determine the strength of the enemy there. The news they came back with was far from encouraging. They could not get close enough to the village without risking being detected but their best guess was that there must be over a thousand Adren camped in and around the village.

The warriors, with little else to do, digested this news and discussed how that might affect Arthur and Cei's plans. It seemed unlikely that the Adren would send any more than two hundred to investigate Branque, leaving over eight hundred still at Eald. Even split, their forces were too numerous to attack.

Balor bore the waiting worse than any among either the Wessex or Anglians and his mood became more sullen as time wore uneventfully on. He was in favour of an all out attack and the others thanked the gods he was not the one in charge and did not hesitate to point out to him that was why he was not the warlord.

Mar'h's arm was healing, thanks largely to Ceinwen's solicitous care and Morgund was fashioning him a leather gauntlet which he could securely strap his shield to in order to prevent the same kind of slip that could easily have cost him his arm. The brief skirmish with the Adren Captain's guard had revised their opinion of the fighting capabilities of the Adren, which they had previously and inaccurately based on their raid upon Branque. They were not as dangerous individually as Uathach raiders but they had a ferocity and a complete disregard for their own lives that made the warriors reconsider their fighting styles. If faced with two Adren, one seemed quite prepared to attack blindly if it gave the other an opportunity to press home an attack. They did not seem to care if they died and this was something new to the Britons.

Word finally came back to the camp that the Adren were moving down the roadway. They were still a day's journey away and they came in numbers. There were three hundred of them in an ordered column with an advance guard riding a mile ahead of the main body. The moon should have lit the forests in a pale light but the heavy snow clouds still lay overhead and the land was dark.

The hollow sprang into life. Tents were taken down and all the surplus gear was packed onto the wains, which immediately began their journey north through the forests, paralleling the road. Groups melted into the darkness as they made their way to the ambush point.

Arthur led thirty through the forest towards the advancing Adren and positioned them five yards apart from one another on a bank overlooking the road. Cei took the same number and set up on the opposite bank. Once again they waited.

Although the long wait had been frustrating, they had put the time to good use. Their plan was to divide the Adren column into two halves with felled trees. At two separate points on the roadway and to either side, deep notches had been cut into the trees. Blocks of wood had been hammered into these notches as supports. When half the Adren column had passed the first point these blocks would be knocked out and axes would quickly deepen the cuts. Ropes had been attached to the trees to make sure that they toppled in the direction they had been cut. If the plan worked then there would be a line of felled trees across the roadway and on into the forest on both sides of the road. Arthur hoped that this would divide the Adren force into two and prevent the front half of the column from turning on the raiders.

At the same time trees would be sent crashing across the rear of the enemy line. The raiders would be flanked by the Britons on either side of the roadway and caught between the two obstructions. In the few minutes of confusion that would follow, they would send hundreds of arrows into the trapped portion of the Adren force then race for their horses that would be waiting for them well beyond the felled trees at the rear of the Adren column.

Arthur wanted the whole ambush to only last a minute or two and he hoped with so many arrows firing down into the confined width of the roadway that most of the second half of the column would be annihilated. The barrier of trees, the suddenness of the ambush, the darkness and the confusion should prevent the first half of the column coming to the aid of the trapped Adren in time.

Everyone knew what they had to do and they waited, checking the strings on their longbows, laying out the arrows for rapid firing or checking the blocks of wood and guy ropes on the pre-cut trees.

Osla peered into the darkness trying to see back up the roadway. He was a young warrior in the Anglian spear riders and this was his first battle. Much to his disgust he had been placed on duty guarding the camp when his friends had gone off to attack Branque. He had complained bitterly to Roswitha, one of the more experienced Anglian warriors, and she had patiently borne his ranting and told him his time would come; there would be more than enough Adren for her younger friend. She had been quickly proved right and now his time had come. He could not decide if he was more nervous or excited but whichever it was he could not stop his knee from trembling as he squatted in the snow. He glanced sideways to Leah. She was securing her shield across her back. She wanted some protection if she had to turn her back to the enemy. Osla had left his shield strapped to his horse and regretted the oversight now. Looking to his other side he saw Herewulf doing the same.

'Why didn't you tell me to bring my shield?' Osla hissed at him.

Aelfhelm came out of the darkness behind him and told him to be quiet, he would know to take his shield next time.

'If you get a next time, lad,' Herewulf said softly once Aelfhelm had moved on.

Osla glared at Herewulf who grinned back. Leah was drawing her full longbow repeatedly, keeping her arms warm as the snow continued to swirl around them.

Aelfhelm came back down the line, 'Remember, five arrows only. Pick your target, fire and move on to the next. Don't be tempted to fire more or stay longer.' As he said this last bit he rested a hand on Osla's shoulder.

'What's Arthur's aim? Sting them? Why don't we charge who's left once we've fired the arrows?' Osla said across to Leah.

'You do as Aelfhelm says. There'll be one hundred and fifty Adren crashing through those barriers as soon as they fall. We won't have long,' she answered.

'Arthur's just trying to keep you alive, lad,' Herewulf added from his other side.

Aelfhelm came striding back towards them, 'Do I have to gag you fools? I said *quiet*. We'll hear them before we see them but only if you shut up.'

They spoke no more. Each of them strained their eyes in the darkness and tried to listen above the sound of their own hammering hearts.

Trevenna waited by the first barricade of trees with Cei who was hefting his war axe, readying for the swing that would knock out the supporting block of wood from the tree trunk. He looked across at Trevenna.

'Just make sure you run the right side of the tree,' he said quietly to her. She was to haul on the rope that was to make sure the tree fell the way it was cut and intended to fall. Running the wrong way would put her on the Adren side of the barricade. She smiled back to Cei and jokingly pointed the wrong way for confirmation. Cei shook his head vigorously before seeing her smile broaden. He went back to hefting his heavy war axe, his hands sweating despite the cold. They had tested what they were about to do a few days ago, deeper into the forest and it had worked well. It did not put his mind at rest though. If this barrier did not work they would be in a lot of trouble. He hoped it would not go wrong here or on the other side where some of Arthur's band were to do the same.

Suddenly the waiting was over. They heard the muffled sound of marching feet and the soft creaking of armour. The head of the column was right below them. There had hardly been any warning at all. Cei tried to count them as they passed slightly below, wondering where the advance guard was and if they could have possibly missed them. He quelled his rising excitement and prepared himself to guess when the right moment was.

He stepped away from the tree and nodded towards Trevenna who took the slack up on the rope. With a mighty swing he sent the supporting block flying back into the forest and immediately swung the blade back into the deep groove to finish the task. The tree groaned under its own weight as Trevenna and two others hauled on the rope putting their whole strength and bodyweight into it. The tree splintered and cracked deafeningly and slowly began to topple over before crashing into the next pre-cut tree. The forest was suddenly alive with the cacophony of falling trees. Screams and curses erupted from the roadway as the column was divided into two.

Leah was cursing that they had not lit the forest road somehow. It was not easy to pick out individual targets but they could tell where the Adren ranks were and they loosed their arrows into them. Then they were up and running madly for the rear of the column.

When they reached the second barricade at the rear of the Adren column they paused and fired five more arrows each into the milling ranks below them and once more sprinted along the bank. Once clear of the barricade they jumped down the embankment and sprinted back up the roadway the Adren had just come down. From the opposite bank Arthur's band were doing the same and they laughed wildly as the groups met and ran together towards their horses.

Ahead, Leah could hear Arthur shouting out different groups' names to see they were there and then sending them galloping off up the roadway.

She reached the horses and heard Arthur roar out, 'Aelfhelm!'

Aelfhelm looked around, counting his band off before replying, 'We're here, Arthur!'

Arthur flung his arm out to point up the road and Aelfhelm's group galloped off.

When all the groups had left Arthur took one last look around, only Morveren and Cei were with him. He grinned at them and tore off after the others. He sent Morveren off to get ahead of the others and make sure no one missed the point where they were to turn off into the forest.

A few miles up the road Arthur and Cei came to the turning point. Morveren moved out of the shadows.

'Everyone through?' Arthur asked.

'Yes.'

'Anyone missing? Did we lose anyone?' he asked and even through the billowing clouds of his horse's breath he could see Morveren's white teeth grinning in the darkness.

'All safe, Arthur.'

Cei thumped him on the shoulder in celebration. He wheeled his horse around once more but there was still no sign of pursuit. They led their horses off the roadway and into the forest.

Ceinwen came out of the trees and started to erase the tracks leading into the forest. There was not a great deal she could do other than shovel snow over their tracks and hope the still falling snow would bury the evidence of their passing before anyone else reached here.

Ceinwen led them on to where the others were gathered some miles into the forest. Cheers erupted when Arthur and Cei emerged into the clearing, restrained in their volume but not their passion. No one had any clear idea how many Adren they had killed and they all realised that they could have killed more if they had stayed longer but they had attacked a force four or five times greater than their own and not suffered a single loss. The plan had worked and it had worked well enough.

Rope was passed down the line and secured to each saddle so that no one would go astray. They made their way in single file, walking their horses through the darkness of the forest. They were heading for a high hill to the South of Eald and they followed the scouts who had already travelled this way.

Their spirits were high despite the cold, wet snow that settled on their cloaks and steamed from their horses' flanks. Their hushed talk was lively and full of hope despite being so far from home. None of them would remember it as such but this was the last time they journeyed together with such hope.

Chapter Eight

Their camp on the wooded hill was well chosen by the scouts, secluded and far enough away from Eald to be beyond any Adren patrols. During their ascent they had come across an opening in the forest that afforded them a view down into Eald. There was no unusual or hurried activity and they considered risking a charge right through the heart of the Adren camp before any news of the attack on the road to Branque reached the Adren. Arthur had eventually discounted the idea, not only was the risk of losses too high but it would only serve to show the enemy how small their force was.

Once they had made camp, Arthur went back down to the viewpoint with Cei, Aelfhelm and Mar'h. Ceinwen joined them at Arthur's request as she was more familiar with Eald and the surrounding country than anyone else was. The snow had stopped, leaving a light covering on the cold forest floor and they made their way slowly and with caution down to the wide ledge. The clouds above them were breaking up and they drifted like heavy smoke across the waxing moon sending their shadows gliding over the pale winter landscape below.

Eald lay below them and about a mile or so distant. The forest had been cleared all around the village by previous generations for their crop fields and pastureland for their stock. Ceinwen had been at the village not that long ago but it was now almost unrecognisable to her. More of the forest had been cleared and from their elevation it looked as if the whole area was one large camp. Hundreds of small fires dotted the fields around the village, adding points of colour to a world cast in the grey shades of winter. Eald itself seemed dwarfed by the army camped around it.

Aelfhelm stirred from his position and said, 'We were wrong. There's more than a thousand camped down there.'

'Say there's ten to each fire. Four, five-hundred fires?' Cei said.

'That's just not possible. How can they feed an army that size? That's half the size of Caer Sulis at the Gathering.' Ceinwen was incredulous at the scene below.

'Well, we know where their army's camped,' Aelfhelm said.

Arthur shook his head slowly and said, 'This is only part of their army.'

Cei rested his forehead on the snow-crusted ground. The other two stared at Arthur.

'There's more than this?' Aelfhelm finally asked.

Arthur nodded in reply, still studying the valley below.

'We're only a few hundred strong, at best. How can we fight them all?' Ceinwen asked.

'We don't,' Arthur replied then fell silent.

Cei raised his head and turned to look at the other two, 'We need to delay them until the tribes return from the West. We need to arm and train the peoples for war. We need time. If we can't fight them all then we'll fight them band by band and group by group, never staying long in one place and never engaging in open battle. Ambush after ambush, just like earlier.'

'We could fight them like that for a hundred years before we bring the numbers even,' Aelfhelm pointed out.

'If that is what it takes then that is what we will do,' Arthur replied and they fell silent once more.

After some time they noticed sudden activity in the valley. News of the ambush on the road to Branque had reached the camp.

They were about to draw back into the forest when Cei pointed and said, 'What's that line to the North of the village?'

'Where?' Aelfhelm asked trying to follow the line of Cei's outstretched hand.

'Through the trees, about two miles beyond the village. Looks like a river cutting through the forest but it's straight,' he replied.

'Looks like there's fire burning down there too,' Aelfhelm added.

'It's the roadway east. There must be hundreds travelling on it - and carrying torches,' Ceinwen said quietly.

They lay on the ledge as the snow melted under them and watched as the light from distant torches advanced along the straight line that cut through the forests.

'Then that must be the East Road that Merdynn and Lord Venning spoke of. It must be the roadway that eventually leads to the Shadow Land City. Their supplies and armies must all come down that road,' Arthur said, thinking about the thousands of miles between where they were and the second Cithol city.

They studied the distant line that cut through the forests and Aelfhelm pointed out a faint glow several miles behind the first one they had spotted.

'If we could block that roadway and prevent the supplies reaching their forces...' Cei said, thinking aloud.

'But against those numbers? How?' Ceinwen asked.

'Even if we could choke their supply lines, wouldn't that just force them to come across the Causeway sooner?' Aelfhelm ventured.

The others nodded and considered this. Arthur was lost in thought and did not notice them looking at him.

'Arthur?' Cei said.

Arthur rubbed his hands across his face and got up on one knee, 'We'll need a camp deeper in the forests. Much deeper. Fifty miles or more and preferably on the North side of the East Road. This whole area will become patrolled soon. The supply columns will be heavily protected this close to their base so we'll have to hit them much further up the roadway. We'll take an hour's rest here then take a wide sweep to cross the East Road. Let the others know.'

They stood up to return to the camp but Arthur called Cei back and they talked on the ledge overlooking Eald while the others rested. Below them they could see the torches of the patrols as they fanned out from the encampment, looking for the raiders loose amongst them.

They set off in darkness without waiting for the clouds to clear. It would be a slower journey but they wanted to put some distance between themselves and the Adren camp before the moon was unveiled and lit their passing in what was now a hostile land. They left behind the carts that had accompanied them so far, loading onto the ponies as much as they could carry.

The war band's ebullience had been sobered by the sight of so many of the enemy in the Valley of Eald. As they made their way through the dark forests under a cold, cloudy sky they felt alone and far from home and each was conscious that every step was taking them further away.

After some hours they reached the East Road and waited while scouts were sent to check for signs of the enemy. The trees that had been cleared lay discarded on either side of the roadway. They were recently felled and the sight of such an undertaking only served to heighten the overwhelming feeling that they were but a small band in the land of a numerous enemy; an enemy that could cut straight roads through miles of forest in order to supply the forces that were now arrayed against Britain.

The scent of pine was thick in the sharp air and Ethain, with his head resting on one of the felled trees, was just drifting into a dream when Ceinwen came back announcing the road was clear. He heaved himself to his feet and leading his horse, trudged through a gap in the trees behind Elowen. As he crossed the wide forest track he did not bother looking right or left as the others automatically did. Nor did he hurry across. He was exhausted. He had not slept much at any of their rests since their raid on Branque. If he slept he dreamt of the Adren who had been about to skewer him with his curved sword before Tomas had swiped him aside. He had frozen when faced by the black-armoured Adren and were it not for Tomas he would have died with that curved sword in his stomach. It was the second time he had faced the Adren, the first time it had been Balor who had saved him.

He thought about the aftermath of the recent battle and how he had watched from a distance as Sawan had writhed on the earth at Branque, scrabbling on his back in the dirt desperate to escape his agony. Ethain did not want to die and he certainly didn't want to die like that. He had no hope that he would be returning to Britain, he just hoped that when he died it would be quick and he would not know much about it.

He would have been glad to suffer the shame of asking to return home but he knew that neither Arthur nor Cei would permit it. Even if he asked and even if they let him he did not think he would survive the journey home alone. He was desperate not to let his friends down, particularly Morveren, Tomas and Elowen but he feared that if the worst happened he would probably stand helplessly by and just watch it unfold, unable to intervene or come to their aid.

He had no idea why they were still heading north and deeper into the Adren held land. He found it hard to believe they were going to the Belgae villages still. He felt sure everyone there had been slaughtered too and probably cannibalised just as those at Branque and Eald had been. His despair deepened and cut its own rut through his soul as his doubts and fears circled themselves, driving the ruts deeper until they could turn neither left nor right and settled instead upon each other in suffocating confirmation. He stared blindly ahead, lifelessly following in Elowen's footsteps. Even Balor's enthusiasm had cooled and set to a bloody-minded determination for what lay ahead. He walked by his horse, silently cursing the tree roots and fallen branches that conspired to entangle his cold feet. The clouds had begun to shred and the intermittently revealed moon sent shafts of pale light through the forest canopy but it illuminated little and only seemed to add further shadows to their path.

Arthur had sent Trevenna and Ceinwen ahead with Cael to prepare a cauldron of hot broth, which they handed out as the warriors went slowly past them. Trevenna alone seemed impervious to the doubts that were sinking steadily into the war band like the creep of winter cold. Her cheerful talk and the hot soup raised their spirits temporarily as they continued north, ever deeper into the forest.

Behind them Trevenna and Ceinwen packed up the cauldron and covered the remnants of the small fire. Ceinwen had been quietly studying Trevenna as the warriors paused to take their hot drink. She wondered again at the difference between Arthur his sister. Her cheerfulness was infectious and never seemed to be forced. No matter what the circumstances she acted as if she was entirely happy and confident in her surroundings and that confidence spread to those she talked with. Strangely the same complete confidence emanated from Arthur but without the cheerfulness or ready smile. His was more forceful and more purposeful.

It was hard to doubt Arthur but Ceinwen had been shaken by the cold way he had ended Sawan's suffering. In fact, many things about Arthur jarred with her memories of him as a young man. She wondered if the years as the Wessex Warlord had entirely stripped away from him the qualities that had once attracted her so, yet, on the other hand, there had seemed to be a closeness, almost a tenderness, between him and the Cithol girl, Seren. She remained undecided but she had to acknowledge that she was more wary of Arthur now than she had ever been before.

She involuntarily thought about the Adren Captain they had captured and the look on Balor's face after he had executed him. She asked herself if there had been any trace of cruelty in the Arthur she had once known and couldn't think of a single example of such a trait. She felt sickened that she could even be thinking of Arthur as cruel after what had happened to the people of her village. She quickly pushed the thought away before the questions returned about the fate of her own family.

As she packed away the bowls they had used for the food, it dawned on Ceinwen that Arthur could no longer make decisions based on individuals. Having seen down into the Valley of Eald she now truly realised for the first time that the fate of Middangeard hung on the balance of Arthur's decisions.

She realised Trevenna was waiting for her. Together they left the small clearing and joined the back of the column as it continued its journey north. Twenty hours after crossing the East Road they finally made camp.

Even though they were deep in the forest and far from Eald, Arthur still posted sentries around the camp. Those not on guard duty set about unloading their horses and the ponies. A small glade between the trees was cleared of brambles and fern and the large tent was erected using cut branches as holding poles and guy ropes were slung around tree trunks at each corner. It was big enough to sleep forty in marginal comfort but it was generally used to provide a place in which to gather and eat, sheltered from the winter harshness. Its greatest benefit was that a fire could be lit inside providing warmth and heated food without the usual dangers of a fire being seen from afar. The Wessex warriors had used it each winter for many years and the inside had become smoke-blackened and it reeked of countless cooked meals. The walls were patched and roughly sewn where innumerable tears stood testament to its years of service.

Smaller tents sprang up like mushrooms between the trees around the main marquee where soon the only permitted fire was lit inside. The familiar mechanisms of the camp fell into place. Water was collected from the nearby small stream, still unfrozen but ice cold. Latrines were dug a hundred yards downhill from the camp. Food and stores were unpacked and an inventory taken of supplies, particularly the amount of arrows they still carried. Much of this would have been Llud's responsibility but since his death on the Westway, Morgund had taken over most of this organisation. Once the essentials were completed and a meal had been taken, they crawled into their tents and slept while those on guard tried not to.

Only the howling of wolves troubled the guards and that was distant. Aelfhelm tirelessly patrolled the camp's perimeter, keeping the guards awake and allaying their concerns about unexplained movements in the strange forest and settling their tired nerves which were starting to fray with the unfamiliar and unearthly cry of the wolves baying across distant forest valleys. When the first watch was replaced by more rested warriors then Aelfhelm too retired and he immediately fell asleep.

Once everyone had rested and eaten again, Arthur called them all together in the main tent and they discussed what they had seen in the Valley of Eald and on the East Road. They talked of the best way to delay the Adren onslaught on the Causeway without precipitating it. They weighed what advantages they had and how best they could use them.

Arthur kept silent, except to prompt someone's opinion, and let everyone say what they thought was best to be done. As each stratagem was put forward and then countered he sat with head bowed, listening closely to what the warriors were saying and how they said it. Every view and plan was considered and argued, and even those plans with little merit were given time and talked through.

Finally everyone who wanted to speak had spoken and the warriors who were crowded around the fire went quiet. No one looked at Arthur but they waited for him to speak. After a minute he looked up at the faces in the flickering firelight.

'If courage, honour and skill in battle were enough then I'd gladly lead you in a glorious charge into the Valley of Eald and tear out the heart of the enemy before they put a foot on the Causeway.'

Some cheered lustily at this, Balor and Cerdic loudest among them, others kept their silence waiting.

'If we were outnumbered five or ten to one, still I would go to battle with the Adren and think our chances of success good.'

More cheered at this, claiming victory was assured, shouting for battle. Some still kept their peace and watched Arthur.

'Even if it meant that each of us would die. As long as it meant utter defeat for the Adren and that Britain were safe then that is a price any of us would pay.'

They clamoured it would be worth the price and those who were silent nodded agreement.

'No one doubts the courage of any warrior here. No one doubts the battle skill of any warrior here. No one doubts the heart of anyone here.'

Everyone bellowed agreement.

'It isn't enough,' Arthur said and the noise died quickly.

'We are less than eighty warriors. They number eight thousand or more and that's just from what we've seen. Balor, Cerdic, any of you, no one doubts you would stand before a hundred Adren each.'

Balor and Cerdic loudly claimed they would.

'Yet would you win? For if you didn't then nothing stands between the enemy and Britain. Even if you slew ninety before falling you would have failed and Britain would be lost.'

Cerdic looked at his hands and Balor's bluster trailed into silence.

'When we have a thousand or more to their ten-thousand then I'll face them in open battle at a time and place of my choosing but I will not throw Britain and its peoples to the Adren by casting aside our lives in a battle we cannot yet win.

'No. We will fight the enemy on our terms, not theirs. We'll fight where we choose to fight, not where they choose. If we have to we'll kill them all one by one.

'Nowhere will be safe for them, whether on the roadway, on patrol or in their camps. They will come to realise death is only moments away. They will come to fear the forest and the unseen enemy it harbours.

'And we'll show them the mercy they showed Eald and Branque.

'None.

'We'll travel the East Road and raid their supply columns. We'll slow their preparations for crossing the Causeway until the summer and when they do come to Britain we'll be there waiting for them with every man, woman and child armed, trained and prepared to defend their land with their lives. And each will count for more than twenty of the enemy who live to cross the Causeway.

'Every day they'll pay in blood for coming to Middangeard. Every step they take on the Causeway will cost them dearer and if they take a breath on our shores it'll be their last.

'And it will start now. Death will stalk their tracks and silently take them. We'll teach them what it is to know fear and what it is to know despair. Together we will make a tale that will last forever!'

None stayed silent, they roared their approval, and they yelled out their battle cries, swearing to defend Britain to the death and cursing the Adren for the flesh-eating cowards they thought they were.

Arthur divided them into seven groups of ten and gave each one an area to raid over the next month. Each group had an experienced warrior appointed as leader and they collected the supplies they would need. They were all to make their way back to this camp by the next full moon.

They went their separate ways with boasts of who would kill the most and cries of good fortune and good hunting. They were to carry out lightning raids and ambushes. To kill as many of the enemy as possible but never to be drawn into battle against heavier odds and, most importantly of all, to come back alive for without the Wessex and Anglian war bands, Britain would surely fall.

So it was that over the following days and weeks, under the winter sky and in the dark forests, the Adren were attacked time and again. Scouting parties did not report back and patrols sent to investigate would later find staked heads fixed on the roadway. Camps were raided and guards left dead. Supply columns were ambushed in rapid attacks. Arrows flew out of the darkness from the warriors' longbows claiming captains or taking down the beasts used to haul carts. When the Adren charged into the forests after their attackers they found spiked traps waiting for them and their assailants gone. Bands of a hundred or more Adren were sent into the forests to hunt down the raiders but became the hunted instead.

Gradually the camps became better guarded and the columns turned to small armies inching back and forth along the leagues of the East Road. The raids slowed and became less effective as the Adren adapted to the new hostile environment.

Then the snows came out of the West and fell heavily across the forest, ladening the trees and weighing their branches downwards to the deep blanket layered on the forest floor. The snow drifted, restlessly looking to fill hollows and gulleys where icy streams froze from their surface downwards and only the swiftest remained free to run their course a while longer.

Thick low clouds covered the heavens denying the stars and moon to the land below. Deprived of light and bound under snow the land became still, held fast by the deepening cold.

The Adren camps waited, no longer sending scouts or patrols out after the raiders. The supply columns slowed to a crawl as they dug their way along the East Road. In the forests the raiders and the wolves watched for rare opportunities to strike.

Then one by one the bands turned to feel their way, landmark by landmark, back to the main camp. First they, and then the snow, had accomplished what Arthur had wanted. The Adren were no longer free to move in the land. They were tied to fortified camps and the supplies for their campaign across the Causeway had slowed to a crawl and then ceased altogether.

Arthur's band was the last to return to the camp for they had taken the longer journey to the Belgae villages. The news they brought back with them was as expected but none the less grievous for being so. Although no sign was found of the Anglians who had been there, many among Cei's spear riders now mourned the warriors and friends whom they accepted as lost.

They listened stoically to the news that another Adren host was camped at the main Belgae village. The reports from the other bands all confirmed that the Adren were in Middangeard in vast numbers and that those numbers had been growing before the snow had stilled the land.

During the weeks of raiding they had lost another seven warriors. Four were lost from one band alone when they had the misfortune to run straight into a large Adren patrol while fleeing a hunting party. Despite these losses they all regarded the campaign as a success. They had harried the Adren across an area of two hundred miles and slowed their preparations for invasion. The tallies of Adren dead were totted up and Arthur privately halved the number, not that he thought his warriors were lying or boasting but he knew that not every arrow found its mark and not every wound inflicted proved to be fatal. Even so, the numbers of Adren killed were high and would have been cause for celebration had it not been for the sheer scale of the numbers they still had to face.

As Arthur's band took their place by the fire they recounted their news from the Belgae villages. There had been no sign that the Adren were building boats or ships to sail across the sea and so bypass the marshes. Even though Arthur had maintained that a sea crossing was unlikely he was nonetheless relieved to confirm that the Adren must be planning their attack along the Causeway.

Leah, who, much to Morgund's chagrin, had been selected to be with Arthur's band, discovered the longboats that the Anglians had used to cross the sea and with which they planned to take the Belgae villagers back to Britain for the Gathering. The boats had not been found by the Adren who had not known anything about them or their planned use. So Arthur's band had moved the boats one by one to a more secluded beach and covered them as best as they could.

As they sat and stood around the fire they discussed whether they should use the boats to send their horses back to Britain and return with further supplies. Their stock of arrows was particularly low. A winter crossing in the longboats was not a prospect that appealed to the Wessex warriors. Even the large ships that sailed from the Haven struggled in heavy winter seas.

Whether they sent all or some of their horses back Arthur wanted the longboats safely hidden in case the route back to the Causeway was no longer possible. The boats could prove to be their only hope of returning to Britain in the spring.

The question of whether or not to send back their horses was a vexing one. They were hardy beasts and used to the deprivations of winter travelling but now that the heavy snows of winter had fallen it might be quicker for the warriors to move through the land without their horses. It would be easier to stable and feed them back at the camps in Britain too. Against this was the need for their horses once the snows melted in spring. Certainly without them they could not hope to reach the Causeway and cross it without having to fight their way through the Adren hordes.

Cei maintained that it would not be a problem for the Anglians to man the longboats in spring and take both the warriors and their horses back across the seas. They had done this many times in ferrying the Belgae to Britain for the Gathering.

They left it undecided for the time being and Arthur's band trudged tiredly to their tents, wrapped themselves in their furs and slept soundly for the first time in weeks.

They woke to the sound of hammering. Morgund had begun work on constructing a basic wooden shelter that would provide a covered place for both themselves and their horses.

Arthur crawled out of his tent and pressed a handful of snow on his face to take the sleep from his eyes. The moon shone down from clear skies and he could see several people using axes to cut and strip branches. Wiping the snow from his beard he walked across to them.

'Thought we could use a shelter if we're staying here for a while,' Morgund said as he approached.

Arthur nodded in approval.

'He's not a craftsman, that's certain. Next heavy snowfall and this whole thing will collapse,' Mar'h said as he passed by carrying a bundle of branches.

'Sorry for the noise but we thought you'd all slept enough and there's a guest waiting for you,' Morgund said to Arthur. Arthur raised his eyebrows and Morgund nodded towards the main tent.

Arthur strode across and entered to find Merdynn hunched by the fire warming his hands. He raised his old eyes and stared at Arthur over the fire, rubbing his hands together slowly above the flames. Arthur dunked a mug into the nearby barrel of water and sat down next to him. One of the warriors came into the tent dragging a makeshift sledge of snow and began packing it into another barrel placed by the fire.

'I'm too old to be travelling in winter,' Merdynn finally said.

'Did you have trouble finding us?' asked Arthur.

Merdynn shook his head slowly and splayed his hands before the fire.

'Adren patrols?' Arthur questioned as he sat opposite Merdynn.

'Surprisingly few. You must have scared them into staying in their camps.'

'Good and they won't be re-supplied now until the spring frees the East Road.'

'The Belgae?' Merdynn asked.

'There's an Adren army camped there.'

Merdynn sighed and took his eyes from Arthur, gazing instead at his age worn hands.

'Have you decided yet which course to take, Arthur?'

'Yes.' Arthur looked around the tent. Morveren was the only other person inside. She was sitting to one side, her long, dark hair falling across her thin face as she cut arrows from a collection of trimmed branches. Her face was pale and dark smudges lay below her eyes in light bruises. She looked older.

'Morveren, find Cei and bring him here,' he said to her.

She got lightly to her feet and pulled her thick sheepskin cloak around herself before leaving the tent. Arthur and Merdynn sat in silence with their thoughts. Minutes passed before Cei came in and threw his cloak to one side.

'Merdynn! Good to see you so far from home,' he said and poured himself a hot drink from the pan by the fire. Cupping his hands around the beaker he sat and looked from Merdynn to Arthur.

'No one has talked much of the numbers of Adren we've seen over the last few weeks,' Arthur stated.

The silence engulfed them again and Cei drank from his mug.

Eventually Arthur continued, 'There must be as many Adren here as there are people in the three tribes. Twenty thousand or more. And the East Road will bring more come spring.'

'Even if we prepare the people for war...' Cei said and shook his head.

'It won't be enough,' Arthur finished for him.

'No, it won't. They're stout hearted,' and Cei nodded to those outside, 'but they've realised they can't defeat an army that size.'

'Not by battle alone. So we have to defeat them another way.' Arthur said.

'How?' Cei asked, fearing the answer.

Arthur rubbed his hands up and down his face and looked directly at his friend of so many years.

'Their food supplies?' Cei asked.

'Yes. It takes a lot to feed an army that size.'

'Attack their supply columns?' Cei asked again.

'That won't be enough,' Arthur answered, reluctant to explain further.

'So, you plan to do as we discussed?'

'The Shadow Land City. Like the Cithol, they have some ancient magic, some ancient power. It's why they can produce enough food to feed such an army. It's why they want the Veiled City,' Arthur replied.

'And if the Shadow Land City or the source of their power could be destroyed then there would be no more supplies,' Merdynn finished. 'If we can keep the Adren from crossing the Causeway long enough. Keep them from the Veiled City. Keep them from the stores we have in Britain,' Cei said and Arthur nodded.

The silence returned and each stared into the fire between them. Merdynn absently added a log onto it and used his staff to push it further into the heart of the fire. The entrance to the tent opened and Leah and Ceinwen came in laughing. When Leah saw the three by the fire and their distant looks she clutched Ceinwen by the arm and motioned for them both to retrace their steps back out of the tent.

The interruption stirred Cei into life, 'If we can't raise an army large enough to defend Britain, how can we raise two? One to defend the Causeway and one to attack this Shadow Land City?'

'We can't raise an army large enough to defend the Causeway against these numbers. And we can't raise another army to march east.'

'This doesn't sound too promising,' Cei said and smiled.

'Dark days...' Merdynn began.

'Bring dark choices,' Cei finished.

'Whatever army we can raise will have to defend Britain from the Adren onslaught. Those that go east will be few in number and will go in secret,' Arthur said.

'And I am to lead them.' Cei looked at the other two. Arthur nodded.

'Where am I to lead them to?' Cei asked.

'I've been consulting with Lord Venning and his lore keepers,' Merdynn said.

'And?' Cei asked.

'And, well, we're not entirely sure,' Merdynn said, shifting uncomfortably.

Cei raised an eyebrow.

Merdynn started to suck on a piece of dried beef that he had been thawing by the fire before saying, 'We have some ancient maps, writings and so on. I haven't been there for a long, long time but I'm fairly confident it lies on the Kara More, somewhere beyond the Middle Sea, if memory serves.' He nodded to himself as if the matter was explained.

'Oh, there. Well, that's not so far then,' Cei said.

'Merdynn will go with you. He'll remember more as he travels the road,' Arthur added.

'I'm not sure that will be a great help. How many do you think should go?' Cei replied.

'Twenty, thirty at the most. Merdynn, unroll your maps and let's see what we have to face.'

The three of them settled to one side of the fire and examined the copies of the maps that Merdynn had brought with him from the Veiled City. They reckoned the distance to be two thousand miles. Neither Arthur nor Cei had any idea of what might lie along those miles. Only Merdynn had travelled that far into the East and then many years ago.

Arthur grew more heavy-hearted as they discussed what might be the best route to take. He had previously decided that his place was defending Britain but he wavered as he considered the prospect of sending Cei and the others on such a journey across so many unknowns. Even if they got to the Shadow Land City they had no idea what to expect there or indeed if it would be possible to enter and destroy whatever the Adren were using to underpin their invasion.

Cei appeared to be taking the task with a considered pragmatism but as they talked Arthur realised with increasing certainty what a desperate venture it was. When he weighed the matter coldly he knew twenty more warriors defending the Causeway or the Veiled City would make little difference and if this journey had even the remotest chance of success then it had to be gambled. But it felt like he was asking Cei, Trevenna and the others to take on an impossible task and die unsung and far from home somewhere deep in the Shadow Lands.

Yet Arthur knew they could not hold back the massed Adren ranks forever. Their only chance was to hold them long enough for Cei to choke their supplies and if Cei failed then they too must surely fail and then there would be no one left to sing of either tale.

Never far from his thoughts were the questions of the king and what his unknown plans were. He would not be able to gather the tribes for war unless the king gave his consent. There was much that was still uncertain in Britain and Arthur knew he could not lead a company east without knowing his land was in safe hands. He did not trust the king's hands.

He silently considered once again whether it would be better to keep Cei and Merdynn for the defence of Britain. Both would count for much in persuading the king and the council to do what was necessary. Yet he could trust no one else with such an undertaking. It seemed to him that each choice was ill-fated. The Adren numbers were too great to be able to hold off indefinitely, all they could do was hold on long enough for Cei and Merdynn to succeed and then deny the Adren the harvests of Britain. It was their only hope and it had some small chance of success as long as the Adren did not know that a company was going east.

Arthur said this to Cei and Merdynn and the three of them talked about who should know of this undertaking and who need not. The more people who knew of the plan, the greater the risk of someone being captured and the information coming into enemy hands.

Arthur did not want to keep the truth from the war band but Merdynn convinced him that too much relied upon their mission remaining undetected. So they decided that those who were going would be initially told that the aim was to travel deep into the east to attack the Adren supply columns in spring. Once on their journey the true nature of their purpose would be revealed. Only a few among those that remained would know the truth of why their friends had gone east.

Arthur was not comfortable with this plan but Merdynn's point was undeniable. To tell those remaining would be to endanger the venture even further, and to tell those going east the truth from the start would be to risk them telling the others. Cei did not feel he could ask people to volunteer for a purpose that was being hid from them. Arthur agreed and they decided instead to choose the members of the eastbound company.

To Merdynn's growing impatience they found it difficult to decide which of the warriors to send on what seemed such an impossible task. Cei wanted to select most from the Anglians but baulked at the thought that he might be consigning each one to a death far from home. Finally Arthur rose cursing and strode from the tent to call all the others together.

News had spread among the warriors that Merdynn was back and was deep in conversation with Arthur and Cei. They were not surprised when Arthur shouted out for them to all gather in the main tent. Most were working on the rough wooden shelter that Morgund had been organising and they had been doing so in high good humour. Few of them had much skill working with wood and it was beginning to tell. They dropped what they were doing and made their way expectantly to the tent where Arthur was holding open the canvas entrance, looking at each one as they passed on inside. Only a few did not meet his eye, among them Ethain and Ceinwen.

Once they were inside, standing or sitting as best they could in the cramped space, Arthur addressed them.

'We've all seen or heard how many Adren are camped on these coasts and what that means for Britain. We are too few to stand against them and defeat them. We've decided,' and Arthur gestured to Cei and Merdynn, 'to divide this company into two.

'One, under me, to harry the Adren here before sailing back to Britain and raising an army with which to hold the enemy.

'One, under Cei, to go into the East and do whatever is possible to stop their supplies reaching the main army. Merdynn has knowledge and maps to help with this and he will travel with Cei.

'You've all lived together and fought bravely together yet it would only be right for you to follow your own warlord on the path they have chosen. No doubt all the Anglians here would want to follow Cei eastward yet it is also right for you to defend your own land against the enemy when the time comes.'

Cei stood up and addressed the warriors, 'Only sixteen will come east with Merdynn and I. The way will be long and the chances are that few who start upon this road will return back down it for there are many dangers and it takes us far from home. Who would choose the East Road and who would choose to aid Hengest at the Causeway?'

In the clamouring that followed it was decided that among those to go with Cei and Merdynn would be Trevenna, Leah, Cerdic, Herewulf and Aelfhelm as Cei's second-in-command.

Much to Ceinwen's surprise, Ethain argued to go with Cei, pointing out that his eyesight was better than most and that it might prove an advantage for them. Cei had agreed.

They had one last meal together where long orations and extravagant boasts were swapped between the two companies. Balor and Cerdic exchanged ever increasingly unlikely stories, talking and laughing in the face of the fear they both felt but could not express. Tomas and Elowen spent the time talking to a distracted Ethain. Neither Morgund nor Leah were in the marquee and it was a testament to their subtlety that no one had noticed when they had left or if they had left together. Arthur sat with

Ceinwen, Merdynn, Cei and Trevenna and they spoke of times they had shared in a past that now seemed trouble free and golden.

When they had finished their meal, and when Morgund had reappeared to divide out the supplies the two groups would need, it came time to part. Arthur stopped Trevenna as she was leaving the tent and slipped the Elk Stone from around his neck. After a moment's hesitation he offered it to her and she took it and studied it with a smile.

'It's beautiful. Where did you get it, Arthur?'

'It's supposed to offer good fortune for the wearer,' he replied.

Trevenna waited for a further explanation and when none was forthcoming she looped it around her neck and tucked it under her tunic. 'I'll bring it back to you,' she said, still smiling at her brother. On her way out she caught Ceinwen's eye and raised her eyebrows at Arthur's uncharacteristic gesture and its significance. There had been some idle speculation about where the pendant had come from. Arthur was not known to wear the ostentatious torques or rings that some of the warriors favoured. Trevenna remembered hearing Ceinwen say that someone in the Veiled City must have presented it to him as a gift. Morgund was wagering heavily that it had been the Cithol Lord's daughter, Fin Seren. No one had yet asked Arthur.

The two bands stood outside the tent in the small glade under the moonlight which cast the forest in cold hues of blue. The farewell was quiet and Arthur took Merdynn to one side, 'Look after them Merdynn. Bring them back,' he said with a quiet intensity.

'I will do what I can, as you must Arthur. If it is possible then I will send you some token of whether or not we have succeeded.' Merdynn shook Arthur's hand before adding, 'It's been a long time Arthur, fare well.'

Merdynn donned a sheepskin cap with thick earflaps hanging loosely to either side. He patted it down once, smiled at Arthur and turned to lead his pony along the line of warriors who were impatient to be away. Arthur felt a dread finality in that parting and looked for Cei and Trevenna along the line waiting to begin their journey through the snowed forest. Trevenna was smiling at him and Cei raised a hand in farewell and they too turned and headed off into the darkness.

Chapter Nine

In the days that followed Morgund quietly resumed work on the ramshackle shelter that they had started. He didn't think they would be there long enough to make much use of it but the alternative was to dwell on those who had departed for the East.

The camp was quieter now, more subdued. The warriors who remained went about their business in silence and any conversations that were held were short and spoken in undertones.

The skies remained clear and the land froze deeply under the innumerable stars of winter. Everyone spent as much time as they could in the main tent as close as possible to the fire and the warmth it offered. Ice and snow were continually melted over the fire to provide water and even the food had to be laid out around the hearth to thaw.

Those on duty outside were wrapped in their sheepskin cloaks and wore their fur gloves and caps and still they froze. Sentries paced between the trees attempting to keep warm, deepening pathways in the snow as their breath trailed behind them and hung in wreathed clouds in the cold, still air.

Morgund watched Cael as he made his way along the line of horses now tethered in the makeshift shelter. He was doling out feed before the horses and those he had not yet got to were becoming increasingly restless. Cael nodded to Morgund as he passed him.

'How are they, Cael?'

'Well enough but they need exercising soon. They'll not go too hungry at least,' Cael answered.

'Worried the same isn't true for us?'

Cael patted his belly, made even more bulky by the layers of clothing, 'Laugh now, Morgund. If we run out of food, I'll last longer than any of you.'

'Perhaps, but you'll be a prime captive for the Adren. Keep them fed for a week.'

'You shouldn't joke about that,' Cael replied and strode off towards the main tent, leaving the feedbag on the ground.

Morgund shrugged, not too concerned by Cael taking umbrage at his remark, and picked up the feed to continue down the line of horses. Ceinwen joined him a few minutes later.

'Need any help?' she asked.

'No. Just finishing off feeding them.'

'Just bumped into Cael - he hasn't got much good to say of you.'

Morgund turned his pale eyes towards her and smiled, 'He can't take a joke,' he said and started to move once more along the line.

'Maybe Sawan's death has taken away his sense of humour,' she replied tersely.

'He doesn't seem to be the only one in an ill-humour.'

'What do you mean by that?'

'You didn't seem too keen on Arthur releasing him.'

'Arthur killing him you mean?'

Morgund stopped once more and put down the feedbag. 'Sawan was a dead man anyway. Arthur just put him out of his agony. I hope he'd do the same for me if it came to it. You're not a warrior so I can understand how you feel but you are a healer, so you should understand that Arthur was just making it easier for him.'

'That's right, Morgund, I am a healer but I'm not an executioner.'

Morgund sighed, 'Well, think what you like, Ceinwen, but if I'm lying there with my guts sliced open I hope Arthur gets to me quickly.'

'I'll be sure to point the way,' Ceinwen replied and left the shelter.

'Who needs the Adren?' Morgund said to the horse in front of him. He continued along the row of impatient horses and as he neared the end, two figures darted from behind the stalls. He started and dropped the feedbag, reaching for his sword before recognising it was Tomas and Elowen.

'Gods! Is there nowhere to be alone?' Elowen spat at him as she fastened her cloak about herself. Tomas smiled and shrugged apologetically as he let the smaller Elowen drag him away by the hand.

Morgund closed his eyes, ran both hands up and down his face and took a deep breath. He finished feeding the horses and made his way back to the main tent, careful not to slip on the snow which the constant treading had compacted to ice.

He saw Arthur and Mar'h talking outside the entrance and joined them. 'Whatever I say next isn't meant to get either of you angry,' he said.

'Been making friends again have you?' Mar'h asked smiling.

'Only with the horses. Everyone else just seems to get angry.'

'It's time we moved. Staying here with the others gone is just making everyone restless,' Arthur said.

'Home?' Mar'h asked.

Arthur folded his arms and nodded, 'Yes, but we'll go via the Belgae villages and pay the Adren camp a visit. Then we'll take the longboats back across the sea.'

Mar'h and Morgund exchanged uneasy glances.

'Don't worry, the Anglians know how to handle them,' Arthur said.

Neither Mar'h nor Morgund looked reassured.

The atmosphere in the camp changed immediately once they heard that they were moving north towards the Belgae villages. Morgund decided he would pull down part of the newly built shelter and fashion sledges from the cut timber. It would be a quicker way for their horses to carry their stores across the snow and it would save burdening them further. Morgund found he had no shortage of willing hands to help build the sledges.

They set out under a winter sky dappled with slow clouds drifting across from the West. Ceinwen was some way ahead, picking the best route through the darkness while behind her teams led groups of horses reined two abreast through the deep snows that carpeted the forest floor. After a mile or so the front team would stand aside, let the others pass, and then rejoin at the rear so passing the hard work of forging a path onto the next team in line.

At the back of the column were the rest of the warriors with several horses pulling the sledges laden with their supplies. The going here was much easier as the horses in front of them had ploughed a path through the snows. Some of the warriors even took off their snowshoes, which resembled small-latticed baskets with one central ridge that could be used to slide across hard snow or ice. Arthur had posted flanking scouts but they found that making their way alone through the snow was too difficult and they inevitably fell behind the column. Rather than risk being lost in the darkness they abandoned the attempt and word was passed that everyone needed to be on their guard for they journeyed blindly.

They stopped every ten hours or so for a few hours rest and to take a main meal. No fires were lit and they had to pick at food that was half-frozen. They were half-frozen themselves despite the layers of bulky clothing that they wore and even the horses had cloaks and blankets fastened over their backs in an attempt to keep the heat in.

They continually packed snow into their leather water bottles and tucked them under their sheepskin cloaks to melt enough to provide a mouthful of water. They wrapped woollen strips under their close-fitting sheepskin caps and around their faces leaving only a narrow gap across their eyes and they gazed blankly at the ground immediately before them as they trudged wearily through the snow-drifted glades of a forest that seemed to stretch on forever in the winter night. They would have made an easy target to ambush but they were only a band of fifty and in the frozen expanse of a dark, empty landscape they travelled the miles unseen and unnoticed.

The days passed with long trudging journeys and short-lived breaks that were intended more to rest the horses than the warriors. Finally Arthur called a halt. As the others set up the main tent and unloaded supplies he left with Ceinwen and Morgund and scouted through the forests to the West. They were fifteen miles from the Belgae villages where an Adren army had settled for the winter. Arthur had been here before with his raiding party and knew enough of the terrain to get them close enough to observe the camp.

Under the pale starlight they surveyed the Adren positions from the edge of the forest. Unlike Eald and Branque the land here was flat. Before them stretched a plain of cultivated land where the forest had been cleared many hundreds of years ago. Three villages were set along the river that meandered widely across the long stretch of cleared land. Snow lay in depth on fields that would go to fallow in the summer to come and, now that the Belgae were gone, the forest would gradually, year by year, reclaim the land as its own once more.

The Adren camp stretched across all three villages and covered nearly all the ten-mile length of the plain. Their fires and shelters were spaced out and roughly followed the winding river that was now frozen over.

Morgund shook his head in disbelief, 'There must be ten to fifteen-thousand of them out there.'

'I've never seen so many people, not even at Gathering,' Ceinwen said softly.

'Certainly explains why none of Cei's lads made it back,' Morgund added.

'We need to find where they keep their stores,' Arthur said and he started to make his way through the trees that fringed the plain. The crescent moon cast the colourless expanse before them in a cold light. The nearest shelters and fires were set back a mile or so from the surrounding forest, a lesson learnt after Arthur's raids. They could pick out some movement along the line of the river but most of the elongated camp was still. Every now and then they would stop and silently study the camp, hoping to see one area busier than elsewhere, a central storage point.

It was at one of these stops that Ceinwen noticed some tracks leading back into the forest and, crouched over, she followed them some way off into the trees. She returned and frowning, squatted down beside them.

'What is it?' Arthur asked.

'I'm not sure but I don't think they're Adren tracks. They come up to this point, about four or five people, then turn and go back on themselves. Surely Adren tracks would come or go to the camp?'

'A patrol?' Morgund suggested.

'Perhaps, but strange for the same reasons. Was your raiding party here, Arthur?' Ceinwen asked.

'No. We worked our way round to the other side of the plain.'

'I'd like to follow them further,' Ceinwen said looking back into the forest.

'We need to find their supply centre,' Arthur said. He turned back to study the camp once more and Morgund did likewise.

'It could be that the tracks were left by some of Cei's men,' Ceinwen pointed out.

Arthur looked directly at her. If there was any chance that some of Cei's men survived then he would have to explore the possibility. He got up and looked at the tracks himself but knew that Ceinwen could read them better than he could ever hope to.

'Are you sure they aren't Adren?' he asked her. To him they just looked like a confused trampling in the snow.

'As sure as I can be. The people who left these tracks were taller for one.'

'Their captains perhaps?' Morgund asked.

Ceinwen shrugged and looked to Arthur who eventually nodded his assent. They unslung their bows and fished out the bowstrings that were kept inside their clothing to stop them freezing. They fitted them with difficulty, Morgund bending Ceinwen's shorter bow while she set the string. Ceinwen led the way, following the tracks in the broken moonlight that fell in shafts through the tall trees. Arthur and Morgund fitted arrows to their longbows and strained their eyes searching through the darkness in front and to the sides of them, ignoring the tracks and following Ceinwen. Occasionally Ceinwen would lose the trail and scout ahead, scanning the ground until she found the signs that would lead them on. The arced moon shadowed their path as they slowly made their way deeper into the forest. Arthur was about to call a halt when Ceinwen suddenly stopped in front of them, dropping to one knee and signalling the other two to do the same.

Three hundred yards ahead of them they could see a glow from a fire. They would have seen it from much further away but for the moonlight that cast the forest in winter light. They waited, watching for any movement and listening for any sound but they were too far away to see or hear anything of what lay ahead. Still they waited motionless trying to detect any sign or presence of guards.

Ceinwen looked to Arthur who silently signalled her forward. As she crept forward twenty yards the other two drew their bows and searched the forest ahead of her. There was plenty of cover and plenty of shadows in which a guard could be concealed.

They repeated the advance with first Morgund then Arthur joining Ceinwen. Slowly they drew closer until they could see the fire itself. Bivouacs and crude shelters circled it. Several figures were sat or slumped around the fire and none of them were moving. They were not Adren.

Arthur looked at the other two. Ceinwen shrugged and Morgund shook his head. They drew closer together.

'Belgae?' Morgund suggested quietly.

'I don't think so, they look more like warriors than villagers,' Ceinwen whispered.

'I think they're Uathach but what they're doing here...' Arthur left the question unfinished.

'Whoever they are, there's a lot more of them than us. We can come back with the war band and then ask them who they are,' Morgund said and made to move back the way they had come.

Arthur stopped him and said, 'No. We'll find out now. They don't look like there's much life left in them. We'll get closer then I'll walk into the camp while you two cover me with your longbows.'

'Arthur, there could be twenty or thirty of them there,' Morgund pointed out.

'Then you'd better cover me well and shoot quickly if it comes to it.' Arthur started to slowly make his way towards the fire ahead.

Morgund exchanged a glance with Ceinwen and swearing softly, followed Arthur. They divided to either side of him, twenty yards apart and stopped at the edge of the clearing as Arthur strode towards the fire at the heart of the clearing.

No one looked up or noticed that a stranger stood by the fire. There were twelve people sat or slumped by the low burning wood, others lay still in their bivouacs or in the crude shelter of lashed together branches. Still no one looked up at the figure that had approached the fire.

Arthur studied them. They were bundled in layers of clothing but the cloaks and clothes they wore were not fit for travelling in the long, cold night of winter. They looked gaunt and starved, each isolated in their own exhausted torpor. Arthur saw a shield half buried in the snow, and on it the Uathach device of the black bear. He recognised it as the emblem of Ablach's tribe. Their territory was to the North of Anglia and for many years they had proved a thorn in Cei's side. They were known for their swift and brutal raids along the Anglian coast. The sight of their sails and the sound of their oars had struck fear into the hearts of villages along the shores and rivers of Anglia for several generations but this band of twenty or so did not look like they would ever raid another village again.

Arthur was about to turn and walk away, leaving them to their inevitable fate when he saw one of the hunched figures staring at him. He was dressed much the same as the others, inadequately for the winter but his hair, though rimed with frost and snow was unmistakably straw coloured and he wore the distinctive Anglian circlet around his head. Arthur stared at the bearded face and something about the small, brown eyes and broken nose brought a name from his memory.

'Berwyn?' Arthur asked, walking across to him.

'Arthur? Arthur of Wessex?' the man asked in a cracked voice. He tried to get to his feet and Arthur, reaching out, helped him to stand. The others around the fire began to stir from their frozen repose and take an interest in the exchange.

'Yes. I'm Arthur. How did you come to be amongst these Uathach?' Berwyn's cracked lips began to work but no sound came from them. He ran a bare, frostbitten hand across his face, dislodging ice from his beard and eyebrows. Relief flooded though his eyes and he put both hands on Arthur's shoulders.

One of the Uathach lurched to his feet and made to draw his sword. Arthur turned swiftly, holding up a hand to stop Morgund or Ceinwen loosing an arrow. He studied the man who had risen. His eyes were weak and almost closed and the cheeks above the twin plaited red beard were sunken and hollowed. He took a step towards the Uathach while the others watched.

'Are you the Uathach leader of this band?' Arthur asked.

The man stood there uncertainly, looking from the two archers on the edge of the clearing and back to Arthur, his sword still half drawn.

'I am Ruraidh and yes, I lead this band. You're Arthur of Wessex?'

'Then sheathe your sword Ruraidh unless you wish to hasten your death. We are both a long way from our homes and a common enemy lies between us and our land.'

The others around the fire rose stiffly to their feet in clothes that cracked with frozen moisture. Morgund and Ceinwen drew their bows to three quarters and shifted their aim from target to target. Arthur ignored those around the fire and placing another branch on the flames, squatted down to warm his hands over the growing blaze.

'You can die here, frozen and starved or you can live. You decide, Ruraidh of Ablach's clan,' Arthur said without looking at any of the figures around the fire.

Ruraidh let his sword slide back into his scabbard. More of the Uathach stumbled from their bivouacs and gathered around their leader.

'You have food? You can get us back across the Northern Sea?' Ruraidh croaked.

'Yes,' Arthur answered then turned to Berwyn, 'How come you to be with the Uathach?'

'Myself and Saewulf were the only survivors when the black army attacked the Belgae.' Berwyn gestured across the fire to another Anglian who nodded to Arthur. 'The villagers were massacred and we fled into the forests. Ruraidh and his men found us there and allowed us to join them.'

'Join an Uathach raiding party?' Arthur asked.

'We had no other choice but to starve or be hunted down.'

'And you were here to raid the Belgae?' Arthur asked Ruraidh but it was another of the Uathach who answered him,

'Who are you to make accusations, Arthur of Wessex? You who have plundered and raided our villages for years. You should realise you are alone out here.'

Arthur turned to look at the woman who had spoken with such venom. She was a young woman but a harsh life had etched itself clearly on her pale, lined face. Her dark red hair was unkempt and long but her hazel flecked eyes were sharp and showed hatred.

'And who may you be?' he asked.

'Gwyna, daughter of Ablach,' she replied in a strong, proud voice.

'You take after your father, Gwyna, but you should realise it is not I who am alone in the Shadow Lands in winter, nor is it I who starve and wait idly for a cold death.'

'I would rather that than take help from you or your kind,' she spat back.

'You have his pride too,' Arthur turned from her and addressed Ruraidh again, 'Why did you let these two Anglians join with you?'

'We came here to supplement our meagre harvests. The black army took everything and killed everyone. Then they feasted on the dead. Neither Berwyn nor Saewulf seemed to be the enemy after that. They found our boats and burned them. We had no way back across the Northern Sea and we didn't see any hope in reaching or crossing the Causeway. Were you the one who raided the black army on the plain?'

'Yes, with some of the warriors that are now camped not far away,' Arthur replied.

'You have your war band here in the Shadow Lands in winter?' Another of the Uathach asked.

'We've been raiding the Adren from here down to Branque and along the East Road.'

225

'The Adren?' the same man asked.

'Yes, the Black Army, the Adren.' Arthur stopped and signalled Morgund and Ceinwen to join them. He looked around at the gathered Uathach and said, 'These people aren't fit to travel to the camp. Go and collect some supplies and whatever spare winter clothing we have and bring them back here.'

'I can wait here, Arthur,' Ceinwen offered, unwilling to leave their warlord alone in the Uathach band.

Arthur stared at Ruraidh for a moment then replied, 'No, you two go back.'

Morgund and Ceinwen turned and were soon lost in the dark forest. Arthur gazed around at the gathered Uathach.

'Well, you have the hated Wessex Warlord here in your camp. You've offered what help you could to Berwyn and Saewulf and now I'm offering to you what help I can. If any of you still think of me as your enemy then now would be your best chance to attack, but first I suggest you go to the edge of the forest and take a look out over the plain.'

The Uathach warriors looked to Ruraidh and after a moment he sat back down by the fire, gesturing for Arthur to do likewise. The others sat too, waiting eagerly for the promised supplies, all except Gwyna.

'You fools! They'll bring his war band and slaughter us!' she said.

'If that's what he wanted don't you think he'd have done so already?' asked Ruraidh.

'Your hatred won't feed you Gwyna, it will only consume you,' Arthur said to her.

Gwyna sat down by the fire, staring at Arthur who gazed levelly back at her until she turned her head to one side. Arthur continued to gaze at her. She was no older than Morveren but even without her obvious vitriol she had a hardness to her. Life in the Uathach lands was not easy. Laws and rules did not exist and one clan was often at another's throat. The land was hard to farm and stayed locked by ice for longer than the southern country and froze sooner too. With better organisation and cooperation they could produce enough to support themselves during the long winter but they chose instead to raid each other and the more productive lands to their south. Arthur thought that Ruraidh and Gwyna portrayed two Uathach characteristics quite accurately between them, a pragmatic approach to survival on the one hand and a fierce independence on the other. The irony was that one was often pitched against the other. The cold and their hunger had quelled their more violent nature, for now.

Arthur turned his attention to Ruraidh, 'You haven't posted guards.'

'No, they've stopped patrolling since your raids. You must have hurt them,' Ruraidh replied.

'We needed to hit their supplies. We wanted to delay their advance on Britain until after the winter. And we wanted to find out what happened to the Belgae and Cei's men.'

'We had no warning, Arthur. They just swept across the plain from all sides and slaughtered the villagers,' Berwyn said his eyes glazed in memory.

'Branque and Eald fell the same way. We didn't know it was going to happen and there was nothing we could do to stop it even if we had. It will be yours and my land next, Ruraidh.'

'What would they want with our lands?' Gwyna asked.

'They want everything,' Arthur answered.

'You're just trying to drag us into your own war. We've nothing they want. We have no lands worth farming.'

'Do you think the Adren will settle down here and farm these lands? Do you think that's why they've slaughtered everyone they could on this side of the Causeway?'

The force of Arthur's questions took Gwyna aback and she did not reply. Ruraidh looked uncertain, remembering the way they had watched the Adren army massacre the Belgae. The Uathach fell silent and waited for whatever Arthur's warriors would bring them. Some feared that Gwyna was right, that the war band would fall on them and kill them even though they knew that if Arthur had wanted it so, he would have waited for his warriors and done so without risk to himself. Berwyn and Saewulf questioned Arthur about Cei and news from home. Arthur was aware that despite their obvious plight neither of the Anglians had told Ruraidh about their own longboats and he told them quietly that he had found and moved them. He told them that Cei and some of his warriors had gone down the East Road to intercept the Adren supplies but that some of Cei's spear riders had remained with himself and that they would soon meet them.

They waited, huddled around the fire, the gaunt and haggard faces beginning to fill with hope after the cold death they had thought inevitable only hours before.

Eventually they heard the approaching members of Arthur's war band as they neared the edge of the clearing. The Uathach stood warily watching as ten of Arthur's warriors stopped just inside the cover of the trees. Arthur stood and waved them on. The two groups, enemies all their lives remained watching each other, anticipating the first indication of an attack.

Arthur strode to his band and hauled one of the sledges towards the fire.

'Winter clothing – what we can spare,' he said.

The Uathach gathered around the sledge and started to unpack the bundles stacked on it. Ceinwen led the others into the clearing and Cael set up a cauldron over the fire to start making a broth for the starved group. Balor and Mar'h stood to one side watching the Uathach, finding it difficult to accept or understand why they were helping people who they regarded as enemies.

As the broth started to cook, the Uathach stood eagerly around the fire, awaiting their first proper meal in weeks. Arthur, unwilling to take any chances, posted guards in the forest towards the Adren positions while the Uathach devoured the hot food put in front of them. Even Gwyna put her pride to one side and ate as greedily as her companions.

Arthur stood to one side with Mar'h and Ceinwen, letting the Uathach eat undisturbed. As the light around them dimmed, Mar'h looked up at the sky. High clouds shrouded the moon above them and the stars were blurred behind their thin veil.

'Storm coming in,' Mar'h said absently.

Arthur looked up at the ringed moon and immediately thought of Seren at their parting in the Winter Garden. He wanted to see her again, soon. He needed to see her soon. He thought of the Cithol City and the warmth and safety it offered. Like the rest of his warriors he was weary, hungry and cold to the bone. They had been cold and tired for weeks now and it was wearing them down. It was time to go home. His thoughts jumped to Cei and Trevenna and their journey east to the Shadow Land City. All he could do was hope Merdynn would guide them soundly and safely. It was not enough and he rubbed the heels of his palms in his reddened eyes.

'Do you think so?' Ceinwen asked Mar'h.

'Yes.'

'When?'

'Soon.'

'What?' Asked Arthur distracted from his thoughts.

'Storm coming in,' repeated Mar'h.

'Do you think so?' he asked.

'Yes.'

'When?'

'Soon.'

Ceinwen burst out laughing. The laugh rang clearly across the clearing and people looked around, unaccustomed to the sound of laughter. Arthur looked at them both, puzzled by their smiles.

'What?' Arthur asked.

'Storm coming in,' Mar'h said grinning.

'Gods! Not again, please.' Ceinwen said.

Arthur understood and said, 'I was far away, I didn't catch it first time round.'

'Lucky you. Take me with you next time,' Ceinwen replied and she realised she was smiling at Arthur for the first time since Sawan's death.

'If Ruraidh has finished, ask him to come across here,' Arthur said.

Mar'h ambled across to the fire and cautiously knelt by Ruraidh.

'How's his arm?' Arthur asked, nodding after Mar'h.

'As mended as it will ever be. His left hand won't be much good for anything,' Ceinwen replied.

Arthur grunted as Mar'h returned with Ruraidh who was wiping his mouth and beard with his hands.

'It's a strange turn of events,' Ruraidh said and Arthur raised his eyebrows in question. 'We came here to raid the Belgae of whatever food stores we could. These Adren, as you name them, slaughter everything in sight and destroy our boats. We're left stranded here in the Shadow Lands in winter. We come across two of the Anglian spear riders sent to protect the Belgae from us and help them as best as we can. Then just as hope is gone and we face a slow cold death, the hated Warlord of Wessex turns up with food to save us. The gods are busy with their dice.'

'The dice haven't finished rolling yet, Ruraidh,' Arthur said.

'I have no doubt of that but I'll be harder to surprise in future.'

'How are your band?' Arthur asked.

'Fed. Warmer. Alive. I didn't ever think I'd be thanking the Warlord of Wessex for saving our lives.'

'And I hadn't thought to be saving them. But everything is now changed. The Adren won't see a difference between Uathach, Wessex or Anglian. They want us all dead.'

'You name us Uathach, we don't call ourselves by that name.'

'What name do you use?'

'We don't, each clan is separate from each other, and each clan has its own name.'

'And there lies your downfall and perhaps our own. When the Adren come you'll stand and fall individually.'

'If they come for us. As Gwyna says, why should they?'

'If you believe nothing else, Ruraidh, believe this; the Adren will destroy your homes and land and they will slaughter each and every one of you. They spare no one,' Arthur said.

Ruraidh looked away, back to his warriors around the fire. Arthur stared at him and the watching Ceinwen saw his eyes become unfocussed and dead. Arthur blinked and the life came back to his gray eyes as he said, 'Say what you will, you know the truth.'

Ruraidh looked back at Arthur and nodded slightly.

'Now, you came here to get stores for your clan. We came here to take or destroy the Adren stores. Do you know where the Adren have their main supplies on the plains?'

'Yes. We hoped to raid it but it's too well guarded,' Ruraidh replied.

'Good, then perhaps we can do together what we came here to do individually.'

'Raid the Adren on the plains? You're mad. There's thousands of the black army down there.'

'Yes, raid the Adren. Yes, I am mad and yes, there are thousands on the plain but if you want your winter supplies and passage home on our boats then you will help. Talk to your warriors. You can stay and starve here if you prefer, it won't disturb my sleep,' Arthur said and walked away.

Mar'h and Ceinwen followed Arthur and as Mar'h passed Ruraidh he said quietly, 'Can you hear those dice?'

They left the Uathach to discuss the proposed raid among themselves. Arthur would return to the clearing with his warriors to learn their answer before commencing with the raid. They left the Uathach with enough food for another meal and returned through the forests back to their camp under a winter sky robbed of its myriad stars by the snow-laden clouds rolling in from the West.

When they reached the camp the news of their encounter with the Uathach quickly spread among the others. Morgund was highly suspicious and suspected that the Uathach would either plan an ambush or somehow betray them to the Adren. He said as much to Arthur who told him it would not be so but that they would in any case send an advance scouting party to be sure.

As Morgund was voicing his doubts, Gwyna was trying to persuade Ruraidh to do exactly as Morgund feared. Ruraidh pointed out to her that Arthur's war band would number over a hundred and that they were only twenty. Even if he had known Arthur's war band was only half that number he still would not have decided to try an ambush for they had no way home without the help of the men from Wessex. Gwyna tried briefly to argue that they should barter with the Adren, Arthur and his warriors in exchange for enough food for the winter but she did not really believe the Adren would barter for anything. She had seen the way they had massacred the Belgae.

Berwyn and Saewulf, who had stayed with the Uathach until Arthur's return, assured Ruraidh that Arthur was a man who could be trusted to act as either a friend or an enemy and clearly he regarded the Adren as the enemy not Ablach's clan whom he had, after all, provided with food and winter clothing.

Ruraidh finished the argument by saying that their only way home was with Arthur. The only way they might be able to take winter stores back to their clan was with Arthur. Whether they liked it or not this was the only way. As if to reiterate the conclusion he had reached they made their second meal from the supplies left to them.

Arthur's war band struck camp and made their way towards the plains where the massed Adren army was busy securing their sprawling encampment from the gathering wind and increasingly heavy snowfall. When Arthur's warriors had covered the fifteen miles, their scouts found that the Uathach had not set an ambush, nor were the Adren waiting for them. The Anglians among Arthur's band greeted Berwyn and Saewulf joyously, thinking they had been killed and were eager for news of the others who had gone to help the Belgae. Ruraidh came out to meet Arthur.

'Have you decided?' Arthur asked.

'Yes. We'll join your raid on your Adren if we can keep some of the stores we take and if you'll give us passage across the sea on one of your longboats.'

Arthur shook his head and walked into the midst of the Uathach band.

'Understand this. It's not a question of you doing something for us and then we help you. We don't need your help to raid the Adren, with or without you we will do this. With or without you we will return across the sea. This is a question of whether we can put aside our hatred and fight together against our common enemy. You and your people have cause to hate us. Likewise we have cause to hate you and your people. We were enemies. We were. The Adren have changed this. The question is, are we enemies still or are the Adren our common enemy?'

Both the Uathach and Arthur's warriors were silent and uneasy.

'Is there anyone here who is my enemy?' Arthur asked, searching the faces around him and settling on Gwyna.

'Is there?'

The question rang through the clearing as both bands stood facing each other in the falling snow. Still no one answered.

'If the Adren are our enemy then we are allies. If we are allies then we help each other. If we are enemies then let's finish it now. Here.'

Ruraidh had no other option but to step up to Arthur and hold out his hand.

'Allies,' he said.

Arthur took his hand and both groups took their hands from their weapons though neither would ever trust the other. Arthur began to discuss the raid and the Uathach began to pack up their scant belongings. As Mar'h massaged his left hand, made useless by an Uathach arrow, he recalled Talan lying dead in the mud with his sister weeping over him. Gwyna watched Ruraidh and Arthur, poisoned by her own memories, then spat in the snow and turned away from them.

Chapter Ten

The falling snow was beginning to sweep horizontally through the trees as the wind strengthened further. Ruraidh had pointed out to Arthur where the main Adren stores were located and both groups were struggling through the edge of the forest that ringed the plain as they made their way round to the far side.

They were about ten miles from the coast and the cove where Arthur's raiding party had hidden and secured the Anglians' longboats. It had puzzled Arthur that the Adren had not searched for the boats that Cei's men had used to reach the Belgae and it was not until Ruraidh had revealed that his own boats had been destroyed that he understood. The Adren had assumed that they were the only boats to have made the journey and the Uathach raiding party must have thought the Anglians had come across the Causeway.

Arthur planned to send half his war band and half of Ruraidh's band straight to the cove to prepare the boats for the crossing. They would take the horses with them and the remains of their winter supplies and load and secure both onto the boats. The other half of both bands would raid the Adren camp under the cover of the snowstorm. Arthur would have preferred to burn the Adren stores but in this storm and with the amount of oil they had left it would have proved impractical if not impossible. He decided they would use the last of Merdynn's poison instead.

They battled against the elements as they forged their way in a long half circle to the point nearest to the Adren stores. Retreating some way into the forest they set up their main tent and crowded inside to shelter from the developing blizzard. Arthur divided the group into two as they set about preparing a last meal before the raid. He decided that the Anglians among them would all go to the cove as his Wessex warriors had little experience of handling the boats. Ceinwen would lead them to the cove then come back, making sure she could find the way easily for she would need to lead the raiding party back to the boats with the possibility that the Adren would be following hard at their backs.

Once they had eaten, the coast-bound party departed with the horses and sledges that carried the supplies. They left the main tent for those that remained to shelter in as Arthur planned to allow several hours for them to reach and prepare the longboats and they also had to wait for Ceinwen to return to lead them to the cove after the raid. It meant that they would leave the tent behind which some were reluctant to do as it had served as their home during many winter campaigns but it was either that or wait exposed to the blizzard.

They spent the hours warming themselves by the fire and discussing the raid. Once again Arthur stressed the importance of not being drawn into a battle that they would only quickly lose. It was to be done as stealthily as possible, their aim was to poison as much as they could of the Adren food stores and only that.

Morgund was concerned that they might lose their way on the plain in the blizzard and they discussed how they might cross the mile or so to the Adren camp and get back without going helplessly astray in the darkness and flying snow.

Tomas suggested laying a line of rope to guide them back but a quick check showed they had nowhere near enough to cover the required distance. Mar'h put forward the idea of stationing people with burning brands to guide the raiders back and he and Cael went outside into the blizzard to see how far apart they would be visible in the storm. It turned out to be not far enough. They would have needed hundreds of people and hundreds of brands to cover the distance. One of the Uathach suggested planting branches in the snow as they made their way to the Adren camp but Mar'h, still sweeping snow from his cloak, said the snow was so furious outside that the branches would be covered by the time they made their way back and that they would have needed too many branches.

In the end Arthur decided that they would all head out across the plain together except for Ceinwen who would remain at the camp and set out, at the edge of the forest, ten burning brands every hundred yards to either side of the camp with markings to show whether the returning raiders were to the left or right of where they needed to be. They would only burn for an hour so Ceinwen would delay lighting them until after the raiders had left. They were all aware of the risk that the Adren chasing them could use them too but each thought it was worth it. The brands would use up their remaining oil but as they planned to get to the longboats as quickly as possible and leave then Arthur did not see any more use for it on this side of the Causeway.

Ruraidh drew a rough map of the part of the Adren camp which held the stores and Arthur allocated tasks for the three groups, those that would go into the camp carrying the barrel of poison, those that would take up the covering positions and those that would comprise the rearguard. Arthur would lead the group to enter the camp, Balor the covering bowmen and Morgund the rearguard. The Uathach were spread among the three groups with Ruraidh and Gwyna in Arthur's band. They set about stringing their longbows and preparing their war gear.

Eventually Ceinwen returned and went straight to the fire as Arthur outlined to her the part she was to play in the plan. She nodded her understanding, too frozen to talk and the others left the warmth of the tent and in single file began to cross the plain, bent almost double against the howling blizzard.

They soon realised that any plan involving rope or brands to guide them back was completely unworkable as they could barely see ten-feet in front of them in the darkness and driving snow. They realised too that this meant the Adren could not see them from more than ten-feet away. Arthur's main concern was whether they could find the right part of the Belgae village where the supplies were stored.

They stumbled on, forcing their way through the deep snow with the wind roaring in their ears and the frozen snow stinging the exposed skin around their eyes. Morgund thought they may well miss the camp on the way back but as long as they kept their backs to the wind then they could not miss the forest at least. He did not find it a great comfort.

It took them an hour to reach the village. Suddenly the wind lessened slightly and the dim light from the village fires outlined the black wall before them. Already exhausted they crowded in the lee of the village wall, breathing hard and freeing their weapons. Arthur stumbled down the line until he found Ruraidh.

'Do you have any idea how close we are to the stores?' he shouted to make himself heard against the still buffeting wind.

Ruraidh pointed to the right, 'There's a gate that way, I think.'

They formed into their groups, the rearguard led by Morgund stayed where they were at the base of the wall. The other two groups moved along the wall to the right until they came to the gateway. The gates were wedged open with drifted snow lying deeply against them. Arthur and

Ruraidh crossed to the far side and studied what they could see inside the compound. There was not much movement as almost everyone was inside the various roundhouses and barns sheltering from the storm. Fires burned in corners out of the wind throughout the compound and each fire had two or three Adren huddled close to it. Arthur guessed that these were supposed to be on guard duty.

Ruraidh pointed alongside the wall, 'Most of their stores were packed in the buildings along this wall.'

Arthur nodded and crossed back to speak to Balor. His group slipped inside the gate and climbed to the parapet that ran along the inside of the wall where they crouched down, trying to scan the ground around the buildings below them.

Arthur then led his group boldly through the gates with Tomas and Mar'h hauling the sledge with the barrel of poison tied to it. Elowen, Morveren, Ruraidh and Gwyna slipped into the darker recesses between the buildings. Arthur hoped that any Adren spotting them amid the storm and among the buildings would assume they were just soldiers collecting stores on the sledge.

Arthur went to the first building and hauled the door open. Once out of the wind he lit the small oil light he had taken from the sledge. The single-room building, probably a stable previously, was full of weapons, swords, spears and the bows the Adren used. He left and placed the oil light on the sledge where its light could not be seen by anyone in the compound.

They moved onto the next building and both the shadows between the buildings and those on the wall above moved along with them. This one was packed with sacks of grain and rice. Tomas and Arthur hoisted the barrel off the sledge and rolled it into the wooden hut. Pouring some of the liquid into a bucket they opened the sacks and began to douse the grain.

Outside, one of the Adren had noticed Mar'h waiting by the sledge and started to walk towards him. Mar'h turned to face him and scanned the immediate area to see if anyone was watching them. As the Adren neared and started to ask questions an arrow flew past Mar'h and slammed into the Adren's chest, sending him flying onto his back. Ruraidh and Gwyna raced out of the shadows and dragged the body through the snow and back into the darkness between the buildings. As Arthur and Tomas brought the barrel out and lifted it back onto the sledge, Mar'h once again scanned the nearby fires for any movement towards them. There was not and they moved on to the next building.

They were going through the same process when Ruraidh and Gwyna came through the doorway. Arthur and Tomas spun round to see who had entered.

'What about our winter supplies? We need to take as much as we can,' Ruraidh said.

'If you loaded up with supplies you'd have to go back out through the gates and then haul the sledge across the plain and to the coast. You wouldn't make it,' Arthur said.

'I told you this bastard would betray us!' Gwyna hissed as she drew her sword.

'I'm not betraying anyone. Now we are here it makes no sense trying to take stores for your winter – it's too difficult, you'd die trying,' Arthur said watching her carefully.

'Many in our clan will die this winter if we don't try but at least news of your death will warm them,' Gwyna said and lunged forward. Arthur twisted away from the sword and struck Gwyna hard across the face with the back of his hand sending her flying against the wall. Ruraidh drew his sword but Arthur was upon him too quickly, forcing him back against the wall, one hand pinning his sword arm the other around his throat.

Gwyna knelt looking from her sword that lay on the floor near the barrel to Tomas who stood with his own sword drawn and pointing toward her.

Arthur spoke as he pinned Ruraidh to the wall, 'Listen, both of you. I said we were allies. It's us against the Adren, nothing else matters to me. If you want to try to haul your supplies back then go ahead and die. It's not possible. But allies help each other. You need supplies for the winter? I'll send supplies to Ablach's clan once we're back across the seas. You have my oath on that. If that's not enough then try for your swords now.'

Arthur released Ruraidh and stepped back, facing them both. They remained still, stunned by how quick Arthur had moved and how easily he had disarmed them both.

'Load the sledge with supplies and try your fortune, use your swords now or we carry on with the plan and I will send supplies to your clan. Choose.' Arthur stared at Ruraidh as he spoke. Ruraidh hesitated, torn between taking the opportunity of killing Arthur and taking his word that he would send supplies. He hesitated because he thought the chances of killing Arthur were slim. Gwyna had no such hesitation and was steeling herself to launch an attack against him when Mar'h burst through the doorway.

'What in hell's name is taking so long? There's a group of Adren approaching!' Mar'h shouted to them. He stood in the doorway staring wildly around at the figures facing each other as the wind drove the snow around him and into the room. Arthur strode to the doorway. There were five Adren making their way to the sledge. Suddenly arrows shot down from overhead and all five of the Adren crashed backward into the snow.

Arthur raced forward and dragged two of the bodies back to the building and Ruraidh and Gwyna passed him to do the same. Tomas was carrying the barrel back to the sledge while Mar'h slung the harness over his slim shoulders once again to drag it towards the next storeroom. Together they quickly poured the contents over the stacked meat that they found in the hut.

Arthur went to join them and several things happened at once. He heard screaming coming from the next hut in line, Gwyna was hit in the shoulder by an Adren arrow, rope dropped from the parapet above them and arrows flew from overhead to meet a dozen charging Adren. Elowen and Morveren sped from between the buildings.

'Get her to the wall!' Arthur shouted to Elowen as he pointed to the fallen Gwyna.

'Kill them and get over the wall!' he shouted to the others and they moved to meet the Adren charge whose numbers had already been halved by the bowmen above them.

Arthur raced to the next building and kicked open the door. The small hut was lit by a dozen large candles and the screaming continued as he stopped cold in the doorway. For several seconds his brain refused to take in the sight before him.

There were nine Adren in the hut but it was not the Adren that sent him into a blind rage. It was the three women chained in the room, one to the wall and the other two on crude wooden beds. Tattered shreds of clothing clung to their emaciated limbs. Their bodies were covered in ugly, deep bruising and open welts. Their wrists and ankles were open bloody sores where the manacles had cut deeply.

One of the women seemed dead already, her head hanging against her chest at an unnatural angle. Another stared sightlessly at the dim ceiling above, her body utterly still except for her hands that twitched uncontrollably. The third was screaming. It was her screaming that Arthur had heard. A dry scream that came from vocal chords that had been shredded hoarse. To the amusement of those gathered around her she had been bucking and writhing violently in an attempt to rid herself of the Adren who was on top of her.

Now she lay thrashing her head from side to side on the hard bed, her long hair, matted and filthy, flying back and forth. Her screaming had stopped and as Arthur and the Adren stared at each other, the only sound in the room was the heavy thudding of her head on the hard wood. It lasted for a few heartbeats then Arthur's rage broke upon them. They scuttled for their weapons in a panic but few had the time to find them and those that did were torn apart by Arthur's sword before they could try to defend themselves. Blood, gore and limbs flew about the room as Arthur hacked his way through all nine Adren. As the last one died, Morveren and Mar'h burst into the hut breathing hard.

'Arthur! Get out now! Now!' Mar'h shouted to him then paused, looking at the nightmarish scene around him. Someone was laughing. A mad, broken cackling was coming from the heap of bodies scattered across the room. Looking around the bloody chaos he saw where the laughter was coming from. In an uncertain voice he repeated that they had to leave and leave quickly. Arthur looked at them both and for a second they saw an unquenchable hatred burning in his eyes. Then Arthur turned and knelt first by one woman then the next.

'See if she's still alive,' he said to Morveren, pointing to the third who lay under the bodies of two dead Adren.

Arthur brushed the long matted hair from the bruised face of the woman who was laughing madly. It was not a woman, it was a girl and her ordeal had plunged her mind into an abyss of insanity. For a moment her eyes cleared and focussed on Arthur, 'Breward?' she croaked.

Arthur stared at the disfigured face and realised who it was. 'Yes Caja, it's Breward. I've come to take you away from here,' Arthur replied. Caja's eyes clouded once again and she began to laugh shrilly.

'This one's dead, Arthur,' Morveren said from across the hut.

'They're all dead,' Arthur replied and placing the point of his sword above Caja's bloody breast, jabbed it downward. The cackling stopped. He did the same to the woman next to Caja, her hands twitched for a second longer then stilled.

'Arthur, we have to leave,' Mar'h said again.

As Arthur had expected, the Adren had already blocked the way back to the main gate and they would have to go over the wall to get out of the camp. They left the hut and ran towards the group by the wall. Their position was becoming desperate. Elowen had reached the parapet and had helped the injured Gwyna over the other side. She was now with Cael and the rest of Balor's group firing arrows rapidly into the melee below them. At such short range they only needed to half-draw their longbows and arrows flew from the wall in quick succession.

Ruraidh and Tomas were still at the foot of the wall, outnumbered and pressed hard by a group of Adren who had got through the hail of arrows from above. Arthur, Morveren and Mar'h threw themselves at the Adren, cutting into them unexpectedly just as Tomas fell under two attacking Adren. It was a chaotic few seconds, the snow blinded them in the darkness and swords clashed and swung as they fought for enough time and space to climb the ropes up to the wall.

Arthur's rage carried him into the thick of the Adren and he cut about himself with wide, lightning sweeps of his sword. Suddenly they had some space and Mar'h wrapped a rope around his good arm and Cael and Balor dropped their longbows to haul him upwards. Ruraidh started to scale another rope. Arthur looked about him and saw Tomas slumped against the foot of the wall, an Adren spear through his stomach. Tomas was staring at it in puzzled disbelief, the shock still preceding the pain even as his life drained away. Arthur dragged Morveren away from her fallen friend and propelled her towards the ropes that led to safety then he heard a cry from above and Balor shouting. The cry was from Elowen who had just seen Tomas at the base of the wall. Balor was shouting a warning. Arthur looked out across the compound and saw why. More and more of the nearby Adren were becoming aware that their camp was under attack and one of their captains was marshalling dozens of them, ready to charge the wall.

Arthur looked once more to Tomas who turned his eyes up to Arthur in glazed shock. Tomas started to scream. The cries above were becoming more urgent. The Adren had begun their charge. Arthur quickly looped a rope around Tomas's arm then hauled himself up another as the arrows flew once more from the wall.

Again Balor and Cael hoisted up the rope, this time lifting the screaming Tomas. Something slipped. Tomas went crashing back to the ground and his screams redoubled. Suddenly free of the load, Balor and Cael fell backwards as the suddenly weightless rope jerked upwards. Arrows began to thud and hiss around them as the Adren neared the wall. Balor's covering group began to descend the other side of the wall.

Elowen looked panic-stricken, 'We can't leave Tomas!' she screeched at the departing figures around her.

'He's dead girl!' Balor shouted taking her by the arm. She wrenched her way free and slid down one of the ropes just as Arthur gained the top. He looked down in despair as Elowen stood over the dying Tomas, her feet planted firmly apart and her sword held before her. Tears ran spilling from her eyes and her lips twisted into a snarl as she faced the Adren charge. A hail of arrows shot at her and plucked her off her feet, sending her flying lifelessly against the wall.

Balor cursed and leapt for a rope to get over the other side of the wall. Arthur cut all but one of the remaining ropes then followed Balor. Mar'h was waiting with Balor on the other side.

'Is there anyone else?' he shouted into the wind.

Arthur shook his head.

'Elowen?' Mar'h shouted.

Arthur shook his head again.

They started to run back across the snow, following the tracks of the others. They caught up with Morveren who was dragging the injured Gwyna away from the fighting. Mar'h joined her and together they half-carried the unconscious Gwyna across the snow. Balor kept yelling out to Morgund, identifying themselves. When they passed his group,

Morgund asked if there was anyone else left then the rearguard turned and followed the others back towards the forest edge, stumbling in the driving wind that forced them onward and fighting against the sapping depth of the snow.

After thirty exhausting minutes of thrashing their way through the snow they reached the forest edge. They could not see any of the burning brands. Morgund's group, who had been just behind them, arrived a few minutes later. They had been following the tracks left by Arthur and the others.

'Are they following?' Arthur asked. He had to shout to be heard above the wind. Morgund was bent over with his hands on his knees, fighting for breath.

He looked up, 'One group nearly caught up with us. Ten, maybe fifteen. We shot most of them. The others disappeared in the storm. Don't know about the rest. Where are we?'

Arthur looked round but saw nothing familiar.

'Mar'h, take the right – go five-hundred yards then come back here. Balor, take the left and do the same,' he shouted to them.

They started off immediately and Arthur drew the others back into the forest a little way. They lined up under whatever cover the forest could offer and strained their eyes staring into the blizzard that blew in from the plains, waiting for the shadows of their pursuers to emerge from the darkness.

Balor returned first. He had found the first of the brands two hundred yards to their left. Arthur sent them to meet up with Ceinwen and the others. He would wait for Mar'h to return from the other direction. Once they had left, he rested his forehead against the tree trunk he was sheltering behind. The bark was frozen and thinly covered with ice. It felt like it was burning through the numbed skin on his face but he welcomed it. He was reliving the last moments in the Adren camp, the fate of Caja and the other two women from the villages. He slid his forehead from side to side against the iced bark. Tomas and Elowen dead. Perhaps Ethain had been wise to go with Cei but what were the chances their fate would be any different? He wondered if Gwyna had made it to the forest alive and found he didn't much care one way or the other.

He thought of Caja dancing barefoot in her simple white dress with a circlet of daisies in her hair. He thought of her mother, Ceinwen, and decided never to tell her that Caja had survived Branque. He didn't think that either Mar'h or Morveren had recognised Caja but all the same he would tell them not to reveal what they had seen in that hut. An image of Fin Seren, her smiling face turned to the rain, came unbidden to his mind and he wondered if he could stop the Cithol sharing the fate of those who had fallen this side of the Causeway. The Downs and valleys of Wessex, would the Adren swarm over them too? Merdynn, Cei, his sister, all gone into the Shadow Lands of the East on a doomed venture.

He reined in his growing desperation and forced himself to stand straight. Not all was lost. If Cei could cut their lifeblood, if the war bands could hold out against the Adren for just long enough. Then perhaps. He remembered Merdynn saying many years ago that hope can be found at the most unlikely times and in the darkest places. For as long as there was a will to make something happen, then there was hope it might be so and hope only needed a seed. A seed that does not need light and does not need water. Just a will to make it happen.

He scanned the darkness of the plain once more and thought he saw shadowy movement. At the same moment Mar'h appeared among the trees to his right. Arthur called out softly to him and Mar'h joined him.

'Balor's found the markers,' Arthur said.

'Let's go then, I keep seeing shadows in the darkness,' Mar'h replied.

'Did you take the poison barrel out of the Adren camp?' Arthur asked.

'Yes. I buried it under the snow out on the plain,'

'Good. They'll think we were just raiding their stores. And Mar'h, not a word to anyone about what we saw in that hut.'

'Did one of them know you?'

'She mistook me for someone else.'

Mar'h nodded absently, he was wondering if the raid had been worth the price of losing Tomas and Elowen. He put the thought to one side and followed Arthur as they began to make their way back to the camp, constantly looking towards the plain where the snow flew at them from out of the darkness. As they came across the brands that led them to the camp, Arthur upended and extinguished them in the snow.

Morgund and the rearguard were waiting for them. Ceinwen had already led the others off into the forest and towards the cove.

244

'Have you put the brands out?' Arthur called out but before Morgund could answer a cry went up from those around him. An Adren band had stumbled across them. The rearguard only had time to loose off one round of arrows before the Adren were among them.

The roars of the Adren mingled with the sound of weapons being drawn and a vicious, chaotic struggle ensued in the darkness between the trees. Grunts and oaths rang out with the frantic clattering of steel as the rearguard and the Adren scrambled alike in the deep snow, spears smacking into shields and swords flaying at the enemy.

Arthur and Mar'h rushed to join the brutal battle and their sudden onslaught from the Adren flank turned the skirmish in the war band's favour. But they had lost two more warriors in as many minutes.

Automatically they retreated back into the forest, leaving their dead behind and following the obvious tracks left by those that Ceinwen had led. They retreated in two groups. One would hold a line, longbows drawn and searching the forest while the other retreated a hundred yards. In such a way they leapfrogged each other as they covered the distance to the coast.

The Adren had either misgauged the raiders' numbers or were too hastily organised, for their hunting packs were too small to overwhelm the rearguard and the only ones that had found the camp were now lying dead around it. Other packs were searching other areas of the forest edge but none had yet picked up their trail and the rearguard made the cove without further attacks.

Things were not as Arthur had expected. The horses were still corralled to one side, under a jutting bluff that offered some shelter from the blizzard that still howled around them. He had expected the difficult process of boarding them onto the boats to have been completed by now. In fact, he had expected the longboats to be only awaiting the rearguard's arrival. He immediately sent Morgund with his bowmen back to the top of the headland that crouched around the cove in a semi-circle and then looked for Mar'h to find out what the delay was.

He was surprised to find it was Ceinwen who was trying to hasten things along. She was arguing with the adamant Elwyn who had taken on the leadership of the Anglians that had remained with Arthur after Cei's departure. Elwyn was not a great deal taller than Ceinwen but his thickset, powerful figure matched his attitude. It was not easy to make him give ground in either a fight or an argument. Arthur strode across the pebbled beach.

'Why aren't the horses loaded on?' he shouted to them over the noise of the crashing surf. Ceinwen threw her arms up in exasperation and gestured to Elwyn.

'We can't board the boats in these seas! It's too wild and we'd never get the horses aboard!' Elwyn shouted back. He shrugged as if to say it was out of his hands and there was nothing to be done.

'You said you could sail the boats in winter seas!' Arthur yelled back.

'Yes, but not in a storm like this! Not yet!'

Arthur looked to the boats, anchored side by side beyond the shallows a hundred yards out and their bows rose in unison as a wave pummelled into them, sending gulleys of foam down the narrow spaces between their sides.

'We have to wait out the storm?'

Elwyn nodded and Arthur cursed then turned to Ceinwen, 'Get the wounded up into the sand dunes below the cliff face, do what you can.'

Ceinwen looked up at him, afraid he was going to add something but he only jabbed his thumb towards the place he meant. Ceinwen gathered her supplies and the injured and, with Cael and Morveren's help, led them up to the shelter of the sand dunes.

A fierce wave stumbled then collapsed onto the beach, spilling its turbulent burden to race up over the tightly packed pebbles that were worn veterans of countless such storms. It engulfed Arthur up to the waist as it surged up the sharp slope and then dragged at his heavy cloak as the sea sucked it back once more. Arthur struggled to keep his footing then waded on towards Ruraidh and the Uathach who were gathered on the far side of the beach.

'A boat, Arthur! You gave your oath we would have a boat!' Ruraidh said.

'Take a boat but I would wait if I were you. The Anglians say it's folly to launch in this,' he replied.

'And wait for the Adren?'

Arthur shrugged his disinterest in their choice. He pointed to Gwyna and another of their clan who were huddled to one side, both wounded.

246

'Ceinwen can help your wounded. She's up in the sand dunes with ours. If you don't sail now then we could use you on the left up there to guard against an attack.' Arthur left them without waiting for a reply and went to organise his warriors in a defensive ring around the bay. Ruraidh watched him disappear into the darkness then signalled his warriors to help their wounded up to where Ceinwen was. He reluctantly led the others up to the headland where Arthur had pointed; Elwyn was right, they could not launch in this weather and they would not get away at all if the Adren caught them here unprepared. Gwyna would have refused Ceinwen's help too but she was only half-conscious and wracked by enough pain to quell her pride.

Arthur set his warriors below the rim of the headland just before the sloping sand dunes that led down to the stone beach. Even here the snow was two-feet deep and it formed a slight overhang on the edge. Arthur's warriors huddled behind this overhang, clearing away spaces from which to watch the dark forest that encroached to within yards of the drop down to the cove.

Arthur checked on Ceinwen and the wounded. She answered his questions nervously, in constant fear that he would make a judgement on who would and who would not survive. To her relief he left to join Mar'h who was halfway down the snow-covered dunes and sitting alone with his head bowed.

'What's wrong?' he asked.

'Back there, in the camp, that hut...' Mar'h said, then brought both hands up to rub his face.

Arthur nodded but remained silent, staring out over the beach.

'Those poor women. I've seen rape before but...'

'What warrior hasn't?' Arthur replied.

'I know the Uathach take child-bearing women and use them for breeding but at least that shows some kind of respect for life, no matter how twisted it is. But those women back there, they were kept for sport, as, no more than supplies.' Mar'h stopped. The thought was too horrific to put into words. He realised he was shaking. Seeing Llud die, then Tamsyn weeping over Talan, both were terrible as were the deaths of Tomas and Elowen during the raid on the camp and he found it hard to accept he would never see any of them again, not this side of death, but at least there was some understandable explanation and reason for their deaths. They had died in battle. They were part of the Wessex war band and they had died in battle either against the Uathach or against the Adren. Such was their fate. But those women? How could their fate lead them to such an end?

He could not stop the shaking. The initial shock had passed during the flight from the Belgae villages but now the true horror was creeping in and he was not at all sure he could face it. Suddenly he turned to one side and vomited. He was sick until there was nothing left to vomit and still he retched, trying to purge the sickening revulsion from deep inside himself. But the horror ran deep. He wiped his mouth with the back of his hand and scooped up a handful of fresh snow to spread over his face.

Arthur watched Mar'h's shaking hand and stared at his face as his lips worked wordlessly.

Finally Mar'h said, 'You did recognise her, didn't you? The screaming one?'

Arthur sighed, 'Yes. Caja from Branque. Ceinwen was her mother – or at least she had raised her,' Arthur replied not looking at Mar'h.

'She called you 'Breward'?'

'Her lover from the village I presume, or at least a boy she loved. Maybe just a boy who loved her. She was only seventeen. She was dancing in their hall when the Adren swarmed in.'

'Seventeen?' Mar'h asked, his voice shaking again, 'Oh gods.' He clasped his arms around his raised knees and bent his head. His lean frame was shivering as he rocked slightly back and forth.

Arthur stared ahead. Even in the darkness he could make out the rolling white horses on the crests of the waves as they advanced in confused ranks and hammered down in a churning, violent assault upon the steep beach. He realised the wind was now blowing into his face and wondered if he had lost his bearings or if the wind had shifted. He saw Elwyn yelling at Lissa and Aylydd and then all three wading the distance to the boats. Aylydd disappeared under the chaos of white raging water as two waves collided against each other, then she was back up and once more fighting to reach the boats.

Arthur turned to Mar'h and quietly asked, 'Who was she, Mar'h?'

Mar'h looked at Arthur and there was fear in his dark brown eyes.

'Who?' he replied, watching Arthur carefully.

Arthur's face was expressionless as he continued looking into Mar'h's eyes.

'When did it happen?' Arthur asked quietly.

Mar'h's head sunk back to his chest and his eyes closed. 'It happened years ago. A lifetime ago. I wasn't much more than a child. Nor was she.'

Arthur could barely hear him. Finally Mar'h raised his head but his eyes were unseeing, looking instead into the darkness of the past.

'Oh gods, the fear in her eyes.' His eyes filled with tears and, as his gaze shifted from one barrelling wave to another, they spilt down his face unchecked. Arthur remained silent, watching the guilt and anguish of the past persecute the man next to him, waiting for him to continue.

'It was in an Uathach village. We'd just raided them. Breagan, one of Saltran's men, led the raid. I'd only just joined the war band and I'd just killed my first man. You and some of the others were on another raid somewhere to the North of Mercia. It was back when Saltran was still the Warlord. Oh gods, why did I do it?' Mar'h's voice broke and he gripped his knees tightly. 'Why did I do it?' he repeated, slowly shaking his head in disbelief and denial.

'Why did you do it?' Arthur asked.

Mar'h turned to him suddenly as if accused and condemned. Arthur did not recognise the face before him, a face contorted with despair.

'Breagan said he had a reward for me. Led me to one of the buildings. She was in there. Cowering in a corner, crying in fear. He held her down and told me to take her, and, I did. Gods help me, I did.'

Mar'h's shoulders heaved as slow, heavy sobs wracked his chest. He covered his eyes with both hands but could not block out the image of her face as she had cried and pleaded with him. The joy of killing and battle had been upon him and he had looked upon her as his just reward. In quiet moments, over the many years that had passed since, he had kept coming face to face with her.

Arthur remembered Breagan. He had been one of Saltran's men when Arthur took command of the war band. He was the same kind of warrior too, the kind that had been more of a threat to the villagers than a protector of them. Some of Saltran's men stayed when Arthur became warlord and Breagan was one of them. They were weeded out one by one as Arthur gradually changed the nature of the war band and he remembered executing Breagan for raping one of the Branque women. He looked at Mar'h and regretted not killing Breagan sooner.

'I'm no different from those bastards back there,' Mar'h said bitterly.

'You think they'd have been haunted by the things they've done?' Arthur asked.

'Gods, if I could only go back, put it right, take it back, not do it.'

'You can't undo what you have done.'

'What can I do if I can't undo it?'

'What you have been doing ever since. Atone.'

Arthur got to his feet and left Mar'h to wander alone in the dark cave behind his glazed eyes, searching his soul and coming once again face to face with the screaming Uathach girl.

Ceinwen looked up as Arthur knelt beside her.

'They'll mend, mostly,' she answered the unasked question.

Arthur looked around for Gwyna but could not see her.

'Gwyna?' he asked.

'She's a tough bitch. I took the arrow head out, cleaned and bandaged her shoulder and then, when she had finished cursing me, she was off without another word to join Ruraidh and the others.'

Arthur nodded and left her to her work. He climbed the slope up to Morgund.

'How long are we going to wait here?' Morgund asked. He was shivering in the cold and steam curled in wisps from his exposed shaven head.

'Where's your cloak?' Arthur asked.

'Lost it in that skirmish in the forest.'

'They can't get the boats out of the cove safely in this storm.'

'It's lessening, and the wind's veered round too. It's not as if we're exactly safe here,' Morgund pointed out.

'As long as they don't find our tracks we should be safe. They have no reason to think we would head for the coast, remember they think they destroyed the only boats,' Arthur said.

'Just as well,' Balor said from nearby, 'We'd be trapped like rats if they found us here.'

Morgund nodded his agreement, his teeth clenched to stop them from chattering. Arthur unhooked his heavy sheepskin cloak and handed it across to Morgund.

'I'll see if there's another on the sledges. You're no good to us frozen,' Arthur said and got up to go but Morgund stopped him,

'Tomas and Elowen?' he asked.

'Both dead. Elowen jumped back down to help him but he was already beyond help.'

Morgund nodded as he wrapped the cloak about his broad shoulders, thinking of the time he disturbed them in his roughly built shelter and Tomas' smile of apology at Elowen's rebuke. He tried to remember how long ago that was but couldn't quite place it. A lifetime ago for the both of them he thought and returned to watching the forest edge where he expected the shadows of the Adren to launch an attack before long.

Arthur had gone to talk once more with Elwyn who was back on the beach with both Lissa and Aylydd. Elwyn was adamant that the chances of getting the longboats out of the cove safely were only half-and-half. The blizzard had ceased but the wind still drove the stacked waves fiercely into the cove.

'Can't we row them out of the cove to open water?' Arthur asked.

'Perhaps, with experienced seafarers. How many of your warriors have handled boats like these before?' Elwyn asked.

'Not many,' Arthur conceded, 'but if the Adren catch us here in numbers then we'll die in this cove. I'm sending a scouting party into the forest to give us some warning. If the Adren approach here we'll row out, whether it's safe or not. Have the boats ready and have the horses ready too.' Arthur left them looking at each other.

'If it comes to it, we'll captain a boat each and spread our lot among the boats. At least then we'll have some on each boat who know what they're doing - because the Wessex lot don't,' Elwyn said and the three of them waded out once more to the longboats to finalise their preparations.

Arthur sent a scouting party of five, led by Mar'h, into the forests. They were told not to make any contact with the enemy but to return with the earliest possible warning if the Adren were following the band's tracks and making their way to the cove. Arthur thought the risk of entrusting the scouting party to Mar'h worthwhile. It would bring his mind back on the present and the task at hand, nonetheless he sent Morveren with him

251

to keep an eye on him. He told Morveren that Mar'h had let the deaths of Tomas and Elowen, and those of the women in the hut, get to him and that she should stay close and watch him. He also told her to keep the events of the hut to herself. Morveren had accepted this, the pain of losing her friends had affected her too. She could understand how Mar'h must be feeling and she assumed that Arthur must be thinking about the others' morale in wanting to keep the nightmare scenes from the hut just between the three of them.

The scouting party slipped over the lip of the headland and disappeared into the darkness of the forest, retracing the route taken by the rearguard. The rest settled back down to wait for either the seas to calm or the forest to erupt in an Adren attack.

The clouds above them began to break and patches of the bright winter stars could be briefly seen before being snatched away again by the scudding clouds. The snow had stopped but the wind still swirled and buffeted the bay, forcing the serried waves onwards in their endless assault on the beach. The constant tumult of the sea and the rolling and grinding of stones as the waves broke upon them filled the cove with a ceaseless roar, which lulled the tired warriors. Heads nodded and eyes closed in the cold, damp air and Arthur went from group to group to keep them awake and watching the forest.

Elwyn brought the longboats in one by one and with Cael's help, marshalled the horses into them. These boats were designed to carry not only the Belgae villagers but also their stores and stock so each boat had partitioned stalls in which to tether various animals. The horses were unused to this and it took several men to lead each horse up the ramp and into a stall. It was a lengthy process but eventually all the horses and what stores they still had were loaded and the longboats once again rode at anchor, their bows pointing to the narrows that led to the open water.

Elwyn then went round all of Cei's warriors that had remained with Arthur and told them which boats they were to make for. He told the Wessex warriors to follow the lead of the Anglians in their boat and to do exactly as they were told if they wanted to make it out of the cove and across the seas. No one resented the instructions, they were well aware that once in the boats their fate was in Anglian hands.

Next he went to the Uathach band and told them which of the boats they were to take. As they no longer had their horses the stalls on their boat were empty and Elwyn had stored some supplies there for the crossing.

Finally he brought the empty sledges up to where the wounded were. They could be carried to the boats on the makeshift stretchers when the time came. Having done what he could, Elwyn too settled down to wait either for the Adren or for the wind to change. He did not think the wind would change any time soon so he strung his longbow and counted out what arrows he had remaining. He did not have that many and certainly not enough. He sat down with the longbow over his legs, and with his back to the headland he watched the heaving seas and waited.

He did not have long to wait. Within the hour Morveren came sprinting out of the trees and leapt down to the sand dunes below the rim of the headland. Arthur was by her side in seconds.

'Adren?'

'Yes,' she panted in reply.

'Coming this way? To the cove?'

'Yes.' Her face was running with sweat.

'How many?'

'All of them.'

'All of them?'

Morveren shrugged between deep breaths, 'The forest is alive with them.'

Arthur started to yell out orders and groups raced across the stony beach, flinging themselves into the surging water and making for the longboats. Mar'h and the other scouts ran from the trees and took up their positions with the defenders.

'How much time do we have?'

Morveren looked at Arthur shaking her head, 'Not enough.'

Chapter Eleven

The cove was a good place for concealment but a bad place to have to defend. Arthur knew this but there had been no alternatives, concealment had been their best gamble. It had not paid off.

Elwyn and the other Anglians raced for the boats, flinging themselves headlong into the waves that still pounded the beach. Arthur had considered putting bowmen on the boats to give them cover as they retreated but having stood on the decks, as the boats rode at anchor, he realised they were pitching too violently for any kind of accurate aim.

Instead, those of his war band not already making for the boats formed into two arced ranks on the stony beach forming a slightly askew crescent. He put those that could swim in the first rank with their longbows ready and the remaining arrows held by those behind them who had their shields raised. They waited one last time, all eyes scanning along the headland above them waiting for the Adren ranks to come swarming over the rim and down the sand dunes.

Elwyn and his men were working desperately to bring the longboats close enough to the shore for the rest of the warriors to board. Ruraidh and the Uathach plunged headlong into the sea and struck out for their boat. Gwyna, unable to swim because of her injured shoulder, stood by the wounded who were laid out on the sledges at the edge of the beach behind the two ranks of Arthur's warriors. As the waves raced up the beach the sledges lifted momentarily in the surf, half turned and then grounded again. The spent waves eddied around the legs of the waiting ranks and dragged at their feet as it tried to suck them back into the next crashing wave.

Arthur cast a look back over his shoulder to see how close the boats were. They were not close enough yet. He yelled to Ceinwen and Gwyna to float the sledges out as soon as they could. Then the Adren came.

They stopped on the rim above the dunes, at first just a few then more and more joined them until the whole of the headland was crowded with the black figures. From one end of the half circle to the other they looked down on the two ranks of Arthur's war band.

Arthur yelled to the line before him to wait for the charge. He did not want to precipitate the attack, every second the Adren hesitated, the closer the longboats got to the shallows.

A dark cloud of arrows flew from the Adren ranks but they were firing into a strong wind and their bows were far less powerful than the longbows used by Arthur's warriors and they fell short, skittering across the wet stones.

Then with a roar that echoed over the wind and waves the Adren charged down the slope. In front of Arthur the first rank let their arrows fly, then reached over their shoulder for the next arrow to be slapped into their hand by the person behind them. The bowmen could loose an arrow every few seconds this way. It would take the Adren at least forty seconds to cover the two hundred yards over the dunes and sand. Even at two hundred yards the warriors' aim was deadly and the force of their arrows sent those they hit flying backwards. The arrows tore through the packed Adren ranks and over a hundred and fifty fell as they covered the distance to the shoreline but the charge did not falter and others took the place of those that fell.

When the massed ranks of the charging Adren were only ten paces away Arthur roared for the first rank to fall back. Arthur's line closed in front of them with their swords drawn and their shields raised to meet the raging force of the Adren. The shield wall swayed backwards as the Adren crashed into it but it held intact and the furious hacking battle started.

Those that had been in the first rank now waded desperately towards the nearing longboats, the waves breaking over their heads and surging on to crash around the raging battle in the shallows. The surf foamed red with blood as Arthur's shield wall was slowly driven into deeper water.

Arthur stood at the centre of the arced wall with Mar'h to his right and Balor to his left. The Adren were forced upon them by the pressure of those behind trying to reach the hated raiders. As planned, the shield wall slowly gave ground. Arthur and those around him were waist deep in the water now and already the two ends of the curved line had reached a depth where they abandoned the fight and thrashed towards the longboats. In this way the length of the shield wall that the Adren could attack gradually diminished but the fighting grew fiercer as it became more focussed on the centre.

Still shoulder to shoulder and allowing no gaps for the Adren to force their way through, they continued to give ground. Arthur was savagely hacking down the Adren before him, while Balor's axe pummelled downwards to his left and on his right Mar'h's sword jabbed in repeated thrusts over his shield at the faces of the enemy that were pressed towards him.

Still the two ends of the shield wall peeled away as warriors flung aside their shields and floundered to the boats that were almost upon them. The sea was up to Arthur's chest now and the waves lifted friend and foe alike as they swept their way onto the beach. The fight had become desperate and the Adren flung themselves at the nine warriors still around Arthur.

Coiled ropes flew from the nearest longboat and slapped into the water behind the last of the shield wall. Arthur roared the last order and the remnants of the shield wall broke apart as they flung their shields at their attackers and grasped for the ropes in the water behind them. Fending off the hacking Adren swords they wrapped the rope around their arms. Those on the longboat hauled with all their strength and the last of the shield wall surged raggedly backwards as they were pulled out of their depth and beyond the Adren still attacking them. Not all of them made it. Four of those last nine died, hacked down or lost to the sea.

Arthur was hauled up the side of the longboat still tightly gripping his sword. He spilled onto the deck and knelt on all fours, coughing up seawater. Mar'h and Balor were hoisted up over the side and flopped next to Arthur, Mar'h spluttering and gasping, Balor lying still and unmoving. Blood seeped from a head wound where his hardened leather cap had been split.

Arthur climbed to his feet, exhausted from the fighting in the water. He shook Mar'h back to a sense of his surroundings, 'Mar'h! See to Balor, he's hurt,' he shouted hoarsely to him.

Mar'h crawled across to the inert Balor and Arthur looked around the boat, trying to keep his feet as it pitched violently. The boat was being driven back towards the shore and to the Adren who lined the beach firing arrows out over the shallows, enraged that they had been cheated of killing the hated raiders.

Arthur searched the dark bay for the other boats. One was nearing the entrance to the cove, probably Ruraidh's as they were first off. The other two were gradually making headway after Ruraidh's longboat. In his own boat the Anglians at the front were pulling on the oars with all their strength but they were too few and their efforts only served to keep the boat pointing bow-first to the waves.

Elwyn was yelling orders from the stern where he stood on a raised platform manning the rudder. Arthur understood what he wanted even though his words were stolen by the wind. He gathered those around him and they began feeding the oars out into the boiling sea. Following the rhythm of the Anglians in front, they began to haul on the oars. Inch by inch then foot by foot they stopped the drift back to the shoreline. Saewulf, who was near the bows, began a chant and the Anglians roared it out to the strokes of the oars as they put their backs against the sea.

Arthur's men were too exhausted to join in. They shut their eyes and hauled on the long oars in time to the chanting. Their boat began to nose its way forward towards the mouth of the cove where Ruraidh's boat fought to make its way out. Arthur tried to look forward as the boat shuddered violently against the oncoming waves. The open sea looked no nearer but he could only see two boats ahead of them now, bows pointing to the narrower gap that led out of the cove. Either one boat had made it out or it had gone under, turned by a wave then capsized by those that followed greedily after.

Arthur's men, already exhausted by the battle, were tiring rapidly. Elwyn could see that they were not going to make it. He lashed the rudder in place and raced down the wooden planking to where Morveren and Mar'h were pulling on an oar. He jumped down beside them and turned his head away as a wave crashed against the side of the boat and cascaded over them.

'You know how to steer this boat?' he yelled at Morveren.

She nodded violently back, her long dark hair plastered across her face and neck. She had grown up by the sea in the far West of Wessex and had been sailing boats since childhood.

Elwyn flung his arm back towards the lashed tiller, 'Keep her pointed dead centre of the opening!' he yelled as Morveren worked her way past him. She ran lightly back down the boat, seemingly oblivious to the jarring assault of the waves. Seeing that Mar'h could not grip the oar with his left hand, Elwyn quickly lashed it to the oar and turned to yell at those around him, 'Row! Row or die!'

He joined Mar'h at the oar and together they swung it back into the water in time with those in front.

They rowed with arms and backs that burnt with the effort. They rowed with gulping desperate breaths that were not enough to feed their strained, exhausted muscles. They rowed blindly with faces screwed up in pain, crashing into those behind them when a deeper trough robbed their oars of any purchase in the water. They rowed beyond their limits, when their strength was gone and only their will remained. They made the entrance to the cove only for the concertinaed waves to hold them trapped in a boiling fury of white water. Elwyn screamed for one last effort for it was now or be turned and smashed against the cliffs that guarded the entrance. Somehow the Anglians manning the oars in the bows found the reserves to increase their strokes and the ragged band behind them doggedly followed the pace, knowing that another few seconds were all they could give.

It was enough. The longboat pulled through and away from the entrance. Arthur's men collapsed over their oars, fighting for breath while the Anglians sprang to the masthead to unfurl and set the storm sail. It rippled then cracked open and the boat surged to one side. Elwyn took the rudder from Morveren and the longboat leapt forward, diagonally cutting into the waves and rolling wildly from side to side.

Arthur's men were dead to the world and beyond caring whether the storm took them or not. For a long while they existed only in their own individual worlds of pain and exhaustion. Mar'h struggled to untie the rope that lashed his arm to the oar then gave up and drew his knife to cut himself free. He half crouched, half crawled his way back along the boat that tilted to first one side then the other as the heavy rollers of the sea first lifted the longboat then dropped it like a toy. Mar'h's stomach lurched up and down with every rise and fall as the boat fought up to the crest of each wave and then hurriedly slid down into its trough only to start the whole sickening process over again.

Finally he reached Balor who was still unconscious. He dragged him across to the side and propped him up then gingerly removed his split leather cap. The seawater that continually crashed over the sides had doused away the blood and washed the wound clean. It did not look too deep but Mar'h guessed that Balor would be at best badly concussed. He called across to one of the Anglians nearby and together they carried him to the comparative shelter of one of the stalls.

These longboats had no quarters below decks. They were not designed for anything more than a crossing of a few days and then not over winter seas. The warriors who only a short while ago were burning with exhaustion now huddled wherever they thought there might be shelter. The Anglians knew better, there was no shelter on a longboat in open seas and they busied themselves with the running of the boat. They all froze in the unrelenting and biting wind. The gale whipped the water from the tops of waves and the air was drenched with spray that continually soaked them, and their clothing gradually stiffened with ice despite their attempts to keep moving.

They saw no sign of the other boats, even if one or more had been near, the rolling dark hills of water and the winter night would have kept them from sight. Each boat took its own course, tacking widely across the dark, storm-driven seas. Elwyn was hoping to make it to a sheltered bay used by the Anglians and knew the other boats would be making for the same bay. Everyone on the boat had made the journey across the Western Seas on more than one occasion but that was on the ships from the Haven. They were far bigger than the longboats of the Anglians, three-masted and with quarters below decks.

They all recalled the tales of how one Imbolc the ships never returned to Middangeard. It had happened many generations ago and thousands had been lost. No one had survived to tell whether they were lost in a storm on the journey out or back, or whether they had landed on some strange unknown shore and met their fate there. Many tales were told of the lost crossing and many took enjoyment from listening to them but none wanted to be a part of any such tale.

Each spring when the sun rose once more over the Western Seas, the lookouts on the towers in the Haven watched the oceans for the sails of the homecoming ships and each year they celebrated both the homecoming and the Wakening of the Sun. Except for the year when they never came home when the tales tell of whole villages standing empty and fields going fallow. All through that summer they had kept watchers on the towers but the seas remained empty and as autumn approached they chose a new king and prayed to their gods for the thousands of the lost crossing.

The warriors on the longboat did not want to share that fate but could do nothing other than wait and keep out of the way of the Anglians as they went about the task of getting them home. Throughout the journey the wind howled against them as if seeking to drive them back to the Adren armies and the Shadow Lands. Elwyn worked the boat in long tacks, fighting against the wind while each turn took them a little closer to home. They covered six times the distance that the migrating birds took in autumn to get from coast to coast.

Most of the Wessex warriors were sick during the crossing and could not fathom the delight the Anglians seemed to take in their battle against the winter seas. Only Morveren among them took any pleasure in the journey. They watched in puzzlement as she became more carefree, laughing at the waves that often enveloped the boat, climbing the masthead to adjust the storm sail when the rigging became entangled. It seemed her small frame would be easily washed overboard or blown away like a leaf from the heights of the mast but she was surefooted and entirely at home as if she were in a no more foreign or dangerous a place than her roundhouse on Whitehorse Hill. With her long, black hair blowing freely in the wind and her laughter ringing clear and strong it seemed to those seeing her that the past was being unwritten as she storm washed away the horror of losing her companions and friends, leaving her clean and whole again.

Elwyn, who had not paid too much attention to her before, watched her take delight in the storm and he approved of the way she took it as a personal challenge to her ability to overcome it. He readjusted his opinion of Wessex seafaring just enough to admit that at least she knew what she was doing on a boat. And as he watched her, he found himself wondering, much to his surprise, if she were married or spoken for.

Arthur faced the storm in a different manner and in a different mood. He too was sick from the constant rolling and pitching but he remained at the prow, tightly gripping the railing to either side and facing each wave as it bore down on the small boat. He cursed the storm and railed against it, but he was also cursing whatever fate had claimed the warriors that had been lost to the enemy. He cursed at the deaths that had been and the deaths that would surely follow. He cursed the fate that took Trevenna,

Cei and Merdynn deep into the Shadow Lands. He cursed the king for wanting him dead. He cursed the fate that only allowed him to love Seren in such times as these. But most of all he cursed the Adren and whatever it was that had led them to the edge of his kingdom. As the waves crashed around him and the longboat ploughed its way onward he was unaware that he was already regarding the land before them, somewhere in the darkness, as his kingdom.

Balor had regained consciousness but wished he had not. His vision was blurred, the wound on the top of his head burned incessantly and he spent the entire journey retching from an empty stomach. He swore at Saewulf and Elwyn and told them to turn round so that he could find a decent death with his axe in his hand rather than drown like a rat or retch himself to the grave.

Mar'h was not in a much better state and whenever he did manage to slip into a fitful sleep he dreamt of a young Uathach girl with dark eyes, chained in an Adren hut and pleading for him to stop. Over the years his similar dreams had become less frequent and he hoped that perhaps they had left him altogether but since the Adren camp he had only stopped thinking about her when he was in the midst of battle. He could not even bring himself to think of his wife, Della, or his children. His guilt felt like a wet leather shroud shrinking around his soul.

They had spent four dark days entombed or revelling in their individual worlds when Elwyn saw Arthur shouting to him from the prow as the boat climbed up the side of a swelling wave. He dispatched Saewulf to see what it was that Arthur was pointing at while he remained at the rudder, as they were about to switch tack.

Saewulf joined Arthur at the prow and looked down into the sea where Arthur was pointing. The longboat seemed to hang balanced between cresting the wave and sliding back down the slope it had just climbed, and then it tilted forward and lurched towards the next trough. Saewulf could plainly see what was concerning Arthur. The sea around and before them was littered with ice, broken panes about six inches thick and a few feet across.

Saewulf nodded and passed back down the boat, stopping to warn people as he passed them. He was not concerned for the boat, this ice would not trouble the hardened oak planks that made up the hull, but there was a very real danger from the ice if the wind-riven waves sent it flying over the sides of the boat. Some of the warriors took heed and clasped their shields about them as they huddled miserably in the freezing wetness. Others, like Balor, would have welcomed a death by scything ice and ignored Saewulf's warnings.

When Saewulf told Elwyn they both smiled for it also meant something else; if there was ice in the water then land could not be far away. Saewulf went back to join Arthur on the prow and together they scanned the darkness ahead for any further sign that they neared land.

Gradually the ice sheets grew bigger and more numerous, the mountainous seas lessened to hills and they saw kelp and seaweed frozen into the ice. Saewulf reckoned land to be near and reported back to Elwyn. Arthur stirred his despondent warriors with the mixed news that land was not far off but that they would be rowing for it. The thought of getting off the longboat outweighed the dread of returning to the oars and they retook their positions on the benches and fed the long oars out to the sea as the Anglians finished furling the storm sail.

Saewulf set up the chant once more and the oars trimmed the top of the sea, turned, dipped and dug back through the water. The pace was steady with none of the frantic effort and burning pain of before as they nosed their way blindly towards the shore.

The lookout on the prow saw the white crests of waves advancing ahead of them as they rolled their way to the unseen land. Elwyn had no way of knowing exactly where they were landing. They had seen no stars to guide them across the sea. He had measured his speed and kept his timer turned but the rest was down to instinct and experience. He did however know that the rollers ahead of them and the way they were breaking meant that a sloped beach lay ahead of them and not the cliffs he had feared and which would smash his longboat to driftwood in seconds. He watched for any break in the rolling waves that might indicate rocks or outcrops. There were some to their right but none that lay ahead. It looked safe but in the darkness there was really only one way to find out what lay before them.

He shouted out for them to maintain their speed and the oarsmen swept the boat onwards. Just as he could make out the shore they ran aground. Fortune, at last, favoured them. They had found a sound landing place on the first attempt and were spared the work of searching the coastline for somewhere to put in.

The oars were shipped with some relief and the ramp put down into the shallows. Wearily they unlashed and unloaded the horses that had spent the entire journey in a state of panic. Arthur sent a group out under Mar'h to briefly scout the area and gather what firewood they could. The others struggled ashore with their meagre supplies.

Mar'h reported back that nothing stirred around or beyond the beach. They camped down in the snow-layered sand dunes and began the arduous task of lighting a fire from frozen driftwood unearthed from the grip of winter. The land behind the beach was flat fen land and the wind from the West blew across it in a constant ill-tempered gale. It did not buffet or swirl or lessen, it just cut across the fens intent on flattening all that had the temerity to raise its head above the long rushes. The dunes offered some protection but the gale sought out the intruders on the bleak landscape that it owned and cut through their soaked clothing, seeking to freeze them to the ground.

Elwyn organised a group to help him drag the longboat up onto the shore beyond the storm line. They used the stored wooden rollers in the longboat and a team of horses and they finished the job about the same time that the others finally managed to light, and keep alight, a fire. Once they had lit one they started lighting others until small groups sat around five fires among the dunes, everyone inching as close as they could to the flames to dry and warm themselves.

They cooked what they could and had their first hot broth since before the raid on the Adren camp. The talk around each fire was much the same. Where exactly were they? Did the other boats make it across the sea and where are they? Who saw what happened in the battle back at the cove? What happened to friends they had lost sight of and did all the boats even make it out of the cove? The questions were as many as the answers were few.

Arthur made it clear to everyone what the next step was going to be. The Anglians had moved their main camp down to the Causeway and that was south. That was where they would be heading as soon as they had some sleep, something to eat and dried themselves out. They could rest properly and eat properly once they were there. For the time being they had a few hours here to recover from the sea crossing.

Arthur decided to use that time by scouting up the coast to see if any of the other boats had landed just to their north. As he was saddling his horse, Morveren joined him and started to saddle hers.

'Mar'h looks in a bad way,' she commented. She finished saddling her horse first and began to help Arthur with his. Arthur looked across to where Mar'h was slumped by a fire. 'Could you finish this?' he asked Morveren.

She followed his gaze to Mar'h and nodded. Arthur walked back to the fires that were partially obscured by a fine snow that was being stripped from the fens by the incessant wind. He sat down next to Mar'h who did not move or acknowledge his presence.

'Mar'h?'

He looked up at Arthur and his dark eyes had a glazed, distant quality. Most of the warriors around the fires had the same expression and after what they had been through in the past few months Arthur was not too concerned about it. What did concern Arthur was the hunted look that had stolen into Mar'h's eyes since the Adren camp and the discovery of Caja.

'What you've done is in the past, Mar'h. Neither you nor I can change it. You were young and stupid and the raid was badly led by a man who was a curse to those near him. An evil act does not necessarily make a man evil. You are not an evil man. You've tortured yourself over what you did and if you allow what we saw in the Adren camp to re-ignite that torture then you will descend into a pit of recrimination and there you will die. If you choose to follow that path then you turn your back on Della, you turn your back on your children, you turn your back on the people who depend upon you in this war band and you turn your back on me.

'It's not a path you have to take. You can choose another. You've done much that is good and much that is necessary since that raid. You can choose to continue doing so. If you turn your back on this choice too then you compound what you did back then. You've paid for your crime by all you've done since. Your debt is paid. And do not think that what we saw in that hut has anything to do with you for it doesn't.'

Mar'h was staring at Arthur as he spoke and Arthur could see the guilt-driven doubts behind his eyes.

'Leave your guilt here on this beach Mar'h and let the wind take it out to sea or walk instead into the depths carrying it close to your heart and end it now. Choose before I return for I will not watch you tear your soul apart for one wrong act deep in your past. Remember Della and your children, you fight to protect them and all like them, even that Uathach girl you now fight to protect. Remember we fight to prevent what we saw in that Adren hut. Remember that you are no longer a battle-crazed youth lead by such as Saltran. Remember the good you have done and can continue to do. Forget this and the Adren can claim one more victory because it will be four good people who died in that Adren hut, not three.'

Arthur put his hands on Mar'h's shoulders, 'Choose.'

He returned to where Morveren waited with both their horses.

'Is he still grieving?' Morveren asked.

'Yes, he is,' Arthur replied.

They started north up the beach that stretched before them in the darkness. The wind whipped at them and Morveren shook her long hair from her face.

'You enjoyed the crossing didn't you?' he asked her.

She looked out across the bay's water, the waves still rolling shoreward despite the wind that skimmed the tops off the hooked rollers, trying to push them back.

'I love the sea. I always have, for as long as I can remember. I grew up on the fishing boats that sail the seas around Wessex. There's something dispassionate and pure about it. It seethes and storms but not in rage and not caring for anything caught in its tempest. It's the closest to the gods we can reach and to ride such storms, it's like riding the anger of the gods.'

'And that means you can tame them?' Arthur asked smiling at her.

'Oh no, not tame them. But if you can ride their anger then you no longer need to fear them. Perhaps you can even use their wrath. Isn't it possible to harness the anger of the gods?' Morveren looked at Arthur as she finished, unsure how she had arrived at the point where she had disclosed so much and afraid that he would scorn her.

'I don't doubt you could ride their anger and use it too. I saw you on the boat and you seemed to be part of the storm. It fed something inside you and I can understand that,' he replied and thought of the storm above the Winter Wood and how he had cursed the storm at sea too. Then he continued, 'But I don't believe in the gods and I don't believe in fate either, though it doesn't seem to stop me cursing both.'

They rode on discussing the gods, fate and people's superstitions. Morveren was enjoying talking to Arthur in this way, a way she had not done so before. She had been aware of the rumours that Arthur was her true father before she had joined the war band but back in her village no one had ever voiced the speculation so openly to her. The warriors of the war band didn't seem to have any such compunction about putting such questions to her directly. She found the best way to silence them was to tell them to put their questions to Arthur. She did not believe the rumours were true and resented the implication that she had only been accepted because she was Arthur's bastard. She had always been more than a bit scared of the Wessex Warlord and feared he thought of her as little more than a girl who could ride a horse quickly and only useful for sending messages. Whether Arthur was her father or not, he was her warlord and she wanted his respect. She knew the chances of talking to Arthur in such a manner would be limited and she sought to continue the conversation, 'Why then do you curse them, the gods and fate?'

'I curse the gods and I curse fate for the same reasons I curse storms. I don't really believe in them because I can't batter them down and I can't defeat them. I don't trust something I can't understand, control or defeat. It makes me angry that such things should exist.'

The tone in Arthur's voice sharply reminded Morveren why she was wary of the warlord.

'They scare you?' she said then shut her mouth, appalled that the thought had been spoken aloud. She looked at him quickly, her eyes wide in fear. Arthur smiled at her but the corners of his mouth were turned down, it was more a smile of derision, 'There's only one thing I'm scared of.'

Morveren had to ask and did so in a voice that barely carried above the wind, 'What?'

'Horses. This horse particularly.'

She laughed in relief that the moment had passed.

'They're itching for exercise. Let's give them a run.'

They cantered up the beach, the horses' hooves sinking first through the snow then the sand beneath. Arthur marvelled to himself how Morveren could be so light-hearted after the deaths of Elowen and Tomas. They had been a tight-knit group. He was surprised too that their friend, Ethain, had chosen to go east with Cei. Perhaps he had discovered a newfound courage. Perhaps the storm had torn the grief from Morveren. Perhaps they were just young. That was one of the problems of getting older, he thought to himself, you remembered being young and the things you did when you were young but you could not actually remember what it felt like to be young; to be immortal.

It was strange though, Arthur thought, Ethain had been scared, very scared yet he took the bravest choice. Elowen had been far from a generous person yet she had thrown her life away just to stand by Tomas at his death, she must have known he could not be saved. Caja, who had been an innocent village girl, raped and tortured beyond sanity only to die by the sword meant to protect her. Mar'h, who was the most pragmatic of his warriors, spiralling into a pit of regret and guilt. Ceinwen, a healer yet unable to understand why he had ended Sawan's pain. Even helping the Uathach had been an unseen turn of events. He dwelled for a while on Cei and the others before putting the thought of those going east from his mind and his thoughts settled instead on Seren and the Veiled City. Much had changed in just a few months and he wondered how much more would change in the coming months, and how much of that would be for the good.

He spurred his horse to gain ground on Morveren who was some way ahead. The tattered clouds were tearing apart and the half moon looked to be sailing through them as it sent long shadows racing across the fen lands and out to sea. Arthur could see Morveren heading back towards him. His own horse whinnied a greeting and trotted towards her.

'There's a fire ahead!' she shouted as she drew near. 'You can see it from the next headland!'

Together they made their way to the headland at the end of the long beach. The fire looked to be over the water and some miles distant.

'It must be a beacon,' Morveren said, for it must have been a large fire to be seen from where they were. Arthur studied the sweeping bay they would have to follow to arrive at the fire.

'Let's see who it is then,' Arthur said and they set off, side by side, on the long trip around the bay to the next headland where the beacon burned brightly.

They rode mostly in silence across the even ground, not pushing their horses too hard as they were still weakened by the journey across the sea. When they did speak it was Morveren who began the brief conversations. She talked of Talan, Tomas and Elowen but she was not morbid about their deaths, she talked of the good times they had shared. Arthur contributed enough to encourage her to continue, thinking it would be good for her to talk about them but his mind was on other matters.

'Do you think Ceinwen made it away from the cove?' Morveren asked after a quiet few minutes.

'I don't know. Hopefully she got away with the wounded just before the Adren fell upon us.'

'And Morgund?' she asked, feigning nonchalance.

'There'll be a lot of happy husbands if he didn't.'

'And unhappy wives,' Morveren added ruefully.

Arthur turned to look at her but she was looking studiously out towards the dark sea. He smiled to himself and they continued onwards with the wind whipping around them tugging at their cloaks and rifling their horses' manes. The clouds had hurried away to the East where a rolling bank was all that remained of the blizzard, lit by the moon in shades of bright white and utter black. The ground before them was now well lit and only lost definition with distance. The wind had not dropped and it seemed that an autumn mist clung to the ground as far as they could see but it was just the snow being sifted and drifting across the fen lands.

Arthur's gaze kept returning to the moon. Its cold light denied the heavens to all but the brightest stars on their slow journey across the winter sky. His thoughts turned inevitably back to Fin Seren. It seemed to him that since he had last seen her the time had been filled with either fighting the Adren or planning how to fight them and that he had had little time to dwell upon his feelings for the Cithol woman whose heart he could not read. He thought that perhaps that was why he had fallen in love with her so quickly and equally why he had not fallen in love with any of his own people. It struck him as strange that he could only love a person that he could not read. Perhaps it was only because he could not see the whole of her heart that he was free to place his faith in it. His faith could not be contradicted. He felt troubled by the implication that his feelings and judgement were based on faith and not knowledge. Until now he had not put any store in faith, he had trusted only what could be trusted. He wondered if he was making a mistake in abandoning that principle.

They were beginning to approach the beacon so he put the issue to one side and concentrated instead on what lay ahead. Morveren's eyesight was slightly better than his was and she spotted the longboats first, pointing out to Arthur where they were beached to one side of the blazing fire. They realised it must be two of the boats that had made it out of the cove and they quickened their pace.

Bowmen covered them as they approached the beacon until Ceinwen recognised their respective and contrasting riding styles. She called out to Morgund who joined her and they held the horses as Arthur and Morveren dismounted and the two riders exchanged a glance to acknowledge the answer to their earlier questions regarding the two before them.

'Did everyone make it safely out and across?' Arthur asked.

'Yes, we did, at least everyone who made it onto the boats. We haven't seen Ruraidh's boat but I think he made it out of the cove,' Ceinwen answered.

'We got here first on Lissa's boat then set up the beacon to help guide in yours or Aylydd's,' Morgund added.

'We landed down the coast. Are you all fit to travel?' Arthur asked as they made their way to the blazing beacon.

'It'll take us a while to get the horses ready but yes, even the wounded can travel on horseback or on stretchers between horses. Should we wait for Ruraidh's boat?' Ceinwen asked.

'They would have headed for the coast further to the North. Without horses they would have wanted to land as near to their village as they could,' Arthur replied.

'What about Gwyna and the other wounded Uathach?' Morgund asked.

'Where are they?'

Morgund led them to where the wounded lay or sat near the fire while Ceinwen started to organise the saddling of the horses. Arthur and Morveren walked among those who had been injured, exchanging comments and greetings until they saw Gwyna off to one side. Arthur turned to Morgund and asked him to bring them some food then sat down next to Gwyna while Morveren moved closer to the fire to warm herself.

'How's your shoulder?' he asked her.

'It's improving, you have a good healer,' she replied. Arthur was surprised. He had expected another surly outburst from the young daughter of Ablach.

'Good. Can you ride?' Arthur said.

'Yes. If I had a horse to ride.'

'Your companion?'

Gwyna looked at the figure laid out beside her, now deeply asleep after taking one of Ceinwen's powders, and shook her head.

'Well, you can take a horse if you wish and make north, we'll look after your companion.'

Gwyna looked reluctant to take up the offer.

'Or you can both come south with us and take the supplies back to your people when you think he's fit to travel.'

Gwyna looked at him and Arthur saw none of the hatred that had masked her face when they were on the other side of the sea. He noticed the bruising on the side of her face from where he had struck her and he noticed something else in her eyes too, an appraising steady look. Gradually she nodded and lowered her eyes. Arthur was amused by the change in her; clearly the last few days had either knocked the fight out of her or she had been forced to change her opinion of the southern warriors.

'You don't expect a trap? You no longer want to take my head back as a prize for your father?' he asked, enjoying her discomfort.

She remained looking at the ground as she replied, 'You and your war band fought well. All of you. Both at the Adren camp and at the cove. Ceinwen has treated my shoulder well and Mar'h and that one helped me out of the Adren camp and across the plain,' she said nodding towards Morveren.

'They may have helped you across the plain but it was Elowen who dragged you out of the camp,' Arthur replied.

'Then I owe Elowen too,' Gwyna said wearily.

'Elowen died at the camp.'

Gwyna lowered her head further and Arthur thought he saw her sigh. 'I will travel south with you and then take the supplies back to my people, if you still intend the offer,' she said.

Lissa and Aylydd were not happy about having to leave their longboats on the beach but few wanted to board them again and sail south. Arthur pointed out that they would not be able to sail them anywhere near to the Causeway and they would have to beach them somewhere. Once the sun rose in spring they could come back and take them up one of the rivers and into the fens, until then they should be well out of the reach of the winter seas.

They scooped up snow and sand with their shields to put out the beacon and they made their way south, retracing the journey made earlier by Arthur and Morveren. Arthur rode with Morgund and Cael discussing who had escaped from the cove and whom they had left behind. Morveren rode with Ceinwen, Gwyna and the wounded, surprised to find herself slightly resenting not being able to ride alone with Arthur.

When they reached the rest of the warriors, camped around Elwyn's longboat, Arthur sought out Mar'h. He had been busy feeding the horses and saddling them. Arthur did not need to ask him what his choice had been; one look at his face told him all he needed to know. Mar'h was resolved to close a door on the past and face what lay ahead. It only remained to be seen if he was capable of doing so.

They packed what little they had left and headed south to the Causeway.

Chapter Twelve

Of the eighty who had left the Causeway only forty returned. Cei had taken eighteen into the Shadow Lands and the rest were dead. The lookouts on the cliffs above the Gates saw the war band winding their way along the coastal path under a crescent moon. The news of their approach raced down to the Anglian camp and Ruadan and Hengest watched Arthur's warriors snake their way down to the Causeway.

In the cold moonlight Ruadan's eyes darted along the approaching line of horsemen as he softly counted under his breath. He stopped counting at thirty-eight with a curse. His face became grim and he started counting again.

'I made it thirty-nine, not counting the ones on stretchers,' Hengest said as Ruadan continued, desperately hoping they were both wrong.

'And I don't see Cei. Or Merdynn,' Hengest said, then added in a quieter voice, 'or my Father.'

Ruadan drew a hand across his eyes, pinching the bridge of his nose and breathing in deeply. 'Perhaps there's more to follow,' he said without any real conviction. They both descended from the wall to meet the returning warriors.

Arthur led his riders through the gates. All the warriors in the compound, those from Arthur and Cei's war bands who had garrisoned the Gates while their companions travelled the Shadow Lands, gathered to watch them enter. They stood on the battlements and outside the two wooden halls. They watched from the line of tents and they watched from the gates. They all stood silently, looking at the gaunt faces and weary figures as they stiffly dismounted. They stood silently and wondered what stories were behind this band of exhausted warriors, some without shields, some carrying injuries and all of them looking worn and empty. They searched for the faces of their friends and names were spoken quietly, the names of those they could not see among the survivors.

The Anglians were dismayed that Cei was not amongst them. Other names followed, Trevenna, Aelfhelm, Leah, Cerdic, the list went on. Tamsyn stood to one side, searching the heavily cloaked figures for her friends. She finally saw Morveren and she barely recognised her.

Ruadan and Hengest approached Arthur. Ruadan embraced Ceinwen and they held each other for a long time.

'Cei? Aelfhelm?' Hengest asked quickly and then more guardedly, 'Trevenna?'

'Not everyone missing is lost. But first, we have wounded. The horses need feed. We need food and we need warmth and rest.'

'Of course,' Ruadan said and stirred the onlookers into action. Suddenly the watchers moved to their friends and companions and the questions started.

Once the injured were taken from Ceinwen's care and the horses led away, Arthur made for the eating hall. He sat wearily at a table and poured himself a cup of wine. Ruadan noted Arthur's slumped shoulders, the ice melting in his beard, the dried sea salt and blood on his winter clothing and the weary way he poured himself a second cup of wine, but his gaze was not distant nor were his reddened eyes glazed. There may have been dark patches under the gray eyes but they were hard and cold and still uncompromising.

Arthur first asked if there had been any attacks on the Gates and Ruadan told him there had been no sign of the Adren on the Causeway. Satisfied with that news Arthur then related the entire journey through the Shadow Lands. The hall was crowded with as many as could fit in and they sat or stood silently while Arthur related the events from across the Causeway. Heroic deeds, deaths, battles, hardships, the immense Adren armies and camps, the ambushes, the slaughter of the villages and the subsequent feasting upon the dead, all were met in silence as Arthur narrated the tale. The time for questions, praise and expressions of grief and horror would follow later with the countless retelling of the various stages of the sortie across the Causeway but this was the time for listening to the whole tale told by the warlord who would neither understate nor exaggerate. This was the report that could be believed entirely for it told of what happened and why it happened. Other tales would follow from different perspectives, Berwyn and Saewulf's tale of the Belgae, Elwyn's tale of the winter sea crossing, and Balor's boasts of battle.

Then the quieter stories would come, told to only a few at a time. Mar'h would tell of the hut in the Adren camp although he would take a care to keep silent about Caja being one of the victims. Ceinwen would tell of the death of Sawan. Balor would relate what he saw after the interrogation of the Adren Captain. Morgund the meeting with the Uathach. The beheading of the Adren. Individual versions of the battle at the cove and personal opinions on the departure of Cei and Merdynn to stem the Adren supplies. How and where each warrior had died. Countless tales to be told and each would grow in the retelling.

Once Arthur had concluded the tale of the Shadow Lands he got up silently and left the hall to find a warm, dry place to sleep. Gwyna, alone in the hall of her enemies, stood against a wall in the shadows of the hall where she had watched Arthur speak. Her gaze followed him as he opened the door to the hall and walked out into the moonlit night. The noise grew in the hall as everyone started talking at once. Questions were fired at the warriors who had returned from the East and as tired as they were they nonetheless answered them with the eagerness of those at the centre of a tale. As the wine flowed and stories were embellished, Gwyna slipped out of the door unnoticed and followed Arthur.

She saw him walk across the compound towards the lines of tents against the West wall. Fires burned in front of the tents and a canvas canopy stretched over both the tents and the fires to keep the warmth in for those who were sleeping. She looked around furtively but no one was watching her and she made her way to the one that Arthur had entered. She stood outside with her heart hammering in her chest. Still she hesitated, caught in two opposing minds.

Arthur peeled off his heavy winter clothing and lay down between two layers of sheepskin bedding. He stared at the canvas above him as he tried to still his mind from reliving the events and decisions of the past few months. For several minutes he was unaware of the figure deliberating outside his tent before the soft shuffle of pines underfoot alerted him. He watched as the fire outlined the shadow of a figure bending down to unfasten the ties securing the entrance. As the figure crawled into the tent on all fours her face was momentarily lit by the fire outside. Arthur saw it was Gwyna.

'What do you want here, Gwyna?' he asked.

She knelt by his side, her face and intent hidden in the darkness.

'You. I'm an Uathach alone amongst the southern war bands. Here I'm safe.'

Arthur watched her in the darkness as she eased her leather jerkin off her injured and bandaged shoulder then pulled her woollen top off over her head. He watched the curve of her breasts, outlined against the lit canvas behind her as she turned to face him again.

'Move over. I'll freeze out here,' she said with an anxious smile.

Arthur inched over holding up the top sheepskin cover and Gwyna slid between the layers. Hoisting herself off the ground she worked her trousers off and cast them to one side of the low bed. She moved closer to Arthur until her head was resting on his shoulder with her long hair strewn across his chest. She rested her thigh across his knees and slowly slid it over the top of his legs, moving her body closer into him. Arthur watched her shadowed face, only inches away as she drew her teeth lightly across his shoulder. Suddenly her hand whipped round and plunged down toward his chest.

The knife stopped just above his heart, her wrist gripped tightly in his hand. He wrenched the hand to one side and the knife flew free then flung her to one side, rolling on top of her. He pinned her hands to the ground above her head and as she struggled he worked his legs between hers and forced them apart. She ceased writhing and they stopped, both breathing hard. In the faint glow from the fire outside they stared at each other.

Gwyna hadn't really expected to be able to assassinate Arthur so easily and as she stared into his eyes she finally acknowledged that her hatred of him and all he stood for was equally matched by her attraction to the power it represented and to the man who wielded that power. It was that attraction that had drawn her to Arthur's tent.

Still pinning her wrists over her head with one hand, Arthur gradually ran his other hand down the side of her still bruised face and down the length of her throat. Her breaths shortened as his hand continued on down her body and without saying a word to each other they wiped away the memories and fear of the past few months and expressed the joy and relief of surviving with a night of fierce, loveless sex. Some hours later she quietly left Arthur's tent.

When Arthur emerged from his tent he felt content and satisfied. He neither felt any longing for Gwyna nor any remorse over their joint release. Neither did it seem strange to him that she had tried to kill him. He knew that the more extreme a passion becomes the closer it sometimes gets to its opposite. He had no doubt that as Gwyna had knelt outside his tent she had hated him and everything he stood for and that she had meant to kill him if it was possible. It hadn't been possible and sex had substituted as the necessary outlet for the violence they mutually felt. He understood her better, and was perhaps more similar to her, than he would have liked to admit.

The rest of the returned warriors had found their way to the tents after drinking their way through the first round of tales and were still sleeping soundly. Arthur sought out Ruadan and started to organise the supplies that Gwyna would take to Ablach's village, Dalchiaran, somewhere to the North of Anglia. He decided that Mar'h, Berwyn and Saewulf should go with Gwyna and her wounded companion. The two Anglians were now familiar with Ruraidh and the others in his band, and they in turn trusted them. Mar'h would represent Arthur and the Wessex war band and, as he had helped to carry the injured Gwyna from the Belgae village, Arthur felt that Gwyna would trust him. Arthur hoped that between Mar'h and the two Anglians they could stress to Ablach that the Adren armies threatened both of their lands equally.

A few hours later three carts left the Causeway, laden with supplies and heading north. Arthur saw them off through the gates and apart from one exchanged look with Gwyna, it was as if nothing had passed between the two of them.

Once the carts had climbed the paths up to the cliff tops Arthur and Ruadan took their horses and slowly rode east along the Causeway towards the watchers at the far end. Ruadan asked him further questions about the journey in the Shadow Lands, particularly about Cei and Merdynn's departure and their mission. Arthur had already told Ceinwen the true nature of Cei's quest and he now told Ruadan. He asked Ruadan to tell Hengest and that would bring to four those who knew how much depended on the venture deep in the Shadow Lands.

Ruadan was shocked that Arthur felt it necessary to gamble so much with such a slim chance of success. Even though he had listened to the reports of how many Adren lay across the Causeway it was not until that moment that he realised just how precarious their position was. Ceinwen had been shocked too but for different reasons. She had seen the forces arrayed against them and fully realised what they faced but what shocked her was that Arthur was prepared to send so many of those close to him to their certain deaths. She did not think they would be returning and she hated Arthur for throwing their lives away on a foolish hope and she had told Ruadan as much.

Ruadan had hoped to see a difference in Ceinwen's attitude to Arthur once she had gotten over the shock of what had happened at Branque and after she had spent some time getting to know him once again. He had hoped that being with Arthur, Trevenna and Cei would have re-ignited her old friendships and taken away some of the pain of losing her family but it seemed to him that nothing much had changed; she still seemed distant from Arthur and, while the others in the war band seemed to have accepted her, she still carried about her the impenetrable air of grief that would inevitably keep a barrier between her and her new companions. He understood it a little better when she told him about how Arthur had ended Sawan's suffering or, as Ceinwen put it, when Arthur had murdered him. He wondered if the events across the Causeway had only served to deepen her despair when he had hoped that an active role with the warriors might have alleviated her personal pain. He knew that Arthur had only done what was necessary and he believed that deep down Ceinwen knew it too. He worried that his sister's resistance to the brutal necessities of war showed a reluctance to accept what she had lost and an inability or unwillingness to face the reality unfolding around her. He hadn't contradicted her tirade against Arthur and hoped that time would heal what she was unable to heal herself.

He glanced across at Arthur's face as they rode side by side through the darkness and wondered what it took to send your own sister and your oldest friend on a mission that would surely end with their deaths. Ruadan realised that with Merdynn gone as well, Arthur was becoming more isolated and the few who could influence him were now far away. He studied Arthur's face briefly but he didn't look like a man who needed support from those around him. There was a set determination in the expressionless face and a distance in the eyes that spoke of the calculations being weighed and judgements decided. Arthur turned to look at him and for a second Ruadan saw a frozen coldness in Arthur's gray eyes and his heart started in fear, sending slow, deep, resonant echoes through his chest.

The moment passed and Arthur was asking him a question about the watchers up ahead. As he answered he realised that Arthur was alone and perhaps he had intended it to be so. Perhaps he could only do what had to be done if he was alone. At the same moment he realised that Arthur did not need their support or friendship and did not expect or necessarily want it in return, all he needed was their loyalty.

The watchers had nothing to report. Arthur stayed for a while at the small fortification that Ruadan had built across this end of the Causeway. He talked to the guards there and briefly told them the news that had been recounted previously at the Gates. One of the guards mentioned that they had not seen the deer herds this year. For many generations the Causeway Gates had been opened as the sun set in the East and thousands of migrating deer patiently crossed the Causeway in their unhurried journey to leave behind the colder lands of the East. It had become an inherited custom to allow the herds unthreatened passage, an unspoken acknowledgement of the mutual threat posed by the long, dark winter. The warriors would watch the spectacle knowing that they would be hunting these very same deer in the months ahead. It made sense to let them cross the Causeway unhindered for if they killed the deer as they crossed then they would eventually abandon the migration west and the hunters would have to go into the Shadow Lands for their hunting expeditions. It also provided them with a self-satisfied sense of honour. The deer had not crossed this year and the guards guessed that the Adren must have slaughtered the unsuspecting herds as they gathered in the forests beyond the Causeway. The warriors were just as outraged by this as they had been about the slaughter at Eald and Branque. Arthur's mood darkened; the Adren now had a ready supply of meat.

He climbed up the tower and stood looking out into the winter darkness, staring east and wondering how far Cei's band had travelled, whether the Adren were still unaware of their goal, indeed whether they were even still alive.

Ruadan stood beside him and mistakenly thought Arthur was pondering the inevitable Adren onslaught.

'Do you think we can hold them here?' he asked.

'Yes, we have to. It may be the only place where we can,' Arthur replied after a pause.

'We've finished constructing the defences, though we keep adding things as someone comes up with something new.'

'And there's been no sign of the Adren at all?'

'No, nothing. Not even a raid to test our defences. They must be waiting for the sun.'

'Then we still have two months.' Arthur looked around at the outpost then continued, 'I want you to make this the first line of defence. Build up the walls. The marshland protects the flanks here. Once you've done that then build another defence between here and the Gates. I don't want them to gain a yard without dying for it. And always make sure you have the same cutting and bridge system so that each outpost can retreat without being routed.'

Ruadan nodded and started to mentally calculate the wood they would need and how long it would take.

'I'm going to Caer Sulis to inform the king of what we saw in the Shadow Lands,' Arthur said.

'I thought he'd gone west,' Ruadan replied, taken aback.

'We have reason to believe he stayed behind, but we don't know why yet. Whether he is there or not, those that remain at Caer Sulis must prepare for war. There are those there that we can start to train, and others who can help with the making of war gear.'

'Do you want me to stay here with Hengest and work on the defences?'

'Yes, but I will need to take forty or so warriors with me to Caer Sulis and I'll need Hengest to represent the Anglians.'

'He's excellent at organising and engineering the defences,' Ruadan pointed out.

Arthur considered this then said, 'Then I'll take Elwyn as the Anglian leader, with some of his warriors too.'

'You still expect trouble from King Maldred and his Mercians?'

'Yes, but again I don't know what kind of trouble to expect.'

'Take a care Arthur. Maldred is a dangerous man who wants you out of the way, and he's no fool.'

'He may be wise in settling local disputes but I fear that ultimately he is a self-serving fool and one who will lead my people to slaughter.' With that, Arthur descended the tower and they made their way back to the Causeway Gates where Arthur began to prepare for the journey to Caer Sulis.

Arthur delayed their departure as most of the forty that were to accompany him had been with him in the East and he wanted them all to have recovered before they began. He waited as the moon waned until his warriors had rested fully, eaten their fill and recounted their stories from the Shadow Lands. Those that were staying at the Causeway looked to the East, thinking of the size of the Adren armies that would swarm across the Causeway once spring came and they knew that they would be first in the defence of Britain. They set about strengthening and adding to the fortifications with a renewed urgency as Arthur led his band up the cliff paths on the beginning of their journey to Caer Sulis.

Balor had decided to stay at the Causeway and help with the fortifications. Ceinwen had been undecided about staying with Ruadan, which was where she wanted to be, and travelling with the war band where she thought she may be needed. She had a feeling of foreboding about the meeting with the king, a feeling that had been stoked by Ruadan's observations of Arthur, which he had shared with her. She had broached the subject with Morgund back at the Causeway. Morgund had dismissed the king by commenting that he had not seen Maldred in the Shadow Lands, or his precious warriors there either. She began to suspect that both the Anglian and Wessex war bands were beginning to regard Arthur as more than just the Wessex Warlord. It worried her even more that she suspected Arthur felt much the same. She resigned herself to being more embroiled in the affairs of the southern tribes and chose to accompany Arthur's band.

Arthur had set scouting riders out on their flanks, unwilling to make the same mistake that Llud had made, and the company rode, two or three abreast, across the winter-locked land. They had renewed their winter clothing and they wrapped and belted the furs closely about themselves as they crossed iced snowfields and skirted woods and rivers frozen to a deep stillness under a comfortless moon.

A few warriors at the rear of the line, led by Cael's baritone voice, were singing a refrain known widely in the southern lands. It was a winter song, mourning the lifeless land and longing for the sun to re-awaken the trees and rivers and bring back to life the animals and birds that were either sleeping away the darkness or passing the winter far from Middangeard. Although the ballad was doleful, the mood of the warriors was not. They had escaped the Shadow Lands alive when many had thought they wouldn't survive to meet up again with their companions at the Causeway. Their hopes were high that Cei would be able to ambush the Adren supplies on the East Road and still return safely. With just a small band Arthur had raided the Adren forces arrayed against them, hurt them and brought most of his riders home again. They believed he could stop the Adren and protect their homes. Arthur was not so sure.

He planned to make the journey to Caer Sulis with only two stops, one above the Winter Wood at Dunraven, where there was now a semi-permanent camp, and one at Whitehorse Hill where he planned to check on the preparations for war. It would make for a long journey between the two stops but the warriors were well rested and none wanted to linger in the cold lands. When they camped near the Winter Wood he intended to visit the Veiled City. Lord Venning would need to hear about the Adren forces massing across the Causeway and about the venture that Merdynn was undertaking. While those reasons were true there were two other more important reasons why he wanted to once again enter the Cithol City. The one he allowed himself to think about was Fin Seren, the other he barely acknowledged even to himself.

They arrived at the hilltop camp under a cloudless sky and the stars shone coldly on the bare, still trees. Arthur recalled the last time he was here and as Morgund passed him they talked briefly of the storm that had raged about them at this place.

The silence of the copse was soon broken as they began setting up camp. Arthur walked off to one side and stared up through the snow-lined and frosted branches at the cold, hard stars. The waning moon was a thin crescent above the horizon. He heard Ceinwen walk up beside him. She took her thick woollen cap off her head and ran a hand through her sweat-matted hair. She followed his gaze.

'Beautiful isn't it?' she said.

Arthur nodded.

'But so cold and somehow unforgiving,' she added.

Arthur looked at her and for the first time in a long while they smiled with some of the warmth they used to share.

'You're going down into the Veiled City aren't you?' she asked.

'Yes, there are some things I must do there,' he replied.

'And someone you want to see?'

They smiled again and Arthur turned to go, saying, 'I'll be some hours. They can prepare a hot meal and then rest until I return. Do you want to come with me?'

'Oh no, that place scares me more than the Shadow Lands. I'll stay here thank you. But take a care down there, the Cithol strike me as more than they would wish to appear.'

Arthur began the descent down the hillside, searching the distant tree line for the path that wound deep into the Winter Wood. Off to his right a brand was lit and waved slowly from side to side. He headed towards it. His heart beat faster when he saw who held the burning brand. His memory had played him false; she was more beautiful than he had remembered. As he approached her she passed the torch to one of her maids who took it and disappeared back down the winding path.

Fin Seren stood at a gap in the trees clasping a fur cloak closely about her. In the starlight she looked delicate and ephemeral. It seemed to Arthur that the white jewels strung around her neck glinted with the pale light caught from each of the stars in the winter sky. As Arthur struggled through the last of the deep snow she smiled at him and held out her slender white arms towards him. Arthur's embrace lifted her off her feet. He set her down again and they held each other at arm's length, one regarding the other.

'So, the Lord of Wessex returns early and safely from the East?'

'I do but many didn't and some still travel the Shadow Lands. How did you know I was here?'

'The eyesight of your people may be good in the winter-dark but I was born to the winter and can see you from afar.'

'So Terrill saw us coming and sent word to you?' Arthur said with a grin and Seren laughed.

'Would you allow me no secrets, Arthur?'

'Your secrets are one of the reasons why I love you.'

'Strange though it may seem, I feel precisely the same way.'

'And there's another reason.'

'Come. Tell me what happened in the East and tell me of the news from Middangeard.' With that, Seren turned and led him along the path to the Veiled City. Arthur noticed several turnings off their path, dark passageways that twisted away into the woods and he asked Seren where they led.

'False paths, Arthur. Wrong turnings that lead to nowhere or back upon themselves. To find the Veiled City you need a guide. You have a guide, now tell me the tales of the Shadow Lands.'

Arthur recounted the journey from leaving the Causeway to their return across the sea in the storm. Seren listened patiently, occasionally glancing at his face or tightening her grip on his hand at different parts of the tale. She was saddened by the deaths of each of the warriors and felt despair for the fate of Caja and the other two women. When Arthur had finished they walked on in silence, following the path as the brand carried by Seren's maid bobbed among the trees ahead of them like a marsh spirit leading them deeper into the darkness.

Seren walked with her head slightly bowed and the hood of her fur cloak hid her face from Arthur. The faint tracings of her eyebrows were drawn down in a frown as she weighed the news of Merdynn's departure into the East and how her father might react to that. Under her thick fur cloak her right hand absently turned and twisted the necklace that hung around her throat as her thoughts dwelled on the sheer numbers of the massed Adren armies waiting to cross the Causeway.

They reached the stone gateway to the Winter Garden and Seren put her concerns to one side for the present. She stepped in front of Arthur and taking his hands said, 'Let me show you the Winter Garden as it should be seen and for a while we can forget what troubles us.'

Arthur smiled at her impulsive childlike excitement and sudden change of mood. He found himself comparing the ethereal beauty and contagious enthusiasm of Seren with the hard-eyed distrust of the wild Gwyna. He put the Uathach girl from his mind and together they walked the meandering pathways within the high walled garden. The bright constellations of the winter sky cast the carved bowers in pale, strange imitations of the encroaching woods beyond the walls, and their endless reflections glittered like jewels that had been flung upon the frozen fountains and pools. It was as if the stars themselves had been embedded in the crystalled ice. The sculpted stone horses crashing through a stream were locked in time with the cascading fountains splashing up from about their hooves hanging frozen in an endless moment.

The Winter Garden held more than just stone sculptures and Seren led Arthur to a pond where a figure, sculpted from ice, stood with outstretched arms. She knelt down by the edge of the deeply frozen pool and pointed up between the figure's arms. Arthur knelt beside her in the snow and looked in wonder, unable to understand how such beauty could be fashioned from nature. Between the outstretched arms spanned a delicate cobweb like a frosted net and through its intricately circular threads he could see the cloudy rim of the Milky Way pinned with the brightest stars of the heavens.

'I call him the Star Fisher,' Seren said softly. She was filled with the pleasure of showing Arthur the Winter Garden and delighted in his wonder. She led him to a far bower where her maid had lain deep furs and set two blazing fires. Heavy curtains hung across the entrance and inside it was warm and private.

As they lay on the furs the roaring fires warmed them and cast flickering shadows about them. Arthur traced a finger down the side of her slender neck and said quietly, 'I never knew there could be such beauty.'

Seren smiled in delight, thinking he meant the Winter Garden and held him tightly against herself. She propped herself up on one elbow and gazed intently into his eyes as if on the brink of saying something irrevocable but Arthur leant across and kissed her. She decided to wait.

When the fire had burned low, Seren slipped from between the warm covers and began to dress. As Arthur stirred from his slumber she smiled down at him and said, 'Our time is short and my father will want to hear the news you bring.'

He rose and got dressed and together they entered the Veiled City. Once again Arthur descended the wide spiral stone steps and took the passage to the Great Hall. They walked side by side, Seren pointing out various areas and where the myriad tunnels led. Arthur was struck by the warmth of the underground passageways and loosened his heavy winter clothing. The Cithol they passed stopped and stared after them, their High Lord's daughter, the White Star, walking side by side and laughing with the scarred, dishevelled outsider with his tangled long hair and uncut beard and who wore a sword at his side fit for the ancient rulers of Middangeard. Arthur acted as if he was oblivious to their stares and comments and they resented what they took to be his ignorant arrogance.

They walked down the length of the dim Great Hall and passed to one side of the raised, magnificently carved dais taking the route down to the Summer Lake. They crossed a wide, stone bridge that arched over an underground river that fed into the lake and Arthur stopped to stare once again at the wonder of the underground City. Just beyond the bridge a channel split away from the main river and disappeared into the black opening of a small cave. Arthur asked Seren if that was where their household water was siphoned off. She shook her head but explained no further and Arthur suspected he had found one of things he was looking for. Seren took his hand once more and they looked out on the underground valley.

The lake stretched into the distance and on each side stone houses and narrow paths climbed the shores. It was as if a whole valley settlement had been entombed underground and Arthur marvelled at the sight. The lake itself was impenetrably dark and completely still. It seemed to swallow the light shed down from the cavern roof and begrudge any reflections. Something about the City struck Arthur as dead, as if a settlement had indeed been buried here.

Seren pointed out a group of grand buildings along one side of the lake. It was the Palace of the Cithol Lord and his wife, her parents. They crossed the bridge and made their way along the lakeshore. The path was worn smooth by endless usage and the surface of the stone seemed polished by the passing of the centuries. Occasionally they would cross small bridges over rills and streams that cut their way down to the lake between the terraced dwellings.

Suddenly Arthur realised what was missing and he turned to Seren, 'There are no fires here. No smoke coming from any of the buildings.'

Seren smiled up at him, 'No, there's no need for fires in our homes. It's perfectly warm down here at the Summer Lake so there's no need for fires to heat the homes and we all eat in the Great Hall.' She laughed as he frowned, 'Underneath the Great Hall are the kitchens – that's where the fires are for cooking.'

'So you all eat together, in the same place and at the same time, always?'

'Yes. Well, not necessarily at the same time but always in the same place. Does that strike you as strange?'

'We eat together at festivals and we share the same cooking pot in winter sometimes. In the war band we often eat together but in the villages usually each family cook and eat by themselves.'

'How strange. For us it's a time for everyone to be together and share in our tales, our lore, our ballads.'

Arthur felt that the peoples outside the Veiled City did not have that kind of time available to them but he left the thought unsaid and they climbed the steps up into the Palace of Lord Venning.

Captain Terrill was waiting for them at the top of the steps and opened the wide doors that led into a courtyard where a small fountain played in the centre of a dark pool that was fed by a channelled rill coursing through the Palace grounds. The soft rushing of the running water filled the courtyard with a sound that reminded Arthur of the rustling of leaves in a light wind. That was something else missing from this vast cavern he thought, trees.

Terrill left to make Lord Venning aware of Arthur's arrival. Seren leant closer to Arthur and placed a hand below his throat where the Elk Stone she had given him should still be hanging.

'I gave it to my sister – she was going into graver peril than I,' Arthur explained.

Seren nodded in relieved approval and looked as if she was going to say something and Arthur looked down at her enquiringly but with a light brush on his arm and a quick smile she dashed off to one side of the courtyard and disappeared through one of the many doors that opened out into the courtyard.

Arthur watched her go, wondering what she had been about to say. He tried to recall what Ceinwen had said at their parting, something about the Cithol not appearing to be all they seemed or wished to appear. He wondered if the same applied to him.

He was alone now and walked slowly to the fountain and for a moment Arthur felt uneasy. He could not read these people and they could not read him but it was more than that. This was an alien world to him. No sunshine, no moonlight, no winter and no summer. There were no trees in the Veiled City, only the splendid carvings in the Great Hall, no birds, indeed no animals at all.

He crossed to the low wall and looked out on the lake and the far shore. No darkness either. The bright crystals set high above in the cavern roof provided light whether it was summer or winter in the world outside. The Cithol themselves, with their pale almost translucent skin and pool-like eyes, seemingly without iris or pupil, were almost as unlike Arthur's people as were the Adren. Indeed more so. They seemed a race apart.

He had felt the looks the Cithol had given him whenever he had passed them and had seen their curiosity give way to a mixture of revulsion, at what was different, and fear, the fear of something unknown. They were certainly a knowledgeable people and their works and craft, evidenced by this City, far outshone anything done in Wessex or elsewhere in Britain. Arthur's thoughts meandered as he stared out over the black lake; perhaps they viewed his people as uncivilised, lawless and dangerously warlike. Perhaps they felt themselves above such matters as conflict. The Adren will claw them down, he thought, and make short work of their Veiled City if they get across the Causeway. He knew now that the Adren wanted the power that resided somewhere below this cavern. They wanted the power to grow the food to feed their armies; the power to live and harvest whether it was summer or winter. They wanted a city to mirror their own. One in the East and one in the West and everything in between under their sway. Arthur wondered if the Cithol understood that the only thing standing in the Adren's way were his uncivilised and dangerously warlike people.

A gate opened onto the courtyard and Arthur turned to see Lord Venning's wife, Inis, approaching.

'Greetings, Arthur. Lord Venning awaits you.'

She led the way deeper into the Palace along narrow stone hallways. The walls were draped in woven fabrics depicting scenes that Arthur could barely make out in the gloom and those which he could discern he did not comprehend. They entered a long room with unshuttered windows stretching down one side overlooking the Summer Lake. A table made from delicately carved, heavy wood ran the length of the room and Arthur guessed that this must be the Cithol Council room.

Although there were more than twenty people seated at the far end of the table, it seemed to Arthur to be able to seat twice that number and he wondered briefly if there used to be more in the council and why it should be so depleted now. Inis indicated a chair for him and then she joined Lord Venning at the end of the table. Arthur unslung his heavy winter cloak and sat down, looking at the faces lined along the table between him and the Cithol Lord. They were studying him in silence. Arthur recognised Captain Terrill, who nodded in greeting, and then his eyes settled on Fin Seren who alone among the Cithol smiled at him.

'You have returned earlier than we expected, Arthur of Wessex, and without Brunroth, or Merdynn as your people call him,' Lord Venning said and Arthur felt his black eyes and the eyes of the others seeking to find a way inside his thoughts.

He shrugged aside their combined will and once again began to relate the events of the journey into the Shadow Lands. He stopped at the point where Merdynn had gone east with Cei and looked at Lord Venning.

'All at this table can be trusted with whatever truth you have to tell, Arthur,' Lord Venning pronounced.

Arthur searched the Cithol faces before him and his eyes fell upon those of Commander Kane and again he hesitated. Those around the table stirred in anger and impatience.

'This is the council of the Cithol, Arthur, your news concerns all of us here,' Terrill explained.

Arthur shrugged and continued. The Cithol listened intently to the purpose of Merdynn's journey into the East. Lord Venning and the gathered council kept their peace as Arthur's voice filled the room. He looked at no one as he spoke, instead he stared out through one of the open windows with a distant look as he recalled and relived the events in the Shadow Lands.

When he had finished the Cithol were silent, looking at each other and avoiding Arthur. Finally Lord Venning broke the silence.

'You sent Brunroth, with less than twenty warriors, into the heart of the Shadow Lands? To destroy the Adren City in the East?'

Arthur stared at Lord Venning, one eyebrow slightly raised, questioning the tone that Lord Venning took. 'Merdynn is no one's man to send anywhere. He goes nowhere against his will or judgement.'

'And yet he has gone to the heart of the enemy and you didn't stop him and you didn't travel with him?'

Arthur turned his gaze to the Commander who had spoken in the same tone as Lord Venning had.

'Yes,' Arthur replied.

'But why, Arthur? Surely it is a fool's mission?' Terrill looked at Arthur disbelievingly.

Arthur sighed and putting both hands on the table stood up, the chair scraping loudly against the stone floor as he pushed it backwards. All the Cithol were staring at him. He crossed to the open window and looked across at the houses that climbed the far shore. The Cithol exchanged looks with each other, perturbed by this strange and disrespectful behaviour at a council meeting.

'How many of you live here?' Arthur asked, still staring out over the lake.

'What?' Commander Kane said sharply.

'I said, how many of you live here?'

'And what has that to do with what we discuss?' he replied.

Arthur's response shocked everyone there, including Fin Seren who was already concerned at the turn the meeting was taking. He spun swiftly from the window and strode back to the table, planting both fists on it as he leant over them.

'I'll tell you why. Four thousand, five thousand here? Well?'

Terrill nodded, the others were too surprised that Arthur dare raise his voice and take this cold tone with them.

'And how many of you are warriors? How many can fight?'

The table was silent.

'I asked you how many!' Arthur roared, spittle flying from his lips.

'We have, perhaps a hundred guards, hunters,' Terrill replied.

'Did you not hear me when I told you how many Adren lie waiting to attack this Isle?'

Again the room was silent.

'Did you not hear me?' Arthur roared once again.

'We are not your warriors or your people, how dare you to speak to us like this!' Lord Venning shouted back as he rose to his feet.

Arthur walked slowly toward him. The Cithol around the table were appalled by the simmering violence emanating from the outsider.

'No, you aren't in my war band, and no, you aren't my people. My war band have fought already, have died already to protect this land where you live. My people will continue to fight and die too.' Arthur stopped directly in front of Lord Venning and continued, 'That's how I dare. There are more Adren soldiers across the Causeway than all your people and mine combined. Have you begun training for war? Will you meet them in battle? We have a fraction of their number and we'll stand against them to protect this land. Will you do the same? All this craft and magnificence here, can you use it to defend yourselves if the Adren break through us?

'Merdynn and people I've known all my life, people I'm proud of, have risked everything in an attempt to destroy what it is that keeps the Adren army moving. If they don't succeed then what do you think our chances of survival are against those Adren armies? Merdynn and the others have set out to do what must be done. They risk everything, for that's what's at stake here: everything. What, exactly, have your people risked so far? What do you propose to do, Lord Venning?'

Lord Venning stared at Arthur and everyone else watched the two of them.

'Perhaps you are not the one. Perhaps we have chosen ill,' Commander Kane said quietly.

Arthur turned to him, 'You haven't chosen anyone and whether or not I'm 'the one', I'm the only one doing what must be done to defend this Isle and if you want me to help defend this City too then you'd best start considering how you can help me.'

Arthur crossed the room and picked up his winter cloak. As he left the stunned room he turned and said, 'I shall return here when the sun rises once more. You have much to discuss and much to decide.'

Arthur strode back towards the Great Hall in a black rage, ignoring those he met on the paths and passages all of whom quickly got out of his way. Terrill and Seren finally caught up with him as he entered the Great Hall.

'Arthur! Wait!' Seren called out and he turned and stopped.

Seren was clearly upset and her lip trembled as she faced Arthur but there was anger in her green eyes too. Terrill stood uneasily by her side.

'Why?' she asked.

Arthur breathed deeply to control his anger. 'Because you need to realise the strength of the storm about to break upon you.'

'But you hold the Causeway,' Terrill said.

'Over twenty thousand Adren lie on the far side. How many to hold the Causeway? One hundred? Two?' Arthur replied.

'You don't think you can hold the Causeway?' Seren asked. Anxiety had swiftly replaced her anger.

'That's not what I'm saying. I'm saying you should think as if I can't.'

'We need to plan for a defence of the Veiled City and you want us to somehow help defend the Causeway?' Terrill asked.

'It's what you've been telling Kane and my father all winter,' Seren said talking to Terrill.

'Then why haven't they done something? They must realise how finely balanced our fates are?' Arthur asked.

They were quiet for a moment then Seren replied, 'Lord Venning thought Brunroth would have a plan to secure the Veiled City. He thought you and your people would hold the Causeway forever.'

'Merdynn has gone into the East to try to secure this City and I plan to hold the Causeway long enough for him to succeed but if I were Lord Venning I'd do three things: Organise help for the defence of the Causeway, plan a defence for this City and have a plan for abandoning the Winter Wood.'

They both looked shocked.

'Leave here?' Terrill said aghast at the prospect.

'Never. Lord Venning would never leave here. None of us would. We've been here since the beginning. Only here can we keep the winter and darkness at bay,' Seren said taking a step back from Arthur.

'Then you'd better make the first two plans very good,' he replied.

'I'll speak with him and the council. They have to see that hiding will not keep the Adren away,' Terrill said.

'Very well. I'll return with the sun and we'll see if there's a way to do together what we may not be able to do alone.' Arthur stretched out his hand. Captain Terrill shook it then turned and left.

Arthur and Seren made their way across the Great Hall and back up to the Winter Garden.

'Don't be angry with me, Arthur, not at parting.'

Arthur sighed before saying, 'I'm not angry at you Seren. I'm angry with the Cithol Council because they endanger you and all your people. If the Adren break across the Causeway they will head here. This City holds what they want and yet nothing has been done to safeguard it. People are already dying and still they do nothing. If they wait any longer then it will be too late and if we fail then the Adren will be hacking their way through the shores of the Summer Lake.'

Seren led Arthur once again back down the twisting path through the Winter Wood. Arthur commented again on the numerous side paths that branched off the main one, some seemingly wider and more frequently trod.

'Terrill believes that any attackers would find it impossible to penetrate the woods against our will,' Seren said.

Arthur had his doubts but kept them to himself and Seren gradually turned the conversation to lighter matters. They talked of the Winter Garden and the plans that Seren had for improving it as they unhurriedly walked towards the open fields below the grove on the hill. When they reached the end of the path they embraced once more and said their farewells. Seren felt a moment of undecided panic as Arthur turned and walked away from her. She had resolved to tell him at parting but that was before the disaster of the council meeting. Now she was unsure.

Arthur had begun the climb back up to his camp and Seren felt her panic rising again.

'Arthur! Wait!' she called out to him.

Arthur turned to meet her as she dashed towards him. As they met and Arthur smiled at her enquiringly she hesitated then said, 'You will return, Arthur?'

'Yes, after I've been to Whitehorse Hill and Caer Sulis. First I must see what my own king has done in preparing for war.'

'But you will return to me?'

'Of course.'

She watched him go with both hands clasped below her stomach as if to conceal the child that was growing inside her.

Chapter Thirteen

Arthur could see Whitehorse Hill from some miles away as his company slowly climbed the Ridgeway from the East on the final leg of their long journey from the grove above the Winter Wood. The hill fort was lit by fires that burned brightly in the long winter night and the flames reflected in dark reds on the low cloud that spread over the cold country, stretching away to each horizon.

Riders came out to meet them and news was quickly exchanged. As they entered the East Gate Arthur noted with approval that the ditch around the hill fort had been deepened and a new, low wall now circled the entire fort so that any attacker would have to face the slope, the new wall, then the deep ditch and finally the steep climb up to the fort's main wall. The gates too looked as if they had been strengthened.

Laethrig's apprentices had been hard at work inside the camp too. Forges billowed gouts of flame as iron was beaten into weapons of war. Arthur decided to inspect the work later and ordered the horses to be stabled. They all went to the main hall and his forty warriors began eating hungrily, meals on their two hundred mile journey had been few and hurriedly taken. Those who had remained at the Wessex base avidly listened to the tales from the East and the reports of battle with the Adren. The wine flowed freely and before long the warriors were drunkenly seeking their beds. They had not slept during the long journey from the grove.

Arthur sat with Elwyn, Morgund and Ceinwen and they were discussing the defences at the Causeway and Caer Cadarn. Laethrig sat with them and reported on the work that was in progress. Ceinwen yawned mightily and wiped her tired, watery eyes before taking another mouthful of her wine. She triggered a yawning fit in Morgund and they swapped cavernous yawns. Arthur was suggesting to Elwyn that the families of the Anglians that were now based at the Causeway should come to Whitehorse Hill and set up their homes here for the present leaving the Causeway for the warriors to defend. Laethrig added that he could certainly put the extra hands to work and Elwyn agreed it would be a good idea. The talk became sporadic and Morgund finally stumbled to his feet and made his way to the table where Morveren sat, stopping on the way to steady himself on a back of a chair as yawns racked his body.

Morveren smiled up at him and they chatted for a while before Morgund made some parting comment and left the hall. Ceinwen watched as Morveren glanced back at the departing warrior and turned back to the others with an eyebrow raised in question but none of the three were looking at her; Laethrig was intent on draining the beer Morgund had left behind, Arthur was staring at nothing in particular with his thoughts clearly elsewhere while Elwyn was staring grim-faced at the door that had just closed behind Morgund. Ceinwen smiled to herself as she closed her eyes.

Laethrig finished the beer and got up to go too. He caught Arthur's eye and nodded towards Ceinwen who was slumped in her chair fast asleep. Arthur hauled himself to his feet then gently picked her up and carried her out to Ruadan's small roundhouse. He laid her down on her bed and buried her in warm fur covers. He watched her for a moment then turned to go. She was already snoring before he left the hut.

Arthur returned to the hall and retired to his own room where a fire had been lit for him. He lay awake for several hours replaying in his mind the meeting at the Veiled City. Perhaps he should not have precipitated the clash with Lord Venning but they had needed to be shaken from their comfortable complacency. He hoped that over the next few weeks they would come to realise their accustomed comfort and security no longer existed and that the only certainty in their future was the Adren host that wanted the Veiled City for their own.

His thoughts turned to Merdynn and Cei in the East and wondered what their tale would tell. He felt with a dread certainty that should they fail then Britain would eventually fall too. Even if he could unite all the king's people with the Uathach and the Cithol and then forge an army from such an alliance they would still be terribly outnumbered.

As he drifted into sleep he was thinking of the coming meeting with the king and what plans he might have already put in place. The last time he had seen Maldred was at the King's Council and he had agreed to Arthur going east in the hope that he would not return. Tomorrow he would return.

Arthur awoke to a clattering in his room. Ceinwen had brought in a hot breakfast and was heating a drink over a fresh fire she had started. She saw he was awake and threw his winter cloak to him.

'Thanks for putting me to bed last night,' she said with a smile.

'Pleasure,' Arthur replied with a laugh.

'Laethrig is impatient to continue the account of his work while we've been away,' she said with a roll of her eyes.

'That'll send you back to sleep. Tell him I'll be with him shortly, and then feel free to make yourself scarce,' Arthur said and helped himself to the warm food she had brought. Ceinwen nodded and left him to eat in peace.

When he had finished he sought out Laethrig and together they toured the hill fort. Laethrig pointed out the work done in various areas of the fortifications and then took Arthur to the store huts. The wood crafters had cut thousands of arrow shafts and two groups of children sat around a fire, one group fitting the flight feathers and the other slotting the arrowheads into the grooves and binding them with thin strips of leather which they then soaked so that the bindings would shrink to an even tighter fit. The children had been chatting and laughing as they worked but when they saw who had entered they went about their work with a studied vigour and a seriousness that made Laethrig laugh.

'Now I know how to make the buggers work! Just bring the warlord in!'

Arthur knew that under Laethrig's guidance the children would be happy and work well. The blacksmith had raised half a dozen children himself and knew exactly when to be stern and when to be gentle. Arthur inspected some of the work nonetheless and praised them on their work telling them it was important, their parents would depend on the feathers being straight and the arrowhead bindings tight. After they had left it was some time before the children started chatting again and there was less laughter but the feathers were straight and the bindings thorough. They argued about who would be the warlord amongst them when their time came but in the back of each mind was the thought that if the arrow they were working on did not fly true then it may cost their father or mother's life. One of the older Anglian children, Aelfric, began to periodically check the arrows they were making to ensure they were true.

Arthur spent the next few hours inspecting the new swords, shields and spears that had been fashioned while he had been away in the East. He told Laethrig's workers that the warriors were proud of their work and that they knew they could rely on the quality of the weapons they turned out.

Laethrig showed Arthur the thousands of hardened iron strips that were to be fitted into the warriors' stout leather battle jerkins. The Adren swords were curved and used far more for cutting and slashing rather than thrusting. The iron strips bound into the jerkins along the shoulders, upper arms, sides and back could save many warriors' lives.

Finally he checked on the longbows. These were works of great skill and only a few master craftsmen were capable of making them. Half of the longbows were fully sized six-foot bows and the archer had to be both well trained and strong to use them properly. The other half were shorter, between three and four foot in length and these were used by those without the strength to stand for hours firing the exhausting full sized bows. Their range was shorter and their penetrating power was less but at close quarters they were just as deadly.

Before going back to the main hall, Arthur quickly visited the herdsmen and the long barns where their animals were kept for most of the dark winter. The feed supplies would last the winter easily and the animals were in good health. Everything at Caer Cadarn was in order and preparations were well advanced. Arthur was satisfied with the work done and he turned his thoughts to Caer Sulis and King Maldred. It was time to visit the king.

He took with him the forty of the war band that had travelled with him from the Causeway. They left Whitehorse Hill under the same low clouds that still reflected the fires in shades of dark red and as they left the first flakes of a new snowfall dropped from the reddened glow like beads of blood upon the hill fort.

They travelled back down the Ridgeway wrapped in their thick winter cloaks and by the time they reached the Westway the snow had settled into a heavy, silent fall that blanketed the dark world around them and muted their journey to Caer Sulis.

The warriors knew the origins and depth of the dispute between their warlord and the king and a quiet tension filled them as they drew nearer to the king's town. While the Wessex and Anglian warriors had been on good enough terms even before the Adren attacks, neither were comfortable near the king's men, the Mercian war band, and the general distrust was mutual. This friction between the war bands only ever manifested itself in the occasional individual conflict or drunken brawl and had not spiralled out of control in decades. An uneasy but effective peace existed between them.

So it came as a surprise when they found the road down through the hills blocked to them. They had expected guards but not to be denied passage. Arthur had been riding near the back of the line with Morveren and Elwyn when the column came to a halt. He left them to see what the delay was and rode to the front where Morgund and Ceinwen were arguing with some figures in the darkness beyond the barricade that stretched across the road.

'I assure you that he's very much alive,' Ceinwen was saying patiently.

'What's the delay, Ceinwen?' Arthur asked as he rode up.

His appearance at the barrier of felled trees had a strange effect on the Mercian guards. As one man they all took a step backward, some making the sign to ward off evil spirits.

'You're dead apparently,' Morgund answered.

'Oh?'

'Yes, killed in the Shadow Lands,' Morgund added.

'Strange, I don't seem to remember that.'

'And you'd have thought it'd be the kind of thing you would recall really.'

'I remember killing a lot of Adren,' Arthur offered.

'Not the same as being killed yourself though,' Morgund pointed out.

'True.' Arthur turned to the still stunned Mercians, 'So then, how did I die? Well, I hope.'

They were silent.

'Perhaps more importantly, how and when will you die?' There was no longer any trace of levity in Arthur's tone.

'You can't enter, Arthur,' the Mercian leader said.

'Well, that answers my last question then,' Arthur replied looking at Morgund and drawing his sword. Behind him rang the sound of his warriors drawing their weapons in the still winter air.

Arthur dismounted and handed his reins to Ceinwen. He walked up to the barrier and the riders drew close about the barricade. Arthur leapt lightly on top of the trees and jumped down the other side. The Mercians drew their swords but backed away from him.

He stared at them in silence for a minute then said, 'Do you mean to bar the Westway to the Warlord of Wessex?'

The Westway was always open for anyone of the three tribes to travel on and it was one of the duties of the war bands to keep their section of it open and free of Uathach raiders. The five Mercians were unsettled. They had been told that Arthur had died in the Shadow Lands only to find him appearing like a ghost out of the snow. They knew full well that the law of the land demanded the Westway be kept open yet they had their orders from the king to bar it to any of the Wessex or Anglian warriors that might return. They looked to their captain.

'We have our orders, Arthur,' he said, looking past Arthur at the war band he knew he could not stop.

Arthur looked at them once again then called out for his warriors to stay their hands.

'So be it then. Your orders are against the law of this land but if you will not go against them then my war band will turn round and go back - if you and your guards can deny me passage.'

The Mercians looked at one another, five of them against the Wessex Warlord. They took up defensive stances. The mounted warriors lined up jostling along the barricade, each trying to get a better view of what was about to happen. Most of them missed it and those who did witness it were astonished by the speed of Arthur's attack. What astounded them even more was that not a single Mercian had been cut by Arthur's sword. A cheer went up along the line and as they hauled aside the barricade Arthur knelt by the Mercian Captain, the only one still conscious, and told him quietly never again to bar the Westway to legitimate travellers.

As they rode on toward Caer Sulis Morgund asked Arthur why he had spared them.

'They aren't the ones to blame,' Arthur replied.

'Then who is?' Morgund asked.

Arthur was silent and Morgund knew better than to repeat the question. Ceinwen's anxiety increased.

When they reached the outskirts of the town they found their way barred once more, this time by fifty of the king's war band. The Mercians peered through the heavy, slow falling snow at the approach of the riders and called out a challenge.

'Arthur of Wessex, seeking passage to Caer Sulis on business with the king,' Arthur called out in reply.

His appearance had the same effect on these guards as it had on the others a few miles back on the Westway and they stared at Arthur as if seeing an apparition.

'Arthur died in the Shadow Lands,' the captain of the guard replied.

'Here we go again,' muttered Morgund.

'I am here and wish to enter Caer Sulis and see the king.'

The captain stepped closer and recognised Arthur's bearded and scarred face. 'The king is in council and you cannot pass, Arthur. The road is barred to any Wessex or Anglian warriors.'

'As Warlord of the Wessex I'm one of the King's Counsellors. By whose authority do you bar me from the council?' Arthur asked.

'King Maldred's.'

'And who is King Maldred in council with if not his counsellors?'

'The council is disbanded. He talks with the Northern tribes,' the captain did not look Arthur in the eye as he replied.

'The Uathach?' Morgund exclaimed and those around him stirred in anger.

Arthur turned his horse around and walked it back into the midst of the warriors.

'I want as little bloodshed as possible. We'll need every warrior against the Adren. The town is not walled, we'll ride around the barricade to the North, head for the King's Hall,' Arthur said, and then digging his heels into his horse's flanks led the charge around the northern flank of the Mercians.

Arthur's riders dashed madly across the field, snow flying from their horse's hooves as arrows from the guards flew through the darkness around them. Morveren led the faster riders and they grouped around Arthur to protect him as they entered the streets of Caer Sulis leaving behind the Mercian guards.

The people of the town, who had not taken the journey west, ran to the streets and windows of their houses to see what the thundering noise meant. They feared they were under attack but many recognised the Wessex or Anglian warriors and word spread quickly that Arthur was alive and in Caer Sulis.

They reached the King's Hall in minutes and Arthur flung himself from his saddle as his horse slid on the ice in front of the long house. There were two sets of guards in front of the hall, Mercian and Uathach, both drew their weapons as Arthur's warriors careered to a stop and made straight for the hall's doors.

'Stand aside! I have no wish to kill you!' Arthur roared at them as he cast his heavy cloak into the snow and drew his sword, making the alternative clear. Behind him longbows were drawn.

The Uathach raced inside the hall, two Mercians stood to bar Arthur's way and without breaking stride Arthur knocked them both down instantly. The other Mercian guards backed against the wall and lowered their weapons. Arthur sent the hall doors flying open with a furious kick and he strode straight towards the raised dais with the others spilling into the hall behind him.

Those at the top end of the hall rose as one in the sudden silence and stared at the approaching Arthur.

'You! No! You died in the Shadow Lands!' the king screamed at him.

Arthur took the steps up to the dais two at a time and brought his sword crashing down onto the table in a fury that split it in two.

'This council is broken!' Arthur said amid the flying platters of food and beakers of wine.

The king's face twisted in hatred and his counsellors looked aghast as Arthur took his eyes from Maldred and stared at those standing around the debris of the broken table.

Besides the king and his counsellors there were three Uathach chieftains and their advisers. Arthur recognised each of the chieftains. The foremost of the three was Ablach and he stood with his arms folded and his small, black eyes shifted between Arthur and Maldred with a keen interest. He was a bear of a man, as broad as Arthur and even taller, with tangled black hair and a beard greasy from the food that now lay around the shattered table.

To his right was the smaller Hund, chieftain of the lands to the North of Mercia. If Ablach was like a bear then Hund was like a weasel, his nervous, darting hands refused to remain still and a long straight nose sharply divided his heavy lidded eyes. He watched Arthur and Maldred avoiding eye contact as his gaze flicked between them at chest level.

Arthur turned his gaze to the third, ignoring Maldred who had begun to spit more vitriol towards him. The third chieftain was Benoc, a red haired giant from beyond Ablach and Hund's lands. Arthur had only seen him the once, years ago on a distant raid north. He was the only one of the three who appeared on the point of attacking Arthur.

'Don't. Or your tribe will need a new leader for tomorrow,' Arthur said with his sword pointing at the giant's midriff.

Benoc snarled and readied himself to spring at Arthur. Arthur just smiled at him and Ablach unfolded his thick arms and placed a hand in front of Benoc to restrain him.

'Wait,' he said, keen to see what would happen next between Arthur and King Maldred.

Below the dais the hall was divided into two with Maldred's men down one side and the Uathach warriors on the other. There were about fifty of each and now there were forty of Arthur's war band spread out in a semi-circle from the hall's doors, with their longbows half drawn. All the warriors were trying to watch each other and what was unfolding on the dais at the same time.

'You're too late, thief of Wessex, dead or alive you're too late,' Maldred hissed at him, his fine silver hair now hanging around his lined face.

Arthur turned his attention to the king and the Great Hall was completely silent.

'Too late?'

Maldred laughed, 'Yes, too late. You should have died in the Shadow Lands where you were supposed to. I know your plans warlord thief, you've craved the throne for years! Since you were a yelping brat in the Wessex war band you've wanted to be king. Too late! You're not even the Wessex Warlord now! How could you be? There's not even a Wessex Council! I'm the sole ruler of Wessex now and Ablach rules the Anglian lands.'

Arthur looked at Ablach who shrugged with a half smile.

'And the Wessex and Anglian chieftains?' Arthur asked.

'Oh, we'll be sure to tell them when they return from the Western Lands,' Maldred replied, leaning forward on one half of the split table.

'And the Adren? Who will stop them without the Wessex and Anglian warriors?' Arthur asked quietly.

'The Adren? I haven't seen any Adren. Some concoction between you, would-be Lord of Wessex, that old fool Merdynn and the ghost from the Winter Wood.'

'Is this what you think?' Arthur asked, lowering his sword.

'Ah, but I'm no fool, even should there be Adren armies we all know what they really want! The Veiled City! Well, they can have it. You're defeated you witless warmonger, while you were chasing shadows in the East we've signed a treaty, an alliance and the land is divided anew!'

Arthur stared at Maldred and his gray eyes emptied of expression. When he spoke to the king it was without anger and in a flat, cold tone that carried through the hall.

'You are a fool, Maldred. You are unfit to stand as king. Your judgements are insane and you would cast this land to destruction. You would divide this land just as it needs to be united. You are,' and his sword swept out in an arc, 'no longer king.' The king's head remained sitting on his shoulders as his mouth soundlessly formed words, then it slowly tipped forward, rolling down his chest and thudding onto the floor. The king's body slumped over the broken table.

The Great Hall was stunned to stillness and only the crackling of the fires and Ablach's soft chuckle broke the silence. The two war bands stared at their dead king and at Arthur in disbelief. What they had just witnessed was impossible, something that just could not happen. Ceinwen's mind reeled in shock as her worst fears were played out as if upon a stage in front of her. The kingdom would be plunged into warring chaos. Doubtlessly the Uathach were here in strength and would leap at this chance. The Adren would just walk into Britain unopposed. Other minds that were not numbed by what they just witnessed were thinking the same. Not least among them, Ablach.

Six of the Mercians, from the king's personal guard, rushed at the dais in a rage and were flung aside by the volley of arrows that flew from Arthur's warriors. The rest of the Mercians reached for their weapons but stayed where they were as Arthur's longbows covered them.

Ablach signalled the Uathach side of the hall to stay their hands. He wanted to let the southern war bands kill each other.

Arthur faced the Mercians and looked among them for Gereint, their leader, and spoke out to him, 'Our king is dead. Had he lived he'd have led each of you and your families to slaughter. More than twenty thousand Adren lie across the Causeway and come the spring they will attack this land. They will kill every living person in this land whether they be in Mercia, Wessex, Anglia or in the tribes to the North. Unless we can stand against them together.'

Arthur stepped down from the dais and walked towards Gereint and the Mercians.

'If anyone in this hall wants to avenge their mad king then you can challenge me to combat, for it was I who killed him. Not the Wessex war band, not the Wessex Council, I.'

Arthur walked down the length of the Mercian line and no one in the hall had ever felt so much force of will from one person before. Even if they hadn't all known his reputation, still none would haven chosen to stand against him. He returned to the dais.

'I am not your king, I am the Warlord of Britain. Together we will stand against the Adren. Once they are defeated then together we will choose a new king.'

Arthur turned to the Uathach chieftains, 'I have a new deal for you. Stand with us against the Adren and your families and tribes will have right of passage to the Western Lands on the ships that sail from the Haven when winter comes. Once we have defeated the Adren you will have the right to clear land and farm in the southern lands if you are prepared to live according to our laws.'

The Great Hall was again silent as everyone listened to the terms Arthur put forward.

'Doesn't sound as good as the last treaty,' Ablach said with a shrug of his huge shoulders.

'The last treaty didn't take account of either the Adren or I. Make no mistake, the fate of your land depends upon what you decide. Refuse this and we will be at war. I will seek to kill all your peoples and burn your land and homes and I will start here and I will start now.'

Again Ablach shrugged, 'I doubt you have the men to do so.'

'What I leave undone the Adren will finish. Pray you fall to our swords and not theirs.'

'Perhaps Maldred was right, the Adren want nothing in the North,' Hund joined the debate. His eyes were darting between the gathered Uathach warriors and the southern war bands, which may or may not have been divided but which together outnumbered their own warriors. They had over a hundred more camped to the North of Caer Sulis and Hund was keen to quit the hall and return in force.

'You can recall those words as you die and your village burns,' Arthur replied.

'What proof do you have of this Adren host?' Ablach asked.

'Disbelieve what I say and the proof will be in your death and the death of all your people. Seek out Ruraidh and your daughter Gwyna if you need to hear it from your own.'

Ablach was taken aback by the mention of his daughter and his captain. 'I've had word that they have returned to Dalchiaran. I will send for them and then you'll have your answer,' Ablach said and signalled the Uathach to leave the hall.

They warily filed out to return to their camp leaving the Mercian and Wessex warriors still facing each other in the Great Hall of Caer Sulis. Arthur climbed down from the dais and told his bowmen to lower their longbows. Once again he faced the Mercians.

'What is decided here, now, and in the next few days will determine the fate of this land. If you decide to attack us now then this land is lost. If you leave here and entomb yourselves in Mercia then this land is lost, either to the Adren or to the Uathach. If we stand together then the Uathach will not be able to defeat us. If the Uathach and Cithol stand with us then perhaps we can withstand the Adren host.

'Your lands remain your own. Your war band will stay together under a leader you choose. I propose that you choose Gereint. The councils will choose a new king. A king who won't lead us to ashes. I am not your king nor do I wish to be. I will lead this land only for as long as the Adren threaten it.

'First we will build a funeral pyre fit for the king who led us well for so many years. Long years when his rule was just and fair, only age and the darkness of this time finally robbed him of reason. When we have sung his death song retire to your quarters and choose a leader from amongst you and decide which course you wish to set Britain upon.'

Arthur told some of his warriors to build a pyre outside the Great Hall and some of the Mercians left to assist them. Arthur signalled two Mercians to follow him and he turned back to where the king lay. They fashioned a death carriage from white tablecloths, spears and shields and carried the king out of the hall between the two war bands who formed two lines, facing each other to salute the dead king.

In the thickly falling snow they placed the king on the high pyre and put torches to the stacked wood. As they sung the death song, all those left in Caer Sulis gathered around the square outside the Great Hall. News of what had happened in the hall spread quicker than the flames on the pyre and many frightened eyes were turned to the tall figure at the head of the pyre who stood staring into the flames that flickered around the king he had slain.

When the fire had burned low and the spiralling, glowing flakes had subsided to charcoal embers hissing in the falling snow, the Mercians turned away from the pyre and left the square. Arthur watched them go and then addressed the gathered people of the town. He briefly told them of what had transpired in the Great Hall. He spoke of the treaty that Maldred had made with the Uathach and the new treaty he had offered to them with the Adren host poised to strike at the land. He told them to return to their homes and await the outcome of events. He and his warriors retreated into the Great Hall to do the same.

They helped themselves to the food that remained on the tables and rationed out some of the wine. Arthur posted guards at the doors and unshuttered windows. Arthur took the first duty at the doors with Cael.

Inside, the others gathered around the main fire and discussed amongst themselves the events that had resulted in the king's death. None thought that he had deserved anything less than death for the betrayal of their lands to the Uathach and for the way he had spoken to Arthur but they all realised how precarious their position was. The Mercians outnumbered them two to one and the Uathach probably three to one. What concerned them the most was the risk of the Mercians joining with the Uathach and bringing back to life the king's offer. They felt confident they could take either of the factions on in battle, despite the numbers, but combined was a different tale and one they thought would not go well for them.

They argued amongst themselves whether or not Arthur should have killed the Mercians in the hall when he had the chance; it would have halved the Mercian force camped around Caer Sulis. Ceinwen angrily pointed out that the whole gamble was because Arthur wanted as many as possible left standing to fight the Adren, that a war between the tribes now could only end with one result; victory for the Adren. She left the group and joined Morgund who was sitting off to one side.

'Well, can't say I expected that,' Morgund said with a laugh as he shifted along to make room for her.

'It was what I feared. I hope he realises how close to disaster we are,' Ceinwen said and sighed heavily.

'Tired?'

'It's been a busy few months. I'm used to the quiet life.'

Morgund laughed and agreed. 'Still, we're alive and back in Caer Sulis, which is more or less what I promised myself. Thought it might not be quite this perilous mind,' Morgund said and drank another mug of wine.

Ceinwen was appalled that he should be taking events so lightly. 'You're drinking too much. We might have to fight our way out of here,' she admonished him.

'Might? With the Mercians smarting on one side and the Uathach smacking their lips on the other? Certain to be dead before I can finish the wine here and if I'm going to die in the safety of Caer Sulis after tramping around the Shadow Lands then I'd rather do so drunk, thank you.'

'Don't be so sure. The Mercians won't want to battle us. They know we've just fought our way through the Shadow Lands and, in a strange way, Arthur showed more respect to Maldred than was shown to him. I think they'll take Arthur as warlord. If they believe the Adren host is ready to invade then they know as well as we do that Arthur is the best warlord to defend the land.'

'Only one left, you mean.'

'That's what makes him the best,' Ceinwen replied.

'And the Uathach?'

'He's offered fair terms.'

'What? You mean, 'do as I say or I'll slaughter all your people', those fair terms? A masterstroke of diplomacy,' Morgund said attacking another mug of wine.

'It's certainly simple enough for them to understand. But offering safety for their families in the West and good farming land in the South is, well, fair. And no more wine for you.' Ceinwen took the cup away from Morgund and added, 'My life might depend on your speed and ability - so stay sober.'

Ceinwen got up to make sure the others were not getting too enthusiastic with the wine.

'Shame Balor missed this, he'll be spitting fury not to have witnessed it,' Morgund said.

Ceinwen turned and smiled, 'And Mar'h too. They'll never forgive us.'

Outside the hall, Cael was shifting uneasily. He almost wished that the Mercians would attack. He cast a furtive glance at Arthur who stood across the doorway, his eyes scanning the darkness beyond the square. The snow was still falling in thick swirls and was now beginning to cover the polished ice in the courtyard before the hall. Cael thought that Arthur looked unwell, the skin below his eyes was circled darkly and the whites of his eyes were veined red.

'Pay more attention to the shadows,' Arthur said quietly and Cael jumped. Arthur knew he was taking a risk being outside in the open. It would only take a few Mercian or Uathach bowmen to send Britain into a chaos that would ultimately result in its fall to the Adren. He felt that everything had been a risk since Merdynn and Cei had taken the road east. But if each risk paid off then perhaps the Adren host could be stopped. He knew that out there in the darkness beyond the square the people of Caer Sulis would be looking towards the Great Hall and fearing what may happen next. It would give them greater belief if they saw him standing guard in the open rather than skulking inside by a fire. It also showed them he was prepared to face the consequences of his actions.

Besides, it was a quiet place to think through the events both here and at the Veiled City. Everything depended upon what the Mercians and Uathach decided. The Mercians would decide first, Arthur thought. Ablach was waiting for Ruraidh and Gwyna. Arthur hoped they could convince Ablach of the Adren threat. If Ablach wasn't convinced then he may well attempt to deal with the Mercians and Arthur's own warriors here and now and take Britain for himself. Arthur knew Ablach would only agree to the treaty if he felt there was nothing more he could take by force. He might be in a position to destroy the majority of the Mercian, Wessex and Anglian war bands and take the throne for himself with all the farming land and riches that implied but he still could not get his people to the safety of the Western Lands in winter, not without the ships and seafarers of the South and neither could he defeat the Adren alone.

Arthur felt fairly confident that Ablach would convince the other two chieftains that the treaty was in their best interests, at least for now. But he did not know which way the Mercians would decide. He took one more turn on guard then let Elwyn take his place.

When he entered the hall Ceinwen beckoned him over. She had saved him some of the food. Arthur sat next to her.

'You look tired,' he said.

'Aren't we all? And we've got every reason to be,' she replied, strangely calm now that the events she had feared had unfolded. She crossed her arms on the table in front of her and lowered her head to rest sideways on her forearms.

Arthur looked around the hall. Half of the company were sleeping, the other half were cleaning and sharpening weapons.

'Do you think it will work?' Ceinwen asked, her head still resting on her arms.

Arthur shrugged as he ate.

'You've gambled everything haven't you? Your friends, your sister, the whole of Middangeard,' she said, looking up at him.

Arthur took a mouthful of wine and wiped his beard with the back of his hand before replying. 'This land has to be wholly united to withstand the Adren. If it doesn't bind together now then it would have fallen anyway. We die here or on the Causeway or somewhere in-between, it would have made no difference. Maldred might have united the land but he was a fool and sought to snatch what he could.'

Ceinwen lifted her head off her arms, 'You don't feel any remorse at killing the king?'

'No. He was a poison in my land. There's enough enemies on the road ahead without having one at your back.'

Ceinwen nodded and thought of Leah who had said something similar in what seemed like another lifetime now. 'So, what happened at the Veiled City?' she asked.

'A less bloody version of what happened here.' Arthur shook his head slowly and looked at the table, 'We stand on the edge of utter ruin with the Adren hordes massing across the Causeway and everyone here seems obsessed with individual plans and plots for their own petty gain and safety.'

'It's like someone hurrying to bring in dry clothes when the storm that's about to fall is going to blow their house and the whole village away,' Ceinwen said, shaking her head at the folly of it all.

Arthur snorted, 'I should have said that to Lord Venning.'

'Do you think it will work, Arthur?' Ceinwen asked again.

'We'll find out soon enough but even if the Mercians throw their lot in with us, and the Uathach, and the Cithol too. Even if we can hold out until the peoples return from the West and even if we have the time to train them and arm them. Even if Cei and Merdynn succeed. Even then I don't know if it will be enough, Ceinwen, but that's as much as can be done so we'll do that and then we'll see if it's enough to save this land.'

They sat in silence and Ceinwen laid her head back down on her arms.

'You should sleep,' Arthur said.

'Hmm. You too,' she replied already half there.

Arthur stood up to make a round of his warriors and check on the guards before finding a corner to sleep in.

He was shaken awake some hours later by Elwyn.

'What is it?' he asked, instantly awake and getting to his feet.

'The Mercians. They're coming across the square.'

Arthur crossed to the doorway, his warriors forming into a line behind him. Morgund was standing by the entrance.

'How many of them?' Arthur asked.

Morgund gestured across the square and replied, 'The whole lot of them.'

Arthur went though the doors and stood looking out into the courtyard.

There were a hundred of the Mercian war band standing in the square but their weapons were undrawn. Arthur stepped forward and his warriors took up a position behind him against the wall of the hall.

Two men walked towards Arthur from the Mercian ranks and stopped five paces in front of him. Arthur recognised Gereint and his brother Glore.

'Will you take an oath, Arthur of Wessex, that you do not desire the throne and will never take it?' It was Gereint who spoke. Like the rest of the king's war band he wore the royal red cloak and the snow was already settling on both it and on his close trimmed, neat beard.

Arthur took a step forward, 'I take the oath that neither do I desire the kingship nor will I take it.'

'And will you take an oath before the war bands of Britain that you shall abide by the jurisdiction of the council once they return from the Western Lands on their choosing of a new king?'

'I take the oath before all here that the council have rule of this land and that I shall abide by their choice of king when they return.'

Gereint drew his sword and approached Arthur.

'Then until the council determine otherwise, Arthur of Wessex is Warlord of Britain and we place our faith in him to defend us from our foes and keep safe the realm until a king returns.' Gereint knelt in the snow and offered Arthur the sword of the Mercian war band, hilt first. Arthur accepted the sword.

He turned to his own company and raised the sword, 'To the Mercian war band!' he cried.

His warriors drew their weapons and holding them aloft, echoed his cry.

Arthur turned to the Mercians. 'For the defence of the realm!'

Both war bands held their weapons to the snow laden dark sky and roared the reply.

The people of Caer Sulis crept from their homes and made their way to the square and the horror of losing their king and having the Uathach amongst them was washed away by the relief that civil war had been averted and a strong warlord was agreed upon to lead them in troubled times.

Arthur picked three warriors from each tribe and together with himself and Gereint they collected the ashes from the king's funeral pyre and carried them down to the frozen river where they spread them on the snow and ice. When they returned they found the warriors had entered the hall and were attacking the wine stores with vigour as Arthur's warriors told their tales from the East.

'Better to be slaughtering the king's wine stores than each other,' Gereint remarked as they watched from the doorway.

'We may still have to battle the Uathach clans so we need to keep them sober,' Arthur replied and told Ceinwen to see to it. Gereint did likewise and when some order had been attained Arthur sought out Elwyn and the three of them left the hall to visit the gathering places in Caer Sulis. He wanted to tell the people of the three tribes what had transpired and that he would govern the land as warlord until the council saw fit to choose a new king.

They went from the eating-places to the smaller halls around the town and the people took heart that Gereint and Elwyn stood by Arthur. It showed them that the three southern tribes stood united and that order had been restored in the face of the nearby Uathach and more distant Adren hordes.

The last place they visited was deserted but for an old couple eating in one corner. They sat near the large fire that blazed in an open hearth against one wall, shook the snow from their cloaks and ordered some ale.

'Is the Adren threat as bad as you say?' Gereint asked.

'Probably worse,' Elwyn replied and started to recount what they had encountered in the Shadow Lands. Arthur studied Gereint whilst Elwyn spoke. He was a short man, the same height as Balor and just as broad but there the similarities with Balor ended. His short-cropped hair was iron grey as was his trimmed beard and the deep lines radiating out from the corners of his eyes and the creases on his brow spoke of his forty-plus years.

It was customary for the king to act as warlord of the tribe he came from but for many years now Gereint had held that place in the Mercian war band although it had never been officially acknowledged. He brushed his hand through his grey hair as Elwyn finished speaking.

'Twenty thousand you say?'

'It's likely to be more,' Arthur replied.

'And how many do you think you can raise in time to battle them?' Gereint asked in his lilting Mercian accent.

'There's about a hundred of the Wessex and Anglian warriors. A hundred of yours here and another hundred in the West,' Elwyn answered.

'Three-hundred warriors,' Gereint said looking at Arthur.

'We will equip and train another thousand or so from those that return from the West. Plus whatever come from the Uathach and the Cithol.'

'So at best we'll have about three-thousand to face them with?' Gereint asked.

'And at worst, three-hundred,' Arthur replied.

'Gods help us then,' Gereint said and called out for more ale. 'Are you going to be collecting the taxes now?' Gereint added without looking at Arthur.

'The taxes are collected at Lughnasa, some time away yet, perhaps the council will have chosen a new king by then. What we find of Maldred's allocation from the last collection we'll use to pay the craftsmen working through winter,' Arthur answered.

'You'll not find much that he hasn't already sent to the Uathach clans,' Gereint answered bitterly.

'You didn't approve of his plans?' Elwyn asked.

'King Maldred was a fool at the end. He saw you,' and he nodded to Arthur, 'as a challenger for the throne. He thought you'd use this Adren threat to snatch it from him. He became convinced you were dealing with the Ghosts from the Winter Wood, those Cithol, and that you'd divide his kingdom up between you. I told him you would never do that, which just shows how wrong I can be. But it was the treaty with the Uathach that did it. That was madness and luckily for you my lads hate the Uathach more than they do you or you'd all have died in the hall. No good ever comes from dealing with the bloody Uathach,' Gereint replied, pointedly looking at Arthur.

'Well, like it or not, we need them now and if they throw their lot in with us then their families will be travelling west with our own come next Lughnasa,' Arthur responded.

'You mean to keep your word about the promise of safe passage to the West?' Gereint asked, clearly surprised and disapproving.

'Would you have me hold true to only that which suits me?' Arthur asked.

Gereint looked down at his ale and said softly, 'You're the Warlord of Britain, you can do whatever you bloody want.'

'Including taking the throne?' Arthur asked.

'Of course you'll take the throne, I would and I fully expect you to – after all, the king has no apparent successors,' Gereint answered.

'So what was all that about back in the square about oaths of not wanting to be king?' Elwyn asked.

'The king had come from Mercia. Arthur had just hacked his demented head off, and fair enough, someone had to put a stop to him selling off Britain to the Uathach, but it would have looked like Arthur had just killed him to be king instead. A Wessex king instead of a Mercian one. It just gave some credibility to the claim that it was all for Britain's safety and not for personal gain,' Gereint replied.

'Do you think I want the throne?' Arthur asked.

'Of course you bloody do.'

'And the oaths?' Elwyn asked.

'No one's going to be concerned about the bloody oaths if these Adren are all you say they are and Arthur looks like being the only one to stop them. Just you wait and see. The council will be on their knees begging for you to be king. Just as you know they will, Arthur,' Gereint said.

'Believe what you will, Gereint, but I only want to see my people and my land safe,' Arthur replied and stood up to return to the Great Hall to await news from the Uathach clans.

As Arthur left, and the other two got up to follow him, Gereint leant closer to Elwyn and said quietly, 'See? He already sounds more like a bloody king than Maldred did.'

They returned through the snow and torch lit darkness back to the Great Hall. Arthur set about billeting the warriors in the various houses surrounding the square. They settled down to wait in the winter darkness for Ablach's reply to Arthur's proposed treaty. They busied themselves with eating, sleeping and keeping as near as they could to the warmth of the fires. Those that had families who had remained in Caer Sulis, rather than undertake the journey to the West, sought them out while the others scavenged what they could, tended their horses and spent time honing their weapons.

Arthur sent for Laethrig and set him the task of organising the townsfolk of Caer Sulis into groups to help with the work of arming a people for war. Most of those who had remained behind were either part of the king's entourage or too old to make the journey west and be useful there. Still, Arthur reasoned, whatever they could accomplish now would mean less to accomplish later and soon time would become critical. Arthur discussed with the others the merits of sending for the peoples in the West. They would have crops to harvest and bring back to Britain but the sooner they returned the sooner the fit and able could be trained for war.

Arthur was under no illusions about how much training could be undertaken in the few months they would have available. He hoped that while the war bands held the Causeway, some of the villagers and farmers could be taught how to shoot the short bows and how to wield a sword and spear. Even so, the land had to be tilled and harvested. Seeds had to be sown and the crops garnered. Their supply of food was, Arthur hoped, the one advantage they had over the Adren host. So much depended on Cei stopping the Adren supply lines.

He talked at length with Elwyn about the plausibility of sending a longboat from the Haven across the Western Seas in winter darkness to take a message across. Elwyn sent for Lissa and Aylydd and they debated what the chances of success were. They finally agreed that the risks were acceptable, especially as they could return on one of the larger vessels with those who were leaving the West early. Arthur told Elwyn to select as few a crew as possible for the journey but to wait for the outcome of the Uathach treaty.

With the warriors and the townsfolk occupied, Arthur settled back to wait for the coming of the Uathach.

It was not the Uathach who came first to Caer Sulis. Instead it was Berwyn, one of the two Anglians who Arthur had found with Ruraidh's Uathach raiding party in the Shadow Lands and who had travelled with Gwyna and the supplies to Dalchiaran. He burst into the hall and half ran to where Arthur was stretched out, slumbering in his chair by a fire.

'Arthur!'

Arthur woke with a start, sending his half-full cup of wine skittering across the floor. The warriors in the hall moved towards the hurrying figure, eager to hear what news he brought from the Uathach encampment. Arthur studied the figure before him. His long sandy hair was whitened with the snow from outside but his face was sheened with sweat. As he stopped in front of Arthur he took a few seconds to control his breathing. Arthur poured another cup of wine and slid it across the table towards him as he studied Berwyn's face. The man's eyes held fear and urgency but the face showed nothing of the gauntness it held when Arthur had come across him and Saewulf near the Adren camp. The cracked lips and blistered skin had healed and the colour had returned to his narrow face and crooked nose. As he lifted up the beaker to his lips Arthur noticed he had lost two fingers on his left hand to frostbite.

'What is it, Berwyn?' he asked calmly.

'They're going to execute Mar'h. Got him chained up, say he raped one of their women!' Berwyn said quickly.

The gathered warriors swore in outrage as more crowded around to investigate the commotion.

'Quiet!' Arthur barked at them, 'Calm down, Berwyn, and tell me exactly what's happened. Slowly and from the start. Sit down.'

Berwyn sat and started to explain. The journey to Ablach's village, Dalchiaran, had gone smoothly and they were welcomed by Ruraidh who had made it safely across the sea in the longboat. The supplies sent by Arthur were well accepted and the village held a feast to celebrate. There were no problems until a woman, one of Ablach's household was introduced to us by Gwyna and she started to scream at Mar'h, accusing him of raping her years ago during a Wessex raid. They had chained Mar'h and prevented the two Anglians from leaving then word came from Ablach for Ruraidh to join him north of Caer Sulis.

As Berwyn finished, the warriors erupted in uproar, incensed by the accusation against Mar'h. Arthur was silent for a moment then held up his hands for quiet.

'Did Ablach send you here?' he asked.

'He says that he has his answer for you and invites you to witness his justice.'

Without being ordered, Ceinwen left the hall to gather those warriors who had been quartered elsewhere. Minutes later the combined war bands were mounted and ready to ride from the square outside the Great Hall. Arthur raised his hand for silence as his horse half turned beneath him.

'Only act on my command! Do not draw your weapons unless I do!' he shouted above the noise of the milling horses and led the hundred and forty mounted warriors to the North. Beside him rode Morgund, bearing the white horse banner of the Wessex, and Elwyn and Gereint with the Anglian and Mercian flags.

Once clear of the town they could see the fires from the Uathach camp in the hills to the North. Arthur led his warriors straight across the snow-covered fields towards the fires. The Uathach had based their camp around a large unused barn and most of them were gathered around the fires that burned in front of it.

The two sets of warriors, enemies for generations, faced each other in the snow before the barn. The horses of Arthur's warriors sensed the tension and the riders tightened their reins to curb their beasts' nervous excitement. Outright slaughter was only a drawn sword away.

Ablach was standing before the open doors to the barn. He spread his huge arms and called out to Arthur, 'Welcome to my Great Hall, Warlord of Britain!'

Arthur dismounted and signalled Elwyn, Gereint, Ceinwen and Morgund to follow him. As he strode towards the waiting Ablach, the Uathach ranks parted and stayed in two groups either side of the barn doors. Arthur's warriors watched them enter the large wooden building expecting the Uathach to fall on the small group at any moment.

Arthur was not concerned with the possibility of treachery. He knew as well as the Uathach chieftains did that the two sides were evenly numbered and a battle between them now would leave too few alive on the winning side to be counted as any kind of victory. He followed Ablach to the far end of the barn where a group of figures waited by an upturned trough that served for a table. Burning torches were fixed into the floor along the walls and they shed a flickering light on the standing figures, casting their tall shadows on the wall behind them.

Two women sat at the table, Gwyna and someone Arthur did not recognise. Benoc and Ruraidh stood by the bound Mar'h who knelt on the straw covered floor. Hund stood off to one side, his eyes ferreting from Arthur to Ablach and back again.

'How do you like my feasting hall, warlord?' Ablach said gesturing around the empty barn.

'What's your answer to my offer and why have you bound one of my warriors?' Arthur asked.

Ablach clapped his shovel-like hands together and barked out a short laugh. 'Right, no royal airs then, but then you don't have a king do you?' Ablach said, directing the last part at Gereint who did not blink or shift his eyes from Ablach's. 'Get your kings murdered often do you?' Ablach asked Gereint directly.

'I can add northern chieftains to the list,' Arthur replied.

Ablach shrugged and spat on the floor, 'No harm in seeing if the pup would bite.'

Gereint's lip curled in a snarl but he kept his hand away from his sword.

'Do you accept the treaty? Join forces with us against the Adren in exchange for winter passage to the West?' Arthur said.

'And land to farm in the South once they're defeated!' Hund added from the side.

'No harm in seeing if the old man's memory was addled,' Arthur replied.

Ablach's laugh barked out once more, 'You'll do as a son-in-law, Arthur of Wessex.'

'What?' Arthur asked.

'We accept your treaty and as a sign of our new found unity the warlord of the southern tribes may marry the daughter of the leader of the northern chieftains. With this tie, neither will forget what is promised to the other.'

Arthur could not keep the surprise from his face and those behind him were clearly shocked by the unexpected proposal. Ablach was delighted and gestured for Gwyna to join them. She walked across to her father's side with her head held high although whether with defiance or pride was unclear.

'You met my daughter in the Shadow Lands, saved her rebellious carcass it seems. Well, to thank you for that I offer her to you for a wife.'

Arthur fought to keep the image of Fin Seren from his mind as he looked from Ablach to Gwyna.

'Seems you weren't lying about the Adren. Ruraidh here paints an even blacker picture than you do. So we'll fight alongside you for our homes and land while your ships can guarantee the safety of our families.' Ablach folded his arms as he finished.

'And Mar'h?' Ceinwen asked, trying to buy Arthur time to think.

'If we're to farm southern lands under southern law, then what does your fabled law say for a man like that?' Ablach answered.

Arthur's mind was racing and he made a conscious effort to still his thoughts. Clearly Ablach thought Arthur would never relinquish the leadership of the southern tribes, whether it be as king or warlord, and by marrying his daughter to him he thought to share that power or at least his descendants would. Gwyna came as part of the deal that would see the Uathach standing alongside his own warriors in the coming war. If Arthur turned the offer down he would be spitting in the face of Ablach and the Uathach. He quickly realised he had no choice but to accept the proposal, or damn Britain to the Adren.

That decided he turned his thoughts to Mar'h. By some cursed turn of fate the girl Mar'h had raped all those years ago now turned out to be one of Ablach's women and retribution was being demanded. He remembered how he had dealt with the warrior from his war band who had raped one of Andala's villagers. That had been more to set a necessary example to the other warriors rather than to punish the individual but doubtless Ablach would demand the same uncompromising justice.

'Well, warlord? What does your justice say to that? This godless bastard raped a girl – a girl who I later took as one of my wives!' Ablach demanded.

'Bring Mar'h to the table. You and I will sit with your wife and judge him. The rest of you wait at the far end,' Arthur said, pointing to the other end of the barn.

Morgund and Ceinwen helped Mar'h to a seat at the table and stood there unwilling to leave him.

'Go!' Arthur said and they reluctantly joined the others walking to the far end of the barn.

Arthur sat at the table with Ablach, Mar'h and the woman opposite him.

'What is your name?' Arthur asked her.

'Esa,' she replied with a glance at Ablach.

'And you recognise this man as the one who raped you during a raid?'

'I'd never forget the bastard. His face has haunted me for years,' Esa said and spat in Mar'h's face.

Arthur sat back and looked at Mar'h. His face was bloodied and bruised and his hooked nose looked broken. His wiry frame looked thin and brittle and he had not raised his eyes from the floor since Arthur had entered the barn.

'Look at me, Mar'h,' he said and Mar'h at last raised his eyes to Arthur's.

A silence fell on the table as Arthur's gray eyes lost their focus and his thoughts seemed to drift away from the present. The only sound was Esa's hard breathing as Arthur's sightless gaze shifted from one to the other opposite him.

Suddenly he leant forward staring keenly at Esa who recoiled from him.

'Join the others, Esa,' Arthur said to her.

She looked at Ablach who nodded without taking his eyes from Arthur.

'She was the one you raped, wasn't she Mar'h?' Arthur asked.

'Yes,' Mar'h replied quietly.

'Then kill him and have done with it!' Ablach said standing up.

'Sit down,' Arthur said coldly, 'and I'll tell you what you already know to be the truth.'

Ablach sat down uncertainly, rocking the upturned trough as he did so.

'Seventeen or eighteen years ago Mar'h was in a raid on one of your villages. Young as he was then, and led by a cur of a man, he did what you have done many times, Ablach. He took one of the young women as spoils of the raid. It was Esa. Mar'h didn't kill her but he did leave her with child. When she realised she was with child from the rape she went to you, didn't she Ablach?'

Ablach sat silently staring at Arthur.

'Rather than have her outcast as a bearer of the child of a raider you decided to have her as another of your wives. Perhaps it was an act of kindness to save her but you never touched her and she bore no further children. Perhaps you saw only the chance to take a pregnant woman for a wife and claim the child as your own. A child to carry your ambitions. A child none of your other wives could produce. She is Gwyna's mother but Gwyna is not your daughter. She is Mar'h's daughter.'

Mar'h stared wildly at Arthur, 'Gwyna? My daughter?' he croaked.

'Yes. Is it not so, Ablach?'

'Gods, I didn't believe it but the stories are true aren't they? How could you know what happened if not for some ungodly curse from Merdynn? But it makes no difference! He still raped her and should die for it!'

'If he raped Esa, which he did, then Gwyna must be his daughter, which she is. That means she is not your daughter as you've claimed for seventeen years. If this were known how would Gwyna feel to be a rape-child? How would you look having claimed Gwyna as your only descendent for all these years? More importantly, why would I marry Mar'h's daughter? How would it serve your purpose for me to marry the bastard daughter of Mar'h?'

Ablach spat on the floor and his fists clenched and unclenched.

'If you pursue this claim of rape then I will execute Mar'h and reveal what you and Esa already know to be true, just whose daughter Gwyna really is. I certainly won't marry her, you will have no heir to your tribe and you will be no nearer the centre of power in this land.

'If Esa has made some mistake and it wasn't Mar'h who raped her then Gwyna can't be his daughter and therefore must be yours and my marrying her will bring about the alliance you want.

'The choice is yours.'

Ablach's face had reddened in fury, 'Is this the justice of the southern lands?' he roared into Arthur's face.

Arthur pushed him back into his chair and stood leaning across the table until his face was inches from Ablach's and he spoke in a voice that was cold and clear,

'You care nothing for justice, Ablach, your false indignation disgusts me. You've committed far more crimes far more frequently and of a far worse nature than Mar'h's and you've done precious little to counterbalance them. Justice would have seen you dead many years ago.

'You will tell Esa she is mistaken and take her away from here. I will marry your daughter, Gwyna, at the Imbolc festival, in the Great Hall at Caer Sulis when the peoples and council have returned from the West. We will hold a feast in Caer Sulis in ten hours time to celebrate the forthcoming union between the southern and northern tribes.

'Bring your clans here at Imbolc and bring your warriors for we will make for the Causeway directly after. If you come to stand by us then your families will have safe passage on the ships across the Western Seas when the winter comes. Fail me and I'll make sure you and all your people burn with Britain.'

Arthur stood up and freed Mar'h from his chains then helped him to walk back to the entrance of the barn leaving Ablach sitting at the upturned trough staring after them. As they left the barn and rejoined the war band they heard Esa screaming in rage at the husband who had once given her back the life that Mar'h had stolen seventeen years ago.

Ten hours later the feast was held in the Great Hall of Caer Sulis. Torches and fires brightly lit the square outside the hall. Hide awnings had been hung between poles to keep the snow off the trestles where the townsfolk feasted the proposed marriage of Arthur to the daughter of the Uathach chieftain. Most people thought it was just simple political expediency to cement the new treaty between the northern and southern tribes. Arthur's warriors saw it much the same way and if it meant that the Uathach would stand by them against the Adren then they were content with that. The Mercians talked openly that it was what King Maldred should have done rather than turn against his own peoples.

The townsfolk who had gathered outside the hall, young and old, felt uncertain. They had heard first-hand from the survivors of Eald about the Adren onslaught. Then they had seen the Uathach raiders welcomed into the very heart of Caer Sulis by their king and their fears of the Adren had diminished with the sudden arrival of the hated raiders. The king had told them that Arthur had died in the Shadow Lands yet he had returned, some said as an avenging ghost, and he had slain the king. Arthur had declared himself to be the Warlord of Britain until a new king was chosen and had driven the Uathach host from Caer Sulis. He had offered an allegiance through marriage so that now, for the first time in known history, the northern raiders and the southern war bands sat under the same roof in the same hall and feasted together. In the uneventful lives of the villagers more had happened in the last few days than was expected in a lifetime. There was much to debate and argue but on one thing they all agreed, their futures and the future of the land depended on the warriors in the Great Hall.

Few in Caer Sulis saw a group of four cloaked riders leave the town and head west out onto the Westway making for the Haven. Arthur had decided to bring back the peoples from the West as soon as their harvest was in and before the sun rose once more over Britain. He had sent Lissa to the Haven to take the message across the Western Seas. With him he had sent the still shocked and broken Mar'h to make a start on the training of new warriors for the coming war and to keep him from any Uathach seeking their own justice.

The engagement ceremony itself was simple and quick and it was conducted on the raised dais at the end of the hall. Arthur wore his usual war gear, unwilling to give the impression he was taking on the role of king, and he looked no more and no less than a Warlord of Britain.

Gwyna, however, looked like a Queen to be. Her long red hair was untied and flowed down past her shoulders. A gold circlet sat on her head like a small crown and she wore a laced long dress, closely fitted round her slim waist and cut low across her full breasts revealing the edge of the bandaging around her injured shoulder. Some remarked that she looked beautiful that night, with maturity beyond her years and that she carried herself with the dignity of the highborn. Of those in the Great Hall only Arthur and Ablach knew her true heritage. Others thought she looked down on those that approached her with cold malice in her hard, hazel eyes. Some of the younger men in the war band looked at her lithe figure and cool disdain and voiced envy that Arthur would be the one to bed her, not knowing that they had already slept together, and as the drink flowed a few of the younger warriors muttered that such a girl as Gwyna was wasted on a man of Arthur's age. The women among them thought less of Gwyna and reckoned she would bring nothing but ill-fated trouble to the warlord.

From her place among the tables below the dais Ceinwen watched the newly engaged Gwyna and wondered how such a monster as Ablach could produce such a girl. Ablach sat to her left and every time he barked out his raucous laugh, food flew from his mouth. Wine swilled down his beard as he quaffed from his endlessly replenished cup. Ceinwen had no doubt that Gwyna had a hardness and venom to her but next to her father she looked like a woodland spirit from a child's tale. Through her own increasingly drunken haze she noticed that occasionally Gwyna would look into Arthur's face or put a hand on his arm, perhaps to reassure herself that her rise from a poor Uathach village to the head of the Great Hall was truly real but Arthur seemed distant from everything around him including his new wife to be. Ceinwen raised her cup of wine in a drunken silent toast wishing Gwyna good luck, she had seen that look before and remembered it well.

Hours later Ablach and Gwyna left the Great Hall to the cheers from those who had not already slumped into unconsciousness. Arthur walked with them down the length of the hall and as he looked across to the unfastened shutters on the windows an image of the Adren scrambling into the hall at Branque came unbidden to his mind to be followed quickly by images of Caja, chained and insane in an Adren hut in the Shadow Lands. He looked at Gwyna by his side and thought for the first time how she resembled the way Caja had looked that night in Branque but Gwyna seemed older in every way despite their similar age. He thought it strange how one's life had ended much as the other's had begun.

As he watched father and daughter walk out into the snow-covered square he found himself hoping that the fates he did not believe in would be kinder to Gwyna than they were to Caja. But the fates did not care for the hopes of men.

Arthur returned to the Great Hall and waited. He had done all that he could to unite the peoples of Britain to face the coming threat of the Adren. He had stalled the Adren advance and he hoped that he had bought enough time for Cei and Merdynn to reach the Shadow Land City.

He sat brooding upon the return of the peoples and how they and the council would react to the killing of the king. He dwelt upon his forthcoming marriage to the Uathach girl and whether the northern clans would join with them to battle the Adren horde now wintering across the Causeway. He fought to keep away the image of Fin Seren and he sought to bury his love for her. More than all of these he tormented himself with the question of whether or not Merdynn and Cei had succeeded in their only hope. He had no way of knowing that they were already being tracked by the enemy and were heading straight into an Adren trap.

CAUSEWAY

SHADOW LANDS: BOOK TWO

One by one the Kingdoms of the West have fallen to the armies from the Shadow Lands and now those armies are massed across the Causeway, readying to invade the last Kingdom that stands against them.

Arthur has done everything possible to unite the tribes of Britain and their hopes of survival now rest upon holding off the invading army long enough for Merdynn to succeed in his quest to strike at the enemy city thousands of miles to the East, deep in the heart of the Shadow Lands.

But the enemy is already among them.

Causeway, the second book in the Shadow Lands series, is available through all online and retail booksellers or it can be ordered direct from www.simonlister.co.uk